THE SWEETEST THING

SUSAN SALLIS

ISIS

LARGE PRINT

Oxford

First published in Great Britain 2010
by
Bantam Press
an imprint of Transworld Publishers

Published in Large Print 2010 by ISIS Publishing Ltd.,
7 Centremead, Osney Mead, Oxford OX2 0ES
by arrangement with
Transworld Publishers
a Random House Group Company

The moral right of the author has been asserted

British Library Cataloguing in Publication Data
Sallis, Susan.
The sweetest thing.
1. Cornwall (England: County) - - Fiction.
2. Large type books.
I. Title
823.9'14–dc22

ISBN 978–0–7531–8678–7 (hb)
ISBN 978–0–7531–8679–4 (pb)

Printed and bound in Great Britain by
T. J. International Ltd., Padstow, Cornwall

For Jane and Mike
with love

CHAPTER
ONE

Summer 1960

Connie turned the key on the door of the beach hut, registering the grittiness of sand in the lock, praying it would open. She pulled at the door so that its normal creak crescendoed to a scream of protest. She stepped inside, whipped the damp towel and swimming costume from the hook and threw them out on to the beach; one of the deckchairs followed, its canvas billowing helplessly. Then the beach table made from driftwood. She watched it fall; it did not break.

Before she could get a grip on the beach mat and paper parasol, a voice said loudly, "Hang on, miss! Steady as she goes! If you've 'ad a row with the boyfriend don't take it out on the furniture!"

The fact that her anger was so obvious and so childish made it melt instantly and left her cold and shivery inside. It had buoyed her up as she left the boarding house and ran down to the cove, and without it she almost collapsed on to the wooden floor of the hut.

The young lad who looked in as she stood there, rigid, suggested deep breathing. She'd seen him yesterday; he manned the little shop at the foot of the cliff steps and doled out extra deckchairs. It didn't sound as if he were trying to be quizzical or sarcastic. It sounded as if he had made the driftwood table himself and very recently mended the door of the beach hut too. She felt ashamed of her outburst.

She turned and looked at him. He was only about seventeen, appeared younger still in his khaki shorts. She supposed that in a year or two he would look just as ridiculous as William looked — as all men looked — in shorts. Such a pity. Perhaps he wouldn't, though. His eyes were so blue, his hair the colour of straw.

She said, "I'm sorry. I really am."

He stopped talking and opened his eyes wide. He said, "You're not going to cry, are you?"

"Of course not. Don't be absurd. I'm in a temper, that's all. And I hardly ever get into a temper." She felt a tear run down to her chin. He was embarrassed.

"Look . . . I din't mean nothing. Honest. I'll set you up." He jumped from the concrete shelf which held the beach huts and grabbed the collapsed deckchair. "Come and sit down. Come on." He leaned up and took her bag from her and put it carefully by the chair, then held out a hand. She stepped down all of six inches. She felt her nose running. If only he was ten years older . . . maybe five . . . she could have talked to him.

She stumbled into the chair and he made to leave her.

She said loudly, "We're engaged! I mean, *engaged* — doesn't that mean *anything*?"

He paused and thought. "I guess it means you're promised to each other."

She gulped and nodded. Then said, "Are you American?"

"No. Why did you say that?"

"You said . . . I don't know . . . you said 'I guess' and I would've said 'I suppose' . . . I suppose." She glanced up and tried to laugh. "I mean, I think. It doesn't matter."

He said, "I read a lot of American books. I'm reading something by a guy called Raymond Chandler at the moment."

"Oh! I like him too. Did you see Humphrey Bogart and —"

"Sure. *The Big Sleep*."

"There you go again. Saying sure instead of yes." She could talk to him like this because she was older than him; four years, maybe five. And there was something else about him. More than childish innocence. The word "simple" sprang to her mind but it had connotations that did not fit him.

They both laughed. He said, "I'll get you a cup of coffee."

She fished in her handbag. "Get two." She looked up, suddenly diffident. "Unless you're too busy to stop for coffee?"

He grinned and his very blue eyes narrowed and twinkled.

"Why do you think I read Raymond Chandler? They don't trust me with the surfing beach so they gave me this job. Hardly anyone comes here to the cove. I've got loads of time."

She leaned back in the chair, feeling slightly better. She thought of William flirting with Mrs Heatherington and her long cigarette holder. Cigarette holder indeed. And silk gloves. They were in deepest Cornwall in a heatwave. Connie was wearing the espadrilles her mother had brought back from a holiday in Brittany. Mrs Heatherington's rather plump legs ended in peep-toed high heels. Connie knew that her mother would classify Mrs Heatherington as common because the toes that were visible sported blood-red enamelled nails, and although Connie would normally have dismissed such a judgement as old-fashioned, now, in view of . . . things, she was not quite so dismissive.

She lay back in the deckchair and held her bottom lip between her teeth. She told herself she was being oversensitive. In fact — she had to face up to it — she had been her usual stupid self. Ever since William had asked her to marry him she had had stars in her eyes; quite literally she had been unable to see properly. She was ecstatic. This could not be happening to Connie Vickers from the respectable suburb outside Birmingham who was so ordinary she was boring. But — she had heard this countless times from her mother — men did not respect girls who slept with them before the wedding day. And this . . . what was happening now, with William giving all his attention to Mrs Heatherington . . . this was what she had meant.

Tears were gathering again. She searched for the anger that had ejected her from the lounge of the Blue

4

Seas boarding house and down to the cove. It had gone, probably for good.

Sounds of bare feet on sandy concrete; she looked up and around. The boy was approaching with steaming cups wobbling precariously on their saucers. She leaned forward, righted the little table and dug its legs into the sand, then reached up.

"This isn't part of the job description, is it? You're not a waiter. We come to you." She forced a smile as she took the drinks and placed them carefully. He sat on the sand. She said, "My name is Connie Vickers. I come from Birmingham."

"I could tell." She flushed. He laughed. "Everyone thinks they en't got no accent. Why? Is Birmingham an awful place?"

"No, of course not. But my mother wouldn't like to know I had an accent of any kind. Where do you live?"

"Hayle." He made it sound like "hell" and she laughed. Encouraged, he went on, "There's Mum and my three sisters. Bit hard up, like, since Dad died." She held her breath but he went on smoothly. "I wanted a summer job and I 'ad to come down the coast to get it."

"Good for you!" She glanced at him above her cup, wondering whether to mention his father. Then said, "Are you going to college in the autumn?"

"Naw . . . me? You are joking! I can add up, take away . . . I'm what at my school they call a woodwork boy. Good with me hands, not so good with this!" He tapped his head.

She looked at him. "I don't believe that. What about Raymond Chandler?"

"That's diff'rent. Cain't do Shakespeare. Cain't do algebra. Raymond Chandler lays it out simple. Bit like wood . . . specially wood what's come out of the sea. Driftwood. Weathered and salted and making its own shapes." He pointed to the little table with his big toe. "That table wouldn't break that easy. I went with the wood, y'see. Din't try and force it to do what it din't want to do. If you do that with anything — anything at all — it dun't work."

"No." She thought about it. "That's true. That's why . . . that's why . . ." She couldn't go further. She sipped her coffee, which was delicious, and raised her eyebrows. "What's your name?"

"They call me Egg."

She was astonished. "Why?"

"'Cos it's Egbert and Mum dun't like Bert." He wasn't smiling.

"Listen, can I call you Philip?"

"Call me what you like."

She said gently, "The thing I'll remember about you is that you like reading Raymond Chandler. So I won't forget Philip. Philip Marlowe."

"Oh." He looked at her, his eyes alight. "That's . . . real nice."

She laughed. "You know, you really do sound like an American. Perhaps you'll go there one day."

"I might." He drained his mug and put it down, looked at her and then away. "My pa was a Yank. Stationed down Devon. Ma worked there in one of they

6

big houses turned into a sort of hostel for the troops. They was going to get married then he got drownded in a landing exercise. She came back to Hayle to have me and she married a boy she sat next to when she were at school. He were kind to me. Real kind. I cain't very well miss my real pa 'cos I never knew him. But I do miss my dad. I were five when he married Ma. I called him Dad straight off. He died two year past."

She stared at his down-bent head. She was ashamed of her temper, her pettiness. She said, "Oh Phil. I'm so sorry."

He flashed her a smile. "That do sound good . . . Anyway, we're all right. The Pardoes. That's our name. Dad adopted me so I could be a Pardoe too and not illegal no more. There's still five of us going strong! Real strong. Mum were nineteen years old when I was born so she's thirty-five now. Strong as a horse. And Ellie's just passed her scholarship to go to Truro — she's a bit skinny but she'll do all right. And the other two girls . . . daft as brushes but plenty upstairs." He tapped his head again, laughing now.

She asked their names because she did not know what else to say and was suddenly frightened she was going to cry again.

"Denny. Short for Denise. And Barbara. They're tinkers."

"And . . . you love them."

She was surprised by her pronouncement. Boys didn't ever admit to loving their sisters. They put up with them. At the very best they were allowed to be the tiniest bit proud of them.

He said, also surprised, "I guess I do. Ellie . . . Ellie is something else. When Dad told me off about something she told me that I would always be his favourite because I was the only son."

There was a long silence.

Connie cleared her throat. "My dad died in the war too. But Mother didn't marry again and I'm an only child." He looked up, smiling, really listening, as if something significant was about to be revealed. She blurted, "I'm engaged to William Mather. He's quite a bit older than me and Mother approves of him like mad. He's a lawyer and I was a filing clerk, then he made me his secretary. I'm not much good at it. He says I've got the sort of qualities clients like. He's very . . . kind."

"Sounds good." He put his head on one side. "Except I guess you've had a big row."

"You said that before. I thought it was a joke."

He laughed. "Mum and Dad were always having rows. He used to shut himself in the shed. Then Mum would give me a plate of stew and tell me to take it down to him and come straight back. And when I did she gave me another plate of stew and told me to go and eat with him."

She laughed too. She thought Mrs Pardoe must have been very confident of Mr Pardoe.

She said suddenly, "William is sucking up to one of his clients. I didn't realize this was a business trip. I thought it was a proper holiday to celebrate us getting engaged. So . . . that was a bit of a shock."

She supposed it was also one of the reasons she had clung to him when they said good night so that he got the wrong idea. But she couldn't tell this boy that she had slept with her fiancé and thereby lost his respect for ever. She wished she could. She had a feeling he would make everything all right again.

"I'd better go back for lunch otherwise he'll think the worse of me." She started to struggle out of the deckchair. "Philip —" she smiled — "you've been so kind. Thank you for the coffee. Keep reading."

He leaped to his feet and helped her upright then dropped her hands, embarrassed. He said, "Leave your stuff. Come down this afternoon and have a swim when the tide's up."

"He might not want that."

"I'll put the stuff in the hut if you don't turn up. But it's there waiting for you if you want it."

She smiled suddenly. "If he won't come with me I'll come by myself!"

He grinned. "Good for you. Keep your nerve."

She took the sandy steps up the cliff, swinging her bag as if she didn't have a care in the world. When she got to the top he was standing where she had left him on the sand. She waved. And he waved back.

"Scuse me . . ." A small girl barged past her waving a bucket, closely followed by another. A young couple brought up the rear carrying folding chairs and a bag bulging with towels.

The woman said, "Do they sell food at the little shop down there, do you know?"

"I think so. We had pasties there yesterday. And I've just had coffee."

The woman frowned. "They won't do vegetarian food. Maybe cheese sandwiches. It looks ideal. And no one else around."

"There's no surf, you see."

"Even better. The girls can paddle."

Connie watched them negotiate the steps with their loads. "Philip" Pardoe came to meet them and helped them down on to the sand. She left them chatting. Of course he would do that sort of thing with everyone. It was his job, after all.

William was not best pleased.

"It's *not* that I mind you doing things on your own! It's just that I had no idea where you were. You simply left the dining room while I was chatting to Mrs Heatherington and when I went to your room you weren't there either. I searched high and low —"

"For goodness' sake, William, don't keep on! Surely you realized when the beach bag and the key to the hut were both gone —"

"I'd said we would have coffee with Mrs Heatherington so I couldn't come down to join you. You should have told me, Connie. Then I could have said to Mrs Heatherington that I was going to the beach immediately we'd had —"

Neither of them had finished a sentence so far. Connie interrupted him again and said in her mother's sensible voice, "I came back here after I'd had *my* coffee. And here we both are."

He was silent for a moment, frowning at her, then quite suddenly he smiled and looked lovely.

"Oh darling. Wasn't it marvellous? Last night you made me so happy I wanted to sing."

She melted immediately. There was no gradual realization that she had misunderstood his preoccupation with Mrs Heatherington, no regret for a wasted morning. She simply melted, right there in front of him.

She breathed, "Oh William."

He touched the back of her hand. "I love you so much, Connie. You make everything worthwhile again."

Unexpectedly she remembered the day she had been interviewed for the job, two years ago. Filing clerk for Arnold Jessup and Son, Family Solicitors.

Mrs Flowers, who was Mr Jessup's secretary, had sketched out the position. Mr Jessup's father had started the practice and had looked after the families in Selly Oak and Kings Norton, and when he died, young Mr Arnold had taken it on, acted for the university several times and made himself quite a reputation. Then Mr Mather had arrived and that was the reason a filing clerk was needed. Mrs Flowers was quite used to doing two jobs, but three was one too many. Connie had made sympathetic noises but thought Mrs Flowers was letting her down gently.

She had no idea, still did not, that Mrs Flowers liked the noises and she liked the look of Connie too. She was neat and pretty and offered no kind of threat. The previous applicant had been very blonde and very curvaceous. Connie had mouse-brown hair, tea-brown eyes and a schoolgirl figure. Mrs Flowers mentioned hopefully that perhaps she could take on some of Mr Mather's work too. She expanded on Mr Mather. He had been the youngest officer parachuted into Arnhem; he had survived, but not unscathed.

And then it had been Mr Jessup's turn. Connie had been introduced to William when it became obvious that Mr Jessup was going to give her the job. She had looked at him and seen what Mrs Flowers had meant. His eyes were brown too but darker than hers, almost black. Almost haunted. She had wanted so much to help him.

Perhaps that was why last night had happened. She understood suddenly that she too must take responsibility for last night. She went to him now and wrapped her arms around him. He held her tightly. "Don't be frightened, darling. Did I frighten you?"

"No." She wanted to tell him how . . . odd . . . last night had made her feel. As if she no longer belonged to herself.

He kissed the top of her head and down to her right ear, where one of her short brown curls got into his mouth. He spluttered and laughed a little then whispered into her ear, "You are everything that is good and honest in this world, Connie."

The sense of responsibility was weighty. She must grow up somehow. She was five and a half feet tall and she consciously lengthened another inch as if to achieve this goodness and honesty. And then realized she never could.

They went down to lunch and sat at the table in the window. Outside, a gardener pushed a mower carefully around flower beds cut meticulously into the lawn. Mrs Pentwyn came in and asked whether everyone was happy. There were only three of them and they all nodded and smiled through their soup.

Mrs Pentwyn smiled back and said brightly, "Why don't you join Mr Mather and his fiancée, Mrs Heatherington? You get on so well. I can soon lay another place at their table."

Mrs Heatherington raised questioning brows at William, who bounced them on to Connie. She said, "Please do, Mrs Heatherington. There's a good view from here."

There was a lot of settling in. Mrs Pentwyn had to move their place mats slightly to make room for Mrs Heatherington's. They grabbed their cutlery before it could clatter to the floor. The water jug splashed excitedly.

William stood up and brought across a chair and held the back while Mrs Heatherington disposed herself, her handbag, her wine glass. She smiled mistily. "Can you bring the decanter, Mrs Pentwyn? And two more glasses." She looked roguish. "I *know* you will say you do not drink at midday but a siesta in this heat . . . and the wine will help."

It was cabinet pudding and she opted for cheese so William did too. Connie did not want either but she chose the pudding anyway. Mrs Heatherington talked to William through her.

13

"Your husband has been *so* kind, my dear. I am an actress, I know nothing about contracts, why should I, I've never had any difficulties before and I could not have believed that my manager of twenty years . . . like a knife being slipped between my ribs!"

Connie seized the tiny silence and said for the third time, "We are not married yet, Mrs Heatherington."

Mrs Heatherington nodded and smiled indulgently. Connie held on to her spoon and looked away from her. She knew. How did she know? She knew. It was unbearable. Connie was absolutely certain that William would never have said anything, why would he? Perhaps it showed somehow. She raked her fingers through her hair in case it was too set.

Mrs Heatherington patted her other hand. "You are both so wonderfully settled somehow. My husband and I never had that. We were married during the Blitz, the day before he was posted . . . We never saw each other again."

"I'm so sorry," Connie murmured.

"Oh my dear, don't be. I expect he's out there somewhere having a high old time. Rangoon. I imagine him in Rangoon. I was not broken-hearted. I am an actress to the core and I have to be a free spirit."

Connie removed her hand and leaned back to make room for the arrival of the cabinet pudding. Mrs Pentwyn added a small jug of cream and smiled as if Connie were a favourite niece. "These two don't know what they're missing, do they?"

Connie murmured something about the heat and luckily did not comment on the solidity of the pudding as Mrs Pentwyn continued, "I made it with my own fair hands, of course."

William tried to look rascally as he leaned over and took a spoonful of pudding on to his plate. Mrs Heatherington gave a little scream and tried to do the same. Mrs Pentwyn was smugly satisfied.

"I knew how it would be!" she said triumphantly as she left them to it.

William and Mrs Heatherington laughed uninhibitedly. Connie began to eat, stoically.

She had thought she and William would spend the afternoon at the beach hut but it seemed that Mrs Heatherington had brought her stage photographs from before the war, which she thought would provide added ammunition when it came to getting rid of her manager. "I mean I had no idea there was a *law* saying you could not sack an employee for not doing their job!"

William cut some more cheese. "Actually, Mrs Heatherington, I rather think photographs such as those might help his case rather than yours."

She thought about it while she nibbled a cracker between her front teeth like a rabbit. Then she nodded reluctantly. "I see what you mean." Then she smiled. "I would rather like you to see these photographs. As publicity photographs go, they are not at all bad."

"Probably it would be better to keep business and pleasure separate." William had a very nice smile and Connie thought he had won the day.

"Such a shame. You would have enjoyed seeing them too, Miss Vickers. But . . . perhaps you are rather too young to appreciate the fashions then. And you are looking forward to a swim no doubt?" She beamed at William. "It looks like another tête-à-tête then, Mr Mather. Or may I call you William? My father was called William. Such a solid name. Brought from France by William the Bastard, I understand. You don't mind, do you, Miss Vickers? You will have the rest of your life with your dear William."

Connie swallowed. William looked at her pleadingly. She said, "Of course I don't mind. Not at all. Really. Honestly. No, I won't stop for coffee, I can have one from the beach shop. A lovely lunch . . ." She swept her bag from the back of the chair and stood up. Mrs Pentwyn was coming in with a tray of coffee things and smiled at her.

As she said to Philip Pardoe when she reached her deckchair, "They all think I'm such a good girl because I am really cooperative. It's all right, I'm just out of breath. Yes, I've run. Well, of course I was running away! If you could see Mrs Heatherington's lipstick and matching nail polish you would understand exactly why!"

He said, "You've got jam on your nose."

"Oh . . . *hell's bells!*"

She scrubbed at her nose with the towel he passed her. And they both started to laugh. And — almost magically — she forgot Mrs Heatherington and Mrs Pentwyn; she was still cross with William but she understood how difficult it was for him. In a strange way she wished she did not understand; it was part of the ties of loyalty already stretching between them. Part of last night. Part of not being Connie Vickers, single female. Part of giving herself over to someone else. And though it was William and though he was a marvellous human being, he was still . . . someone else.

The cove filled up during the afternoon and Philip Pardoe had no time for reading or sitting by her on the sand. She pulled the brim of her sunhat well down, leaned back in her chair and watched him, smiling slightly, already proud of him for being patient with the two little girls and their bucket of shells, for carrying a picnic basket to the top of the cliff for an elderly man. She thought of his mother, visualized her with her three little girls and this charming straw-haired boy . . . She was not yet forty but was probably grey and thin. Did she know her very special child wanted to go to America and find his father's family? She must ask Philip, warn him to tell her gently. His mother might be delighted because obviously she had been amazingly in love with Philip's father . . . How had she coped with a second man? A second family?

Connie checked herself: she was crying again. What on earth was the matter with her — was this another outcome of sleeping with her fiancé before the wedding day? Those were her mother's words. Was she a replica of her mother after all?

She took on another piece of her mother's advice and "snapped out of it". Philip was now trapped inside his little shop dealing with a queue of people wanting ice creams. She picked up her crisply sun-dried costume and went into the beach hut to change into it. She would have a swim. That's what she and William would have done. It would wash away all her strange doubts and fears.

She was floating on her back gazing up at the cliff top, moving with the sea, conscious of the tingle of the sun, when she saw William beginning the descent to the cove. She started to swim back to the shore; it was as if he was pulling her in. She felt a surge of joy that he had got away from the Heatherington and come straight to her. She watched him stop by the beach hut and reach down to kick off his sandals. Why had she thought he looked awful in shorts? He looked marvellous. His dark hair fell across his forehead. He was probably twice Phil Pardoe's age but he certainly did not look it. She dipped her head beneath the crystal-clear water and watched the weed move languorously on the seabed. The cord that joined them seemed to be shortening of its own accord. She stopped swimming and felt herself still moving towards him. It no longer irked her; she gloried in it. To be part of a whole was wonderful. He had come to her and she would go to him. It was perfect.

She was halfway up the beach when she saw that the small group he had followed down the steps had split off and gone on towards the rocks. Except for one. She was sitting — luxuriating — in Connie's recently vacated deckchair. William had just erected the other chair and was settling himself in it. He flung his hands behind his head, stretched his long and hairy legs, saw her coming . . . drawn by the blasted cord . . . and freed one hand to wave to her.

She stopped where she was, dug her toes into the dry sand and held her arms rigidly at her sides. He called to her.

"What's it like?"

"Fine."

He waited for her to move. "I'm trying to persuade this good lady to dip a toe or two."

She forced herself to move forward.

Mrs Heatherington laughed. "I can't swim. And I haven't got a costume. I think I'll stay here. This is lovely. So relaxing."

"It certainly is." William smiled up at Connie blissfully. "Shall I get another chair, darling?"

Suddenly she knew what must happen. It must. If it didn't then she couldn't possibly marry William Mather.

"I've come to get you. Come on. You know you love swimming." She jumped on to the concrete shelf outside the beach huts and held the door open.

William glanced up at her meaningfully then said to Mrs Heatherington, "What can I do, dear lady?" He began to manoeuvre himself out of the chair.

Mrs Heatherington raised her painted eyebrows incredulously. "You're not considering immersing yourself in the Atlantic Ocean, surely? I thought we were going to look through some more photographs?"

He subsided into the chair and for a moment Connie thought she had lost. Then, quite suddenly and strictly against her mother's advice, she became provocative, more than provocative; she became coy.

"Come on, darling. I'll help you to change into your costume."

He looked up, surprised, nearly shocked. She smiled down at him and began to tighten the cord, certain she was in control of it. And she was. He stood up and positively leaped on to the concrete so that she had to retreat hurriedly into the hut before he grabbed her. But then, as the door closed behind them, he did just that. It was as if he had been waiting for ever to hear those words; magic words. He was laughing and kissing her at the same time. He cupped her wet head in his big hands and kissed her eyes and her nose and her ears and her mouth and her neck.

She laughed too but stopped him there. "Darling, not now. Really. Come on, let's go for that swim. Otherwise the Heatherington will rip open the door and expose us to the world!"

"She would, yes, you're right — she would do that!" He pushed down his shorts and grabbed his trunks and began hopping about. "She acts as if I'm some sort of minion . . . which I guess I am."

"You said guess. Are you American too?"

"No. Are you?"

"No, idiot." The cord was tightly around them. They kissed, but fondly this time, not understanding what the other was saying yet knowing it was about love.

20

★ ★ ★

Mrs Heatherington was probably not the ancient femme fatale Connie had thought. She kept smiling at them and telling them they looked like water nymphs. William fetched a tray of tea and a packet of chocolate Wagon Wheels already gooey in the sun. Connie dried her hands carefully and looked through the folder of old photographs showing Mrs Heatherington when she was Greta Gainsborough, in a variety of cloche hats or Suzanne Lenglen headbands. She had been truly beautiful.

"I keep this one separately." Mrs Heatherington delved into a small leather wallet and extracted a tiny photograph. "It's just a snap. Not properly posed or anything. We were married in a register office . . . It was wartime. Actually I must have been nearly forty then." She laughed, embarrassed by her own honesty. "He was fun, but I didn't really know him. Not properly. I simply did not want to die an old maid and death seemed fairly likely then."

Connie looked at the blurred image. There was Greta Gainsborough in a crepe dress — no colour, of course — big puffed sleeves and some sort of smocking around the high waist, gloves up to the elbow, a pearl cap holding down the huge cascade of curls that tumbled to her shoulders, unidentifiable flowers, high-heeled shoes with — yes — peeptoes. The man next to her was in a loose-fitting suit and a homburg; he might have had very dark Brylcreemed hair and brown eyes. He was smiling widely and showing good teeth; yes, his eyes *were* brown — dark brown; big ears and nose. He seemed to be full of optimism and good humour. And

21

Connie knew that her mother would describe him as a "wide boy".

She felt her own eyes fill with sentimental tears. It was twenty years ago: she had been nearly three years old, her mother still had a husband and she still had a father . . . William had been sixteen, enjoying the ATC, wanting the war to go on until he was old enough to help defeat the Nazis, not even knowing that Arnhem was a place and he would see it quite soon. It was a different world, a different time, a different life. Where had it gone?

They swam again. Connie introduced "Philip" Pardoe and asked him to join them, but there were still people on the little beach who might want something from the shop and he declined, smiling.

Mrs Heatherington said, "You should be an actor. Film, I think. You have a look of one of the . . . what is the name, William? A theatrical family. One of the children looks exactly like this beautiful boy. It's on the tip of my tongue. I could perhaps arrange an audition . . ." But Philip had gone, someone wanted an ice cream.

After the swim they lay on towels and dried off in the late afternoon sun before trekking back to Blue Seas.

The young family were staying there for the rest of the week. Mrs Pentwyn did not normally accommodate children but their landlady in a house further down the sandy road had been taken into hospital with appendicitis and Mrs Pentwyn had come to the rescue.

22

"I drew the line at her cats," she confided to William. "But one of the little girls has offered to keep an eye on them. So what could I say? I do apologize, children are so — so unpredictable. I certainly cannot pander to their odd menu. They will have braised steak and the rest of the cabinet pudding whether they like it or not."

"I'm sure they will thoroughly enjoy it, Mrs Pentwyn," William said firmly, already halfway up the stairs.

Connie said happily, "I can vouch for the pudding, as you know. And the little girls are so sweet, they've been on the beach all day collecting shells. Please don't worry. We'll make sure they're all right."

Mrs Pentwyn looked at Connie almost fondly. "Dear girl," she murmured as she made for the kitchen again.

Mrs Heatherington rolled her eyes. "I'd better stay on your table. We can protect each other."

There were plenty of vegetables with the steak, which was just as well as the Membury family were vegetarian and Mrs Pentwyn stuck to her guns and offered no alternatives. It was Connie who went to the sideboard and carried the cheese to their table. "How about grating some over those lovely carrots?" she said to Rosalie and Lily. "I'll go and find a grater and perhaps some more butter."

She returned with a grater. She had been left in little doubt that she had lost her brief spurt of popularity with Mrs Pentwyn, who said, "The parents are no better than fussy children themselves — should be made to sit there until they've eaten properly." She had raised her voice slightly so that it could be heard in the dining room.

Connie hurried through and grated some cheese on to a side plate, shaking her head slightly as if the words had been said jokingly.

Mrs Membury refused to be apologetic. "Eating animals is no less than cannibalism," she announced to the two little girls, who were sniffing the air curiously as William served steak on the next table.

Mr Membury murmured, "Hardly, darling."

Connie willed her queasiness to go away as she took her seat and spooned some new potatoes next to the pool of gravy on her plate. One of the girls at the office dabbled in vegetarianism so she had heard this kind of thing before and thought about it rather too much.

William smiled at her and tried to change the conversation.

"Did you really think the boy in charge of the cove might become an actor?"

Mrs Heatherington paused, steak on fork, considering. "I don't know, of course. But he is certainly what my generation called a matinee idol."

William turned smilingly to Connie. "What do you think, darling? You know him fairly well, I gather."

She looked at him, surprised. "We chatted this morning. I don't know him. But he would like to be a carpenter, I think. Or even a sculptor. He enjoys making things. Using his hands."

"How old would you say he is?"

Mrs Heatherington and Connie spoke together. "Sixteen." They laughed. Connie said, "He told me he was born in 1944, so I'm not guessing."

"I was." Mrs Heatherington nodded. "He'll lose that beauty in another year."

Connie ate her potatoes, avoiding the steak. She felt a rush of sadness that the boy she had named after a character in a book was suddenly made ephemeral. The little girls at the next table finished their makeshift meal. Mrs Pentwyn brought in the remains of the cabinet pudding.

"Is there animal fat in the cake?" Mrs Membury eyed the plate suspiciously. Mrs Pentwyn said, "I haven't the faintest idea. And it's not cake. It's cabinet pudding!" She swept out.

When she returned with trifle and ice cream for the other table, Lily and Rosalie were eating their pudding with relish and Mr Membury was placating his wife. "It will be margarine, darling. Isn't that made from vegetable oils?"

"I believe so."

Connie remembered the pudding as being very solid and the Memburys obviously were half starved. They left not a crumb. Surreptitiously she passed over a dish of trifle as Mrs Pentwyn brought in the coffee. The three of them thought it was rather a joke but neither the Memburys nor Mrs Pentwyn found it funny.

"May I have a word with you some time, Mrs Heatherington?" The landlady did not wait for an answer but swept out once again.

Mrs Membury said with satisfaction, "Someone else is in trouble now, you see, Harry."

Mrs Heatherington looked from Connie to William. "What have *I* done?" she asked. She looked back to Connie. "It was you who used too much cheese and then gave away your trifle."

It was still a bit of a silly joke and Connie waited for William to defend her. Nothing happened and Mrs Heatherington began to look properly aggrieved. Connie lifted the serving spoon, still smiling. "There's heaps of trifle." But Mrs Heatherington put out a restraining hand.

"My dear, I really shouldn't. Mrs Pentwyn always makes a pudding do for two days. She'll put that in the fridge for tomorrow, I am certain of it."

Suddenly it was awkward. Mr Membury said, "Look, have my cheese. Honestly. You hardly ate any of your steak and you've had no afters at all."

Mrs Membury was belatedly contrite. "Was it me? Harry is always telling me to keep my ideas to myself. I put you off the steak, didn't I?"

"Of course not," Connie fibbed. "I've been a cannibal all my life. My mother tells a ghastly story about me eating ants —" Mrs Membury screamed and the girls squealed delightedly, not understanding what it was all about. William sat there looking . . . proud. She suddenly realized what he had meant when he asked her to be his personal secretary. She had said, "But sir, Mr Mather . . . my shorthand isn't always readable and my filing is —"

"Imaginative," he had supplied. "But I hate bad feeling within the office. We have to deal with it in the course of our work anyway. You are so good at diluting potentially awkward situations. Anyone can write shorthand and file papers but very few can make irritable people smile."

She had not known what he meant but she liked him very much and it would be so wonderful to go home and tell Mother that she had had a promotion. She had felt her smile stretch from ear to ear. And he had nodded and looked rather like he was looking now.

Mrs Heatherington replaced her empty coffee cup on its saucer and began to lever herself out of her chair. William rushed out of his and helped her.

"I think I had better not keep our hostess waiting." Mrs Heatherington smiled at Connie to show that she was teasing, and added, "You do realize it's all your fault, don't you?"

Connie was all at sea and wanted to ask what was her fault, but then nodded and said, "Of course." Mrs Heatherington made her usual theatrical exit, the little girls, happily full of pudding, settled down to dipping the cheese crackers into coffee and William said quietly, "I love you, Connie Vickers."

For two pins Connie could have cried. She surely loved this good, kind man, especially as she had slept with him last night. Had she ever told him so? Perhaps not; and perhaps she should now say, "I love you too, William Mather," but what she wanted to say was "I do wish you did not feel you had to kowtow to Mrs Heatherington." But that was so completely petty that she did not say it. Instead, she smiled, closed her eyes for a moment and quoted the title of a song her mother was forever singing in the bathroom.

"Love Is The Sweetest Thing."

CHAPTER
TWO

The next morning Lucy Pardoe woke at six o'clock as usual and lay quietly for a while, registering the quality of the light coming through the washed-out curtains. She had always lived each day in tune with weather and tides, and still as the years went on she spent those few early-morning minutes thinking simply of the immediate tasks to be done once she swung her legs out of bed. The rhythm of them, the very feeling of them, was linked inexorably with the scents and sounds of the land and the sea. Wind, rain and sun were nearly always friendly and could become part of her; but if they brought a roaring tide along the sandy shoreline of the towans, claiming the land instead of caressing it, hurling waves higher than the lighthouse itself, she did her outside work with head down and hands across her jacket, holding herself against it.

This morning the weather was on the change. For a few weeks now the bleached-out curtains had been no match for the early sun and her bedroom had been drenched in a golden light. Today the gold was less precious and more metallic. But there was still no wind. The tide would be edging quietly into the sand of the beaches all down the north coast. But the holidaymakers would be less energetic and the gulls' voices would become peevish and demanding. And her three beautiful daughters would need telling. They would need telling to get themselves dressed, to clear the breakfast things, to feed the hens in the orchard and be nice to each other. Lucy smiled into the hard-edged sunlight, remembering how Daniel might have sighed with mock weariness which hid enormous love and pride, and said humorously, "It's just one of they days, my maid. We'll all need telling. 'Cept our Egg. 'E'll just get on with what he's got to do."

Lucy nodded in agreement as she always did when she recalled the commonsensical words her husband had so often uttered. In response to them she began to sum up in her head her immediate itinerary. Bathroom, dress, cats, breakfast, Egg. Behind each staccato word were so many other words. The bathroom was the old byre converted by Daniel with help from his son, Egg. Dress did not matter today because she had no visitors. The cats were a whole world in themselves and linked her even more firmly to the sandy soil, the granite rocks, the stunted trees. Breakfast was her first offering of the day, tailored to each individual member of the family . . . and Egg was both his fathers with perhaps a dash of herself and the girls, and something else that was simply him. Perhaps it was because of his disability — and his disability was so much part of him it hardly showed any more.

She smiled, put all that aside and listened to the birds. There was a cuckoo somewhere in the copse and he should not still be there. It was August and he should be well on the way to Spain. August was her birthday month and her mother used to remind her that she would not be hearing any cuckoos by then — "'Tis bad luck if you do!" she would warn. And there was the little tinker again, hoarsely coughing out his signature tune. No shame. No caution. No sense prob'ly.

She reached across the bed to where Daniel's place was still kept. His slippers were exactly where his feet emerged from the sheets each morning, his pillows arranged in an inverted V just as he liked them. "Shoulders do get cold else," he explained to her when he first brought her to the cottage. She had laughed and shaken her head. Egg had not laughed or shaken his head. He had asked for another pillow and angled the two of them that first winter. He still did. Lucy smiled and ran her palm up and down the flat sheet as if it were Daniel's back. If he had lived he might well have had a bad back; she had always been telling him to walk straight.

She cut off. It was something she could do when she saw danger ahead. It stopped the heartache before it could start. Without conscious effort she stilled her hand — though she left it where it was — and wondered what Ellie, Barbara and Denny would like on their breakfast toast. And then she tossed back the top sheet and thin blanket and rolled up and out of bed in one movement. The day had started; the cuckoo had been silenced by the screaming gulls, the tide would be high in the next hour and she wanted to be out picking beans before it ebbed.

There was an ebb in her own rhythm while Egg ate his breakfast. She knew she should leave him to it and start on the beans. If they were picked early enough she could sit in the sun and string them while she watched the girls feeding the hens. Ellie would pack the cut beans in the clear plastic bags the freezer man supplied, weigh them, seal them and stack them in the crate for when the big refrigerated van pulled up in front of the cottage.

But Egg started to talk. He wasn't one for talking. He'd grin and nod and a lot of folk thought he had a screw slightly loose but Lucy knew better. And when he started to talk, however odd it might sound, it meant something. You had to listen. You might find out what it was all about, you might not. But you had to listen all the same.

First off, he checked with her about the apprentice-ship with Chippy Penberthy.

"You're not enjoying doling out ice creams and deckchairs then, my boy?" she asked, pouring him more tea, grinning mischievously.

He grinned too. "I like it. I like it too much, Mum. Most days I got time to read."

"Still on they American books, are you?"

"Yeah."

She said nothing. Her father had accused her of being lazy when she read books. She had started to do the same to Egg when he finally learned to read. She had called his choice rubbish. Cowboy rubbish, detective rubbish. Daniel had stopped her mighty quick.

"Don't take away his excitement, my maid. 'E's just got the 'ang of it and we mustn't put 'im off. Dun't matter what 'e do read s'long as 'e do read."

So she waited and after he had finished his bacon-bread and picked up his tea he said slowly, "Mum, I'm not certain about Chippy Penberthy."

She was surprised. "I thought you liked woodwork, son. You bin doing it for the past two year at school."

"'Cos I cain't do anything else!" He laughed. "I like wood. But I don't want to be fighting it all the time. I want to go with it. An' I cain't see old Chippy letting me do that, can you?" He laughed and so did she. Chippy fought with everything in his life; his wife, his wayward daughter, his tools and his trade.

"So what you got in mind, Egg? This job you got now won't last more 'n about another two — three weeks."

"Thought I might be a deckhand."

She forced herself not to look aghast. The respect she had for the sea was always close to fear. She looked at him and said nothing. And he nodded.

"I know. Both my dads. But I want . . . I need . . . to get across it. Over it. Somehow."

"You want to leave Cornwall? Leave England?"

"Not for ever. Course not." He cradled his mug, took a sip. "Mum . . . I only thought of this yesterday . . . I'd like to see my first dad's family."

She was quite still, staring at him. Then she said, "The American books."

He thought about it. "P'raps that's it. P'raps I like them books because they're about America." He opened his eyes wider. "P'raps I wouldna thought about going there if she hadn't said something."

Lucy was on to it like a terrier on to a rat. "She? Who's she, then?"

"One of they lot on holiday. Her name is Connie Vickers and she comes from Birmingham. She calls me Philip 'cos that's the name of the detective in the book I'm reading."

Lucy wanted to wrap her arms around her son and hold him tight against Connie Vickers and everyone else from Birmingham.

She said quickly, "Well, I bin thinking too. I know what you mean about Chippy. An' there's living enough for all of us right 'ere. Your dad seen to that when he started the bean field."

Egg nodded, smiling. "'E wanted to go in for strawberries too."

"Pigs and strawberries — they always go together. We got the orchard for a pig and there's always room for strawberries."

He heard the desperation in her voice and was silent, looking at her. Then nodding agreement. "It's what Dad 'ad in mind, I know that. Plenty of time for America." He finished the tea. Then looked again at his mother and said, almost shyly, "I'm real 'appy, Mum."

She responded instantly, gratefully. "You always 'ave been, son. It's in your nature. And like you say — plenty of time for America." She got up; she could start on the beans now before the girls woke. This metallic sun would become stifling soon; she needed to make a start.

"It was just something she said. She do remind me of you, Mum. She says things that make sense. This friend of 'ers — elderly lady — something to do with the theatre — she said I should be an actor on the stage. That din't make no sense at all. But when Connie said I should go to America 'cos my dad was from there, that made sense."

Lucy collapsed back into her chair, astonished that Egg had spoken so many words all at once, horrified that he had obviously disclosed everything about himself.

"You told these — these — elderly ladies — about Bert McKinley — about your father?"

He grinned. "Naw . . . course not. There were only one elderly lady. Mrs . . . Mrs . . . I do forget 'er name. I told Connie about my father and about Dad. She listened. And her father did die in the war too."

"The woman from Birmingham?"

"Ah. She's not zackly a woman. Bit like Ellie."

"A little girl."

He laughed. "She got a fiancé. Older than her. Tries to look after her but en't making much of a job of it!" He shook his head, still smiling.

"So she's engaged to be married."

"Not for long, I don't reckon."

Lucy felt her heart thumping. She said, "Be careful, son. Never come between man and woman."

Egg looked surprised. "I en't nowhere between Connie and 'er chap, Mum. I just make them coffee and tea."

"And talk to them by the sound of things."

He laughed again. "Naw. They done the talking. But yesty morning . . . they'd 'ad a row, see. She came down in a huff. I calmed 'er down. We talked then."

Lucy's heart knocked against her ribs. "Men and women . . . they have rows."

"I told 'er that. About when Dad went to his shed —"

"You told some slip of a girl about Dad and me?"

"To show 'er it din't mean nothing, Mum — I din't speak out of turn — honest!"

She forced herself to breathe properly. She picked up his mug and took a long draught of tepid tea. She said, "I know that, my son. I know you wouldn't talk out of turn. It's just that . . . you dun't go in for much talking. And 'ere you are talking to someone old enough to be your mother —"

"She's only a coupla years older than me!"

"Well, your auntie then."

"Just tried to cheer 'er up, Mum. Like Ellie needs cheering up sometimes."

"Ellie's too clever for her own good."

"There you are then. Connie is clever, you can tell. An' I can cheer 'er up 'cos I en't clever."

Lucy said fiercely, "What do clever mean? What do clever matter in the long run? It's what you know about living proper. Ellie comes to you like she went to her dad. To remind 'er 'ow to live proper."

"I dun't know. It's like Ellie can't see straight now and then. Connie was like that too. Not sure whether she do want to be engaged but not liking it when she thought 'er bloke was looking at someone else bit too

36

often!" He laughed. "This woman Mrs whatever-'er-name-is — she's mutton dressed up as lamb — said I was like a mattny idle. Just 'cos I reads dun't make me idle. I nearly told 'er that. But it weren't important. The man was nice enough. But it was Connie what mattered. Connie is kind. She do shine with kindness."

Lucy was suddenly terrified. She could picture it, an older couple flirting in front of a young girl and a younger boy. And the boy saw the girl as some kind of victim. Did he think he had to rescue her?

She said carefully, "Perhaps Connie wants to go to America too?"

"No. She wants to get married. She knows he's the right bloke even if she doesn't quite know whether she loves him. Perhaps she expects too much."

"Perhaps she does." Lucy swallowed and watched him stand up and go into the wash house for his bicycle. She no longer made him sandwiches and filled his thermos as she had done all the years he was at school; he was allowed to choose what he fancied from the beach shop. It was part of the process of untying the apron strings. She had been prepared for it. But she had not been prepared for him to — to — become attached to someone else. Someone from another place. Someone with that peculiar nasal accent. Someone who could well be a little lost and need his simple, straightforward views on life. Someone complicated; like Ellie. Who needed . . . him. And might hurt him.

She went slowly down the garden to the bean field. The orchard sheltered the thick vines from the prevailing south-westerlies and the cottage itself took the brunt of the colder winds from Ireland and the north. Not that there was a breath moving today; the air was heavy with heat. She stopped worrying about Egg and took the top trug from the pile and filled it in the first five minutes. If there was some real weather on the way it could finish the bean patch in spite of all its protection. Today's pick could bring the last of the "bean cheques" this year. It must be a good one.

An hour later Ellie brought Barbara through the orchard. Both girls were dressed in pretty sundresses made by the curate's wife. When Daniel had died, the crew of the PZ 51 had made sure that the Pardoes still had their portion of the catch before it went to Newlyn. Before the village shop shut down they had shared leftovers with the owners: bread and biscuits, dried-up cheese, slightly shrivelled oranges. The curate helped Ellie with her studying when she put in for a scholarship; his wife was a dab hand with a sewing machine. It had always been the way; in the past Daniel and Lucy had helped the people who were now helping them. Lucy would do so again in the future. What went around came around, everyone knew that.

"Mum, I fed the cats an' we've et our breakfast and got ready. Denny won't let me do her plaits."

"Got ready?" Lucy did not stop picking.

"It's libr'y morning down in the village. I got ten littl'uns in my group and Denny won't let me do 'er plaits!" Ellie's voice rose a notch.

"Oh my Lord!" Lucy put down her trug and half her pick fell on the ground. "I plumb forgot about library morning!" For a moment she was completely at sea.

Her staccato reminders of early morning had missed out this new venture of Ellie's. She had proposed to the librarian that during the long summer holidays she would spend an hour every Tuesday morning in the library reading to children aged five and up. It was her special thing, she had thought of it, fixed it up with the librarian, who had advertised it, and had gradually increased the "membership" until — today — she was expecting ten "littl'uns". It was the big event in Ellie's week and her mother had forgotten it.

Mortified and angry with herself, Lucy flew into the cottage, picked up her youngest daughter from where she was kneeling with the cats pretending to lap their milk, plonked her on a chair and grabbed the discarded comb from among the cereal dishes. It all looked such a mess. Lucy had been pretending everything was well under control when none of it was. Egg was caught up with some awful girl from Birmingham and they were going to America, the weather was about to smash the bean patch to smithereens, Denny was trying to become a cat again, the breakfast table was downright unhygienic and she herself had forgotten it was library morning.

"If you go on like this," she scolded, dragging the comb through tangled hair, "one of they cats will give you such a scratch your eye will hang right out on your face!" Denny bawled loudly and Ellie and Barbara retreated into the garden.

By the time Lucy returned from delivering them to the library steps, she had lost twenty minutes of her precious picking time. She had also lost the rhythm of the day. She settled outside the kitchen door on one of the ladderback chairs Egg had repaired, not entirely successfully, and began to cut the six trugs of beans into matching slivers. Gradually the day settled around her again and she had started to pack the plastic bags when the front gate squeaked and Chippy Penberthy appeared around the side of the house.

"Ah, Mrs Pardoe I'll be bound!" he exclaimed, as if he had expected someone quite different to be sitting outside the cottage door. She did not blame Egg one little bit for not wanting to spend his days with Chippy Penberthy.

"Ah, Mr Penberthy," she said in exactly the same tone. She forced a smile. "And what can I do for you?"

He looked faintly surprised. Mrs Pardoe never forgot the second Tuesday in the month. He said bluntly, "'Tis rent day, missis. Tuesday, innit?"

She almost spilled the beans as she jumped up. "Sit down — sit down, Mr Penberthy. It is indeed Tuesday. And I 'as to admit I forgot that it were the second Tuesday in August! The rent is ready, of course. And while I fetch it, shall I put the kettle on for a nice cup of tea?"

He made his usual joke. "What if I said I wanted a nasty cup of tea then, Mrs Pardoe?"

She forced another smile and went into the kitchen. Whatever next? Was she going to forget to make pasties for supper? Had she combed her hair?

She fetched the envelope containing the rent book and money, then poured boiling water into the teapot and almost sobbed when she realized she had not put tea in first. She broke every rule in the book and added a spoonful of leaves to the water and carried everything out on a tray.

"Whatever are you doing, Mr Penberthy?"

He was sitting in her wobbly chair, leaning over the trug.

"I'm a-packing these 'ere beans. Saw the van down the towans. You'm a bit late today, missis."

He was doing it all wrong but he was her landlord and though she longed to snatch the bags from him she did not.

"Why don't you pour the tea for me? I'll soon catch up. I'm glad to have the chance of a word with you . . ." They changed places and he began to stir the pot. "I'd appreciate your advice on a plan I have."

He was flattered. She told him about running a pig in the orchard and renting a bit more land on the sheltered side for strawberries. "Daniel and Egg used the byre to make the bathroom, as you know. But I reckon Egg could knock up another sty if we did decide to . . . What do you think, Mr Penberthy?"

"Pigs and strawberries. Always go together." He was still stirring. She pushed the mugs towards him with her elbow. He put the lid on the pot and lifted it. "I reckon 'tis a good thing to do, missis. Funny. I were going to put off young Egg's serve-time till Christmas. Not much work on till I start on the repairs to the village hall. Looks like you will need him till then anyways."

She felt a weight drop from her shoulders. She had not wanted to offend Chippy Penberthy in any way but

Egg was not the sort of lad to take on a long apprenticeship. By Christmas he would be well established on their smallholding. They could think then about what he wanted to do.

He began to pour tea. It was very strong. "Just like I like it," he said, smiling because he had not wanted to upset Mrs Pardoe and here were things working themselves out for once. He drank deeply. If only Mrs Penberthy knew how to make tea properly; how to organize her life so that everything went according to plan; how to manage to make herself look cool in a working frock with her hair in wild curls . . . Of course Mrs Penberthy was not pretty like Mrs Pardoe.

While she went to the van with her trugs of shining plastic bags, he counted out her rent money. There was sixpence too much. Feeling honest and generous at the same time, he handed it to her and then went on his way.

"Good luck with the pig!" he called. He had been bitten by a sow when he was three years old and tried to pick up one of her feeding piglets. He had been terrified of them since.

"Thank you, Mr Penberthy." She smiled properly. Things were all working out rather well after all. "Thank you so much."

And he wished Mrs Penberthy could be more grateful to him.

Lucy washed her hands, combed her hair, took off her pinafore and set out for the library immediately. She felt the air hardening and moving around her bare arms. It was coming from the south, which meant it would blow straight on to the dunes and carry the sand all over the lettuces and radishes in the garden. The beans would be scorched, hanging and brown, tomorrow morning. The apples would be on the orchard floor but some would still be usable. She hoped Egg would get home before the worst of it. His bike would be blown off the causeway else.

The girls sensed the weather through their mother but they also sensed her changed mood. Ellie asked immediately, "Was Mr Penberthy all right about the pig, Mum?"

Lucy nodded. "Grand 'e were. There were sixpence too much in the rent book and he gave it me back!" Even Denny laughed at that. She might be only six years old but she understood Mr Penberthy just as she had understood *Black Beauty* when it was read to her by her sister.

"Can we have a horse as well as a pig, Mum?"

"No, lovey. The cats wouldn't like a horse."

"Oh." That was all. If Ellie or Egg or Barbara had not liked a horse, Denny would have still gone on and on about it. But the cats' wishes were paramount.

They came to meet them in the orchard, yowling like a pair of Siamese. Their names were Matthew and Mark; they were both ginger toms but Mark had a white mark on his neck. Denny cast herself at them.

Lucy called back, "Don't be long, Denny. It's going to rain and you know how they hate getting wet."

Ellie was telling her about two little girls in the library group who were on holiday further down the coast and were staying with a witch. "She won't let them have any food but there's a good fairy staying in the same house and she gives them her food and makes jokes and talks to them. An' they go paddling in the cove where it's calm and there's a shop there . . ." She paused for effect, then babbled, "Mum, it's Egg's shop and they love him and so does the good fairy!"

Lucy barely heard her because a sudden gust of wind came up from the dunes and flung hard sand into their faces. The kitchen door was open and banging against the dresser. The cats got in first; Matthew went to the saucer and tried to rinse off the sand from his whiskers with milk. Mark leaped into the shallow sink and pushed his face against the tap. A dribble of water did the trick.

"Clever boy . . . clever Mark . . ." Denny turned on the tap and tried to do the same; water spurted everywhere. Barbara spluttered and spat a scream; Lucy closed the door and latched it then passed the roller towel around.

"This is just a little warning. When things settle again, we'll tie hankies over our mouths like burglars and we'll pick as much lettuce and pull as many radishes as we can. Then we'll have hard-boiled eggs and salad for dinner." They all nodded. "*Then* we'll sort out the hens." She looked around at her dishevelled family. "Who wants ginger beer and who wants tea?"

"Is it Egg's ginger beer?" Ellie asked.

That was what was at the back of Lucy's mind. Egg. "It's Egg's ginger beer. And there's enough for all of us. He'll make us some more soon." She fetched it from the larder and unscrewed the top very carefully indeed, wrapping the whole bottle in a tea towel. "And two of your group know Egg, do they?"

Barbara nodded importantly. "The girl called Rosalie is the same age as me and she wanted me to cut my wrist."

Lucy looked at Ellie. Ellie said, "They do it at school, Mum. You know, blood sisters."

"Did you do it?" Lucy transferred her gaze to Barbara's face and thought for a moment it looked yellow then realized it was still sprinkled with sand.

"No." Barbara looked disgusted. "She's eight and she doesn't know what sterilization means. She can't even say it! Even Denny knows about sterilization. Don't you, Denny?" She poked her sister with a sharp elbow, not wanting too much attention from her mother.

Denny nodded. "Soaking teef," she said.

Ellie, always so serious, bent double with a gale of laughter. "Egg told her about Chippy's teeth," she gasped at her mother. "He leaves them soaking in a glass when he works. With some stuff to make them white."

Lucy nodded and shook her head at the three of them.

"Never mind the handkerchiefs. The wind has dropped right away. Let's get our dinner stuff in. Barbara, take Denny and see if there are any eggs. Ellie, we'll pick the lettuce. Ease them out the earth gently. Leave the ones what is hearting. We'll manage with the thinnings."

The two of them bent over the lettuce rows, plucking the small shoots and leaving space for the stronger plants to grow. Behind them the sea glittered, still and waiting. The sky above seemed to be pressing on their backs.

"Now the radish, my girl. Shake 'em gently. That's it." Lucy turned her head slightly and smiled. "You did all right this morning, by the sound of things."

Ellie was surprised. "I just read, Mum. It's the little ones who do all right. They either listen or they don't. Barbara and Denny are used to me reading to them so they set a good sample. Example."

Lucy's smile widened. Daniel had said once, "Dun't c'rreck our Ellie, my maid. Wait for a bit and see if she does it for 'erself."

It seemed that Ellie shared part of the memory. She said, "The two holiday girls . . . they're what Dad would call a coupla tinkers!" And they both laughed, perfectly in tune. And Ellie for a moment stemmed the terrible fear of her new school where she would be one of only three girls awarded a full scholarship. And Lucy, just for the same moment, stopped worrying around the thought of Egg, who seemed to be surrounded by people from Birmingham with no understanding of him whatsoever.

As if they had rehearsed it they spoke in unison. "We'll be all right, won't we?" They laughed and hugged. And the two of them felt the earth tremor and heard Barbara and Denny screaming.

CHAPTER
THREE

Connie got down to the cove before Philip arrived the next day. She did not unlock the beach hut. The weather was brassily hot. She kicked off her espadrilles from Brittany and paddled in the lapping sea. Far out, a pod of dolphins took it in turns to leap out of the water as they streamed along the coast looking for breakfast. She watched them without her usual enthusiasm and wondered why she was here. Did she intend to burden the beautiful straw-haired boy with more of her petty problems, carefully avoiding the one big problem that only she could see was a problem.

She shook her head. She must not do it. He was sixteen, just done with school, the whole world waiting for him. Perhaps he was even now planning a trip to America to find his father's family. Life was exciting but also simple. He saw things simply; either yes or no. Yet that was not true either because yes-and-no people rarely listened. And he listened. And she could not ask him to listen . . . not again.

The last of the dolphins leaped laughingly into the air and the pod disappeared around the headland. She trailed her toes through the sandy sea floor and tried not to think. There were shells in little clusters here and there. She picked up the purple and black mussels, rough on the back, shiningly lacquered inside. She kept two that might well have made a single whole at one time; she dried them on the skirt of her sundress and put them in one of the big patch pockets. She could talk to Phil about the shells. Perhaps. Or just go back to Blue Seas and pretend nothing had happened. The trouble was, if she waited for Phil and tried to talk about mussels she would probably blurt out the whole sorry tale of last evening and there he would be, burdened again. And only sixteen.

She blinked hard just in case she might have been about to cry and looked down at her feet. They were rippling in time to the sea. Encased in the clear medium that people called water they waved to her. And just beyond them was a small jellyfish, like an uncooked poached egg, lifting its skirt coyly as it waved to her big toe. She blinked again and then laughed. She could actually tell Phil about this; it was truly funny. And it was apt too, because he had said his name was Egbert and it was always shortened to Egg. And the little creature even now edging towards her big toe was very definitely an uncooked egg.

She put her hand carefully in front of it, wondering whether she could catch it to show Phil, wondering if it would die out of water, concluding that it was going to be beached anyway as the tide was full and would leave it behind very soon.

She wiggled her fingers enticingly and the unpoached egg twirled itself into a shuttlecock, zoomed on to her little finger and clamped its skirt tightly around the first knuckle. And then the pain started.

She straightened, exclaiming, "Ouch!", trying to dislodge the creature with a vigorous shake. She put her hand under the shallow water again and pushed at its skirt with her other hand, trying not to damage it. The clamp grew tighter. How on earth could such a tiny thing have such a fierce grip? Her eyes were watering very freely now. It was hurting badly. Really badly.

From the cliff path came a "halloo" and there was Phil on his bicycle, racketing along over the tufty sand with no regard for safety. She hallooed back and held up her throbbing hand. There was a pause. He was free-wheeling towards the steps where he would dismount and hopefully run down to her.

She yelled, "Can't get it off! Stinging like mad!"

He understood. He yelled back, "Stay where you are!" and took the steps on his bicycle at full tilt. The sight of it almost took her mind off the clamp on her finger. His bicycle appeared to leap from one long shallow step to the next. It made a horrible noise. He stood on the pedals as if they were stirrups on a horse and held the bike together somehow. It ploughed into the sand, he stepped out of the tangle of bars and pedals and ran to her. She told him afterwards, "I could not even count two, and there you were! Philip Marlowe to the rescue!"

He started to propel her onwards towards the headland, one arm behind her back urging her forward, the other clamped on her hand just below the tiny unpoached egg. They half ran, half stumbled through the shallows. He was saying something about water. Needing water. Which did not make sense when they were actually wading through the ocean. And then she understood. Cascading down the cliff was the waterfall where, at low tide, the swimmers would swill themselves free of the salt.

Philip pulled her whole arm beneath the weight of the fall. For perhaps two seconds, the tiny jellyfish clung tenaciously to her finger. And then it was gone, hurtling down into the sea, disappearing instantly. Connie looked and looked and could see nothing past the foam of fresh water meeting salt water. Philip still held her arm, pulling it right under the little waterfall so that her dress was soaked. Unexpectedly an enormous sob racked her whole body. She blurted wetly, "I killed it — oh Phil, it did not understand — I killed it!"

He guffawed. "Naw! You en't killed that little blighter. Let's get his spit out of your finger and we'll go looking for 'e." He held her arm above the elbow so that her hand fell at a right angle. "You dun't need to worry about the creatures from the deep. They got the sea on their side and in the end the sea do always win."

She stopped blubbing and looked over her shoulder into his face. The morning sun caught the lobe of his ear and the line of his cheek, highlighting the tiny hairs into golden fur. His full mouth was tight.

She said, "That was a strange thing to say."

"Creatures from the deep? It's in a hymn. It just means fish and the like."

50

"I know. But the idea of the sea being so powerful. Like an enemy almost."

"Not an enemy. It can be a friend. 'Tis always the master."

"Oh Phil, you sound . . . sombre. Are you all right?"

"I'm all right. Doubt the bike is though." His mouth curved upwards and he became a boy again. A boastful boy. "Did you see me coming down the steps? It were like riding a bucking bronco. When I go to America I might get a job on a ranch."

"I reckon you could." She laughed, relieved. She could bear all this peculiar business back at the boarding house; it would be too dreadful if Phil was unhappy. It was as if he had been born to be happy. She said, "D'you know, Phil, you are my golden boy."

He looked at her, his eyes changing, becoming wary yet not wary. He said in a low voice, "What do you mean?"

She was aghast, knowing in that instant that he thought he was in love with her. She made herself laugh. "The sun is turning your face to gold, Phil. It's really amazing." He blinked. She said, "Have you started shaving, Phil?"

He looked at her hand drooping under the waterfall. He cleared his throat. "Naw. Mum says I'm a late starter. I just got the bum fluff."

She looked out to sea then closed her eyes against the brassy glare. It was all right. He knew . . . he thought he knew . . . that she saw him as a schoolboy.

She said, "Bum fluff? I'm trying to work out . . . oh *Phil!*" She bent over, laughing inordinately. He pulled her back to the water. She said, "It's all right now, Phil. You've done the trick." It was all right. She was sure of it.

They walked back slowly to the beach huts. He told her that his mother was "good" about him not taking up his apprenticeship. "She'll make it all right with Chippy Penberthy too," he said. "We got to be careful 'cos he's our landlord."

"I think your tenancy is probably protected, Phil. I'll ask William about it. He'll know." Then she remembered that she was not going to marry William after all so she could hardly expect free legal advice from him.

But Philip said, "Aw, Chippy wun't do nothing. Mum dun't know, but Ellie and me, we're pretty certain 'e's sweet on Mum."

"Oh . . . I suppose it's a bit soon but . . . would she consider him, d'you think? I mean if you're going to America it would be nice to think she had someone to look after things." She looked at his suddenly closed face. "Sorry, Phil. None of my business."

"I en't going to America just yet, Connie. Mum's thinking of doing more with the smallholding. Mebbe a pig. And a tunnel of strawberries." He lifted her hand and folded her little finger into his palm. She held her breath. He said, "Do that 'urt? Tell me the truth now."

"It's all right. Honestly. I had forgotten all about it." She smiled, relieved again. "Do you mind? About postponing America."

"No. I want to be here for a bit. Help Mum and that. And Ellie when she do start her new school." He paused. "An' you."

She withdrew her hand gently. "Phil . . . Philip . . . Philip Marlowe, detective extraordinary . . . I wasn't going to tell you . . . using you as a prop . . ." They were outside the beach hut now and she let her hands hang by her side and moved her feet, pushing them into the sand as if they could take root. "But." She looked up and smiled at him ruefully. "I won't be coming here again. I'm not engaged any more and I'm not going to marry William Mather. Which means I'll have to find another job. Not so much money. No lovely long holidays in Cornwall."

He returned the smile, blazingly.

"I knew you wouldn't marry him. I knew."

"Yes. You did. I thought you were wrong." She felt very sad. The truth had been spoken and so must be real.

"You will come with me to America."

She gave that smile again. "No, Phil."

"Perhaps not America. But we will be together always."

"No. That cannot be." She unearthed her feet and climbed the small step to the hut, fitted in her key. "You will make a great success of the smallholding. And I will get another job and look after my mother."

He did not care what she said, he knew she was wrong. "Listen. I'll go and open up the shop and make us some coffee and sandwiches . . . We'll sit in the sun and sleep together."

She looked at him sharply and saw that he was being his usual literal self. He strode off to the shop, where the remains of his bike lay in the sand. She could hear him laughing. All the time. And she thought, I *do* love him! My God, I do. I know him like I know my hand. She held up the hand he had cleaned for her. Put it close to her face. Kissed it. And felt the same kind of joy he was exhibiting as he held up a pair of handlebars and rang the bell of his bike. She waved to him, laughing so that he could hear her. Then she unlocked the beach hut and began to get the chairs out and assembled. It was as if a weight had fallen from her. She did not have to "burden" him. He knew. He was so sweet. So kind. And he loved her and wanted her to be with him always.

She set out the little beach table carefully and sat in one of the chairs and closed her eyes. She had not slept all night.

William had said that he could not sleep without her. "I haven't slept like last night for years and years . . ." He was still half joking, thinking she was being coy. "You can't be so cruel."

But it confirmed her feelings. If he had said that he understood exactly how she felt and he respected her and would happily wait until their wedding day, it might have been all right.

She said, "I don't think you can have heard what I just told you, William." She still felt sick. "Mrs Pentwyn asked Mrs Heatherington to get rid of me. I was using her home as a brothel."

William looked at her. He must be listening now. Before, he had said quizzically, "Darling, I'm sure you're mistaken. Let's go upstairs and talk about this properly." And he had taken her key and gone ahead of her into her room as if he had every right to do that. Just because . . . just because . . .

"And this was . . . when?" He was speaking in his solicitor's voice.

"You know very well when it was. When Mrs P. wanted a private word with Mrs Heatherington and Lily asked me very nicely whether I could find some biscuits and I went into the kitchen and the two of them — Heatherington and Pentwyn — were under the porch with the light on and it was obvious that Mrs Heatherington had been coming here for donkey's years and she — *she* — Mrs Heatherington — herself in person — had booked two rooms, one for her and one for you — and then you had telephoned and asked for another room for your fiancée!" Connie took an enormous breath. "I should never have come. I'm the odd one out. You should have explained it all to me properly. That you would have to spend all the time with her. In effect, you have lied to me about this holiday. And I am the one to be shown the door!" She went to the window and stared down at the dark glimmer of the cove and thought of the boy who was reading American novels and was innocent and honest. She had been innocent too . . . and gullible. She put her knuckles on the window ledge and leaned hard down until the pain took her mind off the two women arguing under the porch.

William was behind her, silent, no longer a lover pleading for love, no longer a lawyer. She said loudly, "I feel shame. I feel grubby. Horrible. I want to go home."

"Connie . . . please. I realize now how awful this is from your point of view. Can you try — please — please — to see it from mine?"

"Tomorrow I will arrange a taxi to the station at Penzance — you can tell them what you like."

He said miserably, "I will drive you back, of course. But I want you to know — I didn't want — oh God, Connie, Arnold thought it would be a good idea if I went along with her — Greta Heatherington. She wanted to talk it all over, away from the grime of the city where the air was clear . . . you know how she goes on. Arnold says she hasn't got a chance with this suit and he reckoned if I listened to her and put in a word now and then, she would drop the whole thing. Then I asked you to marry me and you said yes and I thought . . ."

"Yes." Connie nodded as if she really did understand. "Two birds with one stone. You used me, William. I was making sure poor old — Greta, did you say? — couldn't embarrass you. And as I was just next door, why not try it on? It's quite the done thing now, isn't it?" She took another breath and forced herself to say very clearly, "Sex before marriage. A trial run. Just to see if I was good enough?" She turned, suddenly unbearably weary. "Just go."

He looked terrible. Drooping. He held out one hand. "I will go, darling. But please, don't — don't — cancel everything. Not everything."

She felt herself softening inside again. But then, out of the blue, something made her say, "Am I included on the list of expenses for this business holiday?"

He flinched physically as if she had struck him. Before he could speak she had twisted off her ring, the lovers' knot of sapphires and diamonds, and put it into that outstretched hand. Then she turned away again and listened as he walked across the room, opened the door and closed it.

The boy's voice woke her.

"Connie, are you all right?"

She had twisted in the deckchair and was facing the little driftwood table. There was a cup and saucer sitting on it; coffee with wrinkled skin sealing saucer to cup. The boy's shape was silhouetted against the sky. A yellowish sky. It was very hot.

He smiled into her eyes. "You bin asleep. Solid. I kep' an eye on you from the shop. People comin' and goin' . . . thought they'd disturb you."

She struggled up, held her head and noticed her watch. "Oh . . . good Lord, Phil. It's almost one. Lunch will be on the table. Damn! Damn, damn, damn! I meant to be on the train by now!"

He looked stricken. "I didn't think . . . not so soon?"

"I can't go back there. I really can't. I've got my money and there are spare sweaters and things in the beach hut. I'll get a taxi to Penzance and just wait there for a train." She put her hands on the frame of the deckchair and then fell back with a groan. "Bit of a headache," she said as he crouched by her, full of concern.

"Just close your eyes again. I'll fetch a glass of water and perhaps a sandwich — bet you din't 'ave no breakfast."

She did as she was bid and when he came back with the water she sipped and felt herself coming together again. But the innocence of the mussel shells and the strange, painful exhilaration of the jellyfish had gone. She was left with a heavy weight of depression that was like nausea in her chest.

She glanced around. "Where are all the people, Phil?"

"It's going to rain. They've gone back to their caravans and rooms. It was just too hot."

She nodded, still gazing around the deserted cove. "Did anyone come looking for me?"

"Not as I know of. Dun't think anyone 'ud spot you from the cliff top. Reckon you're safe 'ere."

She was not comforted. Why had William not come to find her? Surely he would when she didn't turn up for lunch? And when he did, what was she going to do? She looked at her watch again and shivered in the heat. If she left right now and phoned from the kiosk not far from Blue Seas, she would be seen. Mrs Pentwyn would be triumphant, her accusations verified by such an undignified departure. And by the time she got a taxi and arrived at Penzance station it would be at least mid-afternoon and the journey was six hours. And her mother was at the other end. She would be good about it, she would stand by her daughter. But she would be so disappointed.

"You need summat to eat. I'll get that sandwich."

And he was right again, she did feel better after the cheese sandwich and another glass of water. He munched away, grinning up at her from the sand.

"Goin' to rain cats and dogs," he said. "We'll be all right. We'll wait in the hut till it gives over. Then we'll get back to Hell for the night. You can get the train tomorrow from there."

"Hayle?"

"Where I live. You en't been lissening, Connie!" But he was still grinning. "Told you. You can sleep with the girls — Ellie will see to it."

She said blankly, "How will we get there? It's about ten miles up the coast surely?"

"Mended the bike in between customers. Good as new. You can go on the handlebars. Take us a couple hours but we got all the time in the world now, Connie." He was slickly confident. Like Philip Marlowe. "Give me a year or two to get things going for Mum an' I'll come and fetch you an' we'll go to America. How's that sound?"

She got out of the chair at last. She would have to go now. Now. At this moment. Lock the hut and leave the key with the boy. And go.

And then something happened. The ground beneath her feet started to move. She stared down at the boy. He stared back.

"'Tis only an earth tremor." But he looked frightened. "Mum do call it the shivers. Comes with the heat."

He uncoiled himself and stood up. The dry sand was falling away in little rivulets. Through the soles of their feet came an ancient drumming. And then the beach hut on the end of the row collapsed and its four plank walls spread themselves flat. The other huts jumped but stayed put. The boy gave a little whimper and automatically Connie put her arms around him and held him tightly. "It's all right, Phil. We're OK. We're hunky-dory! Yes?"

The tremor was subsiding. The rain started. They stayed where they were, clutched together, lifting their heads to the enormous drops of water.

"Mum do say it's all right when it gets to rain. It cools the earth down, like."

"I reckon she's right. Can't feel anything under my feet, can you?"

"Naw." But he was shivering. They were both already sodden with the rain.

She loosened her grip on him slightly. "Shall we shelter in the beach hut, Phil? When it stops we can go to the shop and eat everything in sight!" She laughed and he joined in but uncertainly.

"What if the hut collapses like the end one?"

"We shall get wet all over again." She urged him up the shallow step and into the hut. It was an enormous relief to get out of the way of those heavy drops hurtling from the sky. She looked up at it and noticed it had turned purple.

She released him and he folded into a crouch on the wooden floor. His checked shirt and khaki shorts were dripping everywhere. She was suddenly worried.

"Come on, Phil. Take your stuff off. Here's a towel. I'll turn my back. In fact, I'll dry myself too." Rain drummed on the roof so she repeated her words, pushed a towel into his hands, grabbed another one and went into a corner. He must have heard her but she knew he was not moving. As she leaned over to dry her legs she saw his towel lying on the floor. She seized one of William's enormous sweaters and dragged it over her head.

"Phil, for goodness' sake. You're shivering like a dog! Stand up — let me . . ." She hauled him upright, pushed his shorts down as far as decency permitted, unbuttoned his shirt — realizing that he must be wearing it to look American — and pushed it from his shoulders. She picked up the towel and started at his hair, worked down his neck and chest and turned him to dry his back. Then she eased him into the waterproof jacket William called his "slicker".

"It's American. Look, Phil, see the label?" She turned him again to zip up the jacket and realized he was crying. Tears were pouring down his face, his mouth working uncontrollably.

She said, "Oh Phil . . . oh my dear boy . . . what is it? Tell me — talk, Phil. Please say something." Tears filled her own eyes. She said, "We're together, Phil. Nothing can harm us when we're together."

She cradled him and he sobbed into her neck for some time before words emerged.

"Wanted to look after you. Love you. And you love me. Thought I could go to America. Thought I was a detective. Now you know." He almost choked on his sobs.

She was bewildered. "What are you talking about, Phil? Of course you can go to America. And anyone can be a detective."

"Naw. Naw. Not unless you come with me . . ." He raised his head and looked at her. "I'm . . . I'm MD. You didn't know, did you? You treated me like I was normal. And I looked after you when you was unhappy."

"Phil, you did. I haven't thanked you, have I? Oh Phil, you made such a difference."

He stared at her. "You don't know what MD means, do you?"

"I do. And you are not it."

"Say it, Connie. Say what it means."

"It means mentally defective and you are not that. You are wise and kind and you know what to do when people need help. Those little girls — Rosalie and Lily — they love you. So did Mrs Heatherington and William."

"They knew."

"Mrs Heatherington does gush like that. Probably so that you will know she's an actress. And William . . . he doesn't say much." She held his head in her hands and looked into his eyes. She said, "There is nothing wrong with your mind, Phil. Some of those tests . . . I've seen them . . . they're ridiculous."

"Oh Connie . . . oh Connie . . ."

She whispered, "It's all right. It's all right. Honestly." She put her lips against his.

At some point in the next few minutes she made a decision. After all, it was no great thing to give this boy something he wanted and needed so much. William had shown her how; she was not that silly word, a virgin. So really what was the point of stopping him? They lay in the purple darkness and she showed him what to do. He was so gentle. He could not stop saying her name. The beach hut was full of his whispered "Connie . . . oh my Connie . . . Connie, I love you. Connie." And her responses were her kisses and whispered "It's all right, Phil. All right."

They huddled quietly together and laughed at the thumping roar of the storm on the roof. His happiness filled the tiny space so gently. She whispered, "Feel the air, Phil. It's like silk."

It was strange to turn her head in his shoulder and smell William on the crumpled slicker jacket; to feel Phil's arms around her arms within the sleeves of William's sweater.

He said, surprised, "It's us. We made the silk."

"Yes. Like a cocoon."

They were quiet again within their cocoon. The storm abated gradually though the light was still purple. When it stopped and all they could hear was dripping from the cliff above, she stood up and opened the door. The sand was pitted by the rain; the sea oblivious. The tide was lapping up as usual as if nothing had happened. She peered out. To her left the little shop was intact, even the awning above the serving hatch still there, bowed with its weight of water but in place. To her right the broken beach hut was the only evidence of the earth tremor and the storm.

She looked down at him. "Are you all right, my wonderful detective?"

He nodded. His intensely blue eyes shone in the peculiar light.

She said, "I'm going to have a swim, Phil. Then I'm going back to the boarding house and tomorrow William will drive me home."

He stood up slowly. "Will you be engaged again?" His voice shook.

"No." She smiled at him and took his hand. "I can see now why William did what he did. But I can see I should not have said yes when he asked me to marry him." She shook his hand. "Thank you, Phil."

"Won't I see you again?"

"I don't know." She held his gaze somehow. "I don't know anything any more, Phil. What has happened here —" She swept her gaze around the tiny space. "We found something, Phil. Something natural and real. A sort of . . . a sort of . . ."

"Bench mark," he supplied.

She laughed joyously. "That's *it*, Phil! Just like your driftwood table — we didn't have to change any shapes or cut into anything at all. We were there — we were *there*, Phil!"

He caught her mood. "I'm coming in with you. We'll swim — we'll swim!"

They charged down the beach and into the quiet sea, still wearing their bulky clothing. Connie ducked under and swam four strokes and surfaced. The heavy wool of the sweater was too much. She started to struggle out of it. Behind her, Phil was still in his depth, clutching William's slicker around him and gasping with the sudden cold.

Above them, above the beach huts, came a shout from the cliff. A warning shout. William was there, ridiculously overdressed in his city suit and waistcoat. He was waving his arms like semaphores. But already she knew what was happening. She could feel it in her feet and flailing arms and she stopped fighting with the sweater and began to swim strongly towards Phil.

"Go in!" she screamed at him. "Go in . . . now!"

He grinned at her. "Can't swim!" he yelled back and went on walking towards her and she felt pure terror grip her own body as the weight of the Atlantic lifted her high and she could see his beautiful face below her still full of that joy and then he was gone and she was past him and a back wave was coming at her from the shore and she was sucked into a vortex of water and smashed down until she felt the grit of the seabed rolling her over and over and not letting her up.

Strangely she did not care. All she could remember was that voice . . . "Can't swim!" he had said. So why had he —

The inevitable drag was taking her out again and she would have to breathe very soon. She opened her eyes and saw him. Just for a moment his body rolled towards her. And then he was gone and something had hold of her hair and was pulling and pulling and she was free of the drag and the next wave pushed her up. She was choking but she was being borne to the shore. Her hair was still hurting.

She and William landed right in front of the beach huts far beyond the high-tide line. She couldn't move, couldn't breathe. He got across her and began to push her spine so that water spurted out of her and she could move again. She started to crawl back into the sea. He shouted something at her and she managed to speak.

"He can't swim — he can't swim!"

He looked at her, startled, and stood up. He was still in his suit; it was thick with wet sand. She saw it was impacted in his ears; he spat his mouth clear of it. She wondered how he had done it, held himself against that fearful drag and pulled her on to the incoming wave.

He ran back to where the vortex pulled and pushed as the sea tried to swallow the cove. She crouched and watched him run up and down. Then as one wave receded he started to wade and she struggled up somehow and managed three steps before sinking to her knees. She called his name and he looked round and the next wave engulfed him and brought him to her. She grabbed him by the collar of his jacket and felt the full weight of him as the sea tried to drag them both to itself. It left them with a ghastly sucking sound.

She whimpered, "He's gone, William. I saw him . . . down there. Under the water. I think he was already gone."

She must have lost consciousness for a few minutes because the next thing she knew, the cove was full of people and there was the navy and white of St John's Ambulance and the poles of a stretcher and the coastguards were launching one of their latest fast rescue boats.

Mrs Pentwyn acted as if she was royalty and helped her into a hot bath. Later, William knocked on her door with a tray of food. He was in his dressing gown, the same dressing gown he had worn on Monday night.

He said, "She's put my food on the tray as well. But I can take it away if you would rather."

She said, "Stay, William. I have to tell you something."

"You don't have to tell me anything, Connie. Nothing at all. I did an awful thing, insensitive and underhand. I cannot believe now that . . . Anyway, you don't have to say anything. We'll go home tomorrow." He looked at her. "Everyone knows you risked your life to save that boy's."

"William! You know it wasn't like that."

"I was watching, Connie. I saw exactly what happened."

She said, "You saved my life, William. I'll always remember that. But I am responsible for the death of Philip Pardoe and I will never forget that."

He said, "Think carefully, Connie. If you persuaded him to go into the sea or actually pushed him in, that is one thing. If he made up his own mind, that is quite another." He cut up her meat carefully. "Try to eat something, my dear."

She looked at the food; it was veal. She thought of the calves who were reared especially for such delicacies. She thought of the Memburys.

"Are the little girls — Rosalie and Lily — are they very upset?"

"A bit. They don't really understand. But they met Philip Pardoe's sister this morning at Hayle library. And they are anxious for her. Membury drove over earlier with the coastguard to tell Mrs Pardoe."

"Oh . . ." Phil's mum. They had been very close. Connie squeezed her eyes shut. "How will she bear it? William, she has been widowed twice. And now — what have I done, William? What have I done?"

He held her during that first breakdown. Above her head he stared bleakly at the flowered wallpaper and remembered the day Arnold had first laid the plans for the so-called holiday.

"I had a bit of a fling with Greta," Arnold had said. "Years ago now, of course — during the war. But she's a good egg, William. I don't want her getting caught up in litigation that will leave her penniless. See what you can do. She fancies you like mad. If I ask her to book a couple of rooms down in this special place of hers, she'll be tickled pink."

And it had ended up in this boy's death.

Connie raised her head and controlled her breathing. "I'll have to see her, William. Do you mind if we stop off in Hayle tomorrow? I have to see her."

He looked into her face. He had lost her and he knew there would never be anyone else for him. She was good. Through and through she was good. And if he had needed more evidence of her goodness, he had it then.

"You do understand, William?"

He smiled. "I understand, Connie."

CHAPTER
FOUR

Lucy Pardoe thought — much, much later — that when Joshua Warne turned up in his Morris Minor still wearing his oilskin suit, and closely followed by someone called Harry Membury driving a bigger car, she had probably gone mad.

She had known instantly why they were there and her only thought was to get rid of them as quickly as possible so that she could forget they had been there and go back to waiting for Egg to come in and help her clear up the mess left by the earth-shake. She had been anxious for Egg ever since she and Ellie had felt the earth tremble; he was used to these small midsummer shakes but if he got frightened and had one of his "turns" he might not be safe on his bike. So she stood in the doorway and watched them draw up one behind the other and made no move to let them in. Behind her, the girls, laying the table for tea, peered past her curiously. Ellie whispered, "'Tis only Mr Warne. And another man. 'Tis the man who brought those two little girls to the library this morning!"

Barbara whispered back, "Rosalie and Lily." She lifted Matthew out of the chair where his nose was already investigating what was on the table. Denny did the same with Mark. Both girls buried their faces in soft fur and looked over the cats at the doorway, waiting for their mother to stand aside.

She did not. Joshua Warne stammered, "Mrs Pardoe, this is Harry Membury who is staying at the cove and has been helping us to — to — search. Mrs Pardoe — Lucy — we got bad news."

Harry Membury came forward. "Would it be best if Mrs Pardoe sat down and perhaps the girls could go out and play for a while."

Nobody said anything. Lucy did not move. Ellie came up behind her mother and stood by her. Barbara and Denny, clutching the cats like shields, came the other side.

Joshua Warne clenched his hands into fists. He had been two hours in his dinghy, paddling from one side of the cove to the other, searching the water for some sign. The strange tidal surge that had engulfed the beach huts and the shop had torn weed from the seabed and the rocks and several times he had thought . . . but it had been nothing; a long strand of kelp, a tightly packed mass of weed. He had volunteered to tell Lucy. The rescue boat was still out but all hope of finding the poor kid had gone. His mother must be told properly and Joshua had gone out often with Daniel Pardoe and knew the family well. But he had not realized how difficult it would be. Lucy's eyes were fierce; he felt her dislike — hatred — like a physical blow.

Harry Membury said, "I really think it would be best if we went indoors. I can make us all a cup of tea —"

Lucy spoke harshly. "Is he dead?"

Joshua lifted his balled fists slightly and let them drop. "We cain't find 'im. But 'e must be."

"The search and rescue boat is still out, Mrs Pardoe. Mr Warne here has been trawling the cove all afternoon —"

Lucy's voice rose to a shout. "The sea? The *sea*? 'E'd never go in the sea — 'e were frightened of the sea. It were 'is bike, weren't it? It broke up and 'e . . ."

Mr Membury said quietly, "No, Mrs Pardoe. We understand he went for a swim and there was a tidal surge that swamped the cove."

Lucy was rigid. Denny started to cry. Barbara put Matthew gently on to the kitchen floor, took Mark from her sister and set him down too, then enveloped the small girl in her arms. "It's not true," she said. "Our Egg wouldn't go in the sea, you knows that."

Lucy did not move. "Course it en't true," she said fiercely.

Ellie's small voice came from her mother's side. "You didn't see this happen, Mr Membury?"

"No, my dear. The beach was empty because of the rain. Your brother was there with Miss Vickers, who is staying at the same boarding house as my family and me. Miss Vickers decided to go for a swim after the storm. Your brother wanted to join her. She did not realize he couldn't swim." Harry Membury stopped speaking when he saw Lucy Pardoe's face change.

Joshua said quickly, "'E weren't frightened. The girl says 'e were smilin' as if 'e were real 'appy."

He realized what he had said when Lucy turned her gaze on him. He took a step back. Mr Membury put out a hand. "It's important to know that, Mrs Pardoe. He had no fear. That is so important."

"She is safe." It was not a question. Lucy ignored the outstretched hand and spat out another time, "*She* is safe."

"Her fiancé knew she would be in the cove and after the storm he became anxious and went to look for her. He pulled her out of the sea. He resuscitated her and raised the alarm. The coastguards launched the rescue dinghy from the cove and are still out."

There was another silence, broken by the strange whimpering from Denny. Ellie reached out and took Mr Membury's hand. It had been there for so long, unclaimed, an offer of sympathy. She felt its chill against her own warm palm and began to cry helplessly.

Lucy snatched her back to her side.

"'E'll be 'ome soon. We'll go down the towans in a minute and wait for 'im there."

She bade no farewells. The door was closed in the faces of the two men. Through the window Lucy watched as Harry Membury put his arm on Joshua Warne's shoulder and led him back to his Morris. She realized through the numbness of anger and hatred that Joshua Warne was weeping.

There was no question of tea; the idea of sitting at the table for a meal was irrelevant. Yet there it was; the end of this morning's loaf on the familiar bread board, the butter, oily in the oppressive heat, the tiny lettuce leaves, tomatoes, radishes from the garden and an empty plate waiting for Egg to bring home whatever was left from the shop . . . some ham if they were lucky, a couple of pasties, some slices of cheese. Ten minutes ago the girls had been laying plates and cutlery. Ten minutes. Another lifetime. It occurred to Lucy that a lifetime was not simply the span of a life but a whole way of life. When she had known that Bertie had died at sea and that she was carrying his child, she had started to make a lifetime for that child. And that time had included — marvellously and miraculously — meeting Daniel Pardoe again and giggling about schooldays and watching him play with baby Bertie on the towans and seeing that Daniel loved her son as well as herself. And now that lifetime was gone. Swept away by the sea again. She realized, understood at last, the full extent of her loss. Her wonderful Bertie, her steadfast Daniel, and now . . . but not now, not again, it could not happen again, God could not be that cruel.

She saw that Ellie had stopped crying and was cuddling her sisters. She said briefly, "Eat something. Then go up to bed."

She went through the orchard to where a sandy track led to a stile and then the wilderness of the towans. To her left, in another arm of the six miles of dunes, were caravans and chalets and people and bonfires and sausages and football games. This way, facing the lighthouse and Hell's Mouth, there might be someone walking with a dog or standing looking out to sea. They would go as the light failed and she could scream if she needed to. Already the sun was sitting on the sea in the west; it was two months since the longest day; in a week it would be her birthday and she would be thirty-six. If she was unlucky enough to last for three score years and ten, she was over halfway there. She could not live another thirty or more years like this. Not even God could expect that. Not when he had given her so much, only to snatch it away. Too much time. Too many lifetimes.

The long dune faced her and she pulled off her sandals and dug her bare toes into it as she climbed. It was years since she had come as far as this. They all went to Portreath occasionally to see a cousin, but they took the bus from Hayle along the coast road. Daniel and she had done it with Egg on Daniel's shoulders. Forded the Red River and looked at the lighthouse close to, no longer ethereal, a concrete monstrosity rising out of the sea, covered in gulls' mess.

She came to the top of the dune and faced a long beach below. Not a living soul in sight. Not a cottage or caravan. The house, her childhood home, was out of sight behind the enormous piles of sand and rock. Egg had been born there. Had some quirk of fate plucked him out of the cruel sea so close to his birthplace? The sea was much rougher here, curling on to the sand and sucking back, taking what it could with it. She stood looking down. Egg could have been washed up here, dumped among the rocks at the base of the dunes, left for dead. But who said he was dead? Was it the sea? Had he fooled the sea and saved one breath that would make another breath and another?

She giant-strode down the other side of the long dune and ran as the sand got firmer. There were pools and she splashed her thin frock but there was still the big sun spreading its warmth as it dipped into the sea. She ran — crazily at first, then more systematically. Her bare feet hurt as she searched the shingly patches around the rocks. She thought she had found Egg's shirt but it was a plastic bag. The whole of the beach was stained sun-red. There were shadows; when she reached them they were not Egg. She became frantic and turned and screamed at the sea, "Give him back to me — give him to me — now . . . now . . . now . . ."

The sun went suddenly but the sky reflected its light as she waded in. Somewhere, right at the back of her mind, she had an idea. If the sea took her it would give up Egg. It was so simple and so obvious. She took another tiny step, felt the suck and pull of it, a wave broke over her shoulder. And behind her a voice screamed like the scream of a gull.

"Mum! My Mummy! Don't go!"

She turned her head and looked up at the long dune and saw Ellie. And beside Ellie was someone else.

Even in the half-light the girl's grief was like an aura around her. Ellie saw the whiteness of her mother's face and knew she had her attention. She screamed again and again, unintelligibly, and then began to come down the long slope at full tilt. When she fell and began to roll helplessly, Lucy dragged her own body free of the water; flailing her arms, she waded through the waves and gathered Ellie to her. The other shape had gone. But she knew it had been there and she knew it had been Egg. He had come with Ellie to find her. The knowledge was at once a leaden weight of acceptance and an assurance that he was . . . somewhere. She was not surprised when Ellie spoke through her tears and told her that Egg's body had been found.

"Mum . . . you've got to come back. Mr Warne is at the house. They've found our Egg . . . They want to know if they should bring him home. I said yes. Oh Mum, oh Mum . . . oh Mum . . . oh Mum . . . I said yes."

Suddenly Lucy was Lucy Pardoe again. The hatred, the anger . . . it was still there but she was in charge of it. She gathered her daughter to her and held her, rocking back and forth until the sobs lessened. How had she imagined for one second that she could abandon her girls? She had other lifetimes, other lifespans. She did not want them but there was no choice.

She said, "You did the right thing, Ellie."

They stood up eventually. The sun had gone but an uncaring moon lit the way for them. Lucy knew her feet were bleeding and that her body was chilled but she felt neither pain nor cold. She tried to speak normally.

"Did you eat something?"

"Barbara had a slice of last Sunday's cake. Denny had bread and milk."

"What about you?"

"Some radishes. But I sicked them up. Then I felt better."

They went down the other side of the long dune and up into the smaller hills leading to the village. They turned left and found the stile. Already through the orchard Lucy could see the lights of the cottage. She gripped the top of the stile and bent her head.

Ellie said desperately, "We got each other, Mum."

"I know."

"The girls were asleep when Mr Warne came. They dun't really seem to — to — kind of believe it."

"I know."

"The cats are with them. And Mr Warne downstairs."

"That's good, Ellie. So good." She watched as the little girl walked ahead of her through the orchard. She couldn't see anyone else but she knew he was there.

They put Egg on his bed in the tiny front parlour which had become his room when Ellie was born. He wore his new underpants, bought at the summer sales just last week. A sodden anorak hung from his shoulders. He was not bloated; he was not changed in any way. Someone had said he was happy to be in the sea, to be drowning in the sea, and she had wanted to spit her rejection of such an idea; yet he looked happy. She kissed his lips and could have sworn they were smiling. Ellie came behind her and wailed with terror; Lucy put her arm around her and drew her close. "Dun't be frightened, my maid. Just look quiet for a bit. 'E were a lucky boy, Ellie. Two dads and three beautiful sisters."

Ellie had cried so many tears her eyes were too swollen to see. But she did as she was bid and looked quiet. They stayed, wrapped together in silence. When eventually Ellie whispered, "I just want him to be alive, Mum," Lucy was able to say, without one tremor in her voice, "Perhaps he has been spared a lot, Ellie. It's a cruel world."

Their doctor came in from the kitchen where he had been washing his hands. He had looked after baby Bertie from his rather furtive birth in the family farm on the Connor Downs to this afternoon, when they had called him down to the cove to pronounce the all-too-familiar "death by drowning". He had prescribed the tablets that kept the lad on an even keel.

He said now, "Your mother's right, Ellie. He's had a very happy life here in Pardoe cottage. But nothing stays the same." He glanced at Lucy Pardoe, wondering whether she had heard the rumour of the holiday camp to be sited on the north towans. She returned his look and he saw that she had heard nothing.

He said in the most matter-of-fact voice he could muster, "Say good night to your brother, my dear. Josh Warne has got a jug of cocoa in the kitchen. Have a mug of that with this little pill I'm going to give you. Then go upstairs and go to sleep. I've checked on your sisters and they're both asleep too. Everything will seem better in the morning."

"It cain't never be better, doctor."

With difficulty the doctor separated her from her mother and piloted her into the kitchen, then returned.

"I've got a pill for you too, Lucy."

"Dun't want it. Not being okkard, just dun't want it."

He hesitated, then said, "I'll leave them on the top shelf of the dresser." He looked down at Egg. "He's safe now, Lucy."

"I know. But we'd a kept 'im safe too."

"Maybe not. Things happen." He did not want to burden her with anything else but often "things" happened very quickly. He said, "Listen, girl. Buy this cottage. Just pay Chippy what he asks. But buy it."

She was astonished. If it had been anyone else she would have been angry, told him to go. But this was Dr Carthew.

She said, "We en't got money for buying cottages, doctor! You should know that!" They had been unable to pay doctor's bills back in the days before National Health. Dr Carthew had not bothered even to write them out.

He said, "I'll lend you the money, Lucy. It won't be for long — no need to worry about being in debt. But buy it at any price. And soon."

He was gone. And she turned to Egg. "What were 'e talking about, son?"

His beautiful blue eyes were closed but the smile seemed to widen.

The girl arrived next day. Lucy was both glad and outraged that she did not mention staying on for the funeral. She also felt a stab of surprise at the girl's sheer ordinariness. She had expected a peroxide blonde in a very low-cut top, high heels and layers of Max Factor. This girl — Connie Vickers — wore a blue cardigan over a round-necked natural linen sundress with a matching hat. No sunglasses. Swollen eyes. Could be green or brown. Brown hair pushed tightly behind her ears. She wasn't much to look at; Lucy was surprised that Egg had noticed her. Her fiancé was the same;

brown all over. Older than her. Thin to the point of being gaunt. As she turned away from him she noticed something about the brown eyes. They were kind. And they were haunted. She thought suddenly that her eyes must look like that.

The man was a good man. A bit like Dr Carthew. Older than the girl by quite a bit, which probably meant that later on she would have to live on her own. There would be children of course. Quite soon too, most likely, because of this . . . this . . . tragedy. And they would forget Egg, put him behind them, get on with their own lives. It was what they would all do. Even his own mother.

She said in her new harsh voice, "Say it quickly. Tell me quickly."

Connie peered from under the brim of her hat. She felt Lucy Pardoe's anger but also saw into the bottomless pit of her grief. She grabbed on to her wavering self-control and stepped away from William's protective arm.

"It started with the earthquake." She waited to see if this was the right way to go. Lucy Pardoe's concentration was suddenly intense. Connie said, "It frightened him." She waited again.

Lucy nodded. "'E 'ad one of 'is seizures."

Connie frowned slightly then said, "I suppose . . . yes. Then the rain came. Huge drops. We sheltered. There was spare clothing and we put it on. He was shivering."

Lucy nodded again, remembering the anorak. This girl, silly and ignorant as she was, had done the right thing. Until she had persuaded him to get into the sea . . . until then.

Connie closed her eyes for a moment, unable to meet that concentrated stare. She whispered, "It stopped. Everything was so still. The shop was still there. Just the one beach hut, fallen outwards . . . strange. Like another country, like another world. I said I would have a swim. A dip. To get rid of the sand. He came with me. There was no sign of the tidal wave. None at all. We just . . . ran in." She stopped on a sob and opened her eyes. Lucy Pardoe was waiting. What was she waiting for?

She stumbled on, no longer sorting and measuring her words. "We were still wearing the spare clothes. I trod water and started to get out of the sweater and felt the sea piling up. William was on the cliff signalling. And I shouted at Philip to swim back and he shouted back that he could not swim." She sobbed. "The sea took me. And it lifted him high so that I could see him and he was . . . he looked . . . triumphant. As if he'd . . . won."

She was shivering uncontrollably. William put his arm around her and held her tightly to his side. She swallowed another sob, coughed and said, "There was one more time when I saw him. We were both on the seabed. I think — I'm almost sure he was already gone. But he was smiling." The sob surged again in her throat and she choked out, "He looked . . . oh dear Lord . . . he looked happy!"

There was a long pause while she took William's handkerchief and held it to her face and concentrated on her breathing. When she clutched the handkerchief against her cheek, Lucy said, "And then what 'appened? Why are you here and 'e en't?"

William started to speak but Connie overrode him. "I shouldn't be. The sea was holding us down, both of us. But William had waded right in and as it sucked back to make another wave, he saw my hair and he held on somehow . . . I don't know how . . ." She moved the handkerchief to her eyes again.

William spoke. "Mrs Pardoe, I hadn't seen your son. When Connie told me . . . I went back. But it was hopeless. I am — we both are — so very sorry."

Lucy transferred her stare to the man. "Weren't your fault." She wondered whether the girl knew that Egg had fallen in love with her and if she had jumped off the cliff he would have jumped off with her and still looked happy. Had she known? Had she *known*?

William thought she was absolving them both; Connie felt his grip relax. He said, "We have been over and over it. What always — always — comes out of it is that Philip was . . . happy." Lucy Pardoe narrowed her eyes and he was afraid that he had said the wrong thing again. He hurried on, "If there is anything — anything at all — we can do . . ." He had his card in his pocket and he fished it out with his spare hand and held it out to her.

Lucy wanted to take it and hurl it to the ground; she wanted to attack the two of them with her nails but then something stopped her, literally stopped her. Pressure on her forearms. Then the left arm released. She took the card and stuck it in her pocket without so much as a thank you. And as she did so she noticed something. The girl held the handkerchief with her right hand; she put her left hand to join it. There were no rings on her fingers; none at all.

Lucy looked back at the man. He looked at her. She turned and went into the house and closed the door firmly.

Barbara and Denny were glad to go along with their mother's wishes and "get on with things". The terror of the night before gradually died as the weather changed from heated copper to leaden skies and they sat at the kitchen table and cut out strings of paper dolls and made them dance like the Merry Maidens around the pepper pot. People kept coming. The undertaker, Mr Strange, who would prefer to be called a funeral director, was the first. Then came the vicar, who was new. His name was Matthew Hobson. He wore a navy blue fisherman's jersey over a blue shirt, no sign of a dog collar; he was young and keen and "non-judgemental". In other circumstances Lucy might have grudgingly approved of him, but he was too cheerful now. Too understanding. And he was still under thirty so how could he possibly understand?

He said, "Obviously I know very little of the parish. Could you tell me something of your family?"

He said, "Non-attendance at church does not mean you do not believe in God, Lucy. You work the land. You know God much better than I do."

He said, "Church attendance is at an all-time low. It could be that you would find comfort in St Petroc's. It is open. Stand inside by yourself — or with the children. Listen. See what happens."

He said, "Really, I have no real choice, have I — not with a name like Hobson. I either believe in God or I believe in God." He laughed enormously and then stopped as the girls looked up, frightened. He smiled at them. "It is very easy for me. And I think, from what I hear, that it was very easy for your brother too." He leaned towards them. "Can you tell me why you call him Egg?"

Lucy said, "It was his name. Egbert." She moved to the parlour door. "Does 'e want to see 'im now?"

He followed her in willy-nilly and leaned over the coffin that Mr Strange had supplied. "Ah . . . so young . . . so beautiful." He straightened and began to pray as if he were talking to Egg, getting to know him, saying hello and goodbye at the same time. Lucy felt tears, proper tears, fall down her face without anger. She had not wanted Egg to go back with Mr Strange and wait in what he called his Chapel of Rest, but when Matthew Hobson suggested that he should wait in St Petroc's where Egg and the girls had been christened, she thought about it and nodded once.

"You can go in at any time and be with him." He looked past her at the girls huddled in the doorway. "Ellie tells me you go to Sunday school sometimes so you know the ropes. You can explore wherever you like." He addressed Lucy again. "I will call on Mr Strange right away, Lucy." She made a sound of protest; no one called her Lucy. He misheard, perhaps deliberately. "Tears are good, my dear."

The girls went with him to the lane. Denny confided that one of the cats was also called Matthew and he said it was a good substantial name for a cat and came from the Bible. Barbara said, surprised, "I knew that. He kept a pub, didn't he?" And the man-Matthew gave his loud inordinate laugh again and glanced over her head at her mother, who was smiling. She too had gone to Sunday school and on a much more regular basis than her daughters.

Mr Strange came back with his hearse and took Egg out of the front door. Then the neighbours started. They brought eggs, and a new loaf and a pan of rabbit stew and their children brought bunches of daisies and buttercups and one boy in Ellie's class at school had made a garden in a biscuit tin. The house was full. Lucy polished the table where the coffin had left a scrape mark and put a clean cloth over it and laid out the presents with the biscuit-tin garden as a centrepiece. People looked at that and knew it all represented Egg Pardoe.

At two o'clock it began to rain. Ellie took three sou'westers off the hooks on the kitchen door and the children pulled them well down almost to their shoulders and went off to St Petroc's to see Egg. Lucy tidied and washed and cleaned ready for next week, when it would all happen again after the funeral. There had to be an inquiry first but that never took long. The sea gave them life and it gave them death. The coroner was very used to this kind of inquiry. Death by drowning.

86

She shook mats and ran her mop around the boards of the parlour. She scrubbed the flags in the kitchen. She laid tea on the kitchen table; some of the goodies brought this morning. She would make bacon and eggs too. They had not sat down together for a proper meal since Monday. And that had been a different life anyway.

Someone tapped on the streaming window. She looked up and saw it was Chippy Penberthy. She took off her apron. She fingered William Mather's card in her pocket. She went to the door.

She hardly heard him for some time. She had heard so much of it already, the embarrassed fumbling condolences — one of the farmhands had actually brought a verse from Patience Strong and read it out to her. The strange thing was that until then she had always enjoyed reading Patience Strong's poems.

When Chippy's words came through it was quite a relief to realize that he was talking business. He was talking rent. And somehow he was also talking about his wife. She looked at him properly and realized his face was bright red.

"I wouldn't want 'er knowing, Mrs Pardoe. I wouldn't want anyone knowing in fac'. People do put the worst kind of side to this sort of private arrangement an' Mrs Penberthy'd surely jump to the wrong inclusions."

Lucy frowned. "'Ow would that be, Mr Penberthy?"

"She d'know 'ow much I admire you, dear lady. You kep' two men — and young Egg as well — very 'appy.

An' if you allow it, you could keep a third man very 'appy." He gave her a ghastly smirk. She could not believe the implications behind that and had to physically hold her hands still in her lap to stop them flying up and smacking his face so hard he'd go from red to purple.

But not now. Not yet anyway.

She lowered her eyes. "I'm not very clever, as you well know, Mr Penberthy. Can you just run through again what you bin saying? My 'ead is all over the place and I'm not sure I understood you the first time."

"Course I dun't mind, Mrs Pardoe." But he was struggling. He took a huge breath and blurted, "You wun't be able to run a pig now, will you? Nor try y'r 'and with strawberries nex' year. I cain't do nuthin' about 'elping you that way. But I can 'old your rent down for six months. P'raps."

"P'raps?"

He was becoming purple. "I likes y'r comp'ny, Mrs Pardoe. We gets on."

She looked down at her hands, commanded them to stay still.

"Since I bin a widow, you bin kind to me, Mr Penberthy. Did you mean that come Michaelmas you wun't put the rent up as usual?"

"I do mean that, Mrs Pardoe."

She managed a smile. She had to be careful. What was more important to Chippy Penberthy . . . money or friendship? Plus the opportunity to get away from Mrs Penberthy for a couple of hours each day.

"I'm real glad we're talking honestly together," she began. "An' I'm glad I 'ad already made up my mind to talk to you before . . . before . . ."

"Before the accident, Mrs Pardoe?"

"Yes." She glanced at him and away. She did not want him having a stroke. "Dan'l an' me . . . we put a bit aside whenever we could. 'E wun't one to spend money needlessly." There had never been enough to put anything aside but Chippy weren't to know that. She drew another breath, pushed her hands into the folds of her skirt and crossed her fingers. "I d' reckon there's enough in the Post Office to be a deposit on an 'ouse. An' there's some new 'ouses goin' up in Truro what would be very 'andy now our Ellie is starting 'er new school."

He was silent, amazed.

She risked letting one hand creep up to his shirtsleeve. "We shall miss our neighbours and friends. I shall miss you . . . Chippy. But I kin get a job easy in Truro. Woolworths or the Co-op."

He said, "I cain't see you anywhere else but right 'ere. They do call this place Pardoe Cottage. Dan'l did live 'ere as a boy. It en't right, Mrs Pardoe. It en't right for you to move all that way."

"I could visit. Sundays p'raps."

He started on a long ramble about keeping an eye on the place, keeping an eye on the girls, keeping a very special eye on her. She waited for a pause and then spoke doubtfully as if answering a suggestion he had just made.

"I know what you do mean, Chippy. But this is a big place. The garden, the orchard. And now the bean patch . . ." She glanced up at him again, noted his frown and came quickly to the point. "Our savings en't that good. We couldn't afford to buy Pardoe Cottage." She let her gaze wander over the rows of lettuce and said wistfully, "That's just a dream. No one can make dreams come true. Not really."

He looked at her down-bent head, the centre parting in the thick hair, the coiled plait. He felt breathless somehow. Drunk with power. He fished into the folds of her skirt and found her hand and held it tightly as if he might fall off the old kitchen chair without it.

"I can make that dream come true, my lovely!" She did not withdraw her hand and he saw a wonderful future. A big lump of money in the bank and a woman eternally grateful to him. He could tell Mrs Penberthy he had to go up to Bodmin on business and stay a night or two right here in Pardoe Cottage. He had lusted for this woman ever since she married Dan'l but she was always out of his reach. Now . . . now things were different.

He asked her how much she had got in the Post Office and when she told him he almost laughed, it was so ridiculous. Houses in Cornwall were fetching top prices now, they didn't even call them houses any more, they called them investments.

He massaged her hand. "You'll 'ave to borrow. You know that, dun't you, my lovely?"

The hand twitched within his and her body shook slightly but she nodded and was still again. Then she whispered, "'Ow much would you be askin' . . . Chippy?"

He named his price, smiling down at the parting in her hair as she twitched and shook again. "Less for you, a'course . . . Lucy," he added.

But as he reached for her other hand, she withdrew the first.

"I cain't find that sort of money." She sighed. "It was a lovely thought, a lovely dream, but . . ."

He grabbed for her hand and lowered his price. And at last, doubtfully — oh so doubtfully — she agreed to half the figure he had first named. He was taken aback when she led him into her kitchen and drew up some kind of agreement in the back of Barbara's school exercise book.

She said, "I know this binds me to you, Chippy. But I don't mind — honestly. I trust you completely. When you offered to take on my son for a seven-year apprenticeship, I knew then that we would be tied to you. You are such a good businessman. I've always admired that."

He was completely disorientated. He knew he was a good businessman — seven years of cheap labour from a lad who was simple and would fetch and carry and do what he was told — that was good business. So this must be the same. She was right, of course. He had to bind her to him legally. And this bit of lined paper would do it. He signed it with a flourish. And she signed underneath. Just as it should be. He smirked. "Shall we seal it with a kiss?"

She smiled. "Here are the girls. They've been to the church, Chippy. They will need love and comfort now. Perhaps it's not the time . . . yet."

Denny imploded into the kitchen. She had gathered the cats from beneath the rhubarb and hurled the two of them into her mother's arms, weeping copiously. Lucy held her and sat down in her rocker. The other two came in, holding hands and looking very solemn.

He said, "I'd best be off." He looked at the table to pick up the exercise book but it was not there. Denny lifted her head and wailed her grief despairingly. He picked up his ancient hat and left. The "contract", such as it was, would be safe enough with her. That was the thing about Lucy Pardoe; you could trust her completely.

That night when the visitors had all gone and the cottage was tidy, Lucy told the girls they would have a little walk.

Ellie was astonished. "'Tis dark, Mum. And the girls . . . they're tired out."

"I got to walk up to the phone box in the village, Ellie. I'll 'ave the torch with me. I en't leavin' you 'ere on your own." She took down the cocoa tin which held money for the electric. "We'll get a bag o' chips from the fish shop. Eat them on the way home."

It was starting to drizzle; proper rain, not like the heavy, leaden drops of yesterday. Ellie thought her mother was frightened for some reason and the two little ones enjoyed it all immensely at first. Then Denny's wet feet rubbed in her sandals and she grizzled. Lucy picked her up and joggled her along.

They crammed into the phone box and Lucy fished out William Mather's card, fed in a whole shilling and dialled nought with painstaking care. She read Mr Mather's personal number from the card and waited while she was connected and the ringing started. At last a voice said, "Hello," and she sobbed with relief as she recognized it. She shouted, "Hello," back, then remembered and pressed the button.

"Hello. Is that Mr Mather? This is Mrs Pardoe."

"Mrs Pardoe? Are you all right? I've just come in the door. What a bit of luck."

She had worked out the time carefully. An eight-hour drive and he would take the girl to her own house first and stay a while, explaining to her parents exactly what had happened. He might stay for a meal but most likely not as he was no longer a fiancé.

"I'm in the phone box in the village, Mr Mather. We're all squeezed inside 'cos it's raining. You said you could 'elp me. We do need 'elp. All of a sudden, we do need 'elp."

She let the pause go on while he imagined four bodies in a phone kiosk with the rain running down the windows. Denny started up her wailing again and he must've heard that too.

He said, "I've got a notepad here, Mrs Pardoe. Read off the number on your dial, can you? When your money gives out, the operator will phone you back."

The shilling was plenty of money because Lucy did not waste a precious second of her time.

"I need to borrow money. A lot of money. I want to buy Pardoe Cottage and I want to pay for it quick-like.

Before the landlord can change 'is mine. Is that possible?"

He was just as direct. "Certainly. With cash. You are sitting tenants after all." There was the tiniest pause. Then he said, "I will leave early tomorrow morning, Mrs Pardoe. Be with you at midday. Tell the vendor your solicitor is coming to see you. I take it he would be happier with cash than a cheque?"

She gasped. "Well . . . course. Who wouldn't be?" She could picture Chippy's face as hundreds of pound notes were counted on to the kitchen table.

"I'll see you tomorrow. And within banking hours."

He did not let her thank him. The line clicked and hummed and that was that. The girls were agog. They trailed back, eating their chips, lifting their small faces to the rain just as Daniel had always told them to. Lucy wondered what she was doing, why she was doing it. Dr Carthew had told her to buy her cottage and offered her a loan and she had barely heard him. And then Chippy had offered her his "gift" — no rent rise at Michaelmas and a kiss and a cuddle now and then. And she had been angry in a different way. And the girl owed her something. She might not be engaged to William Mather but in a way that made it harder for her to bear.

When Barbara and Denny were in bed with the cats, Ellie stared out of the window and whispered to her mother, "I cain't believe it will be ours, Mum. Ours. Oh . . . Egg would love it so much. He'll be so happy for us, Mum."

She did not understand why Ellie's words held no joy for her. She thought, with sudden panic, that she could not stay here. Not now.

She whispered back, "We dun't never own anything, Ellie. We just borrows it for a time."

Ellie smiled up at her joyously. "That's what the vicar said to us, Mum. When we sat by Egg's coffin. He said about borrowing things. Like you want to borrow something from Mr Mather."

Lucy hugged her daughter and rocked her back and forth.

"I dun't know what I'm doin' any more, Ellie. I must get and see Dr Carthew in the morning before Mr Mather do arrive . . . Poor man, all that long drive home and he has to turn back straight away again. Poor man." She looked at Ellie's bed, turned back ready for her. "How would you like to sleep in your dad's place for tonight, Ellie?"

They lay side by side, both thinking they would not sleep in spite of the doctor's pills. But within ten minutes they were gone. And they slept the night away.

CHAPTER
FIVE

Rosemary Vickers stared at her daughter's down-bent head as they sat together at breakfast, and wondered for the umpteenth time how a few days could make such a catastrophic difference to a life. Last Sunday, just five days ago, Connie and William Mather had been engaged to be married and had gone off on their first holiday together. Rosemary had kissed Connie goodbye through the open window of the big comfortable car, reassured her with one of their special looks that the natural linen frock and hat were just the thing for the journey and the other, more casual sundresses teamed with the espadrilles Rosemary had brought back from her own holiday in Brittany would be ideal on the beach, then transferred her gaze to William as she said happily, "Look after her, my dear."

William had smiled back just as happily. When he had asked her in his lovely old-fashioned way whether it would be "all right" to ask Connie if she would like to marry him, she had said, "Do you love her, Mr Mather?"

His reply had been careful and precise. "That goes without saying, Mrs Vickers. It's whether she can love me. I am thirty-six and she . . ."

He had hesitated and she had supplied, "Younger than her years?" He had looked as if he might be going to nod. She went on briskly, "I have been overprotective, Mr Mather. Perhaps I have tried too hard to be father as well as mother."

"Ah . . . Mrs Vickers." He had said the right things. The sort of things that mothers long to hear and rarely do. After all, he was a solicitor.

She had smiled and cleared her throat and said, "Perhaps I should call you William. And I would like it if you would use my name — it's Rosemary."

It had all been so . . . ideal. She had ignored the fact that Connie might well be too young for him; perhaps more flattered than in love. Connie kept telling her mother what a wonderful man he was. How he put his clients at ease. How some of the women fell for him hook, line and sinker. It was as if she was trying to convince herself.

And then the phone call last night, only four days later, William tightly withdrawn, Connie . . . incomprehensible. Just four days and the whole wonderful thing was in ruins.

They were tired — of course. It would all blow over. As they levered themselves out of the car — like two elderly people — Rosemary had already gathered from the phone call that there had been an older woman; an actress of sorts — Rosemary had never heard of her. Apparently she had turned up at this boarding house in Cornwall. And the landlady of the place — Blue Seas — sounded a complete dragon. Rosemary had tried to make it all funny and told Connie that seaside landladies had to pass a dragon test before they were allowed to welcome any guests. Connie had greeted this sally with a sob; it was hard to tell as the telephone line to Cornwall was strange. Or perhaps it was Connie being strange.

Then William had taken the receiver and told Rosemary that they were coming home the next day, hoped to arrive between six and seven o'clock and, by the way, they had decided against an engagement. The call was cut off at this point. Rosemary did not believe it of course. A lovers' tiff.

They had both been stiff from the journey. Connie leaned on the car, returning her mother's welcoming hug with one arm. Then, while Rosemary's wildly questioning expression was making her eyes pop, Connie said she needed the bathroom and disappeared indoors.

William stated a few facts very briefly as he carried Connie's luggage into the hall of Fairways. Rosemary gathered they had witnessed a drowning, as a result of which their engagement was at an end. It sounded such a tragedy. But hardly the sort of tragedy to affect them and their engagement?

"I'm sorry, William. So very sorry. But I don't understand why . . ."

William said in his solicitor's voice, "Connie will fill in the details." He had not known whether to call her Rosemary or Mrs Vickers. He had left. They had been driving for eight hours; he looked tired, gaunt. She hovered by the front door, a hand held behind her for Connie to take as she came down the stairs — which she did not — her other hand waving to William and saying, "It will be all right . . ." which he also ignored.

Connie told her another garbled story about an earthquake and a tornado and a beach attendant who couldn't swim but who was a special human being and had drowned in a tidal wave. Rosemary was appalled to hear that the Cornish weather was so dangerous. The brochures extolled the golden beaches and the sub-tropical plants and semi-precious stones and said not a word about tidal waves and tornados. She had to assume that Connie was exaggerating and made up her mind to phone William and get the proper version.

On Friday morning she looked out of the window and saw Connie walking slowly from the back gate on to the footpath that wound through the golf course. She went into the hall and dialled William's home number. There was no reply. She dialled Jessup's number and asked Arnold's secretary whether William was there. The secretary was surprised.

"He's still on holiday, Mrs Vickers. He's not due in the office until Monday week."

Rosemary had to assume that William too was taking a before-breakfast walk. It was another shock to realize he had not told Arnold Jessup that his holiday was over. She gnawed her lip and went into the breakfast room. Connie had laid the breakfast. She heaved a sigh of relief. The poor girl was doing her best.

When Connie appeared half an hour later, Rosemary had grilled bacon and made toast and convinced herself that everything was all right. She asked whether Connie had had a nice walk; she ate some bacon and nibbled toast and poured coffee. Connie stared down at her plate, cut a triangular shape of toast and put it in her mouth.

Rosemary believed in being direct so she asked about William and the engagement. Connie did not even look up. She said in a strange monotone, "We weren't really suited, Mummy."

Rosemary said, "I think you were. Are, actually. You just have to think of him in a different way. Not as — as . . ." This was difficult ground but she pressed on. "Not as an Arnhem survivor. Not as your boss at work — a rather clever solicitor, by all accounts. You have to see him as a partner, my love. Someone you can look after and someone who will look after you."

Unexpectedly Connie nodded. Rosemary felt encouraged. She said in her most matter-of-fact voice, "Darling, you've got another week at home. Then you will go back to work again and things will settle down."

Connie looked up at that. Her stare was blank. She said very loudly, "Mummy, haven't you listened to a word I've said? I can't ever see William again. None of this is his fault and he cannot be burdened with someone like me. Especially in his work." She looked at her mother and Rosemary put a hand to her mouth as she saw anguish fill the blank eyes. Connie said, "I am responsible for Philip's death. He was precious — to his mother and his family and it's possible that his American family do not even know of his existence! And if I hadn't . . . if I'd kept my problems to myself . . . my God, Mummy, I am twenty-two years old, I've worked at Jessup's for two years. I've done nothing with my life until now — and now I have killed another human being!"

Rosemary caught her breath. Almost twenty years ago she had said to her own mother that there was nothing left to live for. And her mother had simply switched her gaze to where Connie was tentatively stroking three tiny kittens in the cat basket. And Rosemary had whispered, "Forgive me."

Now, sitting there looking again at her daughter, her reason for living, she felt a rush of tears and thought at first they were sheer nostalgia; then knew the truth. There was no new life for Connie.

She could think of nothing relevant to say. To feel responsible for someone else's death was absurd, of course. She had to squash that right now. She sat back in her chair, clasped her hands and said, "Darling, I'm sorry to be so obtuse. You haven't mentioned America before. And who is this Philip?"

Connie looked at her for another long thirty seconds, then made a sound of despair, pushed back her chair and ran from the room.

By Sunday — a week after their departure to Cornwall — Rosemary thought she had the full picture. She knew that Mrs Heatherington had been the true motive for the holiday, she knew that Mrs Pentwyn wanted to get rid of Connie because she had found out that Connie had slept with William, she knew that Connie had felt both love and fear about doing so . . . Rosemary refused to be shocked. She could tell that there had been a tenderness, a comfort both taken and given during that night. But she also understood that Connie *had* been shocked by it; shocked to feel that she had given herself to William . . . to another human being. That she might actually *belong* to him. When he had been obsequious — Connie had actually used that word, which Rosemary felt was unfair — towards Mrs Heatherington, she could see that Connie might have felt that she had been deceived, even exploited. And it was very unfortunate that she had overheard the landlady's vitriolic words on that second night. Rosemary shuddered at that.

Then there was the boy. Rosemary was less sure about the boy. It was obvious that Connie saw him as some special creature belonging to the land and the sea . . . It did not fit in with the reality of his job at the beach shop. He was young, Connie made him sound about fourteen. He was a great reader. He liked American crime novels. His father had been an American soldier, drowned in the disastrous training exercise in Devon. His mother had married a local man and had three other children, girls. The man had adopted the boy and they were very close. And then he too had been drowned.

Rosemary did a quick sum and realized the boy was either fifteen or sixteen. Connie made him sound younger. Later, when she spoke of his "seizure", Rosemary thought he must be simple.

She said, "He sounds . . . unique. But perhaps . . ."

Connie said, "He could read. He read avidly. That's why I called him Philip, for Philip Marlowe. He was reading Raymond Chandler. He was named for his father, Egbert. And known as Egg. Somehow I couldn't call him that."

Rosemary suggested tentatively, "Perhaps that was why he went into that dreadful sea when he couldn't swim?"

"It wasn't a dreadful sea when I went in, Mummy. It was completely still. I realize now that it was unnaturally still. But people came to the cove because it was calm. The other beaches were for surfing. The cove was for swimming."

"I see." Rosemary shook her head even so. From the way Connie was talking, this poor boy had been euphoric and the only way he could express it was to go into the very element that had killed both his fathers. Was the euphoria a result of the slight earthquake? Had that sent him into a seizure? Or the drumming rain? Surely not . . . Could it possibly have been a death wish?

She said on an upward voice, "And then William pulled you out. I'll never forget that, Connie. He really is a wonderful man."

Connie nodded with the awful sadness that was emerging from the horror. She said, "He had that light suit on, Mummy, waistcoat and all, because he had taken Mrs Heatherington into Penzance for something or other. He was still wearing it, caked in sand, when he went back in to look for Philip. Oh Mummy, it was so awful. I knew then I couldn't ever marry him, yet he was the finest man I ever knew."

"Listen, darling. I know you won't like this but I have to phone him again. I tried on Friday morning. Don't look like that — I had to know what was happening. He wasn't at home and the office said he was still in Cornwall. But if we care tuppence about him, Connie . . . and surely we do . . . then we have to ask how he is. And later you must see him, Connie. You must try to tell him why you have cast him off —"

"Mummy, I haven't cast him off! Can't you see that before I marry anyone — anyone at all — I have to become a person? Not just a heavy parcel to be carted around and —"

"Constance! Stop talking like that. That is bordering on self-pity, which is something we do not do."

Connie dropped her head again and stopped talking until she had finished the next triangle of toast. Then she said, "If you do telephone William, will you say how sorry I am? Please."

"Of course I will." Rosemary put cups and saucers together on a tray. "But all this guilt is stupid, Connie. I suggest we both get ready and go to church. And perhaps lunch at the golf club." She looked out on the sweep of the Lickey Hills. "You had quite a decent handicap when you played regularly. How about taking it up again?" She almost added . . . until this mess is sorted out. She swallowed the words but she had already said the wrong thing. Connie was giving her that incredulous look again.

"Mummy, I cannot see people. Not yet. I'm still in Cornwall."

"Darling, Mrs Penrose did the ironing yesterday. D'you think she won't have told your friends that you are back?"

"I don't mean I am down there still. What I mean is, in my mind I am not back yet." She shook her head with the despair of being misunderstood so often and picked up the tray. "Let's have salad at lunchtime and I will cook this evening."

"Oh Connie — I don't want you . . ." Rosemary stopped herself. Housework had its place in the healing process; she knew that only too well. "Thank you, darling. That would be nice. Shall we drive to the lakes later?"

Connie nodded and took the tray into the kitchen. Rosemary went into the hall and lifted up the telephone receiver. She already knew that William was not a churchgoer and she prayed that he would pick up her call. It was all so . . . so unsatisfactory. Tragic, yes. But one could cope with tragedy and it was better to cope with it as a couple, surely? When that dreaded telegram had arrived all those years ago, she had had Connie. Now Connie had William. And she seemed to be . . . discarding him.

Six rings went by before William's rather dry voice came down the line. She said, "Oh William, I'm so glad you're there. I tried you on Friday. I thought you might have gone away again." There was a pause and she added, "It's Rosemary. Rosemary Vickers. After hearing more from Connie about what happened in Cornwall I was worried about you. It all seems so . . . unnecessary."

He did not reassure her. "Ah. Yes. Events often have a way of appearing to be unnecessary."

Another pause. She had forgotten the reason for her call. Was it to arrange a reconciliation? She had to say something.

"William, how are you?"

Yet another pause, then he said as if surprised, "Not too bad, actually."

That annoyed her. She thought of Connie's awful empty stare and said, "I rang the office. They told me you were still in Cornwall."

"Yes. Yes, I went back very early on Friday. I have clients down there, unfinished business. I returned home late last evening."

She was so taken aback she did not even notice whether there was a pause or not. She blurted, "Will you go back to work tomorrow then?" If he said yes then she would absolutely give up. Connie was right, he didn't give a damn.

He said, "No. I still have a week's holiday left. I am going back to Cornwall probably on Tuesday. Perhaps Wednesday."

There was a small mirror above the phone, placed there for people to check that their hats were straight before they left the house. She focused on her reflection and noted her eyes were bulbous.

Then he said, "Will you tell Connie that something positive is happening down there. After the funeral, which as I say is either Tuesday or Wednesday of this coming week, I will have more information. I would like to tell her about it myself but obviously if she finds it difficult to see me then I can write to her. I think — I hope — that what is happening will help her to . . . accept . . . things."

She sensed he was about to say goodbye and replace the receiver. She raised her voice. "William, wait. Do you mean . . . your engagement might be . . ." Her voice died as she realized she was well past certain limits.

He did not replace his receiver. After an extra long pause, he said carefully, "I think we both know now that we are not suited. It was one of those moments of — of —" she could almost see his tiny wry smile "— of unrestrained optimism." And then he did replace his receiver. And she looked again in the little mirror and saw her eyes were watering.

He telephoned the following Friday and came for tea. Connie watched from her bedroom window as the familiar grey car turned off the road to Barnt Green and negotiated the lane that ran parallel to the golf course until it reached the small cluster of desirable detached houses, the first of which was Fairways. Her mother had said, "I would like you to answer the door to him, Connie." Then, seeing her daughter's expression, had rescinded the request immediately. "All right, but — darling — please come down and let him tell you what has happened."

"He has persuaded Mrs Heatherington not to sue her manager," Connie said. But then she nodded. "Of course I'll be there, Mummy."

The hot weather had dissolved into rain at the beginning of the week and since then had been suddenly autumnal. Connie wore a white blouse and cotton skirt; it made her feel drab. She had felt drab for a week now; it made no difference what she wore.

She watched as the car did a U-turn before the front door and parked facing the gate; clearly he wanted to leave quickly. Her mother emerged and was there as William opened the driver's door and stepped on to the gravel. He was wearing the lightweight suit he had worn that day, that terrible day when life had changed. She was surprised that it had cleaned up, and shocked that he would choose to wear it ever again. Beneath the window, almost out of her sight, they both hesitated, then William held out his hand and Rosemary took it in both of hers. It occurred to Connie that her mother was on the point of tears and she loathed herself anew for bringing her to this. She registered that Rosemary's hair, newly coiffed every other week, was looking straggly and her skirt seemed to be dipping in the front as if she was stooped. She had dropped William's hand — or he had pulled away — and they both disappeared into the house. For a moment she did not move. She did not want to see William in his suit. He simply reminded her that if she had not been with William in Cornwall, Egbert Pardoe — Philip Marlowe — would still be alive, encased in that childlike happiness that sprang from simply being, simply existing in a beautiful world.

She must have been in her private no-man's-land longer than she thought because Rosemary's voice came from the hall. "William is here, darling. I'm going to put the kettle on now. He can't stay long."

Connie got the message. If she wanted five minutes alone with William then she should come down immediately. And the ordeal was not going to be protracted. She tucked her blouse hard into the waistband of her skirt and went downstairs. William was sitting in the bay window overlooking the sweep of hills. He leaped up as she came in. She remembered that one of the things she admired about him was that he was completely non-judgemental. That was how he looked now but she suddenly saw that his careful lack of facial expression was judgemental in itself. She started to cry. He came forward at a rush and she thought that he would take her in his arms, but at the last second he simply took her hands and held them loosely between his.

"I'm sorry. My dear, I'll leave. I did not want to upset you."

She sensed her mother in the hall and could imagine her rushing into the room and commanding William to sit down — this very minute!

She gulped and said, "It's me. I know I'm overwrought. You. And the suit."

He looked down. "This suit? It's new. I had to get another one and I thought . . . I mean, I didn't think. That it was almost autumn."

She too looked and saw it was not the same suit. "Oh William. I'm sorry. I'm not myself — not one bit. Please stay for tea. My mother will be so upset if you go."

He released her hands and sat back down. "I don't want to go just yet, Connie. I've been back to Cornwall twice and I think that what is happening down there might cheer you up."

She wondered why William and her mother kept talking of cheering her up. As if anyone could be cheered up after causing the death of someone else.

There came the click of trolley wheels and her mother entered, beaming. There were sandwiches and two kinds of cake on the lower tray. The top tray held tea things for two.

Rosemary said, "I'm going to leave you to have a chat and pop next door to see Maria. She's not too good and might need shopping."

Connie looked at her helplessly. William said, "My news is not personal, Mrs Vickers. Please stay and hear it. I think it will encourage you too."

But Rosemary was determined. She knew that general "news" could easily slip into something more personal. It was definitely not encouraging to hear William call her Mrs Vickers but even that could change if the two of them were left to themselves. She went out, closing the back door firmly enough for them to hear it.

Connie left the trolley where it was and sat opposite William. She said, "Sorry about this. My mother still thinks it's just a storm in a teacup."

"I don't think so. But then we disagree on so many things." He looked at her almost sadly. "We worked together for so long and so well, I thought . . . Never mind. Let me tell you what has happened and then I'll go." He glanced out of the window. The house next

110

door was lower than this one. Rosemary was tapping on the window. It was obvious no one was in.

He said, "I have a new client, Connie. In Hayle. Lucy Pardoe." He waited for a reaction. Connie was shocked. Was Philip's mother going to bring a case against her? Manslaughter? Was it possible? In a way it would be good. It would be wonderful.

William said, "She telephoned me that night. The Thursday when you and I drove home. I had just got into the house. She had walked to the telephone box in the village — the three girls were with her and I could hear the little one grizzling. It was raining and her feet were sore." He actually smiled. "Lucy wanted to borrow money to buy the cottage. It had to be a very quick deal. I told her I would be with her the next day before the banks closed. I got the money in cash and the vendor came over in the afternoon and she bought her little cottage as if it were a pound of new potatoes." This time he laughed.

She was horrified. "How could . . . She lost her son the evening before, how could she even think about buying the cottage the very next day? Oh . . . sorry, this must have been planned for some time."

"Not at all. She would have discounted such a thought. They haven't got two ha'pennies to rub together!" He actually smiled. "For a moment on the telephone my reaction was like yours. It was bordering on the macabre. But then . . . I trusted her. She wasn't telling me much because she was determined that the shilling she had put into the phone was enough. And of course —" his smile became wry "— I wanted to help

111

her for both our sakes. At the time I honestly thought that it might make a difference to us. You and me."

Connie felt the treacherous tears again. She would never be able to explain to anyone in the whole world how she had felt about Philip that dreadful afternoon in the beach hut with the rain drumming incessantly. So no one, no one in the whole world must know. Especially not this man.

He said in a low voice, "Connie, do you want me to leave? Now?"

She shook her head and motioned with her hand for him to go on. He looked uncertainly at the hand, then stood up, drew the trolley towards him and began to pour tea. And she managed to smile and thank him and sip the hot liquid.

"I'd like to hear the rest," she said. "There is more?"

"There is."

He told her about the rumour and the way Lucy Pardoe — suddenly realizing what she was asking of him — said, "'Tis only a rumour, though as it comes from Dr Carthew . . . 'E offered the money too. But I thought as you said you wanted to help if you could . . . but it is only a rumour and I might never be able to pay you back."

William passed her the sandwiches and she took one. So did he. They looked strangely formal sitting in the window with the trolley between them.

He said, "The cottage is owned by the local carpenter, a man called Penberthy who had offered Egg a seven-year apprenticeship. He saw the boy as cheap labour. Luckily Egg had already told his mother he did

112

not want to take it up." He sighed and then went on steadily. "I think after Penberthy had come round and more or less propositioned her, she was desperate. And . . . quite frankly . . . at first, she thought we owed it to her. Perhaps she still feels that way. I don't think so. I stayed that night in Hayle and had a long talk with her doctor. John Carthew. He brought Egg into the world and the others too. Ellie, Barbara, Denise." He spoke the names slowly, recalling them one by one. They were becoming real people to him. Lucy, the doctor, Egg — he called him Egg — and the little girls Egg had loved so much. "He couldn't tell me a great deal but he said negotiations to build a holiday camp are already under way with the local council. He also said that if she did not buy the place herself the owner would make the most of it, sell it to the highest bidder. Now it is hers, Lucy will be able to sell Pardoe Cottage for very much more than she has paid for it."

"She won't sell," Connie said.

"I think she will. We both went to see her yesterday afternoon — Carthew and myself. The girls made us tea." He smiled. "Not quite like this but just as formal in its way. She has to make a new start and Ellie is going to school in Truro next month. It will take some doing of course but I think she is wise. Penberthy will pester her. If he suspects she knew about the development plans he might get nasty. One of her husband's friends, chap called Joshua Warne, he's going to keep an eye on things." He folded his napkin and put it back on the trolley. "I drove back late that night. I slept well. And I slept in Cornwall too." He smiled. "I hope that this will help you to sleep well, Connie." He stood up. "I won't see much of you next week. I'm going back to Cornwall either tomorrow or Tuesday." He did not mention the funeral. "I want to talk again to Mrs Heatherington."

She was amazed that he too did not understand she could not work with him any more. She tried to explain and after a moment he nodded. Then he stood up.

She walked to the door with him and watched him leave. She wished she had asked him about the funeral. She wished she could have been there. But invisible. As the car turned downhill and disappeared she realized that she really had loved William Mather. She was still holding the front door and gazing after him as her mother rushed from the side of the house and enveloped her.

"I know, darling. I know. Come along in and try not to think too much."

She got a job in Worcester. She told her mother she was a general dogsbody though as it was at the cathedral it was called something much more dignified. It was a tentative joke and was greeted ecstatically by Rosemary. She kissed Connie and told her she was going to be all right. Connie began to believe it. Each day she knew she loved William more and more. She remembered that night when they had slept together. She remembered his tenderness . . . how he had held her until she slept. But she also knew that in many ways she had not been right for William then. She had been — what was the word — was it petty? Yes, she had been

114

petty in her "feelings" and she had been petty about Mrs Heatherington and downright stupid about the awful Mrs Pentwyn! She had known at the time that the woman's anger was really about the wretched cabinet pudding and the trifle. She should have shared it with William and laughed. And instead she had somehow blamed William.

There were times when self-loathing went to extremes and she wondered whether she had made love to the beautiful Philip to punish William in some way. If only she had not helped him — with her new-found knowledge taught by William — had not shown him how sweet was the comfort and glory of love. If only she had not made him so happy that he wanted to be in that sea as a kind of baptism. If only. Two futile words that helped no one.

But she was stronger after William's visit. Stronger for seeing him, stronger for hearing his news. She knew full well that he hoped his quixotic gift to Lucy Pardoe would expiate a little of the guilt and though it could not do that, it did change things. It enabled her to put the awfulness aside for periods of time. At first just long enough to search the jobs column and find the place at the cathedral. And to make up her mind that, dogsbody or assistant steward, she would do a good job; she would immerse herself in it. Because of what had happened, she was different. Perhaps she was a "better person"? She had no idea. She kept going and got to know every corner of the cathedral and everyone who used it. She was well liked from the outset and knew she had found a niche for herself. One of the stewards, an older woman, talked about the history of the cathedral and Connie took an interest and began to read it up for herself. Mrs Adams suggested a visit to the museum and they went together. Then she wondered whether Connie ought to apply for a place at Birmingham University to read history. It was as if a future was opening up for her, page by page.

Autumn became winter. In November the river flooded and her bus back home was stuck for several hours. She caught a cold.

She wasn't really ill but the cold became a cough and that turned into bronchitis and eventually she was persuaded to visit their local doctor. He had known Connie for years and thought aloud that he would give her the once-over. Then he asked her a lot of questions and took a blood sample. He prescribed antibiotics.

"Once the course is finished you should be fine. But if the blood test shows anaemia you'll have to have iron tablets." He looked at her over heavy spectacles. "I cannot believe you did not know you were pregnant. Didn't the absence of your periods mean anything to you?"

Connie stared at him, brown eyes enormous. She croaked, "I've been low. Assumed . . ."

"As I said before — I cannot believe it, Connie. We were all so pleased you were going off on an early honeymoon, yet it didn't occur to you that pregnancy could be a perfectly natural outcome?" He grinned suddenly. "Cancel your mother's plans. Get thee to a register office, woman. You're a jolly good three months!"

She took the slip of paper and said, "Thank you." She was numb. She walked to the pharmacy and collected the antibiotics, then walked home.

Her mother tried to be pleased. Connie said, "Look, I know it's going to be awful — small village, etc. And you've got to live here, Mummy. I'll get a flat in Worcester. Don't argue about it. Mrs Adams might be able to help and I can be completely honest with her."

"After all," Rosemary said, "it is nineteen sixty."

Connie glanced at her, surprised. She nearly made one of their little jokes — "What has that got to do with the price of beans?" — and then thought better of it. The strange thing was that when the shock wore off, she could be quite pleased about the pregnancy. Except that she knew her mother would hate having to tell people.

She smiled and pecked Rosemary's cheek. She felt a small surge of something akin to happiness. She said, "Oh Mummy . . . let's work out her birthday . . . Well, of course I know, darling! It was August the . . . Where's the calendar? I'll look at the one in the hall."

She left the room and Rosemary listened to her talking to herself as she turned back the pages of the calendar. She seemed happy! She must have been in love with William all this time. Rosemary made up her mind then and there. She would go into Birmingham tomorrow and talk to William. Straight.

Connie came back in. "I reckon it will be May the twenty-fourth. If it's a girl we'll call her May. What do you think, darling? Such a lovely old-fashioned name."

Rosemary guessed that her eyes were bulbous again; she closed them tightly and then turned and smiled at her daughter, who was unmarried, pregnant and very happy about it.

"Lovely," she said.

She insisted that Connie should take the car the next morning and as soon as it had gone she put on her boots, matching fur coat and hat and, feeling like the Cossack she looked, walked down to Barnt Green station and caught the train into Birmingham, leaving it at Selly Oak.

William's new secretary was probably Rosemary's age and seemed unable to smile.

"You've come on the wrong day, Mrs Vickers," she said with a hint of satisfaction. "Mr Mather is expecting his first client in ten minutes and is booked solidly until four thirty this afternoon."

"Much too late," Rosemary said briskly. "I'll take this first ten minutes. Thank you so much."

There were protests which she ignored as she swept into the inner office and said in a voice she hoped the secretary would hear, "You should invest in a charm course for the new girl, William. She has none whatsoever!"

He looked up, surprised then anxious, then hearing her words properly he smiled. Rosemary melted and opened her gloved hands helplessly.

"Sorry. I've come on an errand I am not going to enjoy. Probably neither will you. And if ever you tell Connie I was here, that — that — that will be *it*."

118

"How is she? Is she ill?" He stood up, leaned across his desk and took one of the fluttering hands reassuringly. "Sit down, Rosemary. You're flummoxed."

She collapsed gratefully. He had used her first name. And flummoxed was nowhere near a legal term. It was homely.

She said, "I've got ten minutes. It won't take that long and I might as well come right out with it." She drew a breath and heard it catch in her throat. "Yesterday Connie went to the doctor for some antibiotics. She's had a bronchial cough most of the month." She shook her head at his sounds of concern. "The doctor diagnosed something else besides bronchitis. She is pregnant, William." She waited. He said nothing. He was looking past her at the wall, his face expressionless. She said, "William, I am not shocked. The war . . . moved all of us on. As it were." Suddenly she was embarrassed and when he was still silent she was — just as suddenly — very angry.

"Look here, William. If her father was alive I suppose he might still have brought a horsewhip with him. As it is, I have to appeal to your better feelings. I expect you to run into Connie by chance. She is working at Worcester Cathedral and I'm sure you can think of a reason for going there. You will be looking unhappy — not difficult in the circumstances. You will cheer up immediately when you see her. You will tell her how much you have missed her and you will beg her — I mean *beg* her — to marry you."

"Do you think that isn't my dearest wish?" His face was no longer without expression; it was angry. He was angry with her. He had the audacity to be angry with her. "I have never stopped loving her and she knows that." He leaned across the desk as if she might be hard of hearing and enunciated very clearly, "She is no longer in love with me!"

Once, in another life, she had heard her husband use the word "bollocks" and she longed to use it now.

"Rubbish! It's quite the other way round! When you meet her you will see what I mean. She has been desperately unhappy. Now, carrying your child, she is different. Very happy. Though she has no hope at all of seeing you again, she has something that is yours."

He sat back, frowning prodigiously. She held up her hand as if he was about to speak. "I'm not saying more. I'm leaving." She got up, then turned at the door. "I will just add that this . . . this arrangement . . . has nothing to do with immorality or impropriety of any kind. I happen to think that you and my daughter are well suited and will have a very happy marriage."

She was gone. William sat still for the rest of that ten minutes and then his secretary announced his first client of the day and Mrs Heatherington came in, all smiles and fox furs, and he drew a chair forward.

She said, "My dear boy. It is good to see you again. I have come to tell you that I met Archie just yesterday and let him off the hook. All that terrible business in the summer made my feeble efforts to avenge myself seem paltry. Simply paltry. And you were right, it worked like a charm. D'you know what he did? He grabbed me — actually grabbed me — and kissed me and then he kept right on. And the upshot is, he is

taking me out to dinner tonight at the Lygon Arms."
She laughed like a girl. William heard himself laughing
with her.

She said, "I'm going to Worcester first. There's a little
shoe shop somewhere near the Shambles. I used to go
there a lot when I was younger. I see myself in a pair of
these boots — you know, the sort that Jean Shrimpton
has been showing off."

He wondered who on earth Jean Shrimpton was.

"May I take you to Worcester? I want to drop into
the cathedral. You remember Connie Vickers, my
one-time fiancée?"

"Oh my dear, such a shame. She felt responsible for
that boy's death, didn't she? I thought you might get
together again once some water had gone under the
bridge."

He decided to be frank. "I'm going to have another
try. She works in the cathedral. Shows people round,
fetches and carries . . . I bet she's good at it."

"I bet she is. She was good with those kids, wasn't
she?" Mrs Heatherington was — as Philip Marlowe
would have said — "on the case". "I'll come with you.
Make it look coincidental. Then you can sort of spring
on her. Rather like Archie did on me."

He was slightly doubtful but nodded. He picked up
the internal phone and cancelled the rest of his
appointments. "Mrs Heatherington and I are off to
Worcester," he explained. His secretary said nothing.

CHAPTER
SIX

From the moment she saw William and Mrs Heatherington lurking in the shadows, Connie knew what was going to happen. When Mrs Heatherington exclaimed, "My God, it's Connie!" she was not able to stop the little smile she felt lifting her face. And when William lurched towards her so obviously urged by an elegantly gloved hand, she felt the same melting sensation that she had known before.

She had wanted to tell him about the baby so much. He'd had a rotten deal during the war and he deserved to know that he was going to be a father, though he might think — after what had happened — that she might not make a very good mother. Even as the thought went through her head she dismissed it. She was no longer the girl who did not know about love and sacrifice; not any more. She knew that William loved her and always would. And she had known ever since that terrible accident in Cornwall that she loved him.

He opened his arms, perhaps to keep his balance, but he might still have fallen if she had not reached for him and checked his impetus. Crushed together, they subsided against an ancient pillar which had, quite obviously, been built for that very reason. Mrs

Heatherington, disappearing into the shadows, heard the faint murmurings amplified by the soaring ceiling.

"Oh William."

"Oh Connie. My darling girl. Don't leave me."

"Never. Never again."

"My dearest dear . . ."

And she smiled almost smugly.

They were married just before Christmas. It was a register office wedding, much to Rosemary's disappointment, but she accepted that Connie might be a little embarrassed by a white dress affair and really there was hardly any family left on either side. "What about Debbie? And Ruth Arbuthnot?" They had all been inseparable at school and would surely be hurt at being left out of the wedding.

"I know." Connie turned her mouth down with mock regret. "Especially when they got me in a corner afterwards to ask whether I had put on any weight." She smiled. "It wouldn't worry me, Mummy. I'm really, really happy about it all. I'd announce it from the rooftops if it wouldn't embarrass William." She hugged her mother. "But it would. He's not ashamed, darling — not at all. But he's really very shy. And he wouldn't know what to say to them."

"I know, darling. I know. I'm glad you're not having this quiet wedding because of me. I wouldn't mind being next to you on the rooftops, actually. I can't think why I am being so — so *modern*. I'm sure Maria already knows. Though quite how, I'm not sure."

"Could it be because of this?" Connie held her thick sweater close to her. Mother and daughter looked at each other and began to laugh.

Connie said, "I honestly thought poor Philip's drowning had changed everything. And here we are, laughing together. How can that happen?" She took her mother's hand. "Mummy, you've been wonderful. It must have been awful for you. I'm really sorry."

"Don't say that, Connie. Whatever happened has brought us so close. William too. And now we've got the wedding to look forward to."

Afterwards, Rosemary thought how . . . how . . . *significant* the whole thing had been. She had consulted a local florist and when they went into the register office it was full of chrysanthemums, their distinctive wintry smell completely overriding the normal carbolic. The registrar was all smiles. Arnold Jessup, carrying a top hat and wearing a morning suit, squired Mrs Flowers and Mrs Heatherington. Maria wore an unsuitable gauzy dress — "Organdie, my dear, you rarely see organdie these days." Mrs Heatherington eyed it enviously. She had subdued her usual garish taste on darling Arnie's advice and wore a navy blue woollen suit that now looked dowdy. But other neighbours from the village looked even worse. And Connie's mother wasn't much better in a bottle-green dress and coat with a matching hat that made her look like Robin Hood.

But really no one looked at anyone else when Connie came in on her mother's arm, her whole face smiling at

William so that he stopped looking as if he were at the dentist's and seemed to open his whole being as he smiled right back. Mrs Heatherington drew in her breath; Maria made an oohing sound; Arnold Jessup said audibly, "I say!" and Mrs Flowers put a hand to her mouth.

Connie had once been told that she looked like Snow White and on her wedding day she had gone for the whole thing. From the centre parting in her dark hair to her puffed sleeves and close-fitting bodice and on down to the full skirt made fuller still with the now old-fashioned New Look petticoats, she was a replica of the cartoon Snow White. Her mother had thought it was a clever way to disguise the undeniable fact of the coming baby. But it was Connie's way of shouting it from the rooftops.

Afterwards, there was a wedding breakfast at a hotel near Evesham and then the happy couple left for a night at another hotel specializing in honeymoons. There were four-poster beds and candlelit dinners and a six-piece band who would play almost anything requested. Connie thought it was gratingly synthetic but William had chosen it so she entered into the spirit of the place until she too was loving every minute. She chose Ivor Novello songs and danced with her head on William's chest and her eyes closed.

He whispered, "Are you happy, darling?"

"I am the happiest person in the world." She lifted her head and looked at him and saw a reflection of her own happiness in his eyes. She thought, surprised, that she was happy because he was happy. It was so obvious. But it was a revelation.

William's house was on the main A38 road from Worcester to Birmingham, not far from the famous cricket ground. It had a basement and an attic. A row of bells still connected the basement to all the other rooms; the attic had been the nursery and William's rocking horse commanded the day room.

Connie loved every inch of it. Her happiness was practically tangible that winter of 1960-61; it became a joke between them. William called it her central heating system. When he got in from the office he tried not to hug her until he had taken off his outdoor things and warmed his hands by the fire, but she would have none of it. She wrapped herself around him, sometimes with a potato in one hand and a paring knife in the other. He loved to find her in the midst of domesticity and she knew this. When Mrs Heatherington had cut out a page from a magazine and told her to prop it above the kitchen sink, she had read its advice with a small smile of rejection. William did not yearn for a bandbox wife and pristine house. She watched him relax, open up, respond completely to the slightly chaotic way she took on the house and the cooking. He was glad her mother helped her, coming across country at least three times a week armed with rubber gloves and wrap-around pinnies, but it was always Connie's domain. She turned down his offer of professional help; her mother did not hinder the learning process that was happening in the house. She and William had just a few months to know each other simply by a touch, a look, a shared dislike of spinach. The baby was accelerating a process that — in other marriages — might take years to flower. Yet they felt like children, learning by playing. William told her that she smiled in her sleep. The thought of him watching her asleep was wonderful.

She was a natural explorer and Number Five gave her plenty of scope. She had always loved the space and light of the Lickey Hills, and in spite of the cruelty of its sea she had recognized the amazing wildness of Cornwall. The stone staircases and side chapels of the cathedral spoke to her of the mystery of the past; and now there was this sense of joining another continuum that was held inside this Victorian semi. There was evidence — just here and there, peeping from corners and transoms and cast-iron fire grates — of the other people who had lived here. She found it interesting and amazingly comforting. She had a sense of other mistakes having been made, of other tragedies being lived and absorbed.

She had known for ages that William had been the youngest of three brothers. Mr Jessup's secretary had told her that. William himself told her that the others had died in a battle just outside Tripoli. He had paused and then added that "the parents" had gone to London at the tail end of the war to receive the posthumous medals. One of the infamous doodlebugs had demolished the small hotel near Paddington where they always stayed on London visits. It happened in the early hours of the morning and hopefully they had known nothing about it.

It was Mr Jessup himself who had told Connie quite brusquely that William had parachuted from a plane above Arnhem. He had survived to come home from the war to an empty house and what could well have been an empty life.

And now . . . already the house had filled up. The evidence of the past was still there and it seemed to breathe again as Connie dusted off the rocking horse and scoured the saucepans used by other people with the name that she now had. Mather. People seemed pleased that another Mrs Mather had moved into Number Five. An elderly neighbour telephoned and said she had borrowed Mrs Mather's sewing machine to make blackout curtains. "It's twenty years old, my dear, but it works splendidly and I would so like you to have it back." Her gardener brought it down on a sack trolley and William trundled it into the kitchen, put a new drive belt on the side and Connie treadled away to some purpose, making curtains for the night nursery, delighting in the thought that her mother-in-law had used it — probably to make blackout curtains too.

One day when the snow was arriving horizontally from the north-east, Connie found a rag doll in a cobwebby cupboard. She held it up to the light and saw that the calico was still strong and rough. She washed it carefully, squeezed it in a fluffy towel and sat it by the fire while she had her afternoon rest. Then she went into the kitchen and found remnants from the nursery curtains and settled at the old treadle machine, making a doll's dress. She showed it to William with some pride.

"So many little girls have played with it in this house," she marvelled. "And now . . . ours!" She put the doll carefully on to the rocking horse and sang, "May, May, it's a sunshiny day, won't you please come out to play!"

William chuckled as he entered into the game. "I'm not sure about May, however," he said in his solicitor's voice. "She looks crazy — that smile and those round eyes. May is not a name for a crazy doll, surely?"

"It's the name of our baby! What else can we choose when she will be born in May?" She looked again at the linen face. "The doll . . . well, you're right. It could be Tabitha. Does that sound crazy enough?"

He stared at her, amazed that she was so certain they were having a girl that she had already named her. Then he picked her up bodily and swung her around the nursery. She laughed. William kept doing this sort of thing and it made her feel like a schoolgirl again. She held him to her fiercely until he carried her to the bed. She dismissed the thought of the potatoes boiling themselves dry down in the kitchen. It was so good to lose the terrible weight of loss and guilt and waste that she had been carrying since last August. She was having his baby; she was resurrecting his home; she was making him happy. Nothing could spoil this. Ever.

Mrs Heatherington came two or three times to Number Five for William to reassure her that her decision to drop proceedings against Archie had been wise. She too fell for the old house and what she called its "crooks and nannies".

"I know just how you are feeling, Connie, my dearest. I think we have a special relationship. I have felt your feelings ever since we met."

Thinking this was the beginning of a reminiscence centred around Blue Seas or Mrs Pentwyn, Connie wondered why William was taking so long in the kitchen. "Really?" she asked faintly.

"Really," came back Mrs Heatherington firmly. "And you have felt it too. I watched your face when I showed you my wedding snap. Don't deny it." Connie smiled slightly and did not deny it. "You see? *And* I know that you are hesitant to call me Greta." She leaned forward. "It would make me so happy if you would call me Greta. It's not just that it goes with Gainsborough. It's that . . . it would make us friends."

Connie, with her new-found sensitivity, looked at the made-up face now so close to hers and saw vulnerability. She nodded, accepting the so-called transference between the two of them, though she was far from convinced by the "evidence".

"All right, Greta," she said. "Let's be friends."

William came in wheeling the new trolley laden with tea things. Mrs Heatherington clasped her hands delightedly and told him that he must call her Greta just as Connie did. And then she confided that Archie Fielding had found her a job at a casino in the city and she was having "a little fling" with him to show she had forgiven him.

130

"It won't last," she said realistically, opening her locket to show Connie Archie's picture. "We tried it before. He actually told me the other night that that was when he sold some of my jewellery and stuff. What was mine was his. I said to him the boot is now on the other foot and what is his is now mine. But of course it was mine in the first place so we're still not even."

William laughed but said, "Careful there . . . don't let yourself be upset all over again."

"I don't intend to!" she came back briskly. "So long as he still wants to sleep with me I've got the upper hand. And when he finds someone else, he'll be out of the flat like a greyhound when the trap goes up."

Connie found herself revising all her previous notions about Mrs Heatherington. She had never met anyone quite like this ageing chorus girl — because that was what she had been. Mrs Heatherington did away with inhibitions. It gave Connie the effrontery to ask her who on earth was Archie.

William, still laughing, said, "Greta's manager, sweetheart. You know, the man she was suing for misappropriation."

"We're old enemies. Or old friends. What's the difference?" Mrs Heatherington lifted her teacup too quickly and tea slopped on to her frilly blouse. Connie mopped at her and she said sentimentally, "You're a darling, Connie. A few corners to be rounded." She opened her mouth to say more, then closed it. Then opened it again. "We're two of a kind, Connie. Two of a kind. Too generous, too much conscience, too . . ." She raised her cup and repeated, "Generous."

Connie looked at her. William was smiling at what he saw as Mrs Heatherington's outrageous insinuations. Connie caught her eye as she put her glass on the table and was not reassured when one heavily mascaraed lid closed in a wink.

That night she went to bed early and let herself remember why Egg Pardoe had thrown himself into the sea that terrible day. When William joined her she did not pretend to be asleep. She clung to him as if devils were after her.

He whispered, "Darling, our little May is due in four weeks. Is it safe?"

She nodded desperately and they made love and she thought everything was all right.

"Did Greta upset you in any way, Connie?" He was anxious, smoothing back her hair and kissing her eyes.

"She makes everything sound — in some ways — almost meaningless. But no, of course she didn't upset me."

"She lived with a lot of men during the war, darling. Comforts for the troops — you know how they joke about it now." He nibbled her earlobe. "Trouble is she can't stop it." He chuckled and her ear tickled. "When that snow was about she spent nearly a week with Arnold. They're old friends. He knew her husband."

She was intrigued and diverted. Mr Jessup . . . one of Mrs Heatherington's boyfriends? It really was funny. She chuckled.

"I'm not sure whether knowing her husband has anything to do with anything! Probably the shortest marriage ever. Was it even twenty-four hours?"

132

"Probably not. But she has always called herself Greta Heatherington. And she's got her marriage certificate. She practically brandished it at me when I took on her case." He sighed. "We know so little about people."

Connie felt guilt wash up from her stomach again. She swallowed. "How do you mean?"

"I have a feeling that Greta is still in love with the disreputable Maurice Heatherington."

Connie turned her face into William's neck and he said quickly, "You're not *crying*, are you?"

"Not really. You're such a . . . such a romantic, William. I was seeing Mrs . . . Greta . . . as hard. Perhaps I mean tough. And you have shown me something else. I wonder whether she still loves him. And whether he really is alive and living in somewhere like Rangoon."

"I repeat, Mrs Mather, we never know people."

She laughed and kissed his neck and inhaled the scent of him. Then half asleep she said, "Where is Rangoon?"

And he murmured back, "I'm not sure. But somewhere else."

Two weeks later, Connie gave birth to a boy. It was planned to take place in the big double bed, suitably protected with an orange rubber sheet covered with brown paper and then a cosy towelling sheet over the lot. It duly happened there after a long day of inexplicable discomfort and then six hours of proper labour when Connie did everything she had been told

133

to do at her relaxation classes and then released the helping hands of the student midwife, put her feet firmly on the crouching shoulders of the middle-aged, unmarried midwife, grabbed the rails of the bedhead and went to work. She heard Miss Green say grimly to her student, "She means business . . . Here's the head . . . Tell her to ease up else the baby will shoot through the window . . . Bound to be a boy if he's in this much of a hurry."

It was a boy. They called him Francis after Connie's father but almost immediately he was known as Frank, then Frankie.

After a couple of weeks she put Frank into his pram for the first outing. William fastened a knitted helmet over his sandy hair. Rosemary held a tiny flailing fist and fitted a mitten over it. Connie stood holding the handle of the pram, consciously registering this moment in the hall of Number Five, thinking that she had done something right for once. William was glowing with pride and happiness. Her mother had bought a new hat for this occasion and had excused the extravagance by saying, "I know I've got plenty of hats but nothing quite suitable for a grandmother." And the baby had been born happy, squinting round at them now and then as if checking that he really had arrived in the right place, then closing his eyes, content that he had. He did it now. William was saying something about the weather being quite chilly for May, and the baby opened his eyes wide as if in agreement then let the heavy folds of flesh settle again. Whether he had managed to open them wide, whether it was the strange underwater light of the hall, Connie had no idea. But her precious moment of thankfulness had gone. Frank's eyes, which had been a dirty grey colour, were transformed for that second's revelation. They were intensely blue.

Rosemary Vickers was Frank's godmother, Arnold Jessup the godfather and Greta Heatherington volunteered herself as "stand-in".

"I'll have to be something," she told Rosemary, who exuded disapproval. "I was practically at Frank's conception."

Rosemary did not like Greta Heatherington on several counts. She could see that Connie got on excellently with her now, but at the outset, during that disastrous holiday, she had been a thorn in Connie's side and had not helped the situation at all. But even without that, she was so flagrantly common she grated on Rosemary unbearably. And there was something else. She could accept that the woman had had several men friends — the war had a great deal to answer for — but that now, even now, she appeared to be able to crook her little finger and they would come running was, well, incredible. Connie had told her something that had shocked her. Really shocked her. Arnold Jessup was well known for being as straight as a die and he had been good to Connie and it was only right that he should be asked as godfather to baby Francis. Surely, *surely*, he of all people could not be summoned — yes, *summoned* — by someone as flagrantly promiscuous — yes, *promiscuous* — as Greta

Heatherington or Gainsborough or whatever she called herself? Perhaps she had got it wrong because Connie had giggled uncontrollably when she told her mother about the snow and Archie Fielding letting Greta down . . . Yes, she must have got it wrong because as she had understood it, there was nothing remotely humorous about it. Even so, whatever had happened during the snow, Greta Heatherington was still very familiar with Arnold. But then she was familiar with everyone. She managed to dislodge Rosemary's new hat by kissing her enthusiastically before and after the christening.

Arnold had said, "Oh, don't adjust it, Mrs Vickers. It looks marvellous anyhow but somehow rakish at the back of your head like that." He saw her flush and hastened on, "You look like Connie when she came for her interview back in fifty-eight. Like a schoolgirl. A very nice, well-brought-up school-girl."

Rosemary went from pink to purple in two seconds flat. Greta Heatherington hugged her a little more carefully and said, "Arnold never makes insincere compliments, Rosie."

And Rosemary said faintly, "Was that a compliment?"

"I know," Greta said sympathetically. "He's sincere but not really good at it."

She felt better when they got back to the house and she could start handing round tea and sandwiches. The vicar said, "I cannot believe you are the grandmother, Mrs Vickers! You must have been a child bride."

"I suppose . . . well, yes. My husband had not wanted to get married until after the war and he was very worried when Connie came along. How thankful I am."

You could say things like that to a vicar and this one was special; William had mentioned that he had been among the First of the Few. She imagined him hearing God's call while he was in the cockpit of his Spitfire trying to kill other people. She said quickly, "Of course I was lucky enough to be financially secure. I could look after Connie properly. It might have been dreadful if I hadn't had private means."

"Rather." He nodded vigorously. "I went into the Church for that very reason. A house provided and security for life. I never married so my stipend is adequate." He saw her face change and smiled. "It's the *love* of money that is the root of evil, Mrs Vickers. I take it that like me you are simply thankful for what you have."

She was feeling so mixed-up she hardly knew how she felt. She said, "Well . . . yes, I suppose I am. But there are other things. I have to admit that now that Connie is so happily settled, I shall have to think what I can do with my life."

"You need to be needed?"

"Of course."

"There will be a new role to fill. The position is very much vacant for a grandmother." He smiled at her as he delivered this tactful reminder that she was the only grandparent baby Francis had.

She nodded enthusiastically. "That will be marvellous. But I think I will do some voluntary work. I have put my name down for hospital driving."

The vicar looked pleased. "You will meet people —
on a one-to-one basis. That is good."

She nodded doubtfully. She had already taken one
elderly woman to Worcester for treatment. The woman
had talked all the way there and all the way back and
Rosemary had had great difficulty in concentrating. She
realized that the kind of driving she normally did was
very local.

"And of course," the vicar looked straight into her
eyes, "the church can never get enough help."

She said defensively, "I've always delivered the
magazines and shared a certain amount of pastoral
work with . . ." She heard herself making excuses and
smiled suddenly. "I know what you mean. Yes. I can
certainly help out more than I do." Her newly trained
ear picked up a small wail from upstairs and her smile
widened. "Time for my grandmother role, I think."

The vicar watched her leave the room unobtrusively
and thought what a waste it was that she had never
remarried and then, hard on the heels of that thought,
what a wonderful vicar's wife she would make. Many of
his parishioners thought he was a confirmed bachelor
but he had never taken vows of celibacy. He worked out
Rosemary Vickers's age and decided she was probably
about five years older than he was. When it was time to
go he asked her for a lift as far as the vicarage and was
surprisingly regretful when she told him she was staying
overnight at Number Five. Arnold Jessup offered a seat
in his car. He had to squash in the back with two other
neighbours; Mrs Heatherington sat in the front.

* * *

Rosemary sat with Connie in the nursery while she fed Frank. She had wanted to go on with the clearing up downstairs but William had asked her to let him finish it off while she had an hour with Connie. He smiled at her. "You can follow after me and wash up the bits I've missed — I know you will, so don't shake your head like that!" He sobered. "I think it would be nice for the two of you to have a quiet time together. It's been a very hectic day."

She thought what a lovely man he was. Connie was lucky. And so was she. She went upstairs to "her" room, which was the main bedroom overlooking the tree-lined street. Connie and William had made an enormous room for themselves in the day nursery next door to Frank. She slid out of the pencil skirt belonging to her suit and put on a cotton one and immediately felt more relaxed. She really must stop disliking Greta Heatherington so much; the sight of her cuddling — yes, cuddling was the word — right up to Arnold Jessup in his old Riley had been positively sickening. And that poor young vicar, she couldn't remember his name for the moment, had been thrust into the back with the Brookways, who were both overweight and smelled of their dog.

She changed her best blouse and made herself think of something else. The vicar — what on earth was his name? — must be the same age as William if he had flown Spitfires during the Battle of Britain. He had seemed older somehow. He was nice, but not half so nice as William. He seemed to think that the Church was a job, not a calling. Funny that, dear William had a job but he made it seem like a calling. He must feel that way too because otherwise how could he be nice to someone like Mrs Heatherington? She rinsed her face and hands at the fitted basin and went upstairs to join Connie.

The day nursery was full of the late July sun; she went through it to the night nursery, smiling at the sight of William's rocking horse liberally festooned with cast-off clothing. By contrast the smaller room was almost dark and Connie had switched on one of the bars of the electric fire. She sat by it, blouse unbuttoned, feeding Frank. It created a glow around the two of them and Rosemary smiled sentimentally. "Mother and child bathed — contained — in golden light. I wish I could paint."

Connie smiled too. "You do. You started painting the dining room after the wedding — don't you remember?"

Rosemary laughed but said, "I haven't finished it yet. I'd never have started it if I'd realized what a gigantic job it was."

"Oh Mummy. Sometimes I think of you there on your own and I shiver."

"On my own? You must be joking, Connie. Maria comes in every blessed morning — drives me mad sometimes. I mean, I don't mind listening to her symptoms but they're the same ones all the time! Last week I told her I'd got trouble with my spine just to join in the conversation!"

"You did make it up?"

"Of course! If there was anything wrong with me, d'you think I'd tell Maria?"

140

"What about me — would you tell me? Promise me, Mummy. Promise me now and here that you would tell me."

"It's here and now actually, darling. But of course I would tell you." Rosemary settled herself in the opposite chair and sighed with satisfaction. "It's so wonderful to see Frank having his supper."

"Pudding coming up!" Connie swapped sides expertly, used a swab, covered herself. "He's over two months and the health visitor would like me to start on the strained solids but he seems perfectly satisfied with things as they are."

"What about you though? You've lost weight, love. William thinks you get tired too easily."

"What rubbish! Everybody gets tired when they're looking after a baby."

"Yes. I suppose they do." Rosemary sat back, not entirely satisfied. She told Connie about the vicar and how he was encouraging her to do more church work. "I can't remember his name but he was interesting. I don't think I've met a celibate vicar before," she said, passing a clean nappy.

"Celibate?"

"Well . . . I assumed . . ."

"He's just a typical man. Waiting for the right woman, when he will automatically fall in love. Meanwhile he's got a wonderful housekeeper and can have his own way about everything."

"Connie! So cynical. And still so young. But it did cross my mind that he saw his position as a rather nice job. Status and so forth."

Connie put Frank over one shoulder and he wailed and then burped. Both women laughed. Connie said, "He's a realist. Managed to keep out of the war because of his eyesight and has made his life as comfortable and trouble-free as possible. He realizes that marriage is hard work so he'll have to find the ideal wife before he launches into matrimony."

"Kept out of the war? William told me he was one of the First of the Few!"

"You misheard, darling. William probably told you he was one of the few to sail through the war."

Rosemary felt annoyed to have been wrong on two counts. Connie obviously did not like the vicar. She herself had not been enamoured at first but suddenly was on his side.

"I'm hardly going deaf, Connie, dear. I'm not fifty yet. The vicar said I must have been a child bride and I *was* only twenty-one when I had you!"

Connie laid a sponged baby in her mother's lap and stood back, grinning.

"Grandmother and child," she said in an affected voice. "Bathed in light from an electric fire!"

The baby looked up at Rosemary and opened his eyes wide. She was immediately adoring. "He's so *beautiful*, Connie. His eyes are the clearest blue I have ever seen. I think my grandfather had blue eyes. You took after me and William's eyes are brown too." She put her face close to the baby's. She had the strangest feeling of being somewhere else, somewhere . . . other. Just Frank and herself. She could not pull away from him. His blue, blue eyes were a whole world.

142

She must have looked as if she were about to collapse on to that tiny body because Connie's hands were on her shoulders holding her up. Connie was saying urgently, "Mummy — sit up — I'll take Frank — sit up, darling. Please."

Rosemary did so. She blinked. Everything was as it should be. Connie lifted Frank and went to the cot. She tucked him between the sheets and pulled a loose-knit blanket over him. He started to cry. She said loudly, "He always does this at first. If we're here he will soon stop."

Rosemary looked at her in astonishment. She had shared this bedtime routine several times in the last three months, insisting that William and Connie go out now and then, baby or no baby. Frank never cried when he was put down to sleep. In fact, he rarely cried.

But Connie was right; his heartbroken wails abated into little grumbling noises, he turned his head towards one upflung arm and fastened his mouth on to his own thumb. He was asleep.

Rosemary whispered, "Let's stay here for a while, darling girl. It's so peaceful and you look all in."

Connie sat down again without a word. Rosemary made little clucking noises, trying to clear her throat quietly. She put a hand to her face; it was wet. My God, she had actually cried over her grandson. What on earth was the matter with her?

Connie said, "You know, don't you?"

"Know? Know what, Connie? I certainly don't know what's got into me. Sentimental old fool. I could howl."

143

"You know that something is wrong with Frank." She looked up at her mother's gasp. "I'm the same. I cannot believe it."

Rosemary spoke strongly. "There's nothing wrong with that baby. Don't think I'm crazy, but just now . . . he touched my soul. There's no other way I can put it, Connie. He knew me. As if we had known each other before life. It was just so wonderful. But not wrong. There was nothing wrong about that moment."

Connie stood up suddenly and hung on to the high mantelpiece. She whispered, "He's not William's. He belongs to . . . the boy. The golden boy. The boy I called Philip. He's got his father's eyes. Blue as the sky."

Rosemary had to hold the arms of her chair. She stared up at her daughter as if she had never seen her before. She could almost feel herself working things out. It seemed to take for ever. When she spoke she was still incredulous.

"You mean . . .? He was fifteen, Connie. How could you . . . how *could* you?"

"He was sixteen." Connie's voice was dull, resigned.

Her mother said nothing and after an agonizing time Connie said in the same tone, "I simply cannot understand it. Not now. I cannot excuse it. I was six years older than him. I should have known better . . . I *did* know better. And I still . . . He'd had what William called a seizure. He was terrified of the small earthquake and then the rain. I must have known then that he was still . . . a child. But he could read and discuss what he was reading and he was . . . he was *wise*, Mummy. In a basic, commonsense sort of way.

144

When the jellyfish stung me, he knew what to do. He had comforted me and I wanted to comfort him so I cuddled him to me."

Rosemary felt her first outrage collapse completely and she said instantly, "I do understand. Don't chastise yourself like this, Connie. I do understand. I was a girl before I was a woman."

Connie looked down at her mother and dissolved. Rosemary stood up. They held each other.

After the tears abated, Rosemary whispered into her daughter's hair, "Does William know?"

"No!" Connie's sob caught in her throat. "He taught me about the comfort of sex, Mummy. I was so frightened by the possession part of it I almost forgot the comfort until I needed to use it to help Philip."

"Oh darling." Rosemary held the shaking shoulders. This was why Connie had come home in such a state.

"I knew what to do, you see." Connie went on speaking through renewed sobs. "It seemed so mean and petty not to do it."

Rosemary said again, "I do understand. But William . . ."

"We never speak of Cornwall. I know he is acting for Lucy Pardoe still but he has not been to see her since we were married."

"If he has chosen not to speak of it, then probably it is better if you follow his lead. How do you feel about that?"

"It was how I hoped . . . but of course Frank's likeness . . . There is another thing, Mummy. Philip —

Egg — had some kind of brain damage. I cannot make enquiries. But could it be hereditary?"

Rosemary looked over her daughter's shoulder to where Frank slept peacefully. She remembered those wonderful eyes looking into hers, promising something . . . She tried to recall what it had been.

She said firmly, "There is nothing wrong with that child, Connie. I am completely sure of that!"

She drew back and looked into Connie's tea-brown eyes. And Connie, only too ready to believe her, gave a small sob of relief.

Rosemary spoke firmly. "You are not certain that Frank is not William's son, darling. And William loves him so much. You have to leave things as they are."

Connie nodded through her tears. "You're right, of course. He adores Frank. And . . . and he thinks I'm a good person. Oh Mummy, he's loyal and true and he thinks that is how I am. And I was not. And he must know some time —"

"He need not. And you *are* loyal and true, darling! You did what you had to do at the time."

"How could he *not* know? Those eyes are Philip's eyes — William's are brown, darker than mine. And that photograph of his mother, hers were grey and his father's were brown."

"Darling, don't gabble. It will make you feel more muddled and awful than ever. Let's take it one step at a time, shall we?"

Connie blinked on the hot tears still spilling over. She nodded. It was, after all, the easiest thing to do: absolutely nothing. She had been living in a fool's

146

paradise ever since she got married and it would be bliss to go back to that state.

She and her mother went to the cot and looked down at the tiny contented boy, thumb fallen out of his mouth as he slept. It occurred to Connie for the first time that the strange anomaly of the romantic Philip Marlowe character and the sixteen-year-old who seemed part of the magical world around him and was so prosaically called Egg had not, after all, been annihilated. She could have smiled at the thought, found comfort in it, except that nobody else would. Certainly not dear William, who had had such a rotten time of it anyway. It would make life very much worse than it had been when he was alone. And as for Lucy Pardoe, her hatred for the "foreign girl" would be compounded yet again.

Her mother whispered, "He is so beautiful, Connie. And so very happy."

Connie nodded. Yes, that was how his father had been. So very happy.

She hugged her mother. "Thank you, Mummy. Thank you," she murmured into her ear.

CHAPTER
SEVEN

Arnold Jessup had never married though there had been a number of women in his life with whom he had fallen romantically in love. Perhaps fortunately, none of them had been in a position to marry him; he had chosen the role of bachelor without any trouble at all.

When Greta Heatherington had asked for his help with her fly-by-night manager he had tried to explain to her that, as they occasionally spent a rainy afternoon in bed together, he was unable to represent her. She had glanced out of the window at the perfect July afternoon and said, "Well, I'm blessed! It's actually snowing as I speak! And if I can't undo what we have already done, Arnie darling, we might as well go to bed and keep warm!"

He had laughed inordinately and told her that her opportunism would get her into trouble one of these days. And later he had mentioned that William would probably be able to help her and why didn't she book an extra room at this boarding house she went to every year in Cornwall and he would make sure William joined her.

Arnold had worked for his father in the small legal practice on the outskirts of Birmingham until the outbreak of the war, when he volunteered his services to the Intelligence Corps. If he had hoped for a more interesting life he was disappointed; he referred to his two-year service as "festering behind a desk". During the Blitz he was an air-raid warden in the Leicester Square area of London. It made those two years worthwhile but when his father died suddenly he had no difficulty in extricating himself and returning to civilian life in Birmingham.

While he was still at school, William was born and he was asked to stand as godfather. He was flushed by the honour of it; also he was in love with William's mother and even years later could feel his eyes fill with tears when he thought of her. He looked on William as the son he had never fathered.

When the boy (he always called him "the boy") was demobbed he made it his business to find out about courses for ex-servicemen.

"They're offering emergency training for teachers at the university. Recruiting people like yourself who had to stop whatever they were doing to fight the war. Just two years, then you get your certificate. What do you think?"

William knew that he could not face a room full of children; in fact, he was finding it very difficult to face people at all. He shook his head.

Arnold said, "Right. I didn't think so. In that case you need three years to get a decent degree in law. Your fellow students will nearly all be your age. Small groups. Seminars. You can cope with that. Then you come in with me. My stuff is mostly bits and pieces for the university but I do have other cases I like to take on, neighbours, friends and so on — feel obliged. You understand."

Much later William wondered whether Arnold had "felt obliged" to keep an eye on him, but by that time he knew that he was doing the right thing. During the years at university he saw Arnold at least twice a week and hogged the conversation simply because he had to share his enormous interest in what he was studying. Arnold would stand up occasionally and go to one of his shelves, pull out a book and bring it back. "Let me have it back, for God's sake. I can't practise law without it. Does it fit that particular case?"

Once, when they said good night and shook hands and William got on his bicycle, Arnold said casually, "All right, are you? Knocking about in that tall old house? You can always have a room with me, you know. That's the best of staying single. Don't have to get permission."

William hesitated then shook his head. He said honestly, "I didn't like it at first but it's all right now. People knew us. I like that."

Arnold nodded, quite unable to speak. Six years later, when he was interviewing the girls from the secretarial school, he chose Connie without a moment's hesitation. The position was for a filing clerk and he had no idea how she would perform, but there were other considerations.

He felt personally responsible when they became engaged; even more so when they were not engaged and William tried to explain about the awful event on the little beach in Cornwall. It was wonderful when they patched it up because of the baby and got married. He boasted about them as if they were his own family. And sometimes he wondered whether he ought to have made sure he had a family of his own.

And then Frankie Mather was christened and he had another evening with Greta Heatherington, which was comforting and marvellous at the same time. But more importantly, he met Rosemary Vickers. Not for the first time because she had called for Connie once or twice and come into the office. But it was the first time he had seen her properly.

Rosemary did not sleep that night at Number Five. However much she had reassured Connie, fears and doubts came at her from all directions. There was nothing at all she could do about it, yet she had to do something.

On the drive back home on Monday morning she decided that the only thing she could do was to find out more about the seizures Connie had described. Obviously there was nothing whatsoever wrong with Frankie. You only had to look at him to see it. But if she was still worried it stood to reason that Connie would be too. She would name no names, everything would be hypothetical. But she would question Dr Thomas about it.

She wasted no time. When she had garaged the car and let herself into the house, she made straight for the phone.

Mrs Thomas's voice was gently reproachful. "It's Monday, Mrs Vickers. Unless it's an emergency, my husband does not see patients on a Monday."

"Oh, this is nothing to do with being a patient. This is simply a general question. Hypothetical."

Mrs Thomas, gentle or not, could be firm. "I'll ask him to give you a ring then, shall I? He's actually on the golf course at the moment but will be home for dinner. Or perhaps I can help — is it a crossword clue?"

Rosemary said, "No. I'm not sure about a phone call — but yes, that will be fine. I'm in for the rest of the day." She replaced the receiver with a click, wondering whether Rita Thomas was being deliberately annoying. Crossword clue indeed. They knew each other through the Women's Institute but had never become friends. And Rosemary was a little disconcerted at being bulldozed into a phone conversation with Dr Thomas.

She unpacked her overnight case then made tea and sat by the window overlooking the golf course. Her head was still full of baby Frank. She wondered about his father. And his grandmother . . . She was the one to talk to. But she was probably biased against Connie. Connie had not been able to tell her anything much about the family. And William, who must have seen her several times, did not know that there was anything to tell. Poor William . . . poor Connie. And the boy himself, Philip or Egg or whatever his real name was . . . poor boy. What a waste. And the mother . . . She was the one who would know . . . everything. Lucy Pardoe. Rosemary dried her eyes furiously, topped up her teacup and drank the tepid contents in one go. Just for a moment she had imagined how it would have been if Egg Pardoe had been rescued and Connie Vickers had drowned. She closed her eyes for a second. Thank God for William . . . thank God. She put the cup down and stared out at the July afternoon. It had all happened a year ago. Almost. It had been in August, towards the end. Very hot. Enormous thunderstorms had seen the month out.

Someone was waving. She squinted through the window, wondering whether the wave was for her. No one could see her behind the glass, of course. But someone was definitely waving in the direction of the house, no doubt about that. She reached behind her to the desk where the binoculars were kept for birdwatching. Whoever was waving was still there by the time she had wriggled the glasses from their case and removed the dust caps. She held them to her eyes and focused with the usual difficulty. Then she dropped them into her lap and said, "Damn!" quite loudly. She had caught sight of the dog collar. It was the vicar from the christening and she still had not got his name! She would have to lock the back door . . . not that he would try to come in, surely to goodness? But he was the last person she wanted to see. She backed away from the window and scuttled through the kitchen and the scullery and was about to shoot the bolts as quietly as she could, when there was a light tap from outside and the door opened eighteen inches and there was Maria Selby, her neighbour. She leaped nervously when she encountered Rosemary's face two inches from her own.

"Rosemary! I thought I heard you drive in! Is something the matter?"

"Of course not." Rosemary ushered her in quickly. Perhaps the vicar would go when he saw she had company.

"Only, this morning, quite early actually, well, about ten o'clock, I suppose — you know how long it takes me to get up and dress these days, the pain across my back has been unspeakable — anyway, a vicar was knocking on your door and I dragged myself over and told him you were with your daughter and he seemed to know all about it and it turned out he'd actually done the christening!" She laughed heartily. "He said he'd have a round of golf and call back later, so I thought I'd better warn you. He seemed awfully nice, Rosemary, and quite concerned about you because you live alone. I told him so did I and we looked after each other and he asked about your health and I said you were really strong and did the garden without help — not like me, I have to have Mr Tasker once a week — and he was pleased about that. You being strong, I mean."

"Oh, that's good. The only thing is, Maria, he is coming up the garden path this very moment and I can't remember his name. Did he give it to you?"

Maria was flustered. "I can't quite recall. Marcus something. The Reverend Marcus . . . would it be Vallender?"

Rosemary subdued an urge to shake her old neighbour and nodded briskly. "That's it. Of course. Now don't go rushing away, Maria. Sit down here and

I will make another pot of tea. I think there's some cherry Madeira cake in the tin."

Maria sat down, twittering. "The clergy always like a slice of cake with their tea, and I wouldn't say no."

There was a knock at the back door and Rosemary opened it and smiled.

"Vicar. How nice. My neighbour has just told me to expect you. This is a treat."

He came in and made a thing about wiping his feet. She thought she need not have worried about his name as "vicar" would do nicely, and anyway he said immediately, "Call me Marcus and I will call you Rosemary. I've taken a liberty, haven't I? Arriving without prior invitation. But Monday is my day off and the weather has been so nice I thought I would drive along some of the quieter roads and see where they took me." He shook her hand and then went ahead of her and shook Maria's hand. He sat down in Rosemary's chair and stretched his legs. "This is marvellous. Just marvellous. When I saw your brooch flashing in the sun, it was like a signal. In fact, I think it was a signal." He looked at her roguishly and she was appalled as she realized he thought she had been deliberately signalling to him that she was home. As if she had given him the glad eye or something. And now she had to lug round the chair from the desk . . . she was damned if she was going to make more tea and cut the cake.

Maria twittered again. "Rosemary was just saying that she would make more tea. Such a treat to have a gentleman caller. This little development — four houses

— is home to three widows and one married couple and they are always out and about."

Rosemary sat down with a bump. "I expect you are anxious to get back to the vicarage. Perhaps another time would be best for a cup of tea."

Maria looked bewildered then disappointed. The vicar — Marcus indeed — said, "As I mentioned, Rosemary, Mondays are when I have a day off and I like to make sure I am out and unavailable to everyone."

His words hung in the air of the late afternoon. Maria began to look hopeful. Rosemary stood and picked up her tray. "I won't be long," she said and went into the kitchen.

Never had she made tea and cut cake and put out crockery and cutlery on the trolley with such force. She was tired and anxious and wanted time and privacy to talk to Dr Thomas when he phoned. She knew that not long ago she would have thought this situation funny and tried to grab back that attitude. But it passed her by and she went into the scullery, closed the kitchen door behind her and said viciously, "Damn! Damn, damn and damn again!" Then went back into the sitting room and smiled. Maria was reassured and Marcus had noticed nothing amiss so he simply went on luxuriating in the sun, which now beamed into the window and probably flashed messages from her brooch to the rest of the county. He was a hungry vicar and blamed the round of golf as he finished the last slice of cake.

"This is most pleasant, most pleasant." He had just given them a discourse on brass rubbing; Maria's eyes drooped. "We must do this again, Rosemary. Perhaps a little drive somewhere next week." He gave that roguish grin again. "Didn't I tell you only yesterday that the church needed help?"

Maria twittered sleepily. Rosemary raised her brows. This really was going too far. "Do you mean *you* need help? May I ask what is wrong, Marcus? Are you perhaps not managing very well? Are your problems domestic or spiritual?"

She could have gone on and on and he interrupted quickly. "Nothing is wrong, dear lady." He looked slightly disconcerted. "I was speaking metaphorically. Perhaps, however, I do lack companionship."

Maria was asleep. Rosemary said in a low voice, "I wonder whether you would consider dropping in here on a Monday now and then? My friend Maria here, she rarely gets the opportunity for a drive and I could see how keen she was when you mentioned it just now."

He was master of the situation again. "Why not? We could go to Stratford next Monday if you like."

"She would love that. I'll tell her as soon as she wakes up. I hate to be a killjoy now, Marcus, but I am expecting a very important phone call this evening and I would like to take it in private. I'm sure you understand."

"Of course. And I will see you next Monday." He stood up, picking up his panama from the desk. He looked really pleased with himself. Maria woke up and twittered and stood up too.

Rosemary said, "Probably not. But Maria adores Stratford — don't you, my dear? Marcus is going to call for you next Monday and drive you there — or anywhere else you fancy."

Maria was overwhelmed. There was little Marcus could do about it. He armed her across to her own house and Rosemary waved to them both and then shut the door. Almost immediately there came a knock from the kitchen. It was too soon for Marcus to have galloped round to the back garden. She opened the door cautiously nonetheless. It was Dr Thomas.

She looked at him blankly. "I thought you were going to telephone?"

"Was I?" He looked around. "Mrs Vickers, may I come in for just a moment? I'm on the run!" She stood aside and he slid sideways through the door. "I met a chap in the club house. Pompous type. Selly Oak or somewhere like that. Dog collar. He insisted on giving me a lift home and he went off to get his car well over an hour ago. I hoped very much he had forgotten all about me and I was walking back home, which I had intended to do in the first place, when I saw him outside Mrs Selby's door. If he's going back to the car park, there's no way he can miss me and, frankly, I would prefer my own company." He laughed and after a moment so did she, then she led the way into the hall and they watched through the window as Marcus tipped his hat at Maria and continued towards the club house.

"He's been here for over an hour." Rosemary went into the sitting room, unclipped her brooch and indicated the tea things. "He officiated at the christening of my grandson yesterday. The Reverend Marcus Vallender."

"I think you've got that wrong, Mrs Vickers. Challenger. He introduced himself as Marcus Challenger."

She laughed helplessly. "That's about the hundredth thing I've got wrong over this weekend." She shook her head. "He's probably got a network of middle-aged women who will make him tea and listen to him pontificate! Anyway, he wanted to come again next Monday, which is his day off, and I've managed to fix him up with Maria." The bonnet of a small car gleamed suddenly in the low sunshine and then disappeared down the lane. Dr Thomas stared at her for a moment and then roared with laughter.

"All this drama in such a quiet village! And what's this about a phone call?"

"Do sit down — would you like some tea, I can make another pot very quickly."

He sat down but shook his head at the raised teapot, so Rosemary put it down among the cake crumbs and said carefully, "I thought I might have a word with you about a friend of Connie's. I stayed with Connie and William on Saturday and Sunday nights, to help with the christening — did I mention that?"

"Yes. And several people told me about it last week. Did it go well?"

"Yes. Thank you. As you know, the Reverend *Challenger* did not sparkle but he tried."

"And was trying." They both smiled.

Rosemary said, "A friend of Connie's has a little . . . girl. I can't remember the name. But she is anxious because she and her husband have recently discovered a history of some kind of brain disorder in the family. An uncle, I believe." She described what Connie had called a "seizure" as best she could. "She is so afraid it could be hereditary."

"So you rang me for an appointment and my wife explained about Mondays being my day off and said I would telephone you later." Dr Thomas spoke as if this was a regular occurrence. He waited for Rosemary's embarrassed nod. "Well . . . I cannot advise a friend of an ex-patient, Mrs Vickers. You must know that. But if we are discussing something entirely hypothetical all I can say is that there would probably be two causes for this kind of seizure. The patient could well have sustained brain damage during birth, or indeed afterwards. This might lead to epilepsy. Or the impairment could be inherited. It does sound, from your description of the seizure, as if it is epilepsy." He stopped. "I'm drifting from the hypothetical to the particular. I would strongly suggest that Connie's friend visits her GP as soon as possible."

Rosemary thanked him and he stood up and went into the hall. "Good to see you, Mrs Vickers, thank you for sanctuary!" He grinned as he opened the door then said seriously, "Is Connie's friend hypothetical too? Forgive me, but you arrived back earlier today and phoned for an appointment immediately."

She was flummoxed again. "No — of course not," and then was quite literally saved by the bell. The telephone rang at her elbow and she raised her eyebrows apologetically and closed the door.

"Hello?" she said with some caution. Today was proving much too eventful.

"Rosemary? This is Arnold Jessup. You're home safe and sound then?"

She stared at her reflection and was annoyed to see her hair was an absolute mess. And what on earth was Arnold Jessup doing telephoning her? She had met him once or twice as far as she knew and his reputation was well borne out by his performance with Greta Heatherington. And hadn't he called her Mrs Vickers at the christening?

"Yes, thank you. I do come and go to Number Five quite often, you know."

"Quite. It was just . . . there was a lot to do and I thought you might feel your homecoming was rather an anticlimax. Mrs Flowers swept me out of the office rather brusquely and suggested I telephone you to see how you are."

"Who is Mrs Flowers?" She knew very well who Mrs Flowers was. She had been a good friend to Connie during her three years at Jessup's.

"My secretary. She knows everything. She is very fond of Connie and William. And you are Connie's mother."

"Oh. That is . . . kind. Most kind." For some reason Rosemary felt herself relax tremblingly.

"It went well, don't you think?"

"Oh, it was wonderful. He didn't cry once, did he? And those beautiful eyes . . ." She remembered those beautiful eyes and felt her heart lift. There was nothing wrong with baby Frank. Nothing at all. She propped her hip against the hall stand and smiled at her reflection. "Actually, it's been quite hectic since I got in." She felt a need to confide in someone. "That pious vicar called. His name is Marcus Challenger but I thought it was Vallender — not that it mattered as he insisted we should be Rosemary and Marcus. And he wanted to come again next Monday . . ." She giggled, "And I palmed him off on my neighbour who is already besotted with him and makes lovely gingerbread. And then my local GP dropped in. He's just this minute gone, actually."

Arnold Jessup did not appear to need filling in. He seemed to be listening intently to her laughter and when it stopped he said, "Why don't we try that little pub on the Stratford road? They do the most wonderful risotto — do you like risotto?"

"I adore it. But I think I must be tired after the weekend and everything and my hair is such a mess —"

"We won't make it late and I'll drive, of course. I'll be with you at seven thirty." He put his receiver down and she stood there looking at hers disbelievingly. This was how he must talk to Mrs bloody Heatherington. She gasped because she rarely used the word bloody and never inside her head. She would ring back and tell him that she couldn't possibly . . . He lived "over the shop", as Connie had always put it, so she knew his phone number by heart and she dialled three digits and then stopped and looked at herself in the mirror. *This* was how he must talk to Greta Heatherington.

162

She replaced the phone and went to clear up the tea things. Then she ran a bath and added to it from a bottle of something she'd had from Maria at Christmas. And she sat there, head back, eyes closed, until the water became chilly. She spent ages on her make-up and then started on her hair. It had completely lost its set. She scooped it back severely and made a small bun at the back of her head so that her nape showed. She still had a good neck. And to confirm her absolute difference from anyone else he might know, she put on a strapless cotton frock and topped it with one of Connie's old school cardigans. He arrived and if she had wanted to confuse him she would have been delighted by his suppressed gasp and then his total appreciation. Except that, by then, she had realized that though there was nothing at all wrong with baby Frank, he still did not belong to William.

Arnold actually took both her hands and held her at arm's length, surveying her with an enormous grin that went from ear to ear.

"I did not realize that you were beautiful, Rosemary Vickers. You are always so just right for whatever occasion you are gracing. And now . . . a mixture of siren and schoolgirl. Enchanting. Completely enchanting."

"Mr Jessup, I realize now that I really am so tired. Perhaps . . . a quick drink?"

He tucked one of her hands into the crook of his elbow and they began to walk towards his Riley willy-nilly.

"Call me Arnold, Rosemary. In fact, call me Arnie. And I will call you Rosie. D'you realize that it won't be long before I retire? Most of my friends are fairly stuffy but they are the only ones I have and I shall want to keep in with them because they will be helpful to William. You are much younger than I am but somehow of my generation. Would you take pity on an old man and be my friend? Only instead of being Arnold Jessup and Rosemary Vickers, we will regress and become Arnie and Rosie." He was laughing inordinately. He was so enjoying himself she did not have the heart to freeze him. Besides which, hadn't he just told her that he would be handing the practice over to William? In which case she could not freeze him. And of *course* this was the way he talked to Mrs Heatherington and to half a dozen other women probably.

But she didn't care. She was completely flummoxed by this time. William and Connie . . . William and baby Frank . . . baby Frank and Lucy Pardoe . . . baby Frank. She could have wept then and there, thrown herself on to Arnold Jessup's shoulder and wept for all of them and for her dear husband who had been dead for twenty years. If it weren't for Connie she might have forgotten that she was ever married.

Arnold Jessup said, "Rosie. You're not crying, are you?"

And she tucked herself into the passenger seat and said, "No. Of course not. Perhaps just a little bit." She looked up at him as he held on to the door and smiled much too widely. "I was thinking of Francis. My grandson. It came over me how very much I love him."

164

He smiled back at her. "Of course you do. When you took him from Connie I almost cried. What a sentimental pair we are."

"We're not really a pair, Arnold. We're connected through William, of course, but you could hardly call us —"

"Arnie. Try to call me Arnie, please, Rosie. It makes me feel young again."

"Arnie," she said in a low voice.

He shut her door and came round to the driving seat and settled himself in. "I looked up this place on the map and it should take about fifteen minutes to get there. I rang ahead and ordered two risottos." She opened her mouth and turned to him. He said, "Don't let's talk. Let's just enjoy the countryside and each other. Close your eyes and relax completely."

"How can I enjoy the countryside with my eyes closed?" She managed to sound tart, almost irritated, but he did not respond and she dared not bring up the word pair again. So after a while she did in fact close her eyes and the next thing she knew they were drawing into an old stable yard with a well and a pump in the middle of it and her mood had changed again, mainly because she was suddenly and desperately hungry. In her head she used another swear word, not as awful as bloody but rather racy in its context. What the hell, she thought. And liked its reckless sound. She said it aloud. "What the hell?" And he switched off the engine, looked round at her and said, "Indeed. What the hell, indeed. What have we got to lose?"

She accepted his crooked arm again and they went into the old pub looking exactly like a pair.

He stayed the night, sleeping in the double bed with her in the conventional villa in the conventional Worcestershire development for conventional couples. She had no idea how it came to pass. She must have been drunk quite early in the evening, the wine was good and the food was good and he seemed to think she needed to relax so he plied her with both. Unfortunately she could not remember what she said to him. She did remember him saying to her, "*That* doesn't matter. Not in the least. Not one jot or tattle . . . That doesn't sound right but you get my meaning. We'll go down and see this Lucy Pardoe . . . No, all right, don't panic. Perhaps we'll go and see her GP. I know about confidentiality but there are ways of getting bits of information."

She said, "You've drunk too much. I'll drive."

He laughed again. "You can drive if you can find the car." And of course she couldn't. She could barely walk to the front door when they got back. And then she couldn't find her key and they crept round to the back door where she kept the key under a mat, only to discover that the door was bolted from the inside. She supported him back to the front — or perhaps he supported her — where there was a porch light. He tipped her handbag upside down and found the key caught in the lining and they crept inside as if they might wake someone up. He closed the door and leaned against it and pulled her to him and she did not stop him. He had probably undressed Mrs bloody Heatherington only last night, but she did not stop him pulling off Connie's cardigan and unzipping the back of her frock so that it simply fell to the floor.

"We cannot sleep down here," she said in a shocked voice. "It would be almost depraved. We have to go upstairs. Follow me." And he had followed her, suddenly very wide awake indeed. And she had thrown back her duvet and they had collapsed together in such a neat way that she knew quite definitely when she woke the next morning that he had had plenty of practice.

She remembered bleating something about it being twenty years since anything like this had happened to her and he simply kept kissing her and then conscious thought went. She responded. She reciprocated. She inaugurated. She had never felt so alive and then suddenly so luxuriously sinking into sleep. And for twenty years she had never slept a night through. This time was different. She woke to blinding sunshine, turned her head and saw his face and smiled. He did not open his eyes but he seemed to know and he smiled in return. She studied him for some time; almost . . . fondly. He had a craggy, sort of beaky face. Olive skin, very bristly around the jowls. Mediterranean? The lobes of his ears were furry, they shone in the morning sun. She touched one of them with a gentle finger.

She said, "It's Tuesday. Nine thirty. Have you got a hangover?"

"No. What about you?"

"I feel wonderful."

He touched her back, gently. "Yes, you do. Will you do something for me?"

"No. Not now. That was last night."

"Not that, though it would have been nice. But I would like to do what couples do. I would like to go downstairs and bring up a tray of tea."

"You won't find anything in my kitchen. And we're not a couple, Arnie."

He sat up and swung his legs down and reached for his pants. "Well, I don't intend for that to be a one-night stand, Rosie. And I shall find my way round your kitchen because we're so alike that it is probably a replica of mine."

He did it while she was in the bathroom. She emerged in linen slacks and a shirt. He had put the tray in the middle of the bed. Teapot and strainer, milk and sugar. He had put on his vest but she could still tell he had a very hairy chest.

He said, "You're blushing, Rosie!"

She said, "I should think so. That's what it was, Arnie. A one-night stand. I should think I would blush!"

He smiled up at her and poured the tea. His hair was grey and his eyebrows dark. Was that possible? His eyes were brown, a very clear brown, like milkless tea. And his mouth was . . . delicious.

He said, "My God. You're as red as a lobster! What on earth are you thinking?"

"Nothing."

"It was something." He passed her a cup. "It's definitely not a one-night stand, Rosie, otherwise you wouldn't be that colour!" There was a sound of letters dropping on the hall floor then the bell rang. "Something to be signed for. Don't worry, somebody had left a load of old clothes on the floor. I've put them in that linen basket thing next to the washing machine. You can open the door quite freely."

"What if it's Maria?"

"I won't disturb you. I'll have a bath, if that's all right. Give you half an hour with her. Then I'd better get to work otherwise Mrs Flowers will take it out on me for the rest of the day."

She was at the bedroom door, cup still in hand. "I imagine Mrs Flowers has experience in that way." She shook her head at him. "I can't, Arnie. I really can't."

He said quietly. "Love really is the sweetest thing, Rosie. Don't throw it away."

It was Maria and she wanted to make sure that Rosemary was all right because she had seen her go off in a green car and then come home "in a bit of a state" and thought she must be ill. She turned and stared at Arnie's Riley almost accusingly.

Rosemary smiled reassuringly. "A really unexpected call," she said. "William's boss. Mr Arnold Jessup. It was he who was ill. Not fit to drive. I've put him in Connie's room and haven't seen hide nor hair of him this morning."

Maria was appalled. "Drunk?" she breathed. "How dreadful for you, my dear. Do you need any help in . . . getting rid of him?"

"I don't think so. It was a bit of a celebration actually." Rosemary leaned forward conspiratorially. "Unofficial, of course. But he's retiring shortly and William will take over."

Maria looked at once relieved and disappointed. "How wonderful. But . . . what if he's really ill?"

"Then I will ring Dr Thomas. Don't worry, Maria. He has to go to work soon. I'd better get some breakfast for him. And then, are you free for coffee?"

"Well . . ." Maria grimaced with disappointment. "Mr Gimble has offered to take me into Birmingham to change that dress I got from C & A."

Mr Gimble was the only male in the four houses and an offer like this was never refused. Rosemary nodded immediately. "Perhaps tomorrow? You'll be exhausted by the time you get home."

Maria nodded to both remarks. "Tomorrow would be lovely." She turned to go and then half turned back. "Be careful, my dear," she said.

Rosemary watched her negotiate the slope to the lower level and wondered what on earth she could mean.

CHAPTER
EIGHT

It was a year since Egg Pardoe had gone into the sea; Ellie took Barbara and Denny to the church to "sit quiet for a bit". It had been a difficult year, but maybe it would have been just as difficult if Egg had been here. More difficult in a way because he would not have wanted to move to Truro and they had definitely decided to do that.

Ellie was deeply thankful that they had chosen a house not very far from her new school. Last autumn right through to March had been a private nightmare. She had gone with the milk lorry to Hayle railway station at six thirty every weekday morning to catch the 7.05 milk train to Truro. It stopped at Camborne and Redruth, unloaded the full churns and took on the empties and got to Truro just before eight. She had to run down the long approach road into the city, skirt the cathedral, over the river and down towards the sea, where the tall Victorian houses gave way suddenly to a hockey pitch and tennis courts and a long rhododendron-edged drive to the school. She was nearly always late and the other scholarship girls had to save her a place as close to the side door as possible so that she could slide in without too much fuss. No one, girls or staff, had ever mentioned her late arrival but she felt terrible about it nevertheless. Sometimes she woke up in the night thinking she could hear milk churns being rolled over flagstones. And then she remembered with a fresh pang that Egg was no longer in this world. He would have taken her into the station on the crossbar of his old bike and been there waiting for her when she came home. And she cried anew. But there had been others who had tried to help; Mr Warne and Mr Membury . . . she remembered taking Mr Membury's outstretched hand and feeling the grip of it as if he could pull them all out of grief and back into happiness. And Matthew, the rector.

And, as her mother so often said in that stoical voice so full of knowledge, you can get used to anything so long as you've got food in your belly, a roof over your head, clothes on your back and the health and strength to go with it. And the four Pardoe women had all of those things. By mid-March it was light by the time the train got to Camborne and she could see the lambs and calves in the fields and the rows and rows of daffodils. She forced herself to go to swimming lessons in the school's uniquely circular pool and mastered her fear of the water as soon as she mastered the breaststroke.

The summer term changed everything. Josh Warne had driven them round Truro several times during the Easter holidays looking at houses for sale and they had returned home, all of them thankful that they lived on the towans and not in a town. Josh was as anxious as they were; Penberthy sometimes dropped into Josh's regular pub when his wife permitted it, and some of his

172

stories about Lucy Pardoe bordered on the vicious. Josh had taken him aside and advised him that unless he shut up, he would be shut up permanently by someone else. But when Chippy had had a couple he found it physically impossible to shut up. And Josh had only ever hit one person in his life. Farmer Roach. From over the dunes. No one knew about it and Josh intended to keep it that way. It had taught him that he would never hit anyone else. Ever.

On Easter Monday they visited a cottage on the gaunt tract of land towards St Austell. It was shipshape, it had an orchard and a neat garden at the back. There was a bus service into Truro every hour.

Josh drove them back to Hayle and decanted the girls by the phone box so that Lucy could phone her solicitor. They ran down the road hand in hand like a string of paper dolls.

"You got three lovely girls there, Mrs Pardoe," Josh said, watching them go.

Lucy nodded. "'Tis for them I'm doin' this. And that place was the best we seen so far."

He pondered silently for a while then he said quietly, "Trouble with being right outside in the country like, you en't going to get to know your neighbours and the girls will 'ave the same trouble gettin' in to their schools."

"Girls wouldn't mind. And what would I do with the kind o' neighbours I'd 'ave in the city? If it weren't for the walls I could put out a hand and touch them. An' all they does is watch the television. And those backyards . . . Where would I grow a few radish and lettuce for the table?" Lucy shook her head. "I'm a countrywoman and that's that."

But she did not get out of the car. She held that chap's card in her hand like a talisman or something, but she did not get out of the car. He tried again.

"You managed in that hotel place down Devon way."

She looked at him, startled. Because no one ever spoke of that time to her she assumed they didn't know. He mumbled an apology but she shook her head.

"'Tis all right, Mr Warne. I almost forgot that time. And you're right, I did manage very well there." She thought of Bertie with the usual pang. Then told herself to snap out of it: she had been lucky to know that sort of ecstasy and lucky to have had the wonderful contentment of her marriage with Daniel. She said, nodding still, "And I can do it again. I cain't take Pardoe Cottage with me, so I might as well make a complete change. Never mind the telephone. Let's get back and I'll make you a cup of tea and a cheese sandwich."

He brightened considerably. "There were those two for sale in the terrace near Lemon Quay," he mentioned as they moved off. "They both sold quicker'n a flea hop, so that must mean they're good solid houses. You could go back there and ask around a bit."

"I could. Once the girls are back at school, I'll do that. Thank you, Mr Warne."

When she did find the three-storey house with its glimpses of the cathedral towers from the front and the sweep of the river from the back, she had a feeling

174

about it. She told Ellie it was in Steep Street and Ellie clapped her hands.

"Gussie Trip lives there! I went with her to her house so I know where it is! Oh Mummy, it's about five minutes' walk from school and perhaps she'd call for me. She's got plaits. And a cat! Matthew and Mark would have a friend just down the road!"

Ellie told the Reverend Matthew Hobson all about it and he offered to drive them into Truro that very Saturday. Lucy went to the phone box and rang William Mather on his office phone and she wrote down what she had to do next, which was to give the house agent the name and address of her solicitors and then he would take over.

By Pentecost their offer had been accepted and just before the August bank holiday William came down for two nights, looked the house over, was enchanted with it and contracts were exchanged.

He congratulated her on such a swift purchase.

"Swift?" She was astonished. "Just after Easter I saw it and here we are nigh on September — more than four months. I dun't call that very swift!"

He smiled, delighted by the whole thing. She looked well but the gossip at the little hotel in Hayle was not reassuring. Some of Penberthy's slander was beginning to stick. He had caught the words "no smoke without fire" and knew it was time for Lucy to move the rest of her family right away.

He dined with the family doctor that first evening and as Carthew said over dinner, "If it had been anyone else and in any other circumstances, Lucy's expedience would be seen as sharp practice. She seized her opportunity and it so happened that the opportunity came up on the day after her son's death. I had told her to buy Pardoe Cottage — didn't tell her she would make a fortune from the leisure company. She just did what I told her as soon as she could." He grinned across the table. "Actually, Mather, she did well. Surprisingly well. Bought the cottage with your help, screwed the leisure company for as much as she could get and is moving into a very decent house in Truro all in the space of a year."

William raised his brows. "You surely don't think of her as conniving?"

"Of course she's conniving, man! She has connived all her life — living with her dreadful father — wouldn't be surprised if he didn't beat her on a regular basis — got away from him because of the war and fell in love with a Yank — he's drowned, she has his son — I had to use forceps so it's probably my doing that Egg was like he was — took up with Daniel Pardoe, who had been in love with her since he was nine or younger — had his three girls — lost him — buttered up Chippy Penberthy to let her keep the cottage and take on Egg as apprentice — bloody hell, Mather, she's had to connive. Most women have to connive. It rhymes with survive. Think about it!"

William was astonished that his question had provoked such an outburst and said, "I was not criticizing in any way. I admire the woman more than I can say."

176

"Sorry — sorry, Mather. I see so much . . . Good to have this meeting. I was glad to hear you married last Christmas. It would have been a double tragedy if poor Egg's death had put the mockers on that. And a baby boy, eh? Christening last weekend? Well done, old man." He looked at the man sitting opposite him and was genuinely thankful that the girl hadn't gone flying off the hook after what had happened. Even more thankful that this chap had helped out Lucy Pardoe so willingly. That dreadful delivery . . . Seventeen years ago . . . he must have been the same age as this solicitor chap then . . . No one could have done better, the bloody war was still on and there were no facilities near enough to organize a Caesarean. He said abruptly, "Look, let's have another whisky and call it a day."

William nodded. Carthew was a good chap, unusually interesting too, but it had been a long drive and there was a great deal to do in the next two days.

They moved on the last day of August and school started again on 3 September. Ellie had a new blazer and Barbara and Denny matching pinafore frocks; Lucy found it wonderful that they could all go to the school outfitters' and buy them, not even ask the price. And even more wonderful that Ellie could stay in bed until eight o'clock, eat her breakfast, get herself ready and leave at twenty to nine with a tall, thin girl whose plaits hung like rats' tails over each shoulder and down to what would be her waist if she had one. This was Gussie Trip, who thought Barbara and Denny were "cute enough to eat" and said to them, "Say, when you

177

get kinda used to going to school, how about if Ellie and me drop you off on our way?" The girls turned to one another in a paroxysm of giggles at the nasal accent and Gussie Trip laughed with them and looked up at Lucy. "Mrs Pardoe, I reckon these two could be served at teatime with ice cream!"

Lucy said, "For goodness' sake, don't get them too excited! Don't want tears before school, let alone before bedtime!"

But it was a good start to their new school. And a good start for Lucy too. Ellie had never mentioned that Gussie Trip was American. Lucy remembered that Egg had wanted to go there and find his father's family. She lingered for some time at the gates of the school just in case one of the girls should come flying out again, and let her thoughts go wild. Daniel had loved what he called the "if game" and often started long discussions with "If we could afford a share in the boat, there'd be an income for you if anything happened." And she had always put the lid on anything like that. She reminded him that they were not in debt and didn't intend to be. And nothing was going to happen. But he had never played the sort of if game she was playing now. "If Dr Carthew hadn't told me to buy the cottage and if I hadn't known that William Mather was just waiting to help us out in some way and if the Cornish Leisure Company hadn't wanted my bit of ground so badly . . . we wouldn't be here." And then, "If Egg hadn't gone into that cruel sea . . . we wouldn't be here." And even further back than that, "If Daniel hadn't been and drowned, we wouldn't be here." She shook her head and snapped out of it, something she had learned to do many years ago. If Daniel and Egg had been alive they would not have moved from Pardoe Cottage and that would have been that.

She went back home and started on the cleaning yet again. The trouble with the city was dust. On the towans it had been sand. Sand was heavy and you swept it out, dust was light and flew everywhere and settled again and again. Lucy set to in the kitchen; if the kitchen was all right the rest would follow. And she was comfortable in the kitchen and could work and play a sort of if game. It wasn't her way to fly with her imagination; it seemed wrong. You were dealt certain cards and you worked with them as best you could. It was a waste of time to pretend anything else could happen. But the cards now and then seemed to be pushing her in a certain direction and this was no exception. She had been gently pushed into this house in Truro which happened to be near to another house where the family were from America. And if Egg had wanted to go to America, perhaps she was meant to go for him.

There was a frantic hammering on the door and she opened it hurriedly, knowing already that only family would come to the back door. Truro people used the front door and the big shiny knocker. Sure enough, Barbara was standing there, tears streaming down her face. "It's playtime," she wailed, "and I can't find Denny!" And, as Lucy hugged her middle daughter, she thought grimly that this served her right. If you pushed fate too sharply, this was what happened.

It was a storm in a teacup of course. The reception class was late for recess that morning because the children were busy "showing" their drawings. When Denny got outside and could not find Barbara she started her wailing and one of the dinner ladies was dispatched to Steep Street and met Lucy and Barbara on their way back to the school. It gave them instant fame, which both rather enjoyed. Barbara wrote a story called "Disappearing Denny" and Denny drew a picture which appeared to be completely irrelevant but which she also called "Disappearing Denny". That first morning they found their niches. At the end of the week Lucy had to smile at fate, which had been on their side all the time. Nevertheless she took nothing for granted.

The next day Gussie delivered a message from her mother. Would Mrs Pardoe like to coll for cawfee if she was free?

"Coffee?" Lucy asked. She had often paused mid-morning to make tea. Coffee was something people drank in boarding houses or hotels.

"Please go, Mrs Pardoe." Gussie looked longer and thinner than yesterday. "Mom helps out at the museum and she's got friends there but she does need someone special and when I told her about you and Egg and selling your cottage and everything, she said that you must be some woman. She needs someone like you, Mrs Pardoe. She is so homesick."

The last four words did it for Lucy. She knew that just waiting on the other side of her determined optimism was a homesickness that might make her literally retch into the shining lavatory pan in the shining bathroom.

She smiled suddenly at Gussie, who was looking raw with sincerity. "That makes two of us," she said with an attempt at an American accent. The two girls smiled back at her and Barbara and Denny screamed with laughter. But when they had all gone, the two little ones overexcited at being taken by two students from the Laurels School for Girls, she let her determination weaken just for a moment and felt the emptiness in the three-storey house and the days stretching ahead when it would at last be clean and curtained and perhaps even carpeted and there would be no garden to tend.

She went upstairs and made beds and tidied everything away, though there was no need for such excessive neatness with all the extra space. Then, at ten o'clock in the morning, she had a bath. It was the first time she had used the bathroom. The first time too she had given her body much attention. The flannel wash at the end of each day had been enough, there was so much to do to get straight before school started. And now it had.

She lit the new gas oven in the kitchen and dried her hair in front of it, then pushed the still-damp lengths into exactly the same headband she had always used. She remembered one of the girls giving it to her in the hotel when she went there first. "'Tis only an old stocking but do grip the hair a treat." Nearly twenty years ago. Stockings then were made to last . . . She managed a grin into the mirror. She picked out the grey skirt and cardigan she had worn to Egg's funeral. It was

September after all and the leaves blowing down Steep Street were very autumnal. She told herself she was not sentimental but as she slid bare feet into the black shoes that had gone with the outfit, she felt something of Egg still with her. It gave her the courage to lock up properly — another thing she had to learn — and step into the street as if she had every right to be there.

Gussie and her mother — and presumably her father too — lived at the very top of Steep Street and Lucy soon realized that the higher up the steep pavement she climbed, the wider became the views. She had to pause before she got there just to breathe properly and she hung on to a lamp post and stared out over the city. She could see the white hills of china clay and beyond them the blue shadow of Bodmin Moor. She had been over Bodmin on her way to Devon and before that had heard the tales of the wild men who worked in the clay pits and ravaged anything in skirts, and before that the tales of strange creatures who lived on the moor and seemed to come out only at night. She remembered going home after Bertie had died and her father saying sourly, "One o' they men from the clay, was it? Told you, didn't I?" She remembered her reply too, with sheer incredulity. "It were war work, Dad."

That was what had infuriated him so. He had cuffed her across the room so hard she thought he might have upset her baby. Strangely, that too was the moment when she knew she wanted Bertie's baby more than anything else in the world.

She held on to the lamp post and lowered her head. And then a voice called, "Oh Mrs Pardoe! I sure am glad you've come." She looked up and saw someone long and thin and knew it was Gussie's mother coming to meet her.

In the end they were calling each other Lucy and Margaret and eating bread and cheese in the kitchen, which looked straight down the river towards Falmouth. Margaret made her own bread and it was delicious, the crusts crisp without being tough. Lucy broke off small pieces and topped them with a postage-stamp-sized sliver of cheese.

"This is so . . . nice." She could not be quite as forthright as Margaret yet, but could feel herself unfolding inside. She went a step further. "I thought when you said lunch 'twould be side plates and soup bowls and a lot of cutlery." She grinned. "I worked at a hotel in the war. It was taken over by the American soldiers. We had to lay up the tables for breakfast and for dinner. That's how it was."

"I told you I was a country girl. Michigan. We lived off the land and the lake." She looked through the window. "We were so *happy* — can't tell you! We lived with the weather . . . sometimes in spite of the weather . . . We married, had kids . . ." She looked up and grinned. "Say, have I told you all this just now?"

"Not the same way. Not as if you was hankering for it. But Gussie said something." Lucy too stared through the window. "My home en't so far off as yours, but I'm homesick too." She came back to her plate and broke off more bread. "I try not to think about it. But with the girls off to school each day, 't en't that easy." She looked up. "What about your 'usband — dun't he come home each night?"

"Oh yeah, sure. He talks about his work and I pretend I understand, but I didn't go to college — nothing like that." She laughed suddenly. "Listen to me! I was the one who said let's go to England, it will be an adventure. He was the one who said I'd miss seeing my parents every weekend — we lived just outside Detroit — and I said if we've got each other we'll always be OK. And of course we are! We really and truly are, Lucy! I'm an ungrateful so-and-so. Marvin is so very special. He's clever. He's a designer. He says that's why he fell for me because my legs are of equal size."

Lucy stared, mouth slightly open, as Margaret swivelled on her chair and stuck out her legs, lifting her skirt at the same time.

She said, "He says human legs are slightly longer from knee to ankle than knee to thigh and mine are equal."

Lucy looked at the legs. They reminded her of the herons that fished at low tide in Hayle estuary. "They are very long," she said cautiously.

"They're great for climbing trees. I can practically hook my right leg over the lowest branch and I'm up in a minute!"

"I'm not too bad on rocks," Lucy said. "Bertie and me . . . we used to climb over the rocks and up the cliffs."

"Bertie . . . He was your husband?"

184

"No." Lucy nibbled the inside of her cheek. "He was an American soldier. When I was working in Devon . . . we were good friends. And then he drowned." She cleared her throat. "My husband was called Daniel. He was a fisherman down Hayle way."

"Gussie said you were a widow." The other woman's eyes were wide with apprehension. Lucy could almost see her working things out.

"Daniel was drowned too." She paused, wondering whether to tell this new friend all about Egg, then remembering that Gussie had already told her mother a great deal. Maybe the whole story would be too much even for someone as understanding as Margaret Trip. She thought about the drownings; three of them. She said, "It's strange, I miss the sea. It has been cruel. Yet I miss it." She smiled suddenly. "I feel much safer here, though. And I think it suits the girls."

Margaret said diffidently, "I think by the end of this winter you're going to be settled. Perhaps I will be too. I hope so. We've been here almost a year and at first it was awful. I've tried to be interested in things — voluntary stuff, you know. But I stand out like a sore thumb. I don't fit." She grinned suddenly. "I was dreading this winter, but not any more! Our two girls are friends, Lucy. Shall we try it too?"

Lucy nodded vigorously and thought that no Cornish woman would ever come straight out with things like this, and certainly the Lucy Pardoe from Hayle towans would have been unable to accept such openness. But Bertie had been American too and Egg had loved all things American. She was suddenly convinced that Egg had arranged this whole thing.

She was introduced to Gussie's cat, who was much younger than Matthew and Mark, and left in time to walk down to the little school by Lemon Quay and pick up Barbara and Denny. Denny waved a drawing purporting to represent a vase of flowers, Barbara a bag containing "French knitting".

"It comes out the bottom like a long tail and you stitch it round and round and put a vase on it."

Denny clutched her sugar paper. "You cain't 'ave my vase," she said.

"Not a drawing, silly! A real vase. It's like a little mat for a real vase to stand on."

Lucy said, "You can show your sister how it's done when we get home. Let me button up your cardigans, this wind is cold. Coming from the north."

Her own words and the sight of Matthew and Mark on the old rug from Pardoe Cottage filled her with the nostalgia encouraged by Margaret Trip. She lit the fire and drew the kitchen table close to it, made tea and let Barbara pour it while she took over the French knitting. Ellie came in, Gussie behind her, but after exclaiming over what she called the still life Gussie said she must go.

"Mom worries if I'm late." She smiled at Lucy. "I'm real glad you went round, Mrs Pardoe. Ellie and me — we just knew you would be good friends."

"The long and the short of it." Ellie looked mischievously at her friend and then her mother. And was relieved when they both laughed.

186

They made toast and plastered it with butter and jam. There was heavy cake left in the tin. And more tea. Matthew and Mark were given saucers of milk. Ellie got out her homework and Lucy took the younger girls to the bathroom and then to bed. She felt gratitude flowing through her bloodstream, warming her. Life changed, often tragically, but underneath it all was this domestic routine. Cleaning and cooking were ways of caring and loving. Something she could do with her hands, something she had always done and — please God — would always do. She went down to Ellie and spent an hour threading the wool over the pins of Barbara's French knitting and listening to Ellie reciting her Shakespeare text. She too knew a bank whereon the wild thyme had grown seventeen years ago. And another on which the thrift had blown on the towans . . . Ellie said, "I'll go up now, Mummy. Will you come and say good night?"

"I will, my flower." She lifted her head from the wooden bobbin. "We've done the right thing, Ellie. Haven't we?"

"We've done as Egg directed." Ellie spoke the words gravely. She really did believe that their actions were governed now by her brother. And Lucy nodded.

She riddled the ash from the fire and was about to fasten the guard when a tap came on the front door. She went to it gladly; it must be Margaret because anyone who did not know there were children in bed would have used the knocker.

It was not Margaret. In the wavering light from the street lamp, she made out the figure of a man and

187

began immediately to close the door on him. She had not given anyone her exact address in Truro but Chippy Penberthy was crafty enough to have found out from the postmistress at Hayle and she had been almost waiting for this.

"It's all right, Mrs Pardoe." The man lifted his head. He looked grey and drawn. He was nothing like old Chippy, but he was familiar. "You won't remember me. I was staying at the boarding house — Blue Seas — just for a week in August 1960. My name is Harry Membury."

She remembered; a rush of memory that made her gasp. His outstretched hand — she had not taken it but Ellie had.

She whispered, "You came with Josh Warne. To tell me. You helped to carry the coffin. You and Mr Mather . . ." She cleared her throat and spoke in the harsh voice he probably remembered. "What news have you brought me this time?"

He was silent, staring at her. She had her grey skirt and cardigan beneath a short pinafore. She relaxed her grip on the door. She knew her girls were safe upstairs. Could anything have happened to William Mather? He was a good man; she would grieve for him and for his silly wife and the child too, but her girls were safe.

Harry Membury said at last, "News? I suppose my news is that I have left my wife and children."

She was focused now, staring back at him, noticing his thin coat, no hat or scarf. It was cold; the north wind had continued to blow all evening and cut like a knife down the length of Steep Street. He looked ill. Desperately ill.

She said, "Why have you come here?"

He began to turn away. "I don't know. I'm sorry." He stopped, his face now in profile. "I have never been able to forget you and the children and your son, Egg. You have come between me and everything else. I just wanted to see you again." He turned his back and added, "I am sorry, I shouldn't have turned up like this. I am glad you are well and . . . comfortable."

He began to walk down towards the river. He was shambling. She said, "Wait!" but he went on. So she grabbed her coat from the row of hooks behind the door and ran after him.

She took his arm to stay him.

"Come and sit by the fire and have a cup of tea."

He stayed very still, her hand on his coat sleeve. Then he said, "I had better not."

And she said, "For the sake of Egg."

After another pause, he turned and began to walk back with her.

CHAPTER
NINE

That night he slept downstairs. There was a spare room right at the top of the tall old house but when she got him into the brightness of the living room she saw that he would not be able to climb all the stairs. And she suspected the room and its bed might be damp.

She sat him in the chair she had just vacated and propped him with cushions while she heated milk. He could hold the beaker but she steadied its shaking from beneath. He had been in the north wind for too long. Where had he come from? Had he left his family today? Or last week? Was he seriously ill?

He put his chin on his thin coat for a moment, then lifted his head and managed to smile. He thanked her and kept on thanking her as he started to lever himself up. She put out a hand to stop him but already he had collapsed into the cushions again.

She said, "Don't thank me any more and don't tell me you are a nuisance — I will decide that." She lifted the cats, blanket and all, put them on the floor and pulled and tugged the sofa to a forty-five-degree angle with the fire. She filled the old stone hot-water bottles — used as door stops since they moved — and wrapped them carefully in the pillowcases from the airing rack, crept upstairs and fetched pillows and blankets. He seemed to be asleep already and she hovered, uncertain whether to leave him where he was. Then he groaned and shifted and she took his arm and urged him up. He shuffled where she directed him, turned obediently, sat again. She looked at his feet; he was wearing sandals, no socks. She made clicking noises of exasperation and removed the ridiculous sandals, snatched the cat blanket from beneath Matthew and Mark and towelled the blue, swollen feet vigorously. The cats at last realized something interesting was happening; they began their exploratory sniffing and he breathed a small laugh that was close a sob. "Oh Lucy . . . I swam this morning . . ."

"More fool you!" Matthew started to purr loudly; he was a fastidious animal and would not let Denny touch him when she was grubby. Lucy grinned up into the ravaged face. "Anyway you've passed the test. You're clean!"

She lifted his feet on to one of the hot-water bottles and he lay down gratefully. She gave him the other bottle and covered him over. She went back into the kitchen and put bread and cheese on to a plate, poured more milk and took it in. He was already asleep. She put the food on the floor and stood looking at his face. What had he said . . . that Egg had come between him and everything else? Something like that. She had met him once and had not taken his hand . . . yet he had felt as she had felt; that without Egg nothing would ever be the same. Egg's death — the way of his death — had changed so many lives. Egg, in life and in death, had changed everything.

She put the guard round the fire and fastened the hooks securely. She resettled the cats in front of it and went back into the kitchen to tidy it for the night. Her last job was to take the enamelled pail from the back closet and put it discreetly within reach of this strange and unhappy man. It was then ten o'clock and she'd had enough.

She went to bed. And she dreamed that Egg was alive and with them again. Ellie and Barbara and Denny and Egg danced in a ring. And she watched them. And with her were the others . . . Bertie McKinley and Daniel Pardoe. Josh Warne and that young vicar, Matthew Hobson. William Mather and Harry Membury. Even silly Connie Vickers who Egg had loved . . . And when she woke that was what she remembered, that Egg had loved Connie Vickers. And was now dead.

The girls were agog. They crammed into the bathroom flipping face cloths madly, asking questions, answering each other impatiently, coming at last to the inevitable conclusion.

"He's run away. Hasn't he, Mummy? He's run away from Rosalie and Lily." It was Barbara who spoke for all three of them. Ellie glanced at her mother. She knew that sometimes — not often — the thought had crossed both their minds that Egg had gone voluntarily into the sea. Was that the same as running away?

She said, "They were naughty but not that bad."

Lucy said, "I don't know what has happened. All I can say is he was cold and tired and he fell asleep on the sofa." She dried Denny's hands and smiled reassuringly. "Matthew purred for him, so I knew he was all right." She hung towels over the shiny chrome rail. "Now jump into your clothes and come on down for breakfast. I'm doing eggie bread and there's a big pot of tea and your French knitting has grown in the night, Barbara!"

"Can we go and see him, Mummy? An' can I have my red hair ribbon this morning? And the grey socks tickle behind my knee so can I have ankle socks?"

Lucy said yes without thinking and went on downstairs. She had looked at Harry Membury earlier when she let the cats out. As far as she could tell he had not moved a muscle except to breathe. She checked on that again. A virtual stranger in the house, even though he was male and down and out, was one thing. A dead man was quite another. She closed the door gently and went on down the hall to the kitchen. She poured herself a second cup of tea and put dripping in the pan and turned the four thick slices of bread over in the beaten egg and milk. The cats scratched at the back door and she let them in. They took two of the chairs and closed their eyes, smiling ecstatically at the scent of tea and beef dripping. She smoothed Mark's whiskers and asked the usual question. "Any sign of town mice?" There had always been field mice on the towans and she could bear them because they had as much right to the gleanings from the scrub as any human. But she had a horror of house mice. Town mice who lived in the crowded houses and ate human food. Mark opened his eyes and looked at her and she nodded, well satisfied.

"Now." She sat with her tea. "What are we to do with our lodger?" She waited and then said, "I'll talk it over with Margaret. Cain't turn 'im out, can we, my lovelies. Looks like 'e's part of it all whether we like it or not. But once 'e's on 'is feet, 'e cain't stay with us." She slid into what the girls called "towans talk" just as they all did when speaking to each other.

Denny crept in with exaggerated care. Lucy noted she was wearing long grey socks and a navy blue hair ribbon. Ellie had a way with her.

The girls stood in a row and surveyed the sleeping man, then they all assembled in the kitchen and Ellie asked tremulously, "Is he going to die, Mum?"

"Not just yet." Lucy grinned as she put the first slice of bread into the dripping. "And when he does I hope it's not in our house!"

Ellie smiled back unwillingly. She remembered taking Mr Membury's hand and her mother snatching her away. Had he been asking for help then? Had he come to find them so that he could ask again? She shivered slightly and her mother told her to button her cardigan.

When Gussie did her code knock on the back door, three short, three long and three short again — Save Our Souls — she flung it open and almost pulled her friend inside. Everyone talked at once, explaining about Mr Membury. Barbara said he must be all right because the cats liked him. Denny said with relish that he might die. And Ellie said, "He's come for our help,

Gus. Looked for us and found us." Lucy waited for quiet then said, "You've got plenty of time — would you like a slice of eggie bread, my flower?" And Gussie sat down.

He woke two hours later. The house was quiet at last. When the girls left whisperingly, Lucy cleared up the breakfast things, fed the cats and made the beds. Then she crept in with dustpan and brush and swept out the ashes from the grate and lit the fire. This entailed a great deal of scraping but he did not so much as stir and she began to wonder whether she should send for the doctor. The trouble was she had not registered with anyone in Truro as yet. She knelt on the floor and stared at the flames climbing cautiously among the kindling towards the carefully placed coals and bit her lip. She'd been busy day in and day out but there were enormous gaps still to fill. She had intended to write to Dr Carthew and ask about the doctors in Truro. And the dentists. But the girls were never ill and anyway Dr Carthew used to look them over when he brought the tablets for Egg. She would miss Dr Carthew.

She pushed her legs round and sat more comfortably, still clutching the dustpan full of cinders. She remembered the first time she had seen him. Getting on for twenty years ago. In her father's house on Connor Downs. He must have been mid-thirties then; a good-looking man, not unlike William Mather. She had been in labour for nearly three days and her father had stayed in the pub all his waking hours and ignored her when he came home to sleep. But he must

195

have sent for the doctor on the third day because Dr Carthew was suddenly there, holding her hands and telling her to hang on just a while longer while he went for an ambulance. And then he said, "All right, my girl. I think we're there. No need to fret." And he had gone to his bag and got the forceps and put them in the saucepan while he washed his hands. And then . . . and then . . .

She had told no one how terrified she had been when Ellie was on the way. Daniel was so pleased, so happy, and she could not blight such happiness. But Dr Carthew had known. He had said, "It's not going to happen again, you know, Lucy. I'm going to be there when your waters break and if there's the slightest trouble, you'll have a Caesarean."

There hadn't been the slightest trouble. Nor with Barbara. Nor with Denny. She and Dr Carthew had exchanged triumphant grins and he had said, "Here's to the next one!" And she had blushed and Daniel had roared with laughter.

She needed Dr Carthew now.

Harry Membury's voice, still weak but audible, said behind her, "I think I might have a penny for your thoughts, Lucy Pardoe."

She turned, almost spilling the cinders. He did not move but his eyes were open and he was smiling at her. She scrabbled on to her knees and puffed with exasperation. "You've 'ad us worried, Mr Membury, and no mistake! And you must be about to burst because there en't nothing in the bucket and you bin

196

asleep ten hours, I reckon!" She stood up. "D'you want my arm to the back privy?"

He shook his head and pushed at the blankets. She led the way down the hall and pointed to the "downstairs cloakroom" as the house agent had called it. "I keeps the brooms in there so mind they don't fall on you. There's a washing sink in there too." And she continued into the kitchen and the backyard, where she emptied the dustpan. The cats followed her and sprang on to the wall, then up again on to the washhouse roof, then the bedroom window ledge and finally the roof. They sat on the ridge and looked out to sea. She wondered whether they missed it and then stopped her thoughts sharply. She was doing too much of that since this man arrived. Dr Carthew and all the lot of them. Everything still led directly to Egg. And she refused to let that maverick thought come into her head again. As if Egg could fall in love with a girl from Birmingham . . . a foreigner . . . He was sixteen and she was . . . whatever she was! And he had met her only the day before. It was ridiculous. She banged down the lid of the dustbin with sudden anger. What on earth was she thinking about! She went indoors and found Harry Membury sitting at the kitchen table, looking around him as if he had landed on the moon.

"It's different. I didn't expect you to live in a place like this." He spoke slowly and wonderingly.

She said drily, "I din't expect it myself but we are and settling in all right. Girls like their schools. They're good girls."

He nodded. She said, "I'm going to make a pot of tea. Will you have a cup? And some food too."

"There was bread and cheese by the sofa." He smiled at her. He had a thin, oversensitive face; grey eyes, very flat ears. He said, "I got a lift in a lorry. Avis said if I left I must leave everything. The car, the house, my clothes, everything. So I went to a garage on the A38 and I got a lift in a lorry. I walked from Redruth to the towans. There were diggers in the dunes. Your cottage had gone. No sign of it at all. I thought I would go mad then. I thought you were all dead. I went to the Penbeagle Arms and hung about outside. I had no money. The landlady brought me a sandwich. I told her I was looking for the Pardoe family and she said you lived in Truro now." He smiled. "That was the happiest moment of my life, Lucy."

She put the teapot on the table and sat down with a bump. "You must be mad. They're your family. Those girls, they need you. Don't try to put the blame for this on my son, Mr Membury. He would never . . ." Her voice petered out.

He said quietly, "He did leave you. He left you for Connie Vickers. You knew that and still you survived. Still you drew the rest of them around you and tricked the owner of your cottage into selling it and then you bargained with those developers until you got the price you wanted and you came here to this big place."

She recoiled. She had been sorry for him, willing to like him for his gentleness and kindness then angry with him for what she saw as weakness. She was unprepared for such retaliation.

198

"I'm repeating to you what I heard in that pub."

"From Chippy Penberthy, I'll be bound!" she cried.

"And from Joshua Warne. Different slant but same story."

"Dr Carthew told me to buy the cottage at any price and he would put up the money. And I didn't need him to help me because I knew William Mather would do it and act for me as well. So I did it. The chance came and I took it."

"You did the right thing."

"I did!" She stared at him defiantly. "I did the right thing!"

"So did I. I couldn't think of anyone except you and those girls. Standing there, defying everything, even death. I loved you then, Lucy. I love you more now. You are the most wonderful woman I have ever known. I want to be with you for ever. Will you marry me — let me look after you and the girls — help me to get a job in this little city and come home every night and listen to you talking together? Getting on with things, getting on with life, savouring every last little thing together." He saw the horror on her face and ploughed on desperately. "I know how it looks. But I thought you were still living on the towans, growing your food, living on the land and the sea . . . I thought I could help you, summer work for money and winter work about the house and land." He looked around the kitchen again. "I did not expect . . . this. And Penberthy says you've got money in the bank and need never work again. But I could still get a job, Lucy. I could not live off your

199

money. I could still help out in so many ways. If you would let me."

She did not deign to listen properly. She was so angry she almost threw the teapot at him. He thought she was clever, someone who could plot and plan and make things work for them. He had heard the stories and built the female Pardoes into something they were not. She stood up abruptly.

"I thought as 'ow you were ill in the body and you are ill in the head. Please go. Pour yourself a cup of tea — I'll fetch that bread and cheese and you can eat that. Then go and don't come back. How dare you talk of family love when you have repudiated yours! Hurry back for the good Lord's sake before you lose them for ever."

She went into the living room. The food had dried and shrivelled by the fire and it was possible the cats might have nibbled a corner from the cheese. She built up the fire and put the guard back and took the plate into the kitchen.

"I am going to see my neighbour now. Probably she will come back with me when I tell her what has happened. I don't want to see you here."

He was looking stricken. He started to plead. He apologized. Had he got the wrong end of the stick? She was such a wonderful woman, did she not understand that she was also very beautiful? She was an earth mother. How could he not love her? And how could he stop loving her? She was condemning him to a life of misery. She shut the door after her with a click.

Remembered to pick up her keys. And she walked up the hill to Margaret's house and arrived in tears.

Margaret had some difficulty in fitting together the complicated jigsaw of Lucy's life from her garbled references that morning, the more straightforward outline she had picked up the day before and the even sparser information given to her by Gussie. At the end of it all she was still not sure who Connie Vickers was. "So this Membury guy . . . he is married to Connie now, yeah?"

Lucy said, "No, they were staying at the same boarding house. Egg was working nearby at the cove and he met Connie and he sort of fell for her. He was only sixteen, Margaret — he would have got over it. Mr Membury helped to look for Egg and then came to tell us . . . He's married with two little girls and they came to the library in Hayle when Ellie was reading stories there . . ." She blew her nose fiercely. "Now he's left his wife and the girls and he's down in my house wanting to marry me!"

"Oh my God!" Margaret had known that her new friend had been through a terrible time but this was different. This was high drama of a kind that she had thought did not exist in England. She said cautiously, "Isn't that a kind of compliment, honey?"

"He thinks I've got money in the bank — well, I have but it belongs to my Daniel because it was his cottage really. And . . . oh Margaret, they are saying things about me back home . . . I didn't plan any of it, not really. Chippy Penberthy tried to suck up to me lots of times and I might have . . . you know . . . sort of used that to — to lead him on so that he would agree to me buying the cottage . . . Oh Margaret, I think he must be saying I slept with him or something."

"I don't think so, honey. Otherwise this Membury guy probably would not bother with getting married." She poured more coffee. "Listen, Lucy. Sounds to me as if you had a lot of respect from men all your life. This Bertie . . . he was the father of your son, I guess. He loved you a lot, am I right?" She nodded as Lucy nodded. "Then Daniel . . . you can't deny he loved you too." She nodded again in time with Lucy's sob. "And this William Mather you keep mentioning. And your doctor? And Josh Warne, the man who worked with your Daniel? Seems to me you had a lot of respect from a lot of good men. And even this Membury — he came to help you, honey. He didn't know you had sold your cottage. He thought you were still trying to manage on ten shillings a week widow's pension and a few lettuce leaves!" She laughed and, tearfully, Lucy laughed with her.

"But I cain't have him in the house — not after he asked me to — to *marry* him! Oh my God, Margaret! As if I could marry someone who looks like an undertaker! He does — truly he does! So thin and humble and his ears look as if they have been squashed into his head with wearing an undertaker's hat!"

They both laughed hysterically, clutching their sides. Margaret spluttered, "They're wonderful people, Lucy. Better than doctors sometimes."

"I know, I know. Mr Strange was really helpful."

Margaret doubled over. "Strange? What a name! Was he strange?"

"But seriously, Margaret. What can I *do*? I mean, I cain't turn him out. He's not well and he's miles from home . . . I don't even know where his home is!"

Margaret said, "I'll come back with you. We'll talk to him together. And when the girls come home from school perhaps we could eat together? Then I can ask Gussie's advice."

"Gussie?"

"She's got a thing about people. She sums them up. She's always right. She'll know what to do about your Harry Membury."

"He's not mine, Margaret! And I don't want him."

"OK, OK. Let's go out." She raked her fingers through her hair. "Let's go and get something to eat. Pick up your two from school and go back to your place and see what's what." She slid her arms into a long coat that only just covered her knees and thought of something else. "Hey — he won't hurt your cats, will he? Or smash the place up or something?"

"No — no. Not a bit. He's gentle and kind. He was the first person to offer support. He held out his hand." She looked up at her tall friend, eyes swimming again. "I didn't take it. But Ellie did."

"Come on. First stop is the Apple Turnover. Why do they call it that, d'you think, Luce? I don't get it."

Lucy tried to explain while Margaret locked up. She had to run to keep up with those long thin legs, but at least it stopped her going over and over this silly but distressing incident. They sat in the little cake shop-cum-patisserie and shared a large pasty and listened to the couple on the next table, who were discussing the merits of the various hairdressers in Truro. "That's something we could do," Margaret said in a low voice when the pasty was finished. "We could go Mary Quant together." Then she had to explain who Mary Quant was and why Lucy just had to get a television. "I can't imagine how you have managed without one. Surely the girls want to know what everyone is talking about in school?"

"They might do now. No one had a television back home. In Hayle I mean."

"They use television at the Laurels. It's a kinda teaching aid these days. Listen, I'll get Marvin to fix you up with one and show you how it works."

They went on talking for a while about anything and everything. Lucy thought how good it was to have a friend and knew that Margaret felt the same. When it was almost time to collect the girls, someone came into the shop and greeted Margaret. It was someone from the museum. Margaret introduced her as Jennifer. She shook hands with Lucy and explained that Tuesdays were her days for the cathedral. "I need to be useful."

Margaret gave Lucy further explanations when they walked back to the school.

"She looks after her pa. He has talked himself into being an invalid. She has to get away from him now and then and she is in love with the choirmaster at the cathedral. So it's a double blessing. Old Mr Gardner — her pa — was the curator at the museum and got her the job there. And he can't very well object to her helping out in the cathedral." She smiled. "Jennifer told me once he said she can't go wrong with men who wear dresses to work!"

They came to the school gates and waited until one of the ten-year-old boys came into the playground and rang the bell self-importantly. And as if at a signal, Lucy thought of Matthew Hobson, who had certainly worn a dress at Egg's funeral but out of church preferred canvas trousers and a fisherman's smock.

She received the full brunt of Denny's small body as it hurtled across the playground and through the gate, and took Barbara's hand as she skipped more sedately out of the cloakroom. They swung the girls between them up the hill and it wasn't until they reached the front door that Barbara remembered their visitor.

"He was much better and I do hope he feels well enough to be on his way. He might've already gone."

She knew he was still there when she unlocked the door and opened it wide. She had learned as a girl to know when the house was empty. It was not empty today. He was in the kitchen, almost exactly where she had left him that morning. The girls were delighted. They wanted to know about Rosalie and Lily. Lucy introduced Margaret and took the kettle to the tap. Margaret sat down opposite him and looked at him as he stalled the barrage of questions. He avoided looking back at her.

Lucy made tea and they sat around the table and listened to Barbara explaining about French knitting and Denny explaining about her latest painting. At the first sign of the girls running out of breath, Margaret drew hers.

"And now you are better, Mr Membury, I guess you'll be moving on. There's a small hotel at Charlestown. A very pretty place. I'm sure you'd like it."

Lucy said in a low voice, "No money."

"Gee, I'm sure we can lend you enough money to get you bed and breakfast."

Margaret leaned forward. "You know you cannot stay here, Mr Membury."

He flushed. "I have the most honourable intentions, Mrs Trip, I assure you of that."

"I am assured. Completely. But Mrs Pardoe has not been able to tell you certain . . . arrangements which are going forward."

The girls stared at her. Lucy stared at her. Harry Membury swallowed visibly. "They will come together eventually." Margaret was now completely in command. She smiled around her like a benevolent aunt. "You will all know in good time. But meanwhile I think we must speed Mr Membury on his way."

Ellie came in then, closely followed by Gussie. There were fresh exclamations. Ellie sat next to him, her brown eyes brimming with sympathy.

"We know how you feel. If we hadn't been able to come here we would have been destitute. Mr Penberthy would have sold the cottage over our heads to the holiday company and we would have had nowhere to go."

206

He looked at her, near tears himself. "Would he have done that?"

"Oh yes. He would have called it good business. Dr Carthew and Mr Mather saved us." She put out her hand as he had put out his just over a year ago. He took it with a small sob.

She said, "You need looking after for a while, don't you, Mr Membury?"

He said nothing. Lucy made a sound of protest.

Ellie smiled at him. "We'd look after you if we could. You know that. But you will be much better out on the towans. I think you need space . . . sea and sky and sand dunes." She smiled. "I sound like an advertisement for a caravan holiday, don't I? Perhaps you could try that later on. But for now . . . perhaps the Reverend Hobson would put you up for a while. Later on you could help him." She looked up at Gussie, who nodded approval. Lucy looked at them both with astonishment.

Margaret put her hands together, delighted. "That's a terrific idea, Ellie. D'you think your reverend would agree?"

Ellie nodded definitely. "We got to know him, didn't we, Barbara — didn't we, Denny?" The girls also nodded; they were wide-eyed and unusually silent.

Unexpectedly Harry Membury spoke up. "I don't think I could ask charity from Matthew Hobson. I am not asking charity from you either, Lucy. We are connected — you must understand that."

Ellie looked at her mother. Lucy said nothing; she seemed stunned into silence.

Margaret picked up the baton. She was making it up as she went along but it came so easily it had to be true . . . somewhere or other. And if not, then she would make it true. A dream. Come true.

"As I said before, sir, Mrs Pardoe has other plans." She smiled at them all. "It's all still in the melting pot and will be a big surprise for Mrs Pardoe herself, but I do assure you that she still has family who wish to get in touch with her. She is going to be very busy with them." She beamed the smile on to Harry Membury. "You're not asking charity, sir. You are asking to rent a room in a house." She turned to her daughter. "Come on, Gus. Let's go. We've got a phone and a directory and we will suss out the position at the towans." She squeezed Lucy's arm. "We'll be back soon with news. All will be well. And that's another thing — Marvin will get a phone installed in your hallway."

Gussie allowed herself to be swept to the door, where she turned and rolled her eyes at them all. "Just go with it," she advised. "She isn't often like this but when she is, it's easier to roll."

Ellie laughed, stood up and hugged her mother's arm. "I just knew you'd get on with Mrs Trip." She turned to Harry. "You'll be all right now, Mr Membury."

Lucy sat down because unexpectedly her legs were trembling. She wondered what on earth Margaret had been talking about just now. She wondered whether she had been too hard on Harry Membury, who looked as if he could see the end of the world and it was much too close. And she wondered — marvelled — at her girls, who were now bustling about the kitchen making boiled eggs, chattering like sparrows. Ellie looked more like Daniel every day, Barbara some version of herself, and Denny . . . just Denny. She wanted to cry. Had she treated this man unfairly? Should she, even now, be making up the bed for him in the attic, letting him talk about his wife and girls, telling him he could stay a few days until he found a job and sorted himself out? He was so weak. In every way he was the sort of man she mistrusted. Bertie, Daniel, Egg . . . they had had some inner strength and determination. Dr Carthew and William Mather had it too. Josh Warne. Her father and Chippy Penberthy had not had it. Surely she did not think this man sitting opposite her was like them?

He was propping his head on one hand and she had to lower hers to see his face. He was crying.

She stood up and fetched the bread from the crock and the butter from the marble slab in the larder. She cut bread and pushed it across to him. "Butter this and put it on this plate." Ellie handed him a pile of plates. "Put these round the table. Each one to have a knife and an egg spoon."

She watched him do it and thanked him and he blinked and smiled. She said, "Do the small things and they will pile into big things. Eventually."

His eyes filled again and he said, "Oh Lucy."

And she said quickly, "I'm sorry, Mr Membury. I really cain't help you more."

He said, "No, *I* am sorry. Really sorry. I had no idea you had other fish to fry."

Her sympathy dried up instantly. He had a very unfortunate turn of phrase.

She said coldly, "I en't got no idea what Mrs Trip was on about, I do assure you of that."

Ellie brought the girls to the table and settled them in their chairs. A bowl of eggs appeared and Lucy gingerly fingered them into eggcups and handed them round. Lucy took Denny's egg top off while Ellie saw to Barbara's. They smiled at each other. Ellie used Daniel's words, "Nothing like an egg to cheer you up." It had been his way of teasing Egg and it was the first time anyone had said them for over a year. Ellie watched her mother.

Harry Membury said, "I'm really sorry but I don't think I can manage —"

He got no further. Lucy leaned across the table and decapitated his egg neatly. "You will eat your egg like everyone else."

"But Avis says that even eggs are not proper vegetarian food."

Lucy looked around the room. "I don't see Mrs Membury lurkin' in the shadows. Do you, Ellie? Do you, Barbara? Do you, Denny?"

They all recognized a game when they heard one and they roared, "No!"

Lucy grinned at Harry Membury. "Eat your egg. Get strong again."

Later that night Marvin Trip lay on his back in bed, hands behind his head, watching his wife brush her long hair. She was wearing a new nightdress. Demure but perhaps not so demure as it would look on anyone else. He knew she had not settled properly in England but this new friend of hers had changed her in two short days. Tonight, she was the girl he had met in Detroit. Her length and consequent ungainliness made her at once desirable and . . . tender.

He said sentimentally, "Do you realize we've been married twelve years next month?"

"Actually it's thirteen." She looked at him in the mirror and lowered her eyes.

He laughed and said, "I thought Lucy Pardoe started off with a baby and no husband at all — surely we can stop pretending over here? They're far more liberal and understanding."

"Not all of them. And speaking of Lucy, honey —"

"I know, I know. Television. Phone. Will yesterday be soon enough?"

"Give it a few days. She has to get used to the idea."

"OK. Come to bed, honey. You'll catch cold out there. God, it's September and no frost, certainly no snow. Yet it's as cold as charity."

"Yeah . . . that's what that man Membury meant, I guess. Charity is kinda cold. But this isn't charity . . . this is making a dream come true."

"What is? The phone? The television?"

"No. Something more important than them." Margaret turned on the stool so that her nightdress rode above her knees. He moaned theatrically. She stood up and let him see all her legs and a little bit more. He took his hands from behind his head and held out his arms and she fell into them, laughing.

★ ★ ★

She said afterwards, "About making a dream come true, Marvin. Marvin, are you listening? I'm talking about Lucy Pardoe."

"Again? Darling, I need my sleep. I've got a phone and a television to install tomorrow evening . . ."

"You're in a position to find things out, baby. And you can do it. There must be records still kept in Devon. Names of all the men who were drowned."

"Told you earlier on, baby. It's still classified. It was a ghastly accident and embarrassing to the British. No can do."

"You can do, Marvin. You know you can. You can do anything. And you can tell the truth if you have to. One of those men had a son. He's got family back home, honey, who know nothing about Egbert. Don't you think they deserve to know that he didn't just die? He made a baby, honey. Like you made our Gussie. And if he hadn't been drowned he would have married Lucy and taken her to the States and — and —"

"The boy might not have drowned." Marvin's voice was quietly serious. "Listen, baby, what is the point of all this? It would be worth doing if the boy was alive. But he's not, is he?"

"Marvin, he wanted to go to America. He wanted to find his family. He still wants that."

"You're not going all psychic on me, are you, babe?"

"I don't know. I just know that we have to find out something about Bertie McKinley. We have to, Marvin. We have to find his family and let them know . . . let them know . . ."

212

"That they had an illegitimate grandson — or nephew — or whatever? That he is now dead?"

"Oh Marvin . . ."

He could feel her tears on his shoulder and he gathered her to him, concertinaing her into a small bony child again. He smoothed her hair, kissed her eyes. "Go to sleep, baby. I'll see what I can do."

"Oh Marvin . . ."

CHAPTER
TEN

Greta Heatherington's announcement, made just before Christmas, brought mixed reactions. She told Arnold Jessup first. They were drinking their coffee after a particularly good lunch in Birmingham and he actually choked on his.

"You are what? Marrying that no-good manager of yours so that he can finally fleece you of the rest of your money? Are you mad, Greta? You practically took him to court this time last year, then we talked you out of it — you didn't stand a chance, old girl, so don't look at me like that — and what happens next? You go to bed with him. Then he ditches you and you go to bed with me. Then you and he are on and off like yo-yos. And now he's talked you into getting hitched so that he's got someone to look after him in his old age!"

"You're a fine one to talk!" she retaliated. "You and that Rosemary Vickers! You must be all of fifteen years older than she is. And what you see in her I cannot understand — she's one of those women with a poker up her —"

"Leave her out of this, Greta! You don't know what you're talking about. I am not Archie Fielding. I would not dream of marrying her and tying her down to anything. When she's had enough of me she can walk away."

She had never seen him really angry like this. She had been looking forward to a good slanging match and suddenly backed out of it.

She sipped her coffee and held the cup between her hands as if she were cold. She said, "Arnold. You know me. I need . . . someone. Someone who will be there at the end of the day. Perhaps will put my slippers to warm by the fire. I've landed a decent job after Christmas. Wardrobe mistress at the Cochrane — that tiny theatre behind the station. It's the first regular job I've had for years and I'm going to work at it — what I don't know about clothes isn't worth knowing, so I can do it. But at first I'll be tired. Dead tired, Arnold. No one who hasn't worked in theatre can begin to imagine how tiring it is. The adrenalin highs are all very well but there are usually more lows than highs. Believe me."

"I believe you. I simply do not see Archie Fielding as a support. Think what he's getting out of it, Greta. A good-sized flat in the middle of town, very handy for about six different pubs — and the casino. And as he is your manager — *still* — he will be taking his percentage for every dress you stitch, every hour you put up with histrionic actors . . . Greta, is it worth it?"

She said very quietly, "You are making me sound pathetic, Arnold. But . . . yes, I think it is worth it."

"Oh my dear girl. The last thing I want to do is to make you feel pathetic. My God, I think you are courageous. You're a realist down to the soles of your little feet. This is what you want . . . he is what you want. You know all his flaws and you still want him. So . . . I apologize, Greta. If you want it, you have my blessing."

He tried to smile at her, wondering how long it would last, knowing that when it came to an end he would be unable to comfort her as he had done in the past because of Rosemary. And his own heart warmed at the thought of Rosemary. And then shrank a little with grief because of course Greta was right; he was already an old man and Rosemary was still young. And he could never tie her down now. Somehow or other he had cut her loose from the constraints she had made for herself. To bind her again was unthinkable.

"I do want it," Mrs Heatherington said. "I want it very much, Arnold. And you are a man who knows about love and how very sweet it can be."

She put down her coffee cup and reached across the table and he took her hands in his and remembered saying something like this to William once.

That evening he phoned William and told him bluntly that Greta Heatherington was planning to marry Archie Fielding.

The Mathers had become very fond of Greta, and William called Connie to the phone immediately and told her the news. Connie said loudly down the shared receiver, "Can you come round, Arnold? As soon as Frank is in bed we're going to have fish and chips and sort out the Christmas decorations — there are some gorgeous ones from before the war, real glass. Come before Frank goes to bed, he can actually knee that ball you brought him."

William held her to him and said, "That sounds as if she is in full agreement with Greta's decision. I think it's good too, don't you?"

Arnold said, "Actually, no, I don't."

Connie called, "Neither do I, Arnold. She wants a comfort blanket like Frank has got and Archie won't be any good at all at that."

Arnold smiled to himself. "We'll talk about it. But there's nothing to be done, she is determined."

"Come as soon as you can then," William said. "I need fish and chips. Soon."

He put the phone down and kissed his wife and over her shoulder Frank appeared from the living room and scrambled towards them on hands and knees.

They watched him, smiling like all the doting parents in the world. William said, "We could tell Arnold our news tonight, if you like."

"Yes. I told Mummy this morning. She had to be the first to know."

They leaned down together and with practised ease hauled Frank into their arms. He gave a shriek of pleasure and bent forward to share a three-way kiss. Then William took him, and Connie went for the soft ball Arnold had given him when he started to crawl. He knew what he had to do and butted the ball with a plump knee as they rolled it towards him and then clapped his hands with them. Connie sat on the hall chair and watched, smiling, as the ball skidded towards her across the parquet. She no longer worried about

Frank; she had accepted her mother's assurances that his placidity did not mean he was anything but happy. Her new pregnancy helped. William was even happier about this new baby than he had been about Frank. She had thought her mother might think it was too soon but she too had been overjoyed.

"Darling, don't you see? This is nature's way of getting things on an even keel. And it's so obvious that baby Frank is perfectly all right. You must stop worrying right now and get ready to enjoy your two babies." She had hugged Connie enthusiastically. "I did wonder whether you were pregnant, you know. The day of Frank's christening, you were so up and down — typical symptoms."

"Oh Mummy, you couldn't possibly have known! I didn't know myself till September!" But she returned her mother's hug and then said, "And you're right about Frank. When he started to crawl last week at just seven months, it was obvious he was far in advance of the other babies at the clinic." She smiled, hearing her own words and knowing she sounded like every boastful mother that had ever lived. "When I see William playing with him I am pretty certain I was wrong when I told you . . . what I told you. They are so close, Mummy. It's wonderful to see them together. And William says that his grandfather on his mother's side had really piercing blue eyes!"

"Really? Thank God, darling. I did toy with the idea of going to Cornwall myself and seeing if I could get anything out of the family doctor. But if you really think —"

218

"I do, Mummy. I really do. Please don't ever think of trying to find out any more about Philip — Egbert Pardoe. Promise me you won't."

"I do promise, Connie." Rosemary sounded fervent. So many things seemed to be happening suddenly. She felt enormous relief as she gave her promise. She would probably see Arnold Jessup this weekend and she would tell him they could drop the idea of getting anything out of the Pardoes' family doctor. It would have been too difficult anyway. But it would free both of them to be together without any hang-ups. There were two big hang-ups: Greta Heatherington, towards whom Arnold had an inexplicable loyalty; and Frank's beginnings. She frequently wished she had never told Arnold about Frank. But at least now she could tell him to forget any trips to Cornwall. He might . . . he just might . . . ask her to marry him. Not that she cared. Not really. She had never felt like this about any man, not even her husband. A marriage certificate might actually ruin what they had. And meanwhile, there was another new baby on the way. As she said to Maria when they polished the church brass that same afternoon, "I'm not crying because I'm missing Marcus Vallender, Maria. I'm crying because I'm so happy!" And she told Maria about the new baby. Maria smiled and nodded then said, "Dear Rosemary. Your memory really is bad. Marcus's name is Challenger, not Vallender. I have to tell you every time!"

"So you do," Rosemary said and dried her eyes. Only two more days and Arnie would be here for the weekend. The fish man came on Fridays and she planned turbot and perhaps fresh parsley sauce.

William let Arnold in and closed the door quickly because a typical November fog was creeping across from the cricket ground.

"Wait here," he mouthed and at that moment the ball rolled down the hall. From behind the stairs Connie laughed and applauded, and so did Frank. Then Frank appeared, shuffling on his well-padded bottom across the polished floor. He saw Arnold and lifted his arms with a shriek of delight. Arnold felt the usual rush of happiness at the boy's recognition. It did not matter that there was a question mark over his paternity. He belonged to William and Connie Mather and he loved them and he loved Uncle Arnie as well. Arnold gathered him up and held him high and they both laughed.

The two men put the baby to bed and Connie pulled a small table to the fire and put out bread and butter sandwiches and a cruet. Then William went for fish and chips and Connie and Arnie sat by the fire.

Arnie said, "So we're in agreement about Greta getting married, I gather?"

"Well, if Archie is the only choice . . . William talks good sense as you well know, Arnold. He says second best can often turn out to be first best. Given time." She waited and when he said nothing she went on, "I would agree with him if she wasn't still in love with her husband. And, as William says, he has doubtless been

220

dead for ages now." She sighed. "So it looks like Archie Fielding is second best."

"Would you have settled for second best, Connie?"

"Not once I knew that I adored William." She smiled. "D'you know, Arnold, I don't think I did know even when we were engaged. And then there was that awful drowning in the cove and I knew for certain sure that he was the only man in the world for me."

"When you thought you couldn't have him?"

"That sounds awful. But yes, I think you're right. I was just too ignorant and stupid to see the truth . . . which was, that I couldn't be happy without him." She twisted round in her chair and pulled out her knitting from behind the back cushion. She adjusted the needles and began to knit. "I actually did not want to *belong* to him." She looked up, laughing. "Isn't that the craziest thing?"

He stopped himself from saying yes, then from saying no. Instead he said, "What are you knitting?"

The door opened and William came in with an enormous newspaper parcel. She said, "Darling, Arnold wants to know what I'm knitting. Are we going to tell him before we eat?"

He knew, of course. Rosemary had guessed two months ago, before the lump was visible beneath the loose sloppy joe she had taken to wearing. Rosemary had said, "Oh Arnie, I hope I'm right. Somehow it would make it all right for William." And she was correct in both cases. William was incandescent with happiness. Arnold hugged them both and kissed Connie. She tasted like Rosemary. He wanted to cry.

Good God, what was the matter with him? He hadn't cried since William's parents had been killed by that bloody doodlebug.

"Bit soon?" he suggested.

"Just about a year." William grinned like a damned Cheshire cat. "We thought about a cricket side. In which case it will have to be one a year."

Arnold knew it was a joke but he thought that by then Connie would be thirty-four and probably look ten years older. William would be almost fifty. And Arnold himself would be an old man.

William said, "What's up, Arnold?"

"Goose walked over my grave. Let's get on with the fish and chips. That new baby needs sustenance."

They ate them straight from the greaseproof paper and talked about Greta and then babies and then Mrs Flowers, who was going to Australia to see her daughter . . . and then babies again.

"Girl this time?" Arnold asked, already feeling better for the food.

William nodded. "We thought it would be May last time, so it's bound to be this time."

"I wouldn't be surprised if the medics were able to identify the sex of an unborn baby one day." Arnold wiped his hands on one of the paper towels which were everywhere in readiness for Frank.

"Lord forbid." William was definite. "It's the best surprise in the world. Who would want to spoil that?"

Connie laughed and gathered up the greasy newspapers. She went into the kitchen, put them in the bin and washed her hands. She sensed Arnold's mood with some surprise. He was the steadiest, most urbane man in their world — except for William of course — yet she could feel some kind of turbulence going on behind his dark, narrow face. He was anxious for Greta. Should he be quite so anxious? Especially when he was sleeping with her mother. She frowned, anxious herself now. She had thought he would be happier with their own news about the baby but after that first hug and kiss he had simply gone along with whatever William said. And was he getting at something when he suggested that soon the medical profession would be able to foretell the sex of an unborn baby? Did he think such knowledge could extend to foretelling any congenital defects? She stared at the dark glass of the kitchen window and shivered. It surely was not possible that her mother had . . . said something to him? Something about Frank? Was her mother besotted enough to confide such a terribly precious secret to William's boss?

She made coffee and put everything on to the three-tier trolley, which was a new acquisition because William was afraid she might fall over Frank. Arnold got up and held the door wide and admired the trolley. He was always satisfyingly interested in their domestic arrangements. And her mother had told her that he was always making tea at her house. Connie felt her face warm at the thought; she had had enormous difficulty in accepting the idea of her mother and Arnold Jessup in the big bedroom overlooking the golf course. Sometimes she wished her mother had never told her about it. She had begged her not to tell Arnold that she and her mother "shared everything", as Rosemary blithely put it. But Arnold referred to Rosemary so often it was obvious he thought it was an open secret.

He said now, "I was just saying to William — I had to give Greta my blessing in the end. She knew I didn't mean it. She wanted me to say I would be there for her if anything went wrong. I can't do that any more."

The implications behind his words were enormous. Connie felt her face grow warm again and she busied herself with the coffee cups. Did her mother realize that his commitment to Greta Heatherington went back to the days of Greta Gainsborough? And was he trying to reassure them — and perhaps himself — that he intended to be faithful to Rosemary Vickers? Connie overfilled one of the cups and dabbed with a paper towel.

"Here. Let me." He took the coffee pot from her and she sat down willy-nilly. He patted the trolley as if it were a horse. "I'm glad this thing is good and strong. You realize it will in the future become a train, a bus, a Wild West stagecoach . . ." He laughed and passed her a cup and William took it and put it on the little table, then took her hand and held it in his. She smiled at him. He knew exactly how her mind was working. She felt his understanding flow through her like balm.

They settled again. She picked up her knitting. William said, "She's a pretty resilient woman, Arnold. She may well make this work. And if not . . . you are probably not the only man in her life who has helped her to pick up the pieces in the past."

Arnold looked up from his cup, momentarily surprised. Then he said soberly, "Of course not. She is such an idiot when it comes to men. Trusting. Much too trusting. Forgiving too. Archie has beaten her up in the past."

Connie stopped knitting and William said quickly, "There might be something we could do, you know. I'm surprised it hasn't occurred to you, Arnold."

He had their attention and wished he hadn't started this. It was ridiculous; worthy of a romantic novel. But he had to go on with it now.

"Connie and I . . . we know that the only man she has ever really loved is her husband. I don't even know his name." He smiled, mostly at Connie. "Mr Heatherington," he said portentously. They both managed a laugh and he tried to lighten things further. "Apparently that was literally a one-day affair. And then he disappeared. Went to . . . where was it, Connie?"

"Rangoon," she supplied, and remembered that night when neither of them had known — or really cared — where Rangoon was.

"That's right. Rangoon." He exchanged a special smile with her and went on. "Arnold, it will be your job to find out what Mr Heatherington's first name is. Then we can get in touch with Rangoon and see how he is fixed."

Arnold stared at him. "Fixed?"

"Married. Single. Able. Willing."

"You sound like Aunt Agatha," Arnold said, naming a well-known agony aunt in their local paper. "They're both twenty years older. And he ran away from her in the first place. Probably because she was promiscuous. She hasn't changed in that way. And he's probably dead."

"For God's sake, Arnold." William returned his stare meaningfully. "Greta is a romantic. And so are you. Otherwise why did Connie get a job as a filing clerk? Why am I now a solicitor? Why does Greta Heatherington love you? And why is Rosemary Vickers ecstatically happy?" He turned to Connie and smiled their special smile. "Sorry, my love. But you must see that she is. And it's all down to this romantic reprobate here. And surely it is easier to put up with the slight awkwardness of it all if you recognize that your mother is very happy indeed."

"Oh William. I do love you so."

He changed his smile to a grin and said briskly, "Then that's all right because I love you so too."

Arnold said disgustedly, "Oh for God's sake." He stood up. "So I have to see Greta again and get her to tell me her husband's name. And then how do we start finding out whether he is alive or dead?"

"Leave that to me." William stood up and held out his hand as if they were sealing a bargain. "I don't know how to go about things yet. But I'll do my damnedest. And I'm not doing it for Greta. I'm doing it for you and Rosemary."

They shook hands and Arnold left, smiling as he unlocked his car. Smiling because William had grown into the man who had just taken command of a silly situation and Connie was still the girl she had always been — a peacemaker — but made into a woman who could stand aside and let someone else take over.

"Delegation," he murmured as he started the engine and moved off down the road. And then, quite suddenly, he did a U-turn and took the old Worcester road towards the Lickey Hills.

Rosemary was delighted to see him but anxious too.

"Is something wrong?"

She led the way into the living room, where a fire was burning and the radio was delivering the ten o'clock news. She helped him out of his coat, put her arms around him and buried her face in his shirtfront.

"Tell me. Tell me now."

He said, "I'm old and I've done nothing with my life. If only I'd met you twenty years ago, Rosie. We could have conquered the world."

"My husband might have had something to say about that." She breathed in the smell of him. "We could conquer the world twice over if you can stay the night."

"Listen to you. You wouldn't have said that before you knew me."

"You set me free. I mean that, so don't laugh."

"Was I laughing?"

"No. No, you weren't." She lifted her head and looked into his face. "What is it, darling? A trouble shared. Et cetera."

"I've had supper with William and Connie. No . . . she didn't cook and neither did he. We had fish and chips. It was all very informal. But they seized the chance and told me about the new baby. They are so happy . . . I was frightened. How absurd, Rosie. I was actually scared stiff. They're going into everything as if they haven't got very long! Can't they see what sort of world it is?"

Rosemary pushed him into an armchair and sat on the arm, cradling his head against her shoulder. He said, "I'm not crying." And she said, "Shut up. It's me sitting here, for goodness' sake. D'you think I don't know exactly — *exactly* — what you mean and how you feel?" He started to speak and she repeated, "Just shut up, Arnie. Let's cry together."

They were silent for all of five minutes then he whispered, "May I speak now?" and when she nodded he said, "I think you are crushing my skull, Rosie." And she laughed and slid down on to his lap, kissed him extravagantly, pulled his shirt up to dry her own eyes then mopped at his.

He said, "Time for bed." And the front door bell ping-ponged from the hall.

It was Maria and in tow was the dreaded Marcus. Maria was twittering like a starling, Marcus looking very solemn. Rosemary went back into the sitting room and they all caught Arnold tucking in his damp shirt.

Rosemary said, "Arnold. Let me introduce the Reverend —" For the life of her she could not remember his dratted name. Luckily Arnold stepped forward immediately and held out his hand.

"We've met, Rosemary. Don't you remember, Marcus christened baby Frank last July. The Reverend Challenger, I believe?"

Marcus stopped looking pompous but only for a moment. He waited while Maria twittered about their outing to Cheltenham Spa. "It was so good to see you were still up, Rosemary. And Mr Jessup with you too. I wish Connie and William were here as well. You are the closest I have to a family, you know that. I would have loved all of you to hear our news."

Marcus cleared his throat and literally stepped in front of her.

"As you know, dear Mrs Vickers, this is not my day off. Mondays are my days off. This day is very special leave. We have, just this afternoon, driven to Cheltenham Spa. To make a purchase." He turned, took Maria by the hand and drew her forward. "I think you should make the announcement, my dear. Come along, I will help you out. Why did we go to Cheltenham?"

"To look round the shops, Marcus." Maria was laughing so much she had difficulty in getting out her words. "To look round some very special shops."

"Indeed." He held her to his side and took over. "We have purchased an engagement ring. We are, in fact, engaged to be married."

Rosemary looked wildly from one to the other and then at Arnold. He stepped forward and held out his hands. Marcus tried to extricate his right hand to shake Arnold's but Arnold forestalled him, grabbed his left hand, then Maria's right and stood there shaking them and himself in a gallant effort at offering congratulations. Rosemary thought it looked as if they were all

229

suffering a fit; she gathered herself together and put her arms around her neighbour and wept anew.

For a few moments, emotional pandemonium reigned supreme. Maria's twittering escalated into sobs and then floods of tears; Arnold and Marcus talked at the same time, Marcus practically shouting above Arnold so that the words "happiness" and "ideally suited" shot like bullets from the melee. And then Arnold released his hands and retreated to the chair where his overcoat and jacket had been so casually flung by Rosemary, and collapsed. Marcus looked at the two weeping women now clutching each other and moved to the chair by the window where he had sat once before. Carefully he adjusted the closed curtains, probably recalling how easily he had spotted Rosemary that summer afternoon; then he too sat down. He ran a finger around the inside of his dog collar then felt the radiator next to him, which was red hot; and Rosemary had a fire going too, which he felt was sheer extravagance.

Arnold leaned forward. "Let the girls have their moment then we'll drink to your happiness, old man. Meanwhile, many congratulations. The two of you will have many wonderful years together, I am sure."

"I have waited all these years . . ." He let the words settle into the overheated room and make "the girls" pay attention, then visibly drew himself together and went on in an optimistic voice. ". . . and then dear Rosemary introduced me to Maria and I knew instantly I had found my soulmate."

230

Rosemary sat Maria down and went to the cabinet. "The day of the christening," she said, looking over Arnold's head directly at Maria. "Let me see . . . four months ago?"

"We watched the two of you," Maria said, suddenly calm and horribly honest. "You were so happy. Instantly. And it went on and on. And after we had been to the Remembrance Sunday service at the cathedral, we came home and talked about it. And darling Marcus explained to me that neither of us would be hurting another living soul. And then we prayed together until past midnight. And the weather was so awful I couldn't let him drive home then." She smiled at him so lovingly that Rosemary felt her heart melt all over again, but differently this time. Perhaps this really was a meeting of twin souls.

Marcus was not happy with her frankness and did not return the smile.

"I thought we agreed that was our precious secret," he said. He forced a note of jocularity into his voice as he looked at Rosemary. "Seeing you flowering like a . . . flower . . ." Maria laughed, "was encouraging to say the least." Rosemary felt her sentimental smile dying on her face; this was not funny. She glanced at Arnold. He too was looking extremely uncomfortable. She passed glasses around.

"Maria's favourite," she said. "I always get plenty of ginger wine for you at Christmas, don't I, my dear? Good for the arthritis."

She had not meant it to sound catty but Marcus, quick as a flash, said, "Ah, arthritis is a thing of the past. Since we have been together, Maria has also blossomed like a flower. You must have noticed."

Rosemary knew guiltily that she had not. She had been completely involved with her own affairs.

"That really is wonderful!" she cried with enormous enthusiasm. "Love conquers all!" She held up her glass, Arnold said something and they sipped in unison except for Maria, who drank hers like lemonade.

"That was lovely," she said appreciatively. "Isn't this absolutely wonderful, Rosemary? All these years we have lived next door to each other, grubbing along somehow, all alone, miserable . . . and now we have both found wonderful men to look after us." She turned her beatific smile on Arnold. "We did wonder about a double wedding. Marcus thinks he might arrange something in the cathedral — he gets on quite well with the bishop. It would be such an occasion."

"It would indeed," Arnold agreed. Rosemary said nothing.

Marcus put down his glass and reached for Maria's hand. "We had better leave these good people now, my dear. We have given them a great deal to think about and we have to leave early tomorrow. Saturday's jumble sale in the church hall. It seems an ideal time to introduce my dear Maria to the ladies of St Thomas's."

They made their farewells; Maria clung to Rosemary for longer than usual and Rosemary hung about by the open door to give them light to negotiate the descending paths. She returned to the sitting room, shivering. Arnold was standing with his back to the fire.

He said miserably, "I should go."

232

She said, "Please don't. They will see that too. Please don't go tonight."

"You must not let this spoil what we have, Rosie. You must not."

"Of course I won't." She poured more ginger wine and drank it like Maria had. "What a dreadful thing to happen. Maria . . . tied to Marcus Vallender."

"Challenger," he corrected automatically. "And she seems overjoyed by it so don't waste your sympathy."

"I'm responsible. I practically foisted him on to her last July."

"Don't be silly."

He waited for her to flare up and when she did not he said, "For God's sake, let's go to bed."

It was the first time they had slept together without making love. She lay in the crook of his arm and felt desperately unhappy. And bewildered. And knew it was not really anything to do with Maria.

They watched Marcus drive off the next morning as they ate breakfast and then she stood at the door and waved Arnold off. And found herself wondering whether she would see him again. He had been coming this morning for the weekend; she had turbot in the fridge.

It did not help when Connie telephoned that afternoon and was full of their wonderful plan for saving Mrs Heatherington from a fate worse than death.

"Arnold's going to see her on Monday, Mummy. Get Mr Heatherington's name and anything else she might know about him. Wouldn't it be wonderful if he was still alive and we could bring them together again?"

"It would indeed," Rosemary said.

CHAPTER
ELEVEN

Christmas came. Neither William nor Connie appeared to notice anything amiss. This was doubtless because Arnold and Rosemary were determined they should not. Rosemary took over the big old kitchen at Number Five and insisted that Connie should put her feet up and watch Frankie open his presents with lots of help from William and Arnold. When Connie finally succumbed to boredom and joined her mother for yet another gossip about Maria marrying Marcus Challenger, Arnold took her place in the armchair with a sigh of relief.

"My knees aren't what they were," he said apologetically.

William smiled in sympathy and rolled the wooden locomotive along the floor. Frankie yelled delight and threw himself after it.

"Any news of Maurice Heatherington?" William asked, pretending to come after Frankie, who yelled louder.

"No." Arnold felt no need to hide his glumness on this particular matter. "The Far East Association have been very helpful. But nobody of that name is on their lists, dead or alive."

"What has Greta got to say about it?"

"She's not interested. Probably knows something we don't. He may well have been a bigamist. Or a murderer. She simply says we're making up a story in the hope that it will come true. That's probably exactly what we're doing."

William put his son's chubby hand on the cab of the locomotive, covered it with his own and pushed and pulled the little engine back and forth. "Choo-choo!" he cried. "Choo-choo!"

The child looked up at him and echoed his words clearly. William turned an astonished face towards Arnold.

"Did you hear that, Arnold? He said choo-choo. Perfectly. A whole word — two words, in fact. My God. Nip to the kitchen and tell the girls, will you?"

Arnold dragged himself out of the comfortable chair and went down the hall reluctantly. It hurt him physically to watch Rosemary busying herself domestically now; it had been such a thoughtless pleasure at first. He had liked to muscle in, wrestling a tea towel from her to dry the dishes, coming behind her when she was at the sink and sliding his arms around her while he kissed the nape of her neck; laying the table while he watched her straining vegetables. Everything about her had been a delight. Now he imagined himself watching her yet quite unable to help her in any way; watching her while she cooked his meals and looked after him. Would he become a kind of voyeur like Marcus Challenger? He told himself what a fool he was; that no one knew what awaited them in the future and Rosemary might well need him to look after her. But the cynical business of Greta Heatherington and Archie Fielding had disturbed him first of all and then the sheer awfulness of Marcus Challenger and Rosemary's neighbour had — as he said to himself — put the lid on it. When he began the foolish and fruitless search for Maurice Heatherington, it was in a crazy effort to protect Greta. He knew it was hopeless and it would be much better to give in to his schoolboy urge to take Archie into the garden of Greta's flat and punch him hard on the nose. The whole thing was ridiculous, a wild goose chase. But Marcus Challenger was very much present and was one of the many complex reasons for seeing Rosemary only twice since that momentous night in November. Marcus would certainly sue him if he punched *him* on the nose. He wondered whether it would be worth it. If it somehow solved the problem with Rosemary it would definitely be worth it.

He stood in the kitchen doorway watching her yet again. She had found an apron with a frilled bib that strained across her breasts and had crossover straps at the back. She was making custard, whipping eggs as if her life depended on it. Connie was loading the three-tiered trolley with cutlery, napiery, a tureen of bread sauce, another of cranberry, water glasses and a dish and spoon for Frankie, both shaped like a Santa Claus. They stopped talking and looked at him. Rosemary's face flooded with colour.

He said, "Connie. William wants you to go and listen to Frankie. He said his first word just now. Two words, in fact."

237

She gasped and was gone. He went on watching Rosemary; he could not stop. She stared back at him. The colour left her face and she held on to the edge of the sink as if she might fall over at any moment. There was a hissing noise and then a terrible smell and the milk for the custard boiled over.

He leaped forward and grabbed the saucepan off the hob. A mini-second behind him Rosemary did the same and missed. The handle of the saucepan was red-hot. He dropped the lot. They both took a step back as scalding milk splashed everywhere.

Rosemary's whisper was more of a hiss. "Look what you've done!"

"Darling, I'm so sorry." He nursed his damaged hand. "Are you hurt?"

"Of course I'm not bloody well hurt!" Her hiss was practically a scream of fury. "But what on earth will Connie say? Look at the mess on her floor! And the hob! And I bet you a fiver she hasn't got another pint she can spare!"

"I'd offer to clear up but if I get down on my knees again I'll never get up."

"Best place for you!" She picked up the empty saucepan and felt its heat. "Oh my God! Let me see that hand! Come here — get it under this cold tap — stop being such a stiff upper lip — hold it there — don't move." She whipped to a cupboard at the end of the kitchen and withdrew a first-aid box. "Connie was always brilliant about keeping this kind of thing at the ready. First aid was the first badge she got when she was in the Girl Guides." She withdrew a bright yellow dressing from its packet. "Put your hand here, I'm just going to dab it dry with a tissue so that the dressing will hold." She was not particularly gentle and he flinched several times. "How does that feel?"

"Fine." He stared at her. She was so . . . so . . . perfect. She had almost fainted before the wretched milk had boiled over. He imagined himself kissing and kissing her until she fainted in his arms.

William came in and absorbed the scene in stages; the mess on the floor, the open first-aid box, Arnold's outstretched hand.

He said, "Oh Lord. What happened?"

Rosemary closed the box with a snap and replaced it. Arnold said miserably, "I picked up the saucepan and it was hot and I dropped it. I am sorry. Such a mess."

William ignored the mess. "Is it a bad burn?"

Rosemary said, "No."

Arnold said, "Don't know. Hurts like hell."

William said, "Go in and talk to Connie. She's doing nappies and things. We'll see to this." For some reason he sounded annoyed. Arnold felt very hard done by. Connie was sitting in a low chair with a big basket of nappies and ointments by her side; Frank was flat on his back on her lap.

She said, "Everything OK, Arnold?"

"Yes, thanks. I burned my hand on the saucepan and your mother has put a dressing on it." He displayed the dressing. She smiled as if congratulating him.

"Mummy is super at first aid. When I was a Guide I had to take a test to get my badge and she would show me how to do everything. We used to laugh our heads off."

"Good." He settled in the chair opposite her and felt her knitting needles behind the cushion. "Ouch!" He extracted them. "Gosh, they're sharp."

She said urgently, "Don't move any more, Arnold. Please. All the stitches have pulled off and I'm in the middle of a pattern. If you could stay absolutely still until I've finished Frank I might be able to get them back on."

He hardly dared breathe. "I seem to be accident-prone today," he said, his voice full of self-pity.

She smiled as she fixed safety pins. "If it only happens on Christmas Day we might be able to take it," she said. She put Frank on the floor and he went after his choo-choo. She did not stand up.

"Arnold, will you try to be honest with me, please."

It wasn't a question, rather a command. But he said, "I've never been anything else, Connie."

"I think you have. However . . . are you sleeping with Mrs Heatherington?"

"None of your business," he snapped, thoroughly fed up with the way things were going.

"It is very much my business. But I suppose that answers the question. In which case you owe my mother an apology and then you need to get out of her sight pretty damned quickly."

It was such an untypical speech from Connie he just stared for a moment. Then he moved his throbbing hand and rested it on the arm of the chair.

"Yes, it is your business. Of course it is. I'm sorry. It's just that . . . well, it is now unthinkable, Connie. You must know that I would not be in love with your mother and still sleep with Greta Heatherington."

She visibly relaxed but all she said was "You've now run out at least one line of my knitting. It will take me ages to get that right."

"Oh Connie . . ." He was in despair. "I'm so sorry. I really am. I feel I cannot do anything right. As for the romantic notion of finding Greta's twenty-four-hour husband — well, it's ridiculous."

"I saw the photograph. Same age as his wife and she is still going strong. Let me take the wool . . . now the needles . . . Oh honestly, Arnold!" She sat down again and looked helplessly at the muddle of wool, then picked up a needle and began to thread stitches back on to it. "He's got to be somewhere. After all, he wasn't in the forces so there was no immediate danger."

"How do you know he wasn't in the forces? I've always assumed . . ."

"I saw the wedding snap, remember. He wasn't the sort of chap who would have worn mufti for his wedding day. He would have worn full dress uniform and borrowed a few medals. Mummy would have called him a wide boy."

Arnold smiled. "She would, wouldn't she? Oh Connie, can't you make things right for us? I know the thought of that wretched man and her own neighbour practically spying on her is poisoning our — our friendship . . . Some of the things they said . . . But she is changing, retreating into becoming a professional countrywoman again."

Connie glanced up momentarily, surprised. "Mummy can weather all that, for goodness' sake. She didn't enjoy it but she got over it. It's when you're not there to be spied on — that's what she doesn't enjoy. One bit."

"Well, that can be remedied. It's just . . . it's not the same, Connie. I think she's gone off me. If I could do something . . . special, like find Maurice bloody Heatherington, it might improve."

"She's just done a Florence Nightingale on you. What more do you want?" She threaded on the final stitch and put the whole thing in a bag. "Just don't go anywhere near this bag. All right?"

She stood up. "William and I are now going to take over the kitchen. Mummy and you will play with Frank." She went to the door and turned. "For a clever and sensitive man, you are being so — so *obtuse*! I will just say this to you. Maria and Marcus are getting married."

She left the room.

They gathered around the rosewood table in the little-used dining room; Arnold thought it was unbearably festive, like a scene from *A Christmas Carol*. There were tureens surrounding the holly and fir cone arrangement at the foot of the tall red candle which was burning steadily — "That draught excluder really does work," said William proudly. Rosemary had popped upstairs for her cultured pearls, thereby skilfully avoiding Arnold again, while Connie sat by the high chair and pointed out the glittering tinsel bells looped from the cornice and Frankie clapped his small fat hands with his usual delight.

Arnold felt outside all of it; perhaps not outside — he was recognizing his own self-pity, which quickly changed into self-disgust — but certainly not wholly part of it. He realized that he was used to being in control: he had inherited the practice from his father just before it had died on its feet and he had made it into a good family firm and sought work from the university but kept it well under his own hand. Taking on William after the war had been a gamble, yet he knew it would work. And it had. And he had spotted Connie and taken her on in the face of tight-lipped disapproval from Mrs Flowers, and that had worked too. He had kept a professional and caring eye on Greta, comforting her in the only way she knew. And then had seen Rosemary at Frank's christening. There had never been a doubt in his mind that she would fall for him as he had fallen for her. He simply assumed that she would fall into his arms and — quite literally — she had. And it had been wonderful. The very best time of his life. But somehow, inexplicably, things were starting to fall apart. Greta was going to marry the ghastly Archie, Rosemary was moving away from him, Connie's anger had hit him for six, and William . . . William was the man in charge. Without saying much, he had simply taken Rosemary gently into his family circle. The big bedroom in the front was Rosemary's room and she kept spare clothes and hairbrushes there. Last week when Arnold had taken her to see the Ballets Russes — he did not enjoy ballet but she had said once how she had always wanted to be a ballet dancer — she had said, "Drop me at Number Five, Arnie. I've got my key. It will save you having to drive all the way out to Barnt Green." And of course that had meant he left her at the front door; no nightcap, no discussion about the performance . . . nothing.

Her voice interrupted his gloomy thoughts.

"Arnie! You're in another world — pull this cracker with me, for goodness' sake!" Her face, beautiful yet ordinary, full of laughter, was close to his. Without a second thought he leaned towards her and put his lips to hers and just for a wonderful moment she responded. Then she moved back very naturally and he saw she had a sprig of mistletoe in her hair. "Come *on*, Arnie! Everyone else has got a hat!" And he realized it had meant nothing at all.

The short afternoon drifted away with pudding and trifle and games with the choo-choo and carols round the tree. Then Rosemary and Connie put Frank to bed and William and Arnold washed up. Arnold was frightened he was going to cry at any moment. He cleared his throat and tried to express his gratitude for — for — for — for —

William grinned. "For everything, old man?" He was doing the drying because he knew where things lived and his grin was because Arnold looked ridiculous in Connie's bright yellow gloves with the paper hat from his cracker falling over one ear.

244

"For everything. Yes. And just because I'm going to be retiring in five years it does not mean I'm old, William. Fifty-five is nothing in this day and age."

"When I called you old man it was an endearment." William returned a plate still streaked with gravy. "Though it does rather look as if your standard of cleanliness is deteriorating!" He was teasing, of course, but Arnold chose to take him seriously and snatched the plate from him. The slippery gloves did not hold it and they both looked down as it lay on the floor in two neat pieces. And then William started to laugh and could not stop and after a startled moment Arnold smiled and then grinned and then punched William's shoulder with his sudsy glove and then they held each other by the arms to stop themselves falling over.

After William had picked up the broken plate and put it in the bin and assured Arnold that Connie would not notice because they had at least two dozen of that pattern, he became serious and said, "I've wanted to say something for some time, Arnold. Now . . . Christmas night . . . family time and so on . . . very special." He smiled, acknowledging his own embarrassment. "Don't look worried. I want to thank you for rescuing me — what is it now, fifteen years ago? If it hadn't been for you I think I might have ended up in a psychiatric hospital or even teaching inadequately in a school somewhere!" He tried to laugh. "It's no good you shaking your head. I was a mess, Arnold. And I was scared to death. And you calmly took over from my parents and . . . fixed me up!" He stopped speaking because he saw that Arnold was near tears. He seized on the first subject change that was even minimally relevant. "The hand hurting, old man?"

Arnold choked on a laugh at the emphasis William put on "old man" but then nodded. "It's giving me gyp," he acknowledged. "But Rosemary's done a grand job — she used to help Connie with her first aid, you know. When she was a Girl Guide. Probably these gloves." He peeled off the yellow gloves and opened his palm. The dressing was black at the edges. Where it ended, blisters began.

"Oh my Lord, Arnold. We'd better get you along to Casualty. Rosemary should have let a professional see this when you did it." He pushed Arnold into a chair. "I know you and Rosemary have had a tiff about something but I should have picked up that you were in a bad way. I'll get our coats. Don't move."

Arnold thought how right he had been about William. The boy got him into his outdoor things, stowed him in the car in about five minutes flat and then ran back to yell up the stairs to Connie. He also got him out of the car and into the waiting room in the Casualty ward before he passed out. He came round almost immediately and smiled at the face of the young nurse bending over him. "It's supposed to be Rosie who faints. Not me." And he went again.

It continued like that for some time. It seemed that he was run-down and had one of these fancy new viruses and the burn had just tipped him over the edge. He heard the word septicaemia and thought it might be a new type of iodine. William had gone and come back with pyjamas and a toilet bag and settled him into a bed that was as hard as iron and quite narrow. He imagined what he would look like falling out of bed. He was probably still wearing that daft paper hat Rosemary had insisted on fitting over his ears. "*Respected local solicitor falls out of bed drunk and disorderly.*" He fell into a proper sleep but dreamed he was chasing a man down a long, endless street and he had no shoes on his feet so every now and then he would yell with pain when he stepped on a sharp stone. He had to catch the man. He called out at one stage, "Wait, Maurice! Please wait! She is still waiting for you — can't you do the same?"

William came the next afternoon, clutching the centrepiece from Connie's *Christmas Carol* dining table. The nurses were all smiles as they put it on the table in the middle of the ward where the "walking wounded" had their meals. A great fuss was made of lighting the candle. "You'll be able to blow it out soon, Mr Jessup," said one of the girls, who looked like Rosemary must have looked twenty years ago. He smiled, waited till she was out of earshot and said to William, "Oh goody-goody."

William said, "Rosemary is frantic. I did what you asked — told her you did not want visitors — but she thinks it's her fault. She said she went into some kind of trance in the kitchen and let the milk boil over and then let you rescue it . . . You can imagine."

"Some kind of trance, my foot. Tell her she can visit me if she wants to but not until she can look me in the eye and tell me exactly what happened in that bloody kitchen. Until then, yes, it was her fault."

William frowned but in view of Arnold's delicate state did not follow it up. He was given a piece of cake and a cup of tea at teatime and allowed to stay to hear the wassailers. Then it was time for sandwiches and hot milk and pills and injections. The night spread before Arnold endlessly. He took William's arm. "Tell her to come anyway. Tomorrow. Two o'clock till six o'clock."

William grinned. "All right. Gives her plenty of leeway."

"None whatsoever. I need her at two. And she doesn't go until six."

"You're delirious again. But I'll put it to her."

She did not come at two but Greta Heatherington did. She had two turkey sandwiches wrapped in greaseproof paper which she put in his locker. "The nights are so long. Gives you something to do. Next time I'll bring those chocolate biscuits you like. Trouble is, they'll melt in this heat. My God, it's hot in here. Snowing outside."

"Really?" There was no sign of it on the window opposite his bed. Something was falling. Like gritty rain. He didn't feel so good today.

She said, "Well, almost. Sleet, I suppose. Listen, Arnold. I have to attend rehearsals starting tomorrow. Will they let me come in the morning?"

"Shouldn't think so. Has Archie moved in yet?"

"No bloody fear. He doesn't move in till I've got my marriage certificate framed and on the wall."

"Good. I want you to promise me something."

"Go on."

"Promise first."

"OK. Promise. Only because all promises are cancelled if you die and they say things aren't looking good for you."

For a moment he was startled, then grabbed her wrist and tried to give her a feeble Chinese burn. She giggled.

"Seriously. Just for a minute. Promise you won't marry Archie Fielding until you've spent some time with Maurice."

Her face opened wide; he thought he saw joy. There could have been fear as well.

She said, "You've found him! The swine — was he in Rangoon all the time?"

"I haven't found him. But I feel I'm close. I agree the contract is void if I die. But if not . . . you have given your word. Remember that."

She grabbed his hands and he flinched. "You are not going to die! Do you hear me, Arnie? I'm older than you by seven years and you are not going to die before me — that is part of the bloody contract too!"

He whimpered, "If you go on squeezing my poorly hand I probably will die right here and now."

She gasped and let him go. "Dear boy. I have to go. Wish me luck for tomorrow's rehearsal. I've bought a new sewing machine. D'you remember that outfit I made for myself for 'Moonlight Becomes You'?" He nodded feebly. "Well, I plan to do the same one for the ingénue in this production. But it has to be — basically — a dressing gown." She kissed him. "Good luck to you. My first love."

"Liar."

He could still hear her chuckling as she got to the end of the ward and turned to wave to him. Then he saw the big clock over the door; it was three o'clock, so Rosemary wasn't coming after all. He carefully used his good hand and pulled out a clean handkerchief from the pile William had left, shook it loose and put it over his face for a moment. He must be ill, this was at least the third bout since Christmas Day.

She came at five. She and William had been to his place and she brought clean pyjamas, a pair of flannels and a jumper fit for a polar explorer. "You are going to be sitting out for your meals tomorrow," she said as she stowed the stuff neatly in his locker.

"It's like a hothouse in here all the time," he bleated.

"Clean pants and vest. More hankies. That stuff you like to pat on your face — it costs the earth and it's only eau-de-cologne, you know."

"When can I go home?"

"When the doctor says you are free of this wretched poison. How you let yourself get in such a state, I do not know."

"I thought you were taking responsibility? William said you were in quite a state yourself. Guilt."

She was crouching in front of the locker and she stayed there, head down. He elbowed himself up from the pillow and saw tears on her eyelashes.

He said, "I was joking. Get up and give me a kiss. And tell me what the hell is going on. When are Marcus Vallender and Maria getting married?"

250

"Not for a while. And it's Challenger, not Vallender. I think."

She sat on the edge of the bed and he elbowed himself even further up and grabbed her clumsily and pulled her down with him. They kissed. The man opposite whistled.

Arnold said, "I don't care."

"Well, neither do I. But once that whistling business starts everyone does it. So let me up."

He let her up but tutted with annoyance. "I meant I don't care about Marcus Challenger or Vallender or whatever the hell he's called. I know it's horrible for you, my dearest one, but surely it's not horrible enough to put the mockers on what we've got?"

She looked at him incredulously. "You're supposed to be intelligent, clever, sensitive . . . Listen to me properly: Marcus and Maria are getting married."

"Yes. I know." He mouthed the words with enormous exaggeration. "Is that the end of the conversation?"

"And we are not." She started the short sentence with the same emphasis he had used and ended it on a sort of whimper.

He stared at her for what seemed a lifetime. Then he said, "I thought you said . . . I thought I was setting you free from that sort of petty convention . . . You said . . ."

"I know. I thought the same. But then I wanted to look after you. Like now. I wanted the right — the *right* — to walk into this hospital at any time because you are here. It was when Marcus and Maria said they were getting married. It seemed just awful at first, then I saw what it truly meant. It meant that legally — *legally* —

they would be responsible for each other." She looked at him. Her eyes were swimming. "You don't want that. I know. You want to be free. And you want me to be free. In case I find someone younger. In case you have to care for Greta at some point. And I understand that. But it's not enough for me, Arnie. I want to tell the world that I am committed to you. And I want you to do the same. There, I've said it. Pride in the dust and all that." She tried for a laugh. "I'm going now. You know I love you and you know we can carry on almost like we did when it first hit us. But at least we both know where we stand."

He discovered he was bloody well crying again and in a moment of terror thought he might actually be going to die, here in this hospital. And if that were the case then Rosemary would not have to nurse an older husband.

She was on her feet, gathering handbag, gloves, scarf. He choked, "Rosie. Marry me. Please."

She dashed the tears from her own eyes and looked at him. She drew a quick breath and leaned over him to ring the bell. Her finger was still in place when two nurses came running. Curtains were pulled and she was ejected. She heard the initial hiss from the oxygen tank; soothing words as a mask was fitted. More soothing words. Then one of them leaned around the curtain and said, "He is still agitated. Says he did not hear what you said."

There was so much to say. He did not have to do this . . . She had made it plain that they could go on together if he wished . . . She had wanted him to know how she felt . . . She looked at the young nurse who could not possibly understand, she spread her hands wide and her handbag dangled from one arm like a pendulum measuring precious time. She said helplessly, "I said yes. Tell him . . . yes."

The nurse gave a grin that spread from ear to ear and disappeared. Both of them emerged after another ten minutes. They let her look at him propped up with the plastic mask in place. Incredibly he was asleep. They told her what they had done. An injection. His natural immunity was low.

The one with the wide smile said, "He is going to be all right. Come tomorrow if you can. You will see an enormous difference." She walked with Rosemary to the ward door. "Immediately he got his answer, he was all right. His whole face changed. You must not worry about the tears. He is very weak."

Rosemary fought to control her own tears, touched the nurse lightly on the arm and went without another word.

She drove back to Number Five very carefully, conscious that her concentration was not at its best. The streets already had the awful after-Christmas look about them, and the sleet had bedraggled even the miniature Christmas trees around the shops. She had intended to go back home today but Connie had begged her to stay.

"If we're going to get snow you won't be able to get down to see poor Arnie."

"But, darling, haven't we agreed that it is best if I don't visit him? This latest demand — that I spend the whole of visiting time sitting by his bed — it's just his nonsense, you know."

"I think you should go — if the roads are passable. And be honest with him, Mummy. Seriously. And then come back here. If not for his sake, for mine. The baby is kicking like mad — I don't remember Frankie being so active. I'd like to have a check-up and I hoped you would stay with Frankie."

What could she say? Especially now. His proposal and her reply probably did not mean much but she had to be around. She thought of her house and the expanse of the golf course stretching out from the sitting room window. It was so convenient. And she was tired herself. Bone tired.

And then she thought of Maria next door. She sighed. It was better she stayed in the city. Just for a while.

That evening after Frankie's bedtime routine, the three of them sat around the fire and watched the late news. Connie was doodling on the notepad she kept for shopping lists. Rosemary had taken on the tiny matinee coat so nearly destroyed by Arnie on Christmas afternoon and was using a crochet hook to pick up a missed stitch. William had removed a nail from the funnel of the choo-choo and was replacing it with a screw.

He glanced up and responded to the picture of the eager young American waving out of the screen. "Wonder what this Kennedy chap will be like. He's got a good background, links to this country. Could be all right for us as well as America."

Rosemary glanced up too and nodded. "Very nice smile. Good teeth."

Connie stopped writing for a moment but did not look up. "All Americans seem to have good teeth." She sighed and referred to an earlier announcement. "D'you know, I've really missed the farthing."

William grinned over her head at Rosemary but she said staunchly, "I know what you mean. It was practically valueless but it just fitted nicely into that pocket compass your grandfather had. Supposed to take a sovereign but the mean old so-and-so took that out and put a farthing in its place."

The other two laughed. Rosemary said, "There. Now we're on line two of the pattern. Shall I keep going?"

"Oh, would you, Mummy? I just want to finish this. Then I suppose it's a drink and bed?"

"I'll see to the drinks." William tested the choo-choo and ran his hand over the surface. "That's better. Imagine using nails in a child's toy."

He left them to it and went into the kitchen. He was more anxious about Arnold than he let on. Surely this afternoon's relapse could not have been brought on — and cured — by Rosemary's presence? His parents had always told him that Arnold had not been accepted for the armed forces because of a "condition". He had mentioned this to Arnold once and had been told that it was their polite way of saying he had flat feet. What if that was a form of self-protection? What if he had a blood disorder or a heart condition? William reached for the Ovaltine, the cocoa and the Horlicks, wondering why on earth they all had to have different bedtime drinks. He fetched beakers and spoons and frowned at the kettle. He would ask Arnold. Tomorrow, he would ask him.

Back in the living room Rosemary tucked the knitting away in its bag and leaned back in her chair. "I'll leave it, darling. I'm so tired I'll probably make another mistake."

"You're worried sick about Arnold. But don't be. I dreamed about him last night. He was running down a street. He looked marvellous."

"Do you still get those vivid dreams? They used to mean so much to you. One or two did actually come true."

"Well, one did. I got married in a register office and was really happy about it. That came to pass." She grinned at her mother, ripped off the top page of her notebook and passed it across. "What d'you think about that? I'm going to send it to the Brighton newspapers . . . I'll have to find out whether there is a special paper. Greta will know."

Rosemary read Connie's carefully printed words and her brows rose into her hair with astonishment. She looked up. "How on earth will Greta know?"

"Arnold told me she was always popping off to Brighton with various boyfriends. It was the thing to do apparently."

"Well, he would know!" Rosemary snapped.

Connie looked at her mother calmly. "Yes. He would. Accept it, Mummy, please. He is full of love and she needed him." She held her mother's gaze very deliberately. "That was how it was for me. That's how I know that Arnold is faithful to you." She sighed and shook her head. "Anyway, I asked him. He would not have lied to me about that. He was shocked that the suspicion had even crossed my mind."

Rosemary sniffed. "Oh, damn this blessed crying — I hate myself for blubbing every time Arnold's name is mentioned!" Connie offered no sympathy; in fact, she grinned. Another loud sniff and Rosemary waved the notepaper at her. "I still don't get it. Why would the horrid Maurice hide himself away in Brighton?"

Connie took the paper from her and leaned forward. She was not at all certain about this but she was so excited she knew she had to go through with it.

"This dream last night. Arnold was coming out of a fog. He saw someone ahead of him. It was Maurice — no, I have no idea why I knew it was Maurice, but it was. Spivvy suit — you know — soft trilby, very Raymond Chandler. It was a long street, sort of boarding houses either side. Arnold recognized Maurice and started to run. And then I woke up."

Rosemary, who had been instantly hooked, sat up straight. "For goodness' sake, Connie! A street full of boarding houses? It could be anywhere! And if he was wearing clothes like that, it happened in the 1940s so it could have been a sort of transferred memory. Coming from Arnie I wouldn't be surprised! He probably chased Maurice down and offered him a black eye. Perhaps it was him — Arnie — who forced Maurice to propose to Greta!"

257

Connie looked slightly crestfallen. "It could have been the forties. But, Mum, I have to try. Simply because the last thing I noticed in the dream was that onion dome thing — d'you remember when we went with Grandma that time? The Pavilion — I've never forgotten it because it made England look like the Arabian Nights!"

"That was your fifth birthday treat." Rosemary smiled tightly to stop herself from crying again. She did not mention that it was 1943 when they went to Brighton.

William came in with the tray. Connie got up and took it from him. She said, "I'm just going to ring Greta while my drink cools. We all wish her well for tomorrow's rehearsal, don't we?"

The other two nodded. Rosemary noticed she had tucked the single sheet of paper inside the notepad and the phone was in the hall by the kitchen so William would not hear what was said.

CHAPTER
TWELVE

Nineteen sixty-two saw the first of the Flower People arriving in Cornwall.

At first they were mistaken for the itinerant workers who came soon after every Christmas to pick the early daffodils or pack them for Covent Garden. There were new potatoes and cauliflowers afterwards, spring cabbage, primroses, tiny clusters of violets. Cornish harvests were early, everyone knew that.

It soon became obvious that these Flower People were nothing to do with work. Their clothing was completely different and entirely unsuitable and when they got into the sea, which was often because they thought of it as a daily baptism, they did not bother with swimsuits. As Josh Warne said to the Reverend Hobson in the Penbeagle Arms, "You're pretty free and easy — for a vicar — and you ain't 'ad no complaints from anyone down 'ere. But this lot, they ain't got no shame." He was still hot and bothered after an encounter with a group down at the cove, one of whom was very pregnant indeed.

Josh had never felt the same about the cove since Egg Pardoe had been drowned there almost two years ago and as the four naked girls and half a dozen boys —

some of them no older than Egg — had waded into the still water he had tried to tell them about the single surging wave that had happened out of the blue just two years ago. The sun was setting and the water was blood red. The girls had been scattering azalea blossoms around their pregnant companion. They had other flowers wound into their long, salt-stiff hair and they peered through them as they turned to look at Josh capering about on the beach. They did not hear his words; their smiles were beatific. They made a circle around the girl, held hands, floated on their backs, toes towards her. She held as many toes as she could and floated too. They wailed some song or other then they stood again and two girls towed in the pregnant one, righted her and kissed her. Everyone kissed everyone else. Josh almost ran up the steep cliff path, his neck as red as the drowning sun.

"'Twere clear as day they bin picking them mushrooms again up by Zennor 'ead. Never mind flowers, it's them they're after." He looked over his personal pint mug, which depicted George V and Queen Mary at their coronation. "Cain't you 'ave a word with them, reverend? Them mushrooms can get mixed up with others and kill you in two or three weeks. And the way they're going on — the water cain't be doing that mother and baby much good."

"Strangely enough, Josh, I was reading an article in a medical journal just the other day. Babies are actually being delivered in water. It's something to do with the buoyancy."

"Oh ah." Everyone knew the reverend was a bit modern but was he making things up now? Josh said pacifically, "The cold do get things moving, do it?"

"I have to admit, warm water is recommended." Matthew laughed. "They're not going to get that in the Atlantic, are they? But as a ritual it sounds rather significant, Josh. As if they were making a giant lifebelt around the girl, supporting her, holding her up as it were."

"Never thought of it like that. 'Ere's the doctor. What's he got to say about it, I wonder?"

John Carthew brought his whisky and water over to them and grinned. "I know what you're talking about! Josh, you're as red as a turkey-cock. Either Chippy's been trying to drip poison into your ear again or you've witnessed our daily dose of nudity."

Josh told him what was "goin" on down the cove' and Matthew added his piece about water-birthing.

Carthew savoured two drops of whisky on his tongue then said, "I've got no objection to the girl floating in calm water — the weather is perfect. And the idea of the lifebelt . . . very romantic. Very romantic indeed. I hope they don't try to deliver that baby down in the cove, however. It could be very dangerous."

Matthew turned down his mouth. "Hadn't thought of that. Just a few of them turn up in church now and then. I'd better angle something into my sermons."

"Try telling them too that their nudity does give offence to some of us down here. They will simply laugh, I know that. But perhaps if they kept their

261

swimming until sunset and in the cove — most of the families have gone in for dinner by then."

Matthew shook his head. "I can see their point actually. Where's the shame in the human body and so forth. I'm leaving out that particular issue."

"All right. But you're almost a local man now, Matt, and you know they are risking a lot with these damned fungi they're eating. I've treated two of them for jellyfish stings and mosquito bites and I've told them in no uncertain terms what I think about experimenting with the human body. We're vulnerable. We're bloody vulnerable."

Matthew nodded. "Yes, I can certainly preach about the sanctity of the body. I think they will be receptive to that."

Chippy Penberthy sidled over to them and said conspiratorially, "Your mental case is down on the towans, reverend. Not a stitch on 'im. Flowers in his ears and nose. Ready for the asylum, I do reckon."

Matthew said, "He is not a mental case, Chippy. As you well know. And he is not mine either. He is a lodger in the rectory — he is working on a farm up Gwithian way so I hardly see him. But he walks to and from work along the dunes. I expect your . . . informant . . . has seen him on his way to and from work."

"Seen 'im meself." Chippy was cock-a-hoop with news. "Got a contract with the holiday camp to supply winda frames for them shallies they're putting up. Went to sign up at their site office . . . an' there 'e were. Dancing about like 'e were in a different world. Naked as the day he were born. And flowers everywhere." He

262

smirked and withdrew to tell others that in spite of Lucy Pardoe he was going to be . . . not rich zackly . . . not rich like 'er o'course — but comfortable, very comfortable indeed.

Matthew said, "Oh dear. Poor Harry. One of the more vulnerable among us, I'm afraid." He drew down his mouth. "He's been lodging in the rectory since Christmas, behaving like a careful visitor. It was hard work until he got this job at Gwithian."

"I can imagine." The doctor moved his glass along the bar and held up a hand to the landlady, then turned back, frowning. "Which farm might that be, Matthew? West of Connor Downs, is it?"

Matthew nodded. "Roach's. He had the offer of cowman on the Godolphin Estate — better pay and a cottage thrown in. But he was set on Roach's farm. It's mixed, sheep and cattle and two fields of potatoes. Terribly run-down. I think old Roach is past it. Harry needs to be needed. Like most of us, I suppose."

Carthew looked at Josh Warne, who looked back at him. Josh said slowly, "'E must a died long ago. She never mentioned 'im."

Carthew said, "He's not dead. I had to get him a bed in Hayle hospital not long ago."

Josh turned his attention to the rector. "Does she know where he is working?"

Matthew was bewildered. "What are you two talking about? Does who know where Harry is working?"

"Mrs Pardoe," Josh said impatiently. "Does Mrs Pardoe know where Harry Membury is working?"

"I shouldn't think so. She hasn't been back to the towans since she left last September. And I gathered from that American woman who brought Harry over to me just before Christmas that she did not want to see him again." He sighed sharply. "I'm not sure whether I should tell you this but Harry is wildly, crazily in love with Lucy Pardoe. Ever since that awful time — the year I arrived here — when Lucy lost her only son. That was when Harry first met her. And he hasn't been able to function properly since."

"Is he functioning properly now?" the doctor asked. "Since he got the job at Roach's farm . . . is he better?"

Matthew frowned, thinking about it. "I suppose . . . he might be. He often brings home vegetables from the garden round the farmhouse. Chops 'em up and fries them. We have them for supper. He's a vegetarian, you know."

Carthew looked again at Josh and said heavily, "He must know then." And Josh nodded.

"Know what?"

They both looked at the rector, who was still so young, almost naive.

"Old man Roach —"

"Zeke," supplied Josh.

"Short for Ezekiel. Probably shortened his wife's life by beating her every Saturday night. Wanted to continue the custom with his daughter . . ." Carthew remembered the bruised body, welts across the swollen abdomen . . . No wonder that girl had had such a dreadful labour.

Josh said flatly, "He's Lucy Pardoe's faither."

Matthew forgot himself and called on his heavenly father. "Oh my God."

Carthew nodded and said slowly, "If Harry starts confiding in him about his feelings for Lucy, Zeke Roach will kill him."

There was a long silence. Carthew reached for his replenished glass and sipped at it. Josh stared into his empty mug. Matthew finished his Guinness and put his glass on the bar.

"I can't see how to get round this," he said at last. "There's no way Harry is going to leave that job. He's got his own plan — agenda, whatever. I don't want to upset that."

Carthew said, "I wonder whether Chippy is exaggerating about the Flower Power thing. It sounds as if Harry might be a convert, doesn't it? He might throw in his lot with them."

Josh shook his head. "It do all depend on what he knows about Roach and about Lucy. Or even if he knows anything at all." He nodded at the rector. "Up to you, reverend. Find out what you can."

They talked around it. There was another whisky and another Guinness. Josh watched them making everything more complicated and said his good nights. Then he made for the dunes and once there he lay on his stomach and watched as the dancing died down and someone started playing something on a guitar. Someone else started to sing "Where Have All The Flowers Gone?".

It was Harry Membury.

Josh began to scramble down the long slide of sand to the beach. He was welcomed by everyone, especially Harry.

"I've come to walk you back home, m'boy," Josh said, taking Harry's arm. At least he had his clothes back on.

"Stay here with us, Josh. Sleep under the stars . . ."

"Not tonight, boy. Here, let me button your jacket. 'Tis getting colder as the sun goes into the sea."

Harry turned to the others, tears in his eyes. "It was almost two years ago," he said, "and he was drowned. And everything changed. Because he was drowned."

They looked up at him. Josh tugged on his arm. They began the climb up the dune and when they reached the top, Harry had stopped crying and looked down on the young people with love and fear. "They don't understand," he said.

"And neither do you, m'boy. You must not eat those mushrooms any more."

Harry looked surprised. "Fungi are good. A source of protein for people who don't eat meat. Matthew and I, we've been eating some most evenings."

Josh looked at him and started to laugh.

Christmas 1961, the first Christmas in Truro, was hard for Lucy. The Trips spent two weeks back home, staying for one week with Marvin's parents in Detroit and the second on the farm. Already Lucy was carried away by Margaret and she missed her dreadfully. The American woman with her gangling limbs and her foreign accent and her complete openness towards other people was *exactly* what Lucy Pardoe from the towans needed. Margaret used the verb "to fix" quite often and Lucy was reminded of Bertie McKinley. On their first date — which he had *fixed* when she served him coffee in the old sitting room of the Grange Hotel by saying, "Hey, how you doing? You're off duty in an hour, how about a walk along the beach? Gonna be some sunset!" — she had said stupidly, "I was born by the sea and I've only ever got my feet wet in it." And he had said, "Honey, we'll fix that here and now." And though she had screamed protests she had still let him drag her into the slappy little waves, fully clothed. They had laughed. How they had laughed. War or no war, they had always been able to share laughter.

Margaret brought the same excitement to life. The new phone, sitting in its cradle in the hall, was in constant use. The television was only switched off each evening after the National Anthem had played sonorously to its end.

But first had come the swimming. Straight after Margaret had taken Harry Membury to stay with the Reverend Hobson back on the towans, she gave Lucy one of her "penny lectures".

"He's brought it all back to you, hasn't he, honey? OK, so we can't fix the cause. If only we could. But we can fix some things. We're going to get you to swim, Luce. Don't look like that. There's an indoor pool at the club, warm water, changing cubicles, everything just so. Nobody ever uses it in case it musses their make-up or hairdo, so we can have it to ourselves. And I will teach you to swim. And when you can swim, you will stop being frightened of the sea. I've gotten you a swimsuit for Christmas, bit previous but who cares. We'll start today." She let Lucy have ten seconds of protest then she said, "The car's parked outside. The club supplies towels. You look more than good enough — you come as my guest anyway."

Lucy was so grateful for Margaret's help with Harry Membury that she surrendered herself to the smell of chlorine, the unnatural blue of the water, the peculiar floats that Margaret rootled out from a nearby cupboard — in fact, everything that Margaret fixed during those first two weeks of December.

When the schools closed for Christmas there was a family day at the club and Margaret and Gussie took the Pardoes with them and they all played in the pool and then ate an enormous lunch in the restaurant.

Barbara said dramatically, "I will never forget this day."

Denny said, "I wish we could have brought Mark and Matthew with us."

Ellie said, "We'll miss you. But it's lovely for you to go home for Christmas."

Gussie said, "When we start school again, Dad and Mom and me will have been in England a whole year. I'll always remember how you talked to me that first day, Ellie. You told me your brother had been half American . . . d'you remember?"

Ellie remembered. Christmas 1960 had been terrible; the first without Egg. Meeting Gussie Trip in January 1961 had been the first good thing about Truro, about school, about everything really.

Lucy said, "We'll all miss you. But we'll look after Tad and switch the heating on and off and water the plants."

"And come here every day for a swim. You're members now. And there's a bus goes from the quay at nine every morning. I want you to make friends with the water. All of you. We go home at Easter and for a month in the summer, but when we're here I want you to take Gus and me to your famous towans. I want to swim in the sea. I want all of us to swim in the sea."

Denny clapped her hands. Barbara and Ellie glanced doubtfully at their mother. Lucy said nothing. Three of her family had been taken by the sea; Margaret had no idea what she was asking.

But Truro was lonely without the Trips. They made full use of the pool at the club, though it meant two bus rides there and two back. But they all became expert swimmers and Lucy began to think seriously of swimming in the sea and perhaps breaking some kind of bad luck. The other thing she did, almost religiously, was to trudge up the hill in the mornings and evenings to feed Tad the cat and switch the heating on and off. The "plants" consisted of two fancy pots containing berried shrubs. She asked one of the women at the pool about them and was told they were probably some sort of berberis.

"Ah," she said, nodding. "They do look like the wild stuff back home."

"You're interested in flowers?" The woman was encouraging her two boys to come out of the water.

"Not really. Vegetables now . . . there seems more point to growing vegetables. I had a garden back home."

The boys came to the edge and the woman lugged them out. "I've got an allotment. It's church property. But the council run quite a few allotment areas. You can put your name down for one."

When they got home Lucy told the girls about allotments. "When Margaret comes back, I'll ask her to take me to the council offices. My New Year resolution." She grinned at them.

Ellie was thrilled. "It would be like back home. Let's go to the office this afternoon, Ma! Please. I know where it is. It comes under Estates. We went with the school for citizenship. They're nice."

Ellie won the day and by the time the Trips returned they had been allocated a couple of acres of land within walking distance of the house. Margaret seemed strangely unimpressed by it all.

"Are you regressing, Lucy Pardoe?"

"Regress . . . what do you mean?" Lucy asked. "Are you put out about the allotment?"

"Of course I'm not put out — as you call it — by the allotment! For goodness' sake, I'm a country girl myself, honey. I'm going to buy a hoe and work alongside you. It's just that . . . I wanted to fix something back home and I couldn't. Sorry."

Lucy thought that probably Margaret would tell her about the one thing she could not "fix" and why she was apologetic about it. But she did not and it was soon forgotten.

270

That spring of 1962 they worked like the country girls they were, preparing the sandy soil and planting salad vegetables, potatoes, purple sprouting broccoli and some very early kidney beans. They walked from Steep Street most mornings and after a week or so Matthew and Mark fell in behind them and spent sunny days in the shade of some ancient gooseberry bushes and damp ones in the warm wooden shed hung with tools, skeins of raffia and bags of flower pots. Margaret had to persuade Tad to join them, but once he had actually caught a field mouse hiding in the potato bag he decided to make regular visits. Their picture appeared in the *Cornishman*, too small for them to be identified, captioned "*The Pied Pipers of Truro*". Marvin called them the Cat Women.

It was a lovely spring and brought an influx of visitors, some regulars armed with notebooks and cameras as they walked the wide central aisle of the cathedral and pottered around the quay area or took the ferry down to Falmouth and St Mawes, others more exotic. They were nearly all young people, not all English by any means. A lot of them carried guitars over one shoulder and some had small children in hammock contraptions on their backs. They had a motto and voiced it to anyone who caught their eyes. "Peace, man," they would say, whether you were man or woman. A few of them had obviously seen the newspaper picture of the two women and their cats and thought they might be twin souls; they picketed the allotment sites and were at the gate when Margaret and Lucy were going home in a hurry to meet the girls from school.

"Hey!"

Lucy registered the American accent, looked round from checking on the cats and smiled. "Hey yourself," she responded — just as Margaret so often did.

"You the ladies with the cats?"

Matthew and Mark and then Tad joined them sideways on, interested as always in new people. They groomed themselves on bleached jeans and brown legs. Lucy's smile widened. "As you see," she replied.

Margaret gathered Tad into her arms. "We have to go, honey. School's out in ten minutes."

Lucy sensed her distrust of these people and looked at them anew. There were two girls and three boys, all bone thin but fit enough apparently; they had long hair over their shoulders, and were carrying sheaves of lilac. There was something very childlike about the five of them, standing there covered in flowers. She had seen them gathered down on the quay when she did her shopping; they had made some kind of camp by the river and if the wind was in the right direction she heard them singing when she put Denny and Barbara to bed. They were clean and they did not beg so why was Margaret so unusually cautious?

The girls were passing them sprays of lilac, glorious thick white blossoms like random clumps of snow. Margaret tried to avoid them but still landed up with two sprays in her trug. Lucy gathered them to her and inhaled the strange but intensely nostalgic fragrance with closed eyes. It took her back, as scents do.

To Devon — of course. It had been lilac time when she started dating Bertie McKinley. But it took her

272

beyond Devon, beyond the happiness of Bertie and then Egg and then Daniel and the girls. It took her through the unhappiness of her mother's early death. Another time; a time of childhood, a time of real innocence when her mother had taken her out every day, rain or shine, to work on the farm and to look and look and look at every small thing about her and see their vital importance to the enormous whole of the world. Her mother had identified times and seasons by the flowers. "Holly time". "Snowdrop time". "Primrose time". And eventually, every year, lilac time had arrived. With this scent, these prolific flower heads.

Margaret said, "Come on, Luce. They've cleared off. We'd better put a move on — we'll have to throw this stuff in the bin."

"No!" Lucy could barely see over the flower heads. "No. I've got those old cider jars of Daniel's — we can share the flowers."

Margaret was astonished. "They grow like weeds, honey. If I'd known you liked them so much I could have cut some in my own backyard."

Their arrival at the school gate caused some amusement; others had been accosted but had shrugged away from the flowers. It seemed that the Flower People had decided today was the day to share their peculiar euphoria.

Lucy led the way into the cool house on Steep Street, fetched half a dozen of Daniel's old cider jars and let the girls arrange the flowers. Margaret had to admit they were beautiful.

"I haven't remembered my early childhood for years. It must have been the scent of the lilac. Once my mother died, life was quite different. No beauty, no wonderful smells." Lucy carried the jars into the hall and stood them along the wall all the way to the front door. "Ellie and Gus will wonder what has hit them when they come in." She looked at Margaret. "Why were you so against those children — they were no trouble, were they?"

"They're not really children. You see them all the time at home. And no, I guess they're no trouble, not really. Free love, free speech, that kinda thing. There's something very attractive about them. They share everything, nobody starves. They sing their songs and write their poems." She sighed sharply. "Gus thinks it's all marvellous. But they use a drug, they call it a psychedelic drug. Mostly it's all right. But some of them . . ." She bit her lip and looked towards the kitchen, where Barbara and Denny were still dealing with the lilac. "We've got friends in San Francisco. One of their boys, just sixteen, went to one of the concerts and must have taken a pill. Thought he could fly and he tried it. Off the Golden Gate."

"He . . . died?"

"Yeah. We didn't tell Gus. I think we should but Marvin says no."

"Oh. Dear Lord. This happened at Easter — when you were home?"

Margaret nodded. "We're pretty raw about it. Thought we were coming back here to the sort of simplicity that you and me have got, Luce. Then I see these kids wandering around Cornwall — of all places — in all weathers, obviously taking some drug or other because they're not living in this world, that's for sure."

She stopped speaking because Ellie and Gus came through the front door into the hall and stopped in amazement as they saw and smelled the bower of lilacs.

Gus was delighted. "Ma! You've become a Flower Person!"

Ellie closed her eyes. "This is how heaven will smell."

"We did it — we did it!" Barbara and Denny erupted from the kitchen. Barbara said, "Mum got all Daddy's old cider jars and filled them with water and I cut the ends off like what she showed me and Denny put them in." The older girls praised them extravagantly and Margaret looked helplessly at Lucy and shrugged.

That night, Matthew Hobson phoned Lucy. He sounded odd. Once when Daniel had rescued an amateur diver whose airline had blocked, she had heard that sort of voice. Then it could have been due to an attack of the bends; but also from inhaling helium.

He said, "Lucy. Sorry to bother you. Thought you should know. Harry has not come home for two nights." He gave a small giggle. "He's not tied to me, of course, but he hasn't taken his stuff so he is expecting to be back."

"You think he will come here?" The girls were in bed and Lucy was getting ready to go upstairs herself. She glanced at the door to check both locks.

"Possibly. Though I would think he would have arrived by now."

"Not if he was walking."

"Well . . . he left here on Wednesday morning and it's Friday now."

Lucy felt her heart lift. She had not realized she was anxious for Harry. "In that case it could be that he has gone home. Oh, I do hope so."

"Yes . . . he has become part of this Flower Power thing. I don't know whether you have any of their groups in Truro. There's a large contingent camping just beyond the cove."

"The cove?" The usual thing happened to her heart; it must actually skip a beat, she thought, just like the novelists and poets told you.

"They walk across the bay at low tide and make camp fires in the dunes beyond the towans. No harm in them, not really. They could be a danger to themselves and . . . perhaps . . . Harry Membury."

"How? In what way?"

"He is caught up with some of their ideology. Freedom in all things. And he's been eating some fungi stuff which he says heightens his perception. It's the air down here, well known for being exceptionally clear. Artists can't keep away . . ."

She looked along the hallway at the lilac, almost fluorescent in the glow from the street lamp streaming through the door light. She nodded, understanding.

"Is it dangerous?" she asked.

"It depends. Doc Carthew does not care for it. But then he's quite narrow-minded when it comes to looking after the human body."

"Yes. So you're not worried about Mr Membury?"

"Oh for goodness' sake, Lucy, call him Harry, not Mr Membury! This is one of the good things about the Flower People, their complete informality. Harry told me that they rename themselves in a ritual baptism in the sea. One of the girls is called Sunrise and another Sunset." He paused and then said in a more controlled voice, "I'm not worried for you. I don't think he will ever harm a hair of your head. But I do worry about him if he's thrown up his job and gone on the road with some of these people. I thought he was doing rather well." He cleared his throat and said, "It would be excellent if he has gone back to his family, of course. Thought I'd better put you in the picture." He put down his receiver and Lucy was left holding hers for a moment of uncertainty. He had not asked after the girls. And he had not mentioned the fact that it was nearly two years since the sea had taken Egg.

The next day was Saturday and she and Margaret took their children to swim in the pool. "I quite thought I would be driving you to your wonderful towans this summer," Margaret mourned as they ate lunch in the restaurant. "Why don't you all go over and see that lovely vicar of yours while we're in the States?"

Lucy felt surprised but not shocked. She had assumed that she would never go back to Hayle, just as she had never gone back to Devon. It had been her mother's belief that there was "no going back". She had stated it sadly but then hugged Lucy and added, "Why would I want to go back when I've got you?" But this was different. She would be visiting her local priest, tending her son's grave . . .

She said, "We could do." She looked at Ellie, who nodded enthusiastically. Barbara said, "Can we take Matthew and Mark?" And when their mother shook her head the younger girls shook theirs back.

Margaret said, "Listen. We don't go back home till next week. You two bring the cats and come up to us for the day tomorrow. Let Ellie and Mom go see the vicar. How would that be?"

The girls clapped their hands. It was, as Margaret said, fixed.

Lucy telephoned Matthew Hobson. There was no news of Harry — she remembered to call him Harry — and the doc had been round and told Matthew that both he and his lodger had probably been on a diet of magic mushrooms for the past few weeks and were unfit for duty. "It did not occur to me that I was eating the blessed things, but, of course, as Harry was cooking supper I was having what he was having. Do I sound strange to you, Lucy?"

"No, but your voice was different last night. Sort of . . . hysterical." She had never spoken to a priest so familiarly before. She bit her lip and added, "Sorry, reverend."

"Please call me Matthew. I was — and am — quite worried about Harry. I telephoned Farmer Roach this morning and there was no reply. I drove over immediately and the cows were going crazy to be milked. I let the Godolphin cowman know that there's

278

no one around. He told me that when Roach starts drinking he can disappear for days at a time. He'll see to the cattle. He hadn't seen Harry for a week but that's not unusual."

Lucy said, "Did you say Farmer Roach?"

"Yes." There was a pause then Matthew said, "Lucy. I'm sorry. Josh told me that Roach is your father. I had forgotten." He tried to laugh. "Those mushrooms really are magic."

"Yes." Lucy stared at the lilacs. "Ellie and me are coming over on the bus tomorrow. We were thinking of coming to Matins but perhaps Ellie can do that while I go out to the farm."

"We'll all go. I'll drive us. I've got a different car and it hardly ever breaks down. I'll fetch you after the early Eucharist and we'll go straight there."

Lucy said carefully, "I'd rather go alone."

Another pause. Matthew said, "All right." He cleared his throat. "Will it be all right, Lucy? Will you be all right? I understand that your father can become violent . . . on occasion."

"I will be all right, Matthew."

She put the phone down and stood very still in the lamp-lit hall. Then she went into the kitchen and opened the dresser drawer where she kept bits of string and plastic bags; she took a key from the muddle and pocketed it. Then she packed bread and cheese and a bottle of water. And the carving knife.

CHAPTER
THIRTEEN

Gussie came down for Barbara, Denny and the cats at eight o'clock the next morning. The weather had changed and there was a nasty little wind blowing down Steep Street. Already the piercing whiteness of the lilacs in the hall was dimmed; one enormous fondant was brown on the edges. Lucy and Ellie, standing on the step to wave to the girls as if they were off to America, were both conscious of the weather, as they always had been when they lived on the towans.

They went down to the quay and caught the early bus to Penzance; it wound its way through all the villages en route: Redruth, a loop to Portreath and Camborne. They got off on the edge of Connor Downs before it reached Hayle; from there they could walk across to the first of the sand dunes and drop down to the towans and St Petroc's.

They stood above the church and the sea and looked down to where Pardoe Cottage had nested in the scrubby land. It had gone. The garden had gone. The beans and the arthritic apple trees in the orchard were all part of the sandy landscape. Where the gate opened on to the lane down to the beach, a large digger sat waiting for the morning and its operator. They were levelling an enormous area bounded by the phone box, the church, and the cluster of cottages that included Chippy's workshop, then the single street with its offshoots which comprised the hamlet. Already a new shop had opened and though it was Sunday its front was bedecked with beach shoes, buckets and spades and fishing nets.

"Oh Ma . . ." Ellie took Lucy's arm, distressed. "It's as if we never were here. Daddy's lovely bathroom . . . the bean plot . . . We let them kill our home!"

Lucy put her arms around her daughter and held her tightly, taking as well as giving comfort. Ellie understood that and responded quickly. "It wasn't us, was it? Not really. Chippy would have turned us out and sold the cottage anyway."

Lucy nodded against Ellie's dark hair. She dared not speak. It was nobody's fault. Even if Egg had been with them, he could not have saved Daniel's cottage.

After a moment they started to walk down towards the church. Matthew came to meet them, holding out his arms in welcome.

"Ten o'clock. Time for a cup of tea before Matins. Ah . . . Ellie. Dear girl. Don't cry . . . I do understand how you feel. Your home razed to the ground. But as long as I am in the rectory you still have a home at the towans." He looked at Lucy. "I mean that, Lucy. You will always be welcome here."

She nodded, still unable to speak. They walked slowly back to the rectory, through the churchyard with its leaning stones and the old iron gate that squealed so horribly and into the chilly shelter of the house.

Matthew took them straight through to the kitchen, lit the gas oven and left the door open as he had seen her do, then put the kettle on the hob. A line of socks hung across the window. Towels were draped over the rack above the cooker. He apologized.

"I miss Harry in more ways than one," he admitted. "He kept the fire going in the living room, well damped down but it warmed the house. He brought food in too." He laughed. "I don't think either of us realized that the mushrooms were hallucinogenic." He shook his head. "I think I've got them out of my system now — do I sound normal?"

Ellie looked more cheerful. "Some of the Flower People who are camped outside Truro are high all the time on them. You don't sound like them so you must be all right."

"High?" Lucy asked, surprised because Ellie spoke of the Flower People so casually, so familiarly.

"It's how they describe it, Ma. It means they are transcendent — above all normal constraints and what-have-you. Gussie explained it all — it happened in America first so she's the expert."

Matthew poured tea and produced a packet of biscuits. "It worries our good doctor. People do strange and dangerous things under the influence of drugs."

Ellie sipped. "What sort of things?"

"Well, Carthew had heard of a case at Hell's Mouth. Someone thought they could fly . . . luckily they went into the sea and the inshore boat went out and got them."

Ellie nodded seriously. "That happened to someone Gus knows."

It was another shock for Lucy. Margaret thought she and Marvin had shielded Gus from the awful tragedy that had befallen their friends in San Francisco, but Gus must know for Ellie to know. Lucy said fearfully, "Do you think Harry Membury has done something stupid?"

"I have no idea." Matthew looked from one to the other. "He is caught up with the young people who are camped in the dunes and could well have thrown in his lot with them. The farmhouse is properly locked up but no one was there. Nor in the sheds. No sign of him. And your father has gone too, Lucy."

Ellie was shocked. Lucy said, "Apparently Mr Membury got a job at Roach's farm, Ellie. Ezekiel Roach is my father."

"I thought — I thought — Ma, why didn't you tell us?"

"You thought he was dead. He was to me. And to your father." She glanced at Ellie. "He is not a good man, Ellie. Daddy was afraid he might harm Egg."

Ellie put her hands to her face. Over them her eyes were enormous.

Lucy sipped her tea, trying to make the situation unusual rather than horrific. Why had it not occurred to her that her own children did not know about their grandfather? Did she imagine that they had just picked up the information at school and never asked questions about it?

She said, "Most of the time he is just a dour man, unhappy, I suppose. But on Saturdays he gets drunk." She drew a breath and said woodenly, "That's when he hurts people."

Ellie made a sound. Matthew put a hand on her arm. "He won't have hurt Harry. Harry has grown strong since Christmas when he came looking for you. Before he got this job he walked miles every day. Josh took him out in the boat now and then and he'd come back with mackerel and crabs . . . He worked in the rectory garden and we had cabbage. And then, four weeks ago, he found this job and part of the pay was in kind. Vegetables mostly. Milk and eggs." He grinned. "And of course the famous mushrooms!" He laughed and at last so did Ellie.

She said, still anxious, "But he wouldn't have just gone off without telling you, would he?"

"If he'd had enough of those damned mushrooms he might have done anything! But he would not have let Farmer Roach hurt him."

Lucy said nothing and Matthew turned to her. "I must be getting over to the church for eleven o'clock. If you really want to look around the area I suppose there's no harm in it. It was, after all, Saturday yesterday, so I suppose your father will be sleeping it off somewhere."

Lucy knew where he would be; there was a house on the road between Camborne and Redruth, just north of Lytton village. Ezekiel Roach had been thrown out of it times without number but he was always taken back in, eventually.

Matthew said, "Josh will come with you, Lucy. Then Carthew has invited all of us to lunch there. He says his housekeeper needs the practice. He eats at four. And I will take you home at seven. Is that all right?"

In the face of Ellie's sheer bewilderment Lucy did not want to object, but she had never eaten at Dr Carthew's table. "Is Josh coming too?"

"Of course."

"Then . . ." She smiled at Ellie. "We will be delighted to accept the doctor's kind invitation."

"But Mom." Ellie occasionally used Gus's word for her mother. "I ought to come with you . . . perhaps?"

Lucy smiled and nodded slightly. "One day. Of course. But let me try to find out what is happening at the farm first. Stay with the reverend. Enjoy the service like you used to. I'll try to get some news of Mr Membury."

Ellie, biddable as always, nodded. Lucy hated the lost expression in those brown eyes. Daniel's eyes had been blue but there had been times when they looked just like Ellie's looked now. She should have made some kind of statement — years ago — about the farm and the man who lived in it. Simply "Your grandfather lives four miles up the coast. He is a farmer, but he would rather live on his own." That would have done it. Except that there would have been questions. She never wanted to have to say, "He killed my mother and he tried to kill Egg and me." Because if that was true why wasn't he in prison at this very moment?

Josh arrived and tucked her into his familiar old car. She tried to thank him; it would have taken her most of the day to walk there and back. Josh, never quite easy in her company, said that it gave them chance for a chat, then after asking about the family he could think of nothing else to say and neither could she. They became silent until they turned down the lane on the edge of the Godolphin Estate, when they both commented on the wealth of cow parsley which was brushing the car on both sides. Lucy, who was becoming more and more nervous as they got closer to the old farm, started to ask what they would do if they met something coming towards them and Josh said at exactly that moment, "Let's 'ope we dun't meet nothing down 'ere." They laughed.

The gate on which Lucy's mother had swung her so long ago hung from one hinge and was roped closed. Josh pulled the car in tight and switched off.

"Looks like we got to climb over," he said.

"Stay 'ere, Josh. Please. I know where 'e is and it's not in these parts."

"Aye." Josh spoke heavily. He knew about Lytton too and looked at her as she gathered up her bag. "Why you coming zackly? We've looked for that Harry Membury. 'E en't 'ere, my girl. 'Tis all locked up and deserted."

"I hope he isn't here." She looked at her husband's friend. She almost told him; some scrap of loyalty stopped her. "I don't know why I'm here. Perhaps just to look at the place again. I don't know. Will you wait here for me? I might be half an hour. Not much longer."

"I'll be 'ere. Give us a shout if you need me."

She clambered over the gate and felt in her pocket for the key. The track, heavily rutted, took a right angle not far from the gate and the car was out of sight. She held the key in her right hand and felt with her left for the reassurance of the carving knife. She knew she was being ridiculous; if Ezekiel Roach had killed Harry Membury he would be on the run. And if he hadn't then he was at the Lytton house. Her father was predictable; she had known when she begged him to call Dr Carthew that he would not. He must have thought she was already dead when he went for him that last terrible night before Egg finally arrived.

Another bend in the thick hedge and there was the house. It was low-ceilinged and squat; the windows squinted at her in the pallid light. She knocked and called before using the key. If he was home he would rip open the door and ask her what she bloody well wanted after all this time. The house offered no response. She put the key in the door and turned it with difficulty. She went inside, already feeling sick with the blind terror she knew so well. Her sixth sense told her he was not there but she could not control her breathing or the body-shaking thump of her heart. She muttered, "Dan . . . stay with me now."

She moved cautiously down the narrow passageway towards the kitchen. The smell was heavier, more familiar the further she went. All the doors were open; on the left, next to the kitchen, was the dairy. It was clean. She peered in; a trug of fast-withering cauliflower stood on one of the churns. She stared at it. Harry

Membury was the only one who could have left it there.

It didn't mean anything. But the nausea deepened with dread.

There were other signs of his presence in the old parlour on the other side of the hall: a khaki linen milking smock was over a chair. She picked it up and then put it down quickly. It could have been mud but she knew the dark stains were blood. She closed her eyes and swallowed hard. She almost ran back outside and shouted for Josh but then had to sit down quickly and stay very still. When she thought she was in control of herself again, she put a hand on the smock. She said quietly, "If you have killed him in the same way as you killed my mother, I swear I will do the same to you."

And then she got up, went into the kitchen, put her bag on the cluttered draining board and looked carefully around. If she was looking for signs of a struggle she did not see it and did not look for long. In her mind she could hear that dreaded voice again and again: "Get down into the cellar, miss! Wait for me there. Don't show your face up here again!" She could hear the bolts shot across, she could taste the darkness, feel the sponginess of the wooden steps which would surely give beneath her one day, feel too the weight of guilt. He told her constantly that she was the cause of all his troubles. She could not cook, sew, milk the animals, do anything like her mother did. Everything was her fault and one day she would pay for that.

Sometimes she was five minutes on her own in the cellar. Other times, much much longer. Her release depended on how urgently he needed to punish her. If he decided to go to the Lytton house immediately, it might be days before he came home and remembered that she was due for a beating. Once, not long after it started, she managed to articulate sufficiently to beg him to beat her immediately. He told her to stop whining. "Your mother always kept her trap shut!" he said before he pushed her through the door. That was how she had learned that her mother had taken — absorbed — his treatment to shield her daughter.

Outside the wind had got up and suddenly, shockingly, the door banged. Lucy leaped up and went to the window; the door banged again. She crossed the kitchen and looked down the passage. No one was there, the door swung open and shut like a pendulum. She ran down, took out the key, closed it and locked it.

Then she checked the rooms properly: the parlour, the dairy again, the kitchen. She went upstairs and looked into the two bedrooms. Nothing. The beds were made. Perhaps he no longer slept upstairs.

She went back down and stood in front of the cellar door. At last she reached up and shot the top bolt, then the bottom. Then pushed the door open. The smell was appalling. She choked, closed the door and wrapped her silk scarf around her nose and mouth. Then she fetched the torch and opened the door again. The cellar was the size of the house but she did not have to look very far. The spongy treads had at last given way. Harry lay in a crumpled heap on the floor beneath them.

He was not dead though Lucy had been certain that he was. He had fallen on his right side; the arm and leg that side were both broken. He was dehydrated and there wasn't much of a pulse but the nurse who talked to Lucy and Josh at the hospital in Penzance assured them that they had done all the right things and he stood a good chance of a full recovery.

Josh had run to meet Lucy and they had driven to Godolphin Home Farm and telephoned for an ambulance. The estate manager had promised that the Roach animals would be properly looked after. "Roach is a funny chap," he said, "but he's a good farmer. Cares for the animals. Gets on better with them than he does with people. And that chap he took on was the same. Born to it, I suppose. Any idea where Roach might have gone?" Lucy said nothing. She was so thankful that Josh had said Harry was breathing, she did not care whether her father was alive or dead.

Josh went back with the ambulance and the men cut the padlock and bumped over the rutty track without comment. Harry became conscious as they lifted him on to a stretcher and moaned; Josh was thankful that Lucy had waited at Home Farm. They followed the ambulance and then the stretcher and while Lucy drank tea from a cardboard cup, Josh made another telephone call to the rectory.

Matthew said, "What am I to say to Ellie?"

Josh frowned at the receiver. "Tell her the truth. The steps to the cellar broke and Harry Membury fell on to the stone floor and broke his arm and his leg."

"What about her grandfather?"

"He's disappeared. The police are going to be talking to Mrs Pardoe before long. But I don't think we shall see him again. He might have got away with beating his wife to death. Probably din't have anything to do with Harry's fall. But he'll be made to pay for it at last, thank God."

Matthew was shocked by Josh's grim tone. But all he said was "What about our meal down at the surgery?"

"For goodness' sake, reverend." Josh was reminded of his days as an air-raid warden. "Use your initiative!" He put the phone down with a definite click.

When they saw Harry next, he was connected to a saline drip, his leg was in a sling higher than his body and his arm was splinted at an angle to his shoulder. He looked like a cartoon of a man who had fallen downstairs.

The most important thing was that he was conscious.

"Sister says I am a non-walking miracle." He spoke in a strange grating whisper.

"She also says you must not talk." Sister appeared and smiled at everyone at once. "Mr Membury has had a bad experience. He will need time and careful nursing."

Harry gritted, "Matthew won't be able to manage. He's not very domesticated."

"You will be nursed here, Mr Membury. Now, no more talking." She addressed herself to Josh. "I rather think it might be difficult for my patient *not* to talk. Perhaps you could visit him tomorrow when he will have had a good night's sleep and plenty of liquids."

They were ushered outside and told that Harry might be worse before he was better. "He has probably gone over eight hours without fluid. And his body is in shock from the fall and consequent fractures. I have the Reverend Hobson's telephone number and will keep in touch."

They were dismissed.

Lucy huddled into the passenger seat of the car, her head down.

Josh said, "I think it's over now, my girl. For good."

Lucy was silent, shivering slightly. She saw from the dashboard clock that it was just gone five but the sky was darkening for a storm and so much had happened it seemed like night time.

They turned on to the A30 and Josh said in a low voice, "Thank the good Lord that Daniel got you out of that place afore anything could 'appen to Egg."

She wanted to say that it had happened to Egg anyway and the good Lord hadn't done much about it then. She bunched herself against the shivering and said nothing. They were driving through Hayle before Josh spoke again.

"We'll go straight to the doc's house. Is that all right? I think your Ellie and the reverend will be there and if not I can fetch them. We need some food, my girl, and we know there's plenty there."

She moved one of her arms, pulling it from around her body and on to the seat. She pushed herself upright. "I have to get home. My friend is looking after the girls. I have to get back."

"We can telephone her perhaps?"

"Yes. She has got a telephone. And she has got the rectory phone number."

"Good." He turned off towards the sea and the towans. "You were right to come. You saved 'is life. It were as if you knew . . ." He glanced sideways. "Did you know?"

She met his eyes for a moment, then stared through the windscreen as they came to the first of the houses. "Harry Membury is a fool. But he didn't deserve what he got. I din't save 'is life. Those steps breaking . . . that's what saved 'im. My father pushed 'im, saw 'im go, thought 'e'd killed 'im. An' 'e ran. 'E couldn't a got away with it this time. Like you said back there, 'e's paying for my mother's death."

"But if you 'adn't 've followed it up, Harry woulda died."

She shrugged. "I thought 'e might be dead already. When I went back from Devon Faither said 'e'd get rid of the baby for me, beat me right 'ard and put me down there and bolted the door. Left me for a week."

"Oh Christ . . ." Josh gripped the wheel. Even so, the car veered into the hedge surrounding the doctor's house and surgery.

Lucy appeared not to notice their abrupt arrival. "That's 'ow 'e did it. People wondered why I stayed. I were too weak to do anything else. Dr Carthew saved Egg, saved me. 'Im and Daniel between 'em. Got me into the maternity hospital."

The car ticked as the engine cooled; Josh breathed hard as if he had been running. At last he said, "You

293

made up for it, girl. You 'ad the best marriage I've seen."

"Short."

He looked at her. There were tears in her eyes. He said, "But sweet."

She nodded. "Every day were sweet, Josh. We made it so. Harry Membury dun't understand that."

"No. Well . . . 'e's a foreigner, remember."

"Aye."

The front door opened and John Carthew, Matthew Hobson and Ellie came down the drive. Josh reversed the car out of the hedge and they went inside. Ellie hung on to her mother on one side, and on the other the doctor put an arm around her shoulders. "It really has ended now, Lucy," he said into her ear. "His body was found by one of those flower folk. Put 'em off their swim, I reckon."

She looked up at him and started to laugh. She knew it was hysteria but it came from relief. She reached into her bag and withdrew the carving knife and put it on the table. They all stared at it and stopped laughing.

She said, "Saves me a job, dun't it?" She looked at Ellie and Ellie looked back. It was as if in a few seconds they had complete communion.

Ellie hugged her and said, "Come and have something to eat, Ma."

They went through into the dining room where the long table was laid beautifully. The housekeeper poked her head through a very modern hatch and said, "Are you ready for me to dish up now, doctor? It's all shrivelled, of course, but I've done my best."

"Bring it on, Mrs Kervis. Your best is better than most!"

They sat down. Beneath the tablecloth Ellie and Lucy held hands. They both had a sense of Egg standing behind them and looked round at the same time. No one was there. But they smiled at each other, understanding.

CHAPTER
FOURTEEN

At first Greta was enamoured of Connie's idea. She believed in the dream, especially as one of the few things she knew about her husband was that he came from Brighton. But if it hadn't been for that creased black and white snap of her wedding day, she would not have remembered what he looked like. And if she hadn't got that job at the Windmill she would not have even been in London. He had told her one of the things he loved about her was her Brummie accent. She had been offended — what about the elocution lessons she'd paid for? Anyway, she was an actress and could do any accent. Her favourite was Greta Garbo, of course.

He had laughed and tried to kiss her and she had said, "Get off!" and he had said triumphantly, "There! See what I mean? Say it again — go on!" And she had said it again. And again. And ended up laughing as usual. She had realized later that he might not even have singled her out from the other chorus girls if she had had a London accent. It was all . . . everything up to that point . . . was all about being in the right place at the right time. They were meant for each other.

But then he had gone. Without a word. It had taken her years to believe in his death. She realized now that she had been waiting for him still. It was to rid herself of that particular albatross that she was now engaged to Archie Fielding. It had sounded so darned *sensible* when Archie said, "For God's sake, Greet. Marry me and let's be done with all this flirty-Gertie stuff. We're too old for it now." She had felt tired — so tired — of waiting and hardly ever getting work and consoling herself with Archie and others and being comforted by Arnie when they let her down. There was a sense of surrendering to fate. Why not marry Archie? She knew him through and through. She could manage his gambling and his drinking. And darling William had tied everything up so tightly that if she had to throw him out she would keep her flat and the nest egg her mother had left her. And there was this new job too. They were a small company, old-fashioned, struggling, her sort of people. The playwright was trying to put over a satire on the kitchen-sink era. The costumes were all dressing gowns in various stages of disrepair. She saw the point instantly and produced sketches; "Different but the same," she told the stage manager. "And we should have slippers likewise. Some tatty but sort of Turkish type for Miranda."

Greta felt a whole person again. All the dreadful acrimony with Archie was over and though he constantly grumbled because she put off the date of the wedding, he was still around, still waiting. She liked that. Secretly she liked keeping him on a string — no sex without marriage and no marriage just yet. She did not tell him why. She was in control and that was that.

But the crazy part of her, the romantic part of her, adored the idea of Connie looking for Maurice. She told the stage manager about it. The stage manager was called Lilian and lived with another woman. Greta had never understood such relationships but the theatrical world accepted all kinds of love and she was of the theatrical world. Lilian was very sympathetic but also cautious.

"Why the hell did he pop off like that straight after the bloody wedding?" she asked very directly. "Did he have another wife tucked away in Brighton?" There it was again. Brighton. First Connie and now Lilian. "God, you poor devil, you must have felt like that ghastly Gracie Fields song."

Memories started to return. "I did. I told people he'd been sent to Rangoon. Don't ask me why. It was awful. And actually, Lil, I think I loved him. Properly. Not just for the sex either. Properly."

"The *bastard!*" Lilian said, spitting the word venomously. "I'd tell that daft friend of yours to forget it. Let him stay in Rangoon where he bloody belongs!" She looked at Greta standing there, holding a portfolio almost as big as herself. "Christ, you've got talent — Roger thinks so too. Just be careful, girl."

Those few words of praise for Greta herself did wonders for her. And at the same time made her scared. If Roger — who never had a good word to say for any of them — actually thought she had talent, then she could go far. There would be no room for Maurice or any other upset he might cause her. And anyway, what with Arnie being so ill and the play, which was called *Sink and Swim*, everything was on hold until almost the end of February, when Connie sent a very short advertisement to the *Brighton Gazette* which said simply, *"Will Maurice Heatherington please get in touch. Box number . . ."* Connie's original message had run to twenty-five words but she saw William's point. Keep it short and simple and intriguing.

March and April went by and nothing came from Brighton. Arnie was out of hospital, the opening of *S and S*, as Roger bitterly called it, was in sight, Archie was less demanding and Greta suspected he was in temporary lodgings with another of his female clients. Connie's time was getting closer and she thought they ought to put in another advertisement offering an incentive. She gave Greta another slip of paper and asked her to think about it and let her know and she would do the rest.

Greta phoned Connie and went to see her the next Sunday. It was now May and the lilac trees were dripping blossom over the garden walls, though it was cold and rather damp. Connie answered the door herself. She was the size of a house.

"Is there room for me?" Greta teased, making a big thing of squeezing past Connie's enormous tummy. "You weren't like this with Frankie, were you?"

"No, I certainly wasn't. So it's got to be our girl. May. And she's going to be born in May. Only another two weeks, Greta! Get a new hat because you are in line for godmother this time."

Greta screamed with pleasure and got both her arms around Connie. Then the funniest thing happened. The baby — May — started giving funny little kicks and they transmitted themselves from Connie's abdomen to Greta's. Greta stood very still, mouth open, feeling what Connie was feeling.

Connie said, "OK, Heatherington — enough's enough!"

Greta did not let her go immediately. She whispered, "Connie, the baby is kicking . . . she is still kicking. And it *is* May. And she's going to be a champion swimmer."

Connie said feelingly, "Don't I know it! Now let me breathe."

Greta moved away but her face was still alight. "That is the closest I'll ever come to being pregnant. Oh Connie. Thank you." Suddenly she was in tears.

Connie comforted her as best she could. She and Greta had become very close since Connie had first asked her permission to put the advertisement in the *Brighton Gazette*. Greta had been wide-eyed when she heard of Connie's dream; she believed absolutely in signs and portents and dreams came very much into the category. Now, with eight or nine weeks since that cryptic little message had been published, Connie was feeling somehow responsible for those tears.

"Darling Greta. Please don't get upset. William has agreed to let Arnold take over the advertising thing and we're going to go and see him — yes, now, darling. Well, I know he's still resting but I rather think he is also in need of a bit of stimulation. Let's get him interested in something really important."

Greta appreciated that. She appreciated Connie. She often referred sentimentally to their first meeting at Mrs Pentwyn's horrible guest house. "D'you remember that dreadful vegetarian lot? I know you don't want to think about that time, sweetie, but if you could just see parts of it as . . . amusing? . . . I think it also might become bearable. That's what I do."

Connie had made an effort. "Yes, perhaps. Anyway that was when I met Maurice for the first time and I am determined it won't be the last!"

Greta was bewildered for a moment then said, "Oh, the *photograph*! You can hardly decipher him."

"Well, I know darned well it was him in my dream. So my subconscious must have deciphered him all right!"

The four of them, Connie, William, Frankie and Greta, drove up to Barnt Green where Arnold was blissfully ensconced with Rosemary. He had a day bed in the window which overlooked the golf course, from where he was watching Marcus Challenger teaching Maria how to hold a club so that it did not fly out of her hands.

"He hasn't even got round to using a ball yet!" he marvelled. "He *must* be in love with her. Otherwise he wouldn't be out there in this wind being so patient and — and — *kind*!"

"How are you, Arnold?" William spoke first and waited while Arnold was kissed by Connie and Greta, before shaking his hand.

Rosemary, joggling Frankie on her hip, got in first. "Terrible," she said, smiling all over her face. "Lying there all day demanding food and — and —" he started to speak and she said loudly, "entertainment!"

"She means the television of course." His eyes rolled in his head; he looked so happy Greta thought she might start crying again.

They had coffee and cake and then William went to the village shop for six tins of soup for lunch. He had suggested fish and chips and Rosemary had shaken her head so that William could not see her and said, "It's Sunday, darling. But the shop will be open till midday. How about some soup and rolls? See what they've got, William. In fact, I'll come with you and we can choose between us."

Nobody offered suggestions. Everyone knew that fish and chips were not on Arnold's menu. He said contentedly, "She usually gives me a dry biscuit and some of that ghastly cottage cheese."

"You look very well on it, Arnie," Greta said. Sometimes she felt her heart literally swelling with love for Arnie and wondered whether she should be marrying him instead of Archie. And then wondered whether it would swell for Maurice. When Connie had shown her the advert she thought it had then. But now, after so long and with so many things happening in her life, she was not quite so sure she wanted it to be like that. When your heart swelled it was so difficult to be sensible any longer.

Settled with bowls of soup and hot rolls, William broached the subject, fully expecting back-up for his rejection. "I've told them that they cannot use the firm's name, Arnold. We need to build in an incentive without being so specific. Not that I think it will work but it can't do any harm." He read aloud, "*'Will Maurice Heatherington Esquire please get in touch with blah blah blah when he will hear something to his advantage.'* It's Victorian and typically melodramatic — worthy of Greta and Connie, you have to admit — but we can't have Jessup's name there."

Arnold thought about it. "What do you think, Greta?" he said at last.

"I don't know any more. We've been at this for so long now."

"Six little weeks?"

"More like nine or ten. And I still don't know. You have done this in good faith and I am grateful — for your concern. But . . . Archie is the devil I know. Maurice might be the devil I don't know."

"Listen, girl. Let's just put our telephone number in. Mrs Flowers will be back from Australia in two weeks — she can take the calls, tape record them if they sound at all credible. You can listen and make up your mind then. What do you say?"

"Oh Arnie . . . you're so clever."

"You don't have to sweet-talk me, Greta. You've got what you want."

"I'm not sweet-talking. I am really . . . touched. Everyone . . . sort of . . . cares."

Arnie took the slip of paper, changed it and then held on to it.

"William. Let me take this on. You're going to have a lot to cope with quite soon, by the look of things. And I . . . I'd like to get my hand in again."

Connie glanced at Greta and closed one eye. It was something she had picked up from the older woman. Sometimes it said everything.

That night before they slept, Arnold said casually, "Rosie, I know you're not keen on my friendship with Greta Heatherington but would you mind if I used your telephone number for that insertion?"

She said resignedly, "You can't let go, can you? You were the one who made her promise not to marry Archie Fielding until she'd given this search a go. And now you want to be the one to speak to Maurice Heatherington first."

"Darling, she's like a child. Hopeless and helpless."

"No, she's not. Not one bit. But you . . . you're a megalomaniac."

"You don't know what that means," he said, smiling into the velvet dark.

"I do. I looked it up."

"Then you know it describes you perfectly. No fish and chips indeed."

"Where are you going to get fish and chips on a Sunday, for goodness' sake?"

"Don't know," he said sleepily. "Go to sleep, beautiful soon-to-be wife."

"Love you," she murmured.

"Love you too."

The opening of *Sink and Swim* was a great success mainly because the small theatre was packed with family and friends. Arnold had booked the two front rows and spent a lot of time resurrecting friends and acquaintances to fill them. The rest of the company had done the same, except Roger. He swore he did not want anyone who knew him to see a gaggle of inept actors playing out something that was not amusing or meaningful, and the sooner it closed down the better for all concerned. "Waste of everyone's time," he said, skulking along the back of the auditorium and eyeing the full house with incredulity.

When the leading lady, Miranda, appeared having changed into an even tattier kimono and said to the audience, "I thought I would dress down for you, darlings," Arnold roared with laughter and led the clapping. Everyone followed suit, which gave Miranda time to do an impromptu parade, revealing cigarette burns and patches in the silk and escalating the appreciation to the limit. Roger put his head on the barrier and moaned, "Stop milking it, you stupid cow . . ." But Miranda was by no means stupid and she had at last got a handle on the satire. She realized in an instant that *Sink and Swim* might well introduce a very special new genre. The rest of the cast followed suit. Greta, acting as dresser for everyone, was delighted with the reports that came through. "My God, they absolutely love it, Greet! Your stuff is going down a treat!"

Afterwards, when they had a theatre supper in the pub next door, Miranda stood up and toasted Arnold. "I saw you clapping. I played that whole scene for you."

Rosemary groaned. "Here we go," she said to Connie in a low voice.

"Oh Mummy. You don't mind, not really. Do you?"

"Not one bit. It means he's getting better. It makes up for the fact that poor old Maurice is never going to be found, alive or dead. He wanted to produce him for Greta, like a rabbit out of a hat."

"Nothing so far?"

"Nothing."

Maria came in, twittering madly. It seemed that Marcus had parked his car in quite the wrong place and an ambulance had been unable to get through to respond to an emergency. "They've towed the car away somewhere and there will be a fine and perhaps a court appearance!" Maria was near tears.

Arnold reached up and took her hand. "We will take you home with us, dear friend and neighbour. Where is your intended now?"

"He is outside being told off. Oh Arnold, you are so kind. I really don't know how we would manage without you . . . but the gossip . . . just before our wedding."

"There will be twice as many pictures in the papers, dear girl. I wouldn't be surprised if it hit the nationals. You'll be so proud of those pictures later . . . so will Marcus. Fame is heady wine, Maria. Heady wine."

Rosemary said to Connie, "Here we go, yet again." She looked up at Maria. "He's had too much wine actually, Maria, but he's talking sense. Marcus won't mind the publicity one bit. Go and get him and have something to eat and then we'll leave. I want to get Arnold to bed fairly soon." And that really did bring the house down. And Rosemary, who at one time would have turned crimson from top to toe, simply looked at Arnold and said, "I mean it."

"I know you do, my love. I know."

That night May was born. Greta knew it was going to happen before Connie. She had griping pain right after the potted shrimps and ignored it but as the evening wore on it happened again and again and eventually she timed the pains and they became very regular. She moved her chair next to William's.

"Contractions every eight minutes," she gasped as one of them grabbed her right across her midriff.

"How do you mean?" William was letting himself enjoy the evening of careless euphoria.

"I'm having birth contractions." Greta put her hand on his knee. He winced. "I'm having them for Connie. When I felt May kicking inside my own body I told Connie it was as near as I could come to being pregnant. But it wasn't." She sucked in a huge breath and William closed his eyes as her fingers tried to prise off his kneecap. "Ask her . . . oh God . . . ask her how she is."

His eyes were watering. He turned to Connie on his other side.

"Greta says she's having your labour pains and we should go home."

Connie leaned forward and looked at Greta. Then she nodded. "I think we'd better."

She got the bed ready herself while William phoned the midwife. Greta sat in a chair next to the bed, holding her stomach and groaning now and then.

Frankie's babysitter shrugged her coat on in the hall and said to William, "She's not in labour, you know. Not a single pain has she had. That old girl's got indigestion and is putting it all into her head."

"Probably. See yourself out. Thanks very much." William replaced the receiver and sprinted up to Rosemary's room. They had moved downstairs just two weeks ago for just such a contingency as this. Rosemary was to have had their room and kept an ear open for Frankie. "The best laid plans . . ." William muttered as he took in the scene in the bedroom: Connie, large and unwieldy, flinging a rubber sheet over the mattress; Greta looking smaller than usual, clutching her abdomen and breathing in the exaggerated manner she had seen on television programmes.

He took over the bed. "If you're really up to it, put out the layette and that sterilized pack the midwife gave you and get into your nightie."

Connie looked surprised. "I didn't think you would set much store by this proxy set-up."

"Better safe than sorry."

Greta breathed out on a tiny scream. "Thank you, William. Tell him, Connie."

Connie told him as she undressed, folded her clothes into a neat pile and donned the flowing nightdress with the button-through bodice. "It was some sort of transferral," she said matter-of-factly as she slid into the fresh bed. "Towel, darling. Just underneath me." She stayed very still for a second then drew in her breath sharply. "Was that the door bell? I think it's going to be quick." She closed her eyes and when she opened them they were no longer seeing what was around her; her whole concentration was inside her own body. She closed her eyes again and said, "Thank you, Greta. Don't forget, this baby is half yours."

Greta looked surprised, then she stood up and went to the bed. "It's gone from me, Connie. It's yours now. God bless you, dearest girl."

Connie remembered very little of May's arrival. It was quite different from Frankie's. He had slid quietly and happily into the world, trusting his parents to do the right thing always. May came in three enormous bursts of energy, squinted suspiciously with her nothing-coloured eyes at the man and woman bending over her and yelled furiously. It was as well that they did not know then that it would be a year before they had a full night's sleep.

If Rosemary and Arnold had needed more reassurance about the wisdom of Maria marrying the Reverend Marcus Challenger, they had it that night. Marcus was in a foul mood; he sat in the back of Arnold's car as far from Maria as he could get and studiously avoided all reference to their parking problems but gave a concise and vitriolic review of *Sink and Swim*.

"It was salacious. What they are calling soft porn, I believe. Heaven knows what hard porn is like."

"I think it's when they enact the sexual act on the stage," Maria said helpfully.

"That is called simulated sex, Maria. It would be impossible to do more than represent the act in full view of the public."

"Oh, but it does happen. Before she was taken so ill, Mrs Heatherington was telling me about it. They have to sort of gird themselves up to it before they come on stage."

Marcus was silent, considering this. Maria said, "I just loved Greta's dressing gowns, didn't you, darling? That silky one that was so damaged — it reminded me of the one you bought for me. Just before we became engaged. Not that it was damaged." She giggled. "Not until later anyway."

"Maria!" he cautioned.

But Maria had had three glasses of wine and was unstoppable. "You were reading one of my romantic novels. You called it a bodice-ripper and said that the term was ridiculous because no self-respecting garment could be demolished so easily. And you experimented on the dressing gown." She was convulsed with giggles.

He was silent and Arnold called back from the passenger seat, "Good for you, old man! Didn't know you had it in you!"

There was still no reply. Rosemary, who was driving, angled the rear-view mirror so that he could see the back seats. Maria and Marcus were locked in an embrace. As Arnold said later, "It could have been salacious. I'm not sure."

"Why on earth didn't you switch on the interior light?" Rosemary asked innocently.

"I might have discovered what hard porn really is. He is a man of the cloth after all."

Rosemary woke him with tea and toast the next morning at six o'clock. He groaned and held his head. "I'm supposed to be resting," he complained piteously.

"You can rest and eat breakfast and then rest again." She was glowing. "May has arrived. And guess what — Greta's pains were nothing to do with indigestion. They were labour pains. She had them for Connie. Have you ever heard anything like it?"

"No. But how is Connie? And what about May?"

"Connie is fine. She had three contractions and May positively burst forth." Rosemary took some toast and rammed it into her mouth. "Thee taketh after my father." She chewed fiercely and swallowed. "She takes after my father. My mother called him a professional complainer. Hope she gets over it." She sat on the edge of the bed and drew on stockings. Then stood up, took off her dressing gown and fastened a bra.

"You're doing it purposely," Arnold said.

"Doing what?"

"Dressing. You always dress in the bathroom."

"Because I have to get your breakfast and I know that if I dress in front of you, you will grab at me."

"What makes you think you are safe from me today?"

"First because you know I am practically halfway to Number Five. Secondly because you have a hangover." She leaned over and kissed him. "Listen, I'll take my own car. Marcus is sure to need a lift this morning. Are you up to coping on your own?"

"He can have my car."

"You are a wonderful man. I love you. There's salad in the fridge. Cold chicken. I'll be back to cook for tonight."

She was gone. He listened to her opening the garage, getting out her car, closing the garage, reversing carefully around his parked car and then driving down the lane and away. He must be weaker than he thought because for two pins he could cry. It was because he was so happy. Who would have thought that at his age he would have this wonderful new life? He scrubbed his eyes with a corner of the sheet and poured more tea. And the phone rang.

He almost fell down the stairs into the hall. It couldn't be Rosie, she would only just have got on to the main road. But what if it was William to tell them that something was wrong with the baby . . . or with Connie? The trouble with loving so many people was that it increased your chances of heartbreak. He snatched up the receiver.

"Hello — I'm here — who is it — what has happened?"

"It's Maria. I just saw Rosemary driving away. Is anything wrong?"

The serpents in the Garden of Eden. He forced jocularity into his voice. "Nothing at all. Connie has just had her baby. A girl. May."

"Oh how lovely. Marcus — darling — Connie has had the babe. Isn't that wonderful?"

He came on the line. "Congratulations to you all. Are they all right?" He barely waited for an answer. "I was rather hoping Rosemary would be in a position to take me in to the police station this morning but I can get a train of course."

"Better than that, old man, borrow my car. It's insured for any driver and you can leave it outside my place. Rosie and I will be back and forth for a while and can pick it up."

Marcus was sincerely grateful. "I know that what you said last night made sense, Arnold. But I am still rather nervous about the whole thing. The bishop will not be pleased."

"Sell it to him. Clergy can make mistakes. Makes you one of the people, that sort of thing."

"Arnold . . . your support is very welcome. I feel a little emotional this morning, I do apologize . . . Darling, pass me a tissue . . . Arnold, Maria has breakfast waiting. I hope to see you in an hour or two."

Arnold grinned. Marcus Challenger was having a good cry; he'd put money on it.

The phone rang again and his heart was in his mouth — again. He picked up the receiver gingerly and immediately a voice said, "I am ringing on behalf of Mr Maurice Heatherington. Have I got the right number?"

Arnold felt as if he might explode with sheer joy. Connie's baby at six thirty in the morning, Marcus's tears at seven thirty, and now Maurice Heatherington. He had met Maurice just once but he greeted him like an old friend.

"You certainly have, Maurice! Welcome back to the land of the living! This is Arnold Jessup here. When we met I was old Mrs Gainsborough's solicitor. Now my partner acts for your wife. And we certainly have something very advantageous to tell you."

There was a long pause. Arnold said urgently, "Maurice, don't hang up. I am serious. We've been looking for you since Christmas."

"I'm afraid Mr Heatherington has passed away, sir. That is what I have to tell you."

"Come on, Maurice. You can please yourself, of course. Disappear again if you want to. But you must be interested to have phoned. And you probably know where my office is. So why don't you call? Otherwise the lot goes to Archie Fielding. And you certainly will remember him."

No one replaced a telephone receiver and no one spoke.

Arnold said in the heartiest voice he could muster, "Tell you what, you shrinking violet you, come up to Brum tomorrow. My office number is four seven four seven. Ring me and I'll collect you from the station. We could have lunch."

With enormous will power he replaced the receiver. He hovered, waiting for it to ring again. It did not.

Rosemary did not want him to go. She arrived home in time for tea and was looking forward to an easy tomorrow. "She's like a — a — suffragette!" she said, referring to baby May. "Greta says she was fighting even when she was born!"

"Listen, you can drop me wherever Marcus has left my car then go on to Number Five and do your grandmotherly stuff again."

"You're not supposed to drive, Arnold! Just because this chap calls himself Maurice Heatherington doesn't mean a thing. And anyway, poor old Greta is going to have a hard enough time with a full week of performances, the last thing she wants is —"

"Slippers by the fire. I must tell him that. Darling, you're tired. Sit down and put your feet up — another cup of tea, then you can watch the news while I dish up."

"Oh Arnold. I forgot to get something special. I'm so sorry."

"I took the braising steak out of the freezer and after lunch I cooked it with some garlic and peppers and things and it's been marinating in the sauce ever since."

"I love you," she said with conviction. "You are an absolute catch and I am glad you played the field for so long otherwise you wouldn't have been available when I came on the scene."

"I would always have been available for you, sweet Rosie." He leaned over the back of her chair and kissed her upside down. "I've had a good day, love. This phone call has got me going again. And I think that actually it was you who decreed I should not drive. You're trying to incarcerate me in the house so that I am available at your every whim!"

He was gone before she could hurl a cushion at him. She leaned back, smiling. It was so good to come home. Everything was marvellous at Number Five and May was going to be such a joy. She was dark-haired with mud-coloured eyes, and so like Connie in one way and exactly like a female version of William in another.

It emphasized the fact that darling Frankie was blond, blue-eyed, placid and nothing like either of them. It was good to be home and able to put that at the back of her mind.

Marcus rang later. Arnold's car was outside the office in Selly Oak and he thought he had "smoothed everything over".

Arnold said, "Till the next time."

"What do you mean? How do you mean?" Marcus sounded panicky.

"You've always dealt in other people's problems, old man. Rather like me. Now you've let someone in. Next to you. Part of you. You can't be objective any more and fate knows that. Things will happen." Arnold made his voice sonorous and doom-laden.

"Maria is very placid," Marcus said with a hint of uncertainty. "And I don't believe in fate — not in that way." He paused, cleared his throat and went on, "But thanks so much for the use of your car. Lovely drive. Rosemary can bring you in when she comes to see her new grandchild."

"Oh yes." Arnold waited for Marcus to ask about baby May. He did not. They rang off.

They left early the next morning and ate breakfast in Arnold's sitting room, which doubled as a waiting room during office hours. Mrs Flowers had kept milk in the fridge for William and herself and made them coffee after they had eaten some stale cereal. She had visited Arnold three times since her return from Australia but as he was living in sin she pretended those visits had never happened and launched anew into her holiday itinerary, her face turned to him. She did not exactly ignore Rosemary but simply assumed that she was not interested.

"It was autumn over there, of course. The colours were wonderful. They say Adelaide is rather like an English city only before the war."

Arnold grinned at Rosemary. "Perhaps we could go one day, Rosie." He turned to his secretary. "Any early phone calls, Mrs Flowers?"

"Mr Mather rang, sir. Said he would be late as they hadn't had much sleep."

"Right. I'm waiting for a call which might not come. Mrs Vickers is going on to be with her daughter." Rosemary started to say that she was driving him but he overrode her. "That will free William to come into the office. And I will take all the calls initially." He stood up.

"Thank you for looking after us, Mrs Flowers. I'll see you off, Rosie, then I can sit upstairs. Go through some paperwork."

Rosemary did not want an outright row in front of Mrs Flowers but she did her best. "Isn't that why Mrs Flowers has kept in touch, Arnold? You have been 'going through paperwork' since you came out of hospital!"

"Don't forget your keys, darling. I've got my spare. I'll give you a ring at Connie's, shall I? Say cheerio to Mrs Flowers."

She looked up at him as they went into the hall. As if the prompt had been for her, Mrs Flowers trilled,

"Goodbye, Mrs Vickers — so good to see you," and went on up the stairs. "Goodbye, Mrs Flowers," Rosemary trilled back and then, with quiet venom, "I could kill you at times, Arnie. You haven't driven that damned car for almost five months. It's not safe."

"I'll doubtless be driving it the short distance to Number Five, my love. Stop worrying. Nothing awful is going to happen."

He waved her off, grinning like a Cheshire cat. And then turned and went up the stairs to his office. It was good to be back.

Maurice rang at nine thirty. There were no preliminaries this time.

"I'm at Euston. There's a train in ten minutes. Gets into New Street in two hours. I'll be in the refreshment room. Carry *The Times*."

He had been so cautious last night. Arnold wondered what had happened to change him. Were the police after him? He felt like a schoolboy detective.

"Fine," he said. "I'll wear dark glasses."

"Oh." Heatherington sounded almost affronted. "I'll be wearing them too."

"Looks like we're both on the same track."

Arnie replaced his receiver. Mrs Flowers would have heard every word of that but he didn't care. He dialled Greta's number.

"How are you bearing up after all that heavy labour stuff?" he opened.

"Arnie! Darling . . . how lovely to hear your voice. How are you? I'm fine — I think it kind of freed me in some way. I don't feel such a barren old hag."

318

He guffawed sardonically. "How about audiences for the show?"

"Not bad. Nothing like that first night but word hasn't got round yet. I think we'll be all right, Arnie. The West End won't be interested but we might get a tour of sorts. It's funnier than we thought."

"I plan to be in Birmingham this afternoon — getting my hand back in. Any chance of a cup of tea at the flat?"

"Arnie, that would be wonderful. I don't have to be at the theatre till five thirty."

"OK. No cream cakes. Doctor's orders."

"Rosemary's orders you mean. But she's right."

Arnie put the phone down and went through the outer office and upstairs to his private quarters. Rosie had practically stripped his wardrobe, which probably meant he was a permanent fixture out on the Lickey Hills. He smiled contentedly. He found his old glasses and changed into his office suit. The wardrobe mirror made him look like an American private detective. His smile widened. Things could not get much better than this, surely?

It was wonderful to be behind the wheel of his car again. Wonderful to wind carefully through the traffic and into the car park at New Street station. Wonderful to go underground, locate the refreshment rooms, get his dark glasses from his top pocket and push open the doors. A man was sitting at the bar reading *The Times*. Arnold had forgotten about *The Times*. The man looked round, saw no one in dark glasses and went back to his paper. Arnold studied him carefully, trying to assess whether he could make Greta happy. It was an impossible task. He wore a trilby pushed back and showing a lot of crisp white hair. His sports jacket had leather patches on the elbows — Arnold hated that but accepted that most women thought it showed masculinity. He wore a very heavy-looking gold-coloured watch and shoes with horrible pointed toes. He could be a cad. But Greta must have known he was a cad when she married him. Was he the sort of cad who would forget to put her slippers by the fire? Was he the sort of cad who might punch her in the face if things weren't going well? How could he know by looking?

He went to the newspaper stand and selected a copy of *The Times*, paid for it, put on his dark glasses and went to the bar.

"Maurice Heatherington, I presume?"

The man looked round, took off his glasses and grinned disarmingly. "My God — you are who I thought you were, if you get me. You haven't changed much in the last twenty years."

Surprisingly, Arnold discovered he was accepting this at its face value; mainly because memory suddenly fitted what he saw before him with the nervous forty-year-old standing next to the woman called Greta Gainsborough. The wide face was wrinkled now, of course, but it was still genial; Maurice's big frog-like grins had proclaimed him to be everybody's friend.

"Neither have you," he said tersely. "Which makes me want to punch you here and now. And very hard."

320

The face seemed to collapse in on itself. Maurice removed his dark spectacles and revealed baggy, faded blue eyes; tired eyes. Exhausted eyes. He said, "Listen. I shouldn't have let it get that far. But I'd never felt like she made me feel. Alive. As if something exciting was round every corner. When I realized it was you on the telephone I knew she was dead. It was awful. But then . . . you know, the glasses and catching the train up here . . . I thought perhaps the excitement was still around. Somewhere."

"And you hoped she'd left you something, did you?"

"Hardly. Not after what I did. I needed her so badly, Mr Jessup. And in those days you could not sleep with a girl unless you were married."

Arnold looked at him incredulously. "Those were the very days when you could do that! And she was not a girl. She was almost forty years old. Unmarried because she was waiting for Mr Right. And you were Mr Right!"

The head hung low. "I married Jessie when we were both eighteen. I thought I'd left her when I came to London. But . . . the next morning, after Greta and I were married . . . I wondered how she would get her breakfast, how she would dress herself . . . She had polio as a kid and it left her very weak." The head came up and the blue eyes focused on Arnold. "I couldn't do it, Mr Jessup. Greta was strong and beautiful and there would be others. There wouldn't be for Jessie. I told myself she could sell the shop and go on living in the flat . . . but I still couldn't do it."

Arnold stared into those eyes and saw something that Greta had seen. They were kind. He said as curtly as he could, "So . . . you have kept the shop and your first wife. Fine. You could have written to Greta. She would have understood."

"Yes." Maurice sighed deeply. "I was going to. It was so difficult. We had something wonderful, precious, we both knew that. I was afraid. I'm not a brave man, Mr Jessup. I was afraid."

"Yet you are here."

"It was the . . . mystery. I remembered what it had been like." He shook his head. "I can't do it by myself. When Jessie died, two years ago, I thought I would sell the shop and live abroad. Do something really exciting. Then I was sorting the papers for the delivery boys and . . . there it was. My name." He grinned. "Never seen my name in print before. And when I realized it was you on the other end of the phone I hoped she might have left me a note. Something."

"Oh God . . ." Arnie levered himself off the bar stool. "Let's go and have some lunch, Maurice. And please call me Arnold." They walked out of the refreshment room side by side, suddenly two men in late middle age, chatting amiably.

Arnold said, "I have to tell you, Maurice, Greta is alive. Very much alive. She told everyone you had gone to Rangoon. That's how bereft she was."

"Oh my God, my poor darling. But . . . she's alive! And not ill?"

"She's wardrobe mistress for a theatre company here in Birmingham. We went to the first night on Monday and it was great. The play is called *Sink and Swim*."

322

"That could be us, couldn't it? I thought we had sunk without trace. Perhaps we could learn to swim? What d'you think?"

Arnold told him that it was all a bit chancy but that Greta wanted to see him. Over lunch, which was a pie and a pint — Rosemary must never know — they got into the car and went to the flat. Arnold said, "Look. You know about her, she doesn't know about you. You have to tell her as soon as you can exactly what you have told me." Maurice looked as if he might throw up his lunch quite soon but he nodded. "And . . ." Arnold sounded very serious. "Tell her that all you want to do is to be around to put her slippers by the fire. Got that?" Maurice nodded again.

The door opened before they could ring the bell. Greta's eyes were enormous. She breathed, "I saw the car, I saw him get out. Oh Arnie . . . it is Maurice — it *is* Maurice, isn't it?"

"Yes, my love." Arnie stood aside and Maurice took his place.

Rosemary said crossly, "What d'you mean, they didn't say goodbye?"

"They didn't say goodbye to me. I was non-existent. They stared and stared and delved around in each other's soul . . . My God, it was amazing. I'm not kidding, Rosie, it was just how I felt about you. That night we had dinner. We simply . . . knew."

Rosemary said, "Yes, but you were so bossy. It sounds as if Maurice is rather weak."

"He's been in love with Greta yet looked after his wife for twenty years? You think that's weak?"

She said, "No. That was wrong of me. He must be very strong."

Much later something else occurred to her. They had driven back home separately and she had done a lot of thinking in her car.

She said, "Did you say that Maurice's poor wife died two years ago?"

They were sitting in one armchair watching the evening sky, which was streaked with red and azure. He nodded.

"It might have been around the time that poor Lucy Pardoe's son was drowned. That has to mean something, Arnie."

He kissed her neck. "It does. Connie . . . Greta . . . William. All the boy's family of course, devastated."

"We should try to do something. I don't know what."

"No. Best not interfere, love. But it seems awful that she has a grandson and does not know it."

"Yes." Rosemary thought of May and bit her lip. "Yes, indeed."

"There was another family in that boarding house, wasn't there?"

"I don't think they were very involved."

"No, probably not. And anyway they've doubtless put it out of their minds by now."

He nuzzled her neck again. Then said, "Shall we have supper and go to bed? Or the other way round?"

She held his head. "Are you really all right, Arnie? You looked sort of peaky when you came into William's place."

"I don't know what that means. But I am really all right. Seeing Maurice and Greta — it was just beautiful, Rosie. Gave everything fresh meaning."

"Oh Arnie." She kissed the top of his head. And wished that she could give Lucy Pardoe just a taste of this sweetness.

CHAPTER
FIFTEEN

When the Trips got back from their summer holiday in the States, Lucy tried to explain to Margaret why she felt responsible for Harry Membury lying in Penzance Hospital like a broken doll. Margaret not only failed to understand but she was aghast that Lucy had "gotten where she was".

"Can't you see, honey, that you are looking for sticks to beat yourself with? And in a strange way, the guy seems to be happier since this — this — horror story than he was before when he was all gawny-lovestruck for you!"

"I've got to look after him now, Margaret. Surely you can see that? He can't go back to the rectory. The reverend is useless. He's going to need someone to dress him and wash his clothes and feed him . . ."

"Oh my God." Margaret stared at her friend and saw that she was determined. She said slowly, "We've got to get something out of this. For you. Sackcloth and ashes are all very well but not for too long." She put a finger to her bottom lip, miming concentration, then said, "I know, I'll teach you to drive! Marvin will help you to choose a car. Then you can trundle up and down to Penzance. Better still, you could leave him with

326

Matthew Hobson and go in daily to see that he is OK." She leaned forward. She saw driving lessons as her next project. "What do you say?"

Lucy thought about it and saw that it made sense. But she was still cautious.

"Well . . . I'm not sure." There had been no women drivers in Hayle that she knew of; it was definitely a man's thing.

"I was reading in the paper about the district nurses. That's what you'd be, Luce. His own special nurse. Would that make things better?"

Lucy had forgotten about district nurses. In the war they had managed on bikes but most of them had cars these days. She nodded cautiously and Margaret — being Margaret — went straight back to her place and fetched her car.

That first driving experience was terrifying. Margaret was used to driving on the right-hand side of the road and had to remind herself about being in England over and over again. "I'm not like this when I just drive without having to think," she explained. "It's that I want you to do it the right way from the start." But the next day she took Lucy up to the country around St Austell where the abandoned clay pits provided traffic-free space.

Lucy mastered the mechanics very quickly. She had watched Josh when he had brought her house-hunting and knew how to check the gears before switching on, how to use the clutch and brake. She proved excellent at easing the car around the huge boulders in the clay pits without stalling. She could reverse and do a

327

three-point turn almost immediately. Margaret was cock-a-hoop. She applied for a test much too soon; Lucy failed it and made her weekly visit to Penzance on the bus as usual. "I really wanted to drive there. He'll have to be discharged next month and I won't have time to practise if he has to come to us." She looked at Margaret mournfully. "Now that he's actually coming out of hospital, I don't want him in the house one bit. So much for making amends."

"We'll put in for another test, kiddo. The examiner had to fail you because of going through a red light, but that was the only thing, wasn't it?"

This time she passed. She had never achieved anything "official" before. She was speechless with delight. Without thinking, she threw herself into Margaret's long thin arms. "I love you!" she laughed. "I can buy a car and go anywhere I like and it's because of you!"

Margaret laughed at first and then said seriously, "I love you too, honey. But calm down." She gave her an odd sideways look. "Hope you're not like this with Marvin when you test-drive this car of yours!"

Lucy pestered like a child until Margaret let her drive home and even then she continued to chortle. Margaret could not get over it. "My God, Luce. Give you a taste of power and you go mad! I can see where Denny gets it from. Watch that lamp post — this is my car, remember!"

So a new routine was set up that autumn. Harry Membury moved back into his room in the rectory and Lucy drove there each weekday as soon as she had

328

taken the girls to school. She gave Harry his breakfast, ran a bath, bundled his clothes into a basket for laundering back home and helped him to dress and make his bed. Both arm and leg were out of splints and needed no dressing but he was unable to walk without a stick and Dr Carthew had arranged for a therapist to call and organize exercises for him.

Lucy insisted that Matthew must get his own breakfast and do his own laundry and she left lists for him of everything else that needed doing. He said plaintively, "Lucy, I can't do shopping every day. And you bring enough food for both of us anyway."

Lucy had changed a great deal since the days when she had lived almost entirely off her garden and the orchard. She said, "The food I bring is only for Harry. How can we get him better if we don't feed him properly? I want him to go home at Christmas and be with his family."

"You don't even know where he lives!" Matthew protested.

"I went through his things and found a notebook. It's like a diary but it's not actually a diary — sometimes there are dates, sometimes not. It starts with . . ." she swallowed and said, "Egg. The drowning." A big breath and she went on quickly, "And ends with him sleeping with a girl from the commune. He just had time to write it before he went to see my father, who tried to kill him."

He stared at her, amazed, remembering the Lucy Pardoe who had lived on the towans and suppressed . . . so much.

He said in a low voice, "Lucy, you know you should not have read that book."

"I haven't read it all, just the beginning and the end. I needed his home address, that's all." She grinned. "It's because I've got a car."

"What is? What are you talking about?" Matthew sounded cross; he felt he wasn't coming out of this very well.

"Margaret calls me a megalomaniac. That means I get my power from having money. But actually it's because of the car. I can do anything because of the car."

Matthew grinned unwillingly. "You seemed to do an awful lot before the car came along."

She laughed. "I know. But I didn't even know what I was doing half the time." She looked at him very directly. "Now I know. And I know I have to look after Harry up to a point. But I do not have to look after you."

He took a long, resigned breath. "All right, give me the shopping list." He stared down at it unseeingly. "You know he wants to divorce Avis and marry you?"

"Not in so many words but I guessed."

"I suppose now that you have read that notebook and seen about the Flower People, you don't want to know."

"I didn't want to know before. I'm glad about the Flower People." She finished clearing Harry's breakfast tray. "He was so terribly unhappy when he arrived last winter. And he didn't sound much better when he was with you. The Flower People made him happy."

"Those mushrooms had a hand in it, I suspect." Matthew spoke with a touch of bitterness. He had not relished the laughter from Josh and Carthew.

"Who knows?" She took clean towels from the airing rack and made for the stairs. "Soup for his lunch. And the fruit jelly is from Margaret."

He called, "The good doctor is having us for Sunday. He reckons Harry should be able to walk to his place."

"Check with this man who is coming to give him exercises," she called back.

"It's a woman. But yes, I will."

Matthew gathered himself together and made for his study. He had a Confirmation group this evening in the vestry and needed to plan something that would cover the three fourteen-year-olds and the two in their twenties from the commune. Three years ago when he arrived here he had been full of plans for making God accessible to everyone. It had gone well; a youth club, singing groups, an organist from St Cloud who had taken kindly to using Bing Crosby's "White Christmas" for the carol service. But something was lacking and he did not know what it was. Could it possibly be as simple as resenting Carthew's laughter about the mushrooms? Or the fact that Lucy was prepared to care for Harry Membury. but most definitely excluded him? Or that Chippy Penberthy, suddenly saddled with his feckless daughter's three children, expected him to amuse them for the whole of Sunday? He thought longingly of Ellie Pardoe, who would have told them Bible stories and walked them miles over the dunes so that they might actually ask to go to bed at six o'clock.

But the autumn term was well under way and now that Lucy had this car, they would be off calling on Harry's family, trying to heal the enormous breach that split them when Egbert Pardoe had drowned. That drowning . . . a terrible time that went on and on . . . Ellie going to her school in Truro, so unhappy, white and strained. Eleven years old. And now thirteen and beautiful. They had coped. Lucy had coped. He had helped them but they would have managed anyway.

He drew his papers towards him. He felt useless.

Harry also marvelled at the change in Lucy. In his head he would always have a picture of her standing in that doorway, her remaining children close to her skirt, defying . . . what had she been defying? The knowledge that her only son was dead? At the time it seemed that she had been defying the whole world. Standing there, waiting for the next blow to fall, determined that she would not fall herself.

But after he left the towans and went back home with Avis and the girls, she must have changed. Gone out to meet whatever came and to shape things to her own ends. That business with Penberthy and then the holiday company. He had seen a change in her when he eventually found her in Truro. A different kind of toughness. Not so much stubborn resistance as political manoeuvring.

But now . . . since he had come back to his room in the rectory and she had acted as a daily nurse . . . now it was startling.

She told him it was the car.

"It's like having a key." She was waiting for him to finish with his breakfast tray and she went to the window and looked down on the bottle-green Hillman Minx parked below. "Because I can go anywhere, I think I can do anything!" She laughed at herself and moved to the tallboy to get the day's clothes ready. "It must be a bit like you with those Flower People. That's how they are, aren't they?"

He thought about it, nodding. "Probably, in their case, it has a great deal to do with those damned mushrooms." He tried to grin and sipped at his tea to cover the usual wince of pain. He had caught his cheek on the splintering steps as he fell.

He said, "You know, Lucy, I didn't go to work for your father to — to inveigle myself into your family. The manager at the Godolphin Estate told me that Zeke was your father . . . but no details. I thought it was one of those family splits — like — like Avis and me. Well, not quite. But anyway, I thought I could heal it. But . . . I've heard from Dr Carthew that he was an alcoholic."

Lucy said in her old flat voice, "He killed my mother."

There was a long silence. Lucy put a neat pile of underwear on top of the tallboy. Harry put down his cup and lifted the tray to the side of the bed. Then he said quietly, "I think he pushed me down those steps, Lucy."

She said nothing but nodded and looked at him, waiting.

"We had a terrible row. He didn't care about me dancing and singing. But when he realized — when I told him — that I knew you, that did it."

"Yes." She sighed and turned to close the tallboy. "It would have happened anyway. That's how he was."

"It must have been . . . awful."

"It was. I don't think I realized how awful for a long time. He'd done it to my mother and he was doing it to me. I thought that was how husbands and fathers were. But when the war came everyone was joining up, doing something. He said we were in the front line because we were providing food for people. But the girl from Godolphin Home Farm said she'd had enough of Cornish mud and she'd heard that this place in Devon needed chambermaids and would I come with her. And I did." She laughed and for a moment he could see that wild, unkempt teenager in the face of the mature woman. She said, "He came after me but I was doing war work and that was that." She shuddered. "It made it worse to go back. I shouldna gone. I thought the war would've changed him." She shrugged. "You shoulda given him some of the mushrooms."

He tried to laugh with her and could not. She picked up the tray and made for the door. "Don't let that bathwater get cold."

"No, miss," he joked feebly.

"I hope the physio woman gets you going soon." She turned and looked at him. "I think you know now what you have to do."

He said, "Get going?"

She said tartly, "See if you can patch up your marriage. It's almost a year since you left them."

"They're all right. I do keep in touch, you know."

She did know. Because of the notebook she knew a few more things about Harry Membury. Avis too. Harry had said nothing about Avis's new "husband". It was certainly time he sorted that out.

Lucy took down the tray and laid it again for lunch, then she stuffed the laundry into the boot of the Hillman and closed it firmly. She put the palm of her hand on the shining dark green finish of the car and spoke quietly. "We'll go up to Devon soon. Find that Avis Membury and give her one of Margaret's penny lectures. That should get things moving again." She turned to go back indoors and glanced up at the bedroom window and saw Harry standing where she had stood half an hour before. His striped pyjamas and tousled hair reminded her of pre-war book illustrations of homesick boarding-school boys. She jabbed her finger angrily in the direction of the bathroom and marched back into the kitchen, working out exactly what she was going to say to Avis Membury about the sanctity of marriage. She stuck her head around the study door without knocking. Matthew was holding his head with one hand and a pen in the other, though he did not seem to be using the pen.

She said, "He's just going to the bathroom and he'll need help getting out."

He looked up. "I was just getting going!" he said accusingly.

She said, "Oh good. But don't forget he's up there. I have to go. Good luck with the massage woman."

He had no idea what she was talking about and forgot about Harry until he heard him banging on the ancient radiator in the bathroom. When he leaped upstairs to find him sitting in cold water, Matthew blamed it all on Lucy. His mother used to say, "Better leave a job undone rather than half done." And he saw now exactly what she had meant.

That afternoon, Lucy and Margaret had two hours on the allotment. They were putting it to bed for the winter, collecting slugs from around the sprouts, cutting some of the Jerusalem artichokes, tying bean and pea sticks into neat bundles, putting seaweed around the roots of the currant bushes. They planned to bring all four girls with them during the weekend to create some kind of framework to contain weeds and old stalks for compost. The first frost was forecast for tonight.

Margaret said, "I'm working on Marvin to stay put for Christmas. It's a real long way to go for only two weeks."

Lucy was almost afraid to show how much it would mean to her to have Margaret's company over the Christmas holiday. It might be "only two weeks" to the Trips; it seemed a lifetime to Lucy. She said carefully, "Ellie would love that. Barbara and Denny too. D'you think Marvin will go along with it?"

"Not sure. He can be an awkward cuss at times. I'll have to pay for it." She laughed. Lucy was startled, then embarrassed. Some of the women at the club said things that were a bit near the bone but Margaret was not like that. She bent over the plastic sack of seaweed, lifted out a bundle of odorous bladderwrack and arranged it around a gooseberry bush.

Margaret was similarly embarrassed but brazened it out. "Can't you take a little joke, Luce?"

Lucy shrugged. "It's what my father used to say. That's all over and done with now."

Margaret said nothing. But Lucy was unsurprised when she announced two days later that Marvin wouldn't "play ball" and they were flying over the pond earlier than last year. "Gus will have to miss a coupla days of school, which Miss Harkin will *not* like, but it can't be helped."

"Gus is well ahead of everyone else in her class," Lucy said consolingly. "More important to see her family."

"Sure is."

Neither Ellie nor Gus saw anything odd about the earlier flight. They marched off to school, Ellie holding Denny's mittened hand and Gus linking arms with Barbara, who was in her first year at the Laurels. Margaret had gone into Falmouth with Marvin to get presents for home. Lucy stood on the step and watched the girls go off and felt the day stretching ahead of her endlessly. She went back in, opened her own notebook and dialled the operator for an Exeter number. When Avis answered she said, "This is Mrs Lucy Pardoe from Truro. I am driving to Exeter today and will call on you at midday." She paused, waiting for Avis to respond. Avis did so in no uncertain manner.

"You certainly will not! I have no wish to see any of you lot from Cornwall ever again." She replaced her receiver vehemently.

Lucy stood there, nibbling her lower lip. She did not want to drive over a hundred miles and not be able to talk to the woman. On the other hand this opportunity seemed heaven-sent. She looked at her watch. It was not quite eight thirty. She dialled again.

She said directly, "Do you know that the man you are living with is married?"

Avis's voice was icy. "I do. He is married to me."

"Your divorce is not yet through. And he cannot get one because his wife is Roman Catholic. You are both committing adultery."

Avis had remembered people speaking of Lucy Pardoe as a simple person scraping a living from the sandy soil and bringing up her children in what sounded like a shack. She blustered angrily, "We might not have any certificate to prove it but we are married in the eyes of God!"

"I understand that exactly. However, there is no real security in such a marriage and the fact is he threw your legal husband out without a penny. Since then Mr Membury has worked for board and lodging. There was an accident and he is now staying at the rectory —"

"I know all this, you stupid woman! Do you think you are the only woman in the world he pesters? I get letters asking me about the girls. They are much better off without him but he can't believe it. Tell him if he so much as shows his face here, Ted will put him in hospital again."

Lucy stared at the humming, empty receiver. She replaced it gently and sat down. Poor Harry. Nobody wanted him. For some reason she felt like crying.

The phone rang and she snatched it up. "Yes? Is it you, Avis?"

A voice she recognized said, "No. It is William Mather, Mrs Pardoe. I am glad you have had a phone put in. Good morning. How are you?"

That did it. She felt tears fill her eyes. "I'm well, thank you. How are you?"

"Very well. We are all extremely well. We have a new baby, a little girl we have called May. She sleeps all day and cries all night. Is that unusual?"

Surely he wasn't phoning for advice of that kind? She said, "Egg and Ellie went through the nights. But Barbara and Denny didn't give us any peace for a year."

He laughed. "The voice of experience. Lucy — may I call you Lucy? We know each other fairly well, don't we?"

"Yes. Yes, of course. Yes."

"Good. Thank you. I want to talk to you about the farm, Lucy. I have had some correspondence with your father's solicitors and as there is no will it now belongs to you. You need to sign some papers and then Mr Trumble of Trumble and Trumble in St Austell will hand over the deeds and the keys."

"I have my own keys, Mr Mather."

"Your father's keys will be handed over officially once we have seen Mr Trumble. He also holds the deeds."

She levered herself up from the chair, then held the receiver with both hands and stared at the front door. Margaret had asked about the farm and made wild suggestions for selling it to the Flower People. Lucy had told her soberly that the cows had already gone to Home Farm and she would sell off any equipment left and just let the building be taken by the sands. Standing there holding the phone, she knew she could not do that. It had been her mother's home.

William Mather's voice said gently, "Are you all right? It's just one of those legal things. Nothing to worry about."

"Will you — can you — come with me?" She sounded like a frightened child. One of the cats brushed against her legs and she lifted him on to her shoulder and put her face into his side. He purred loudly.

"Lucy, I have spoken to your doctor. John Carthew. He has given me some background information. I am really sorry. But he tells me you are doing very well in Truro and all the past is . . . in the past." He paused long enough for her to wonder what past he was meaning. Then he said, "Yes, I will be with you. I wondered whether I might come down today — or is that too soon?"

"It would be a good day for it." She sat on the hall chair again and let Mark slide into her lap. Whatever

340

was inside her, coiled so tightly, began to relax. William Mather was coming to see her.

"That's good. I can be with you for one o'clock probably. Take you to lunch in St Austell and on to see the Trumble." He made it sound funny and she laughed. He said, "That's better. I realize the farm has no happy memories for you so we can talk about a sale perhaps."

"I don't think I want to sell it, Mr Mather."

"William. Call me William, Lucy. It's only fair and we are friends."

"We are. Yes, we are." If she was losing Margaret for some reason, then she was gaining William Mather.

"Shall we talk about all of it over a late lunch?" he said.

"Yes, please."

She put the phone down and cuddled Mark hard and he struggled furiously. She was so pleased she was not seeing Harry this morning and that Avis Membury had rejected her so vehemently. It did not matter that Mr Mather — William — was married to that girl either. She need never see her. She could forget she even existed. William was her friend. He was a friend worth having.

She flew around getting ready. A note to Margaret, which she pushed through her door. Another for Ellie. Potatoes to be peeled . . . saucepan on the hob . . . stew in the old-fashioned stockpot which had belonged to Daniel's mother . . . cats fed. She went upstairs for the real luxury this house provided: a hot bath. Then spent some time looking at the clothes she had bought since her move. In the end she went back to her usual outfit, a jumper and skirt with some new shoes that looked like slippers and were red. She was sitting in the kitchen with outstretched legs, admiring the red shoes, when the door bell rang and her insides tightened. For a moment she was appalled at herself. All this dressing up for a young man who was nothing to do with her personally. And yet . . . was.

She opened the door, red-faced but smiling. And there he was, unchanged from the man who had brought that girl to apologize to her and then helped her so much. She said, "Mr Mather."

"William," he corrected.

"William. You must have had a good journey. It's only just gone one."

He noted her voice. Softer. More precise . . . probably for his benefit.

He said, "I was already in Bristol on some other business and there was hardly any traffic. Christmas rush hasn't started probably . . . Lucy. You look very well. It must be well over a year since we exchanged contracts on this house. How has it worked out?"

She was ushering him in as they spoke. He remembered the cats, even their names — he admired the living room — she was aware that he was aware of every small thing she had done in this house. She settled him on the sofa and fetched coffee. The sort of coffee Margaret had taught her to make. He was very appreciative.

"This room reminds me of my own house . . . When I was a boy I could smell Christmas coming throughout the house. I get that same sense of anticipation as I sit here."

She swallowed. How could she have been so low about Margaret's departure when Christmas was waiting less than a month away. Already in this room, it seemed.

She said hoarsely, "I'll just go upstairs and . . ." She cleared her throat. "I am very glad to see you." She smiled and said his name. "William."

They had lunch in St Austell's old coaching inn. The appointment with Mr Trumble was for three o'clock and as his office was just across the square they lingered over coffee until the last minute. She was very taken with the pudding she had just enjoyed, especially its name.

"It sounds like one of those playground rhymes," she said. "I don't think boys had them, did they? We could have skipped to this one . . ." She smiled widely and chanted, "Syllabub, syllabub . . . dub, dub, dub!"

He threw back his head, laughing, and she noticed his throat, the Adam's apple, the strong sinews either side. He said, "We had them all right. I went to a little private school when I was four and I well remember —" he too chanted "— 'The big ship sails on the alley alley oh, on the twenty-fifth of September!' "

She said, excited, "We had that one too and you weaved in and out of arches made by the other children! How — how *strange*. That we were playing the same sort of games all those years ago and all those miles away." She shook her head at her own foolishness.

"Not strange at all really. Children are children the world over."

"Better than strange, isn't it? It's another link. Our lives are so different, Lucy. Yet we are linked in all kinds of ways." He grinned. "I think I will be teaching Frankie and May to sing the syllabub song — make sure the link continues."

"But that is one I made up. You must teach them about the big ship sailing on the twenty-fifth of September. Michaelmas Day."

"I will. Quarter days are important in my life still. But syllabub will link them to you. A personal link."

"Oh William." She did not know what to say. He was part of Egg's death; one of the many kind and gentle parts, Josh and Harry and William. Sent by Egg to give her support even when she rejected it.

He said, "It's nearly three, Lucy. Do you need to powder your nose before we go?"

She did not. He dealt with the bill and helped her on with her winter coat and they left.

She quite liked Mr Trumble in spite of his rather obsequious manner. She wondered, as she sat down opposite him at the enormous leather-covered desk, how William could be just as polite — use the same words probably — and not sound in the least servile. She was very relieved William was with her; she could see that without him she could have been here listening to explanations and adjurations for an hour. William had it "tidied up", as he put it, in twenty minutes and they were all smiling and shaking hands at three thirty and walking out again into the November dusk.

344

"There. That didn't hurt, did it?" He tied his scarf so that his ears were covered. "Shall we have a cup of tea before we go home?"

"I'd rather go straight back. I asked my friend to pick up the little ones from school but I don't want her to have to look after them until Ellie gets in. Not really."

"That's fine. I'd like to see them before I leave."

He tucked her gloved hand into his arm and they strode out to the car park and settled themselves with expressions of relief. He said, "It's going to be a really cold night." And she said, "Probably a lovely day tomorrow. Could you stay overnight? As you can see, we have plenty of room now."

He concentrated on getting the car on to the main road; they paused and he switched on the heater then swung into the line of traffic.

"I thought I'd mentioned to you, Lucy, I am staying with Dr Carthew tonight. I could not impose on you and the girls, it wouldn't be fair." Her silence was full of disappointment and he said, "Actually, I did wonder . . . if it really is a good day tomorrow, may I pick you up? I would really like to see your farm. I don't have to start back until midday."

She was all smiles. "I can do my usual thing. Get Harry's breakfast and sort him out and then pick you up. Will you mind?"

"I'll thoroughly enjoy it."

The girls were in the kitchen, hats and coats still on. Barbara was reading the note her mother had left for Ellie.

"Margaret didn't meet us," she greeted William and Lucy as they came in, stamping and blowing. "We came home by ourselves and found the key stuck on the shoe scraper and we were going to get tea ready for you and Mr Mather." She waved the piece of paper. "Only we didn't know he was here till we read Ellie's note."

"Goodness!" It was the best she could manage as she filled the kettle and reached for the tea tray. Margaret's non-appearance was completely unexpected. But, of course, it was all too easy to get waylaid by Christmas shopping and she and Marvin knew nothing about William's precipitate arrival. The girls bombarded William with questions about his new baby. Lucy wondered about resurrecting the fire in the living room; it might need some wood to start it off again. Then she put the tray on the kitchen table simply because the three of them were sitting around it and Barbara was telling William he just *had* to teach baby May to do French knitting and Denny was earnestly drawing an abstract of a threaded bobbin. She found biscuits in a tin and with her other hand reached down Barbara's bobbin and put it on the table. Barbara flew upstairs to find wool. Denny moved over on to William's lap. Gus and Ellie came in discussing last night's *Z-Cars*: apparently Gus was the driver with the Irish accent and Ellie was the snappy DI Barlow. They dissolved into giggles at their own impressions and then stopped as they saw William. Just for a moment all was bedlam.

Ellie was delighted. She introduced him to Gus. "Mr William Mather," she said importantly. "Our family solicitor."

And he reached around Denny's dark curls and held out his hand. "Augusta. What a lovely name."

Gus grinned. "You gotta have something pretty important to go with Trip. My dad is called Marvin for the same reason."

He laughed and shook her hand thoroughly then said, "Americans are so much better at handshakes than we are. They mean something very special."

"Gee, I like you," Gus announced and even the girls laughed because Mr Mather blinked and looked shy.

They all settled down and spoke in turn. William looked from one to the other, smiling slightly, obeying Barbara's instructions for threading the bobbin, nodding thanks as Lucy slid a mug of tea across the table, accepting a biscuit bite by bite from Denny. He smiled at Lucy, swallowed the last crumb and said, "This will be happening for Connie and me soon."

Ellie said, "I wish you had brought them all with you! Your wife was so pretty. And so nice. It was all dreadful for her but she was brave. Like Ma." She turned her shining face to Lucy, expecting a smile and a nod. Neither was forthcoming. She went on, stumbling a little, not understanding something. "And now she has two babies — almost twins — it — it's a sort of miracle, isn't it?"

Lucy passed the biscuits to Gus. William said, "That's exactly it, Ellie." He did not look at Lucy. "Every time I look at them I know it. And now, looking at you in your new home with your friend and — and — the cats — and your mother driving a Hillman Minx!" He spread his hands and Denny almost fell off his lap and he grabbed her and laughed and at last Lucy smiled.

Lucy had told Harry what was happening and he had asked her to let him know how "the old place" was looking. Sometimes he amazed her; the whole business of being pushed down those rotten steps and nearly dying on the floor of the cellar did not appear to haunt him as Egg's terrible drowning haunted him. During their conversations when she looked after him that autumn, she had tried to "explain" her father. She found it impossible. But he had nodded and said, "When the mind has gone, Lucy, nothing is logical any more. Nothing at all. That space — where the mind was — fills with something else. In your father's case it was a terrible sense of injustice at first, then it was hatred."

She looked at him now as he pulled a clean shirt over his head. He was managing so well; there was no need for daily visits any longer, she made them to assuage her own guilt.

She answered his question with a shrug. "It's not going to look very different, I wouldn't think. I let the cows go to Godolphin Home Farm, of course. There are no cauliflowers this year, no sprouts. Anything that comes up accidentally will be left. I am expecting it to look very run-down."

He said, "It will still fetch a decent price, Lucy."

She shrugged again. Unless William advised her otherwise she knew exactly what she was going to do with Roach's farm.

Harry said, "William came in to see us last night. I wanted to talk about . . . things. But he would not. Matthew never will. And neither will you." He looked at her. "I thought I might work it out like you are doing, Lucy. But of course . . . that went wrong."

"Yes." She looked at him. Everything he did seemed to go wrong and she wondered how on earth he would ever "work things out". She had so wanted him to go back to his family. She could try again of course.

William accepted a lift in the Hillman. "A lovely little car," he said as they bounced down the lane towards the dunes. She put Harry to the side of her mind and beamed.

"I know it's wrong to love material things, but I do so love Minnie. I tell everyone she is my key to freedom!"

He smiled, marvelling yet again how much this woman had changed. And as if she could read his mind she said, "This is how I felt in Devon with Bertie. And before that with my mother when we went blackberrying or picking mushrooms. And, of course, with Daniel. After Egg I thought that happiness had gone for ever but I don't think it has." The car leaped over a tussock in the middle of the track and she laughed. "I really don't think it has!"

"It's just been lying dormant," he agreed, smiling, accepting that such happiness was infectious. "I wish you could meet Arnold Jessup. He is getting on for sixty and he has fallen in love with Connie's mother who is probably a dozen years his junior. And suddenly they are teenagers. They live together and bicker like a couple of children. It's marvellous."

She wanted to ask about Connie. Was she happy with William now? She remembered that morning when they had come to see her — why had they come to see her, to be forgiven? She remembered her own reaction to that ringless finger. She had hoped wildly that the girl had been rejected . . . that her life too was in ruins around her.

Their laughter died and she said quietly, "I am glad you and Connie . . . I really am glad."

"Thank you, Lucy. I will tell her that. She will be pleased."

"She still feels it? Actually seeing Egg in the sea like that . . . probably already . . ." She could not go on.

"Oh yes. She still feels it."

She negotiated the open gate and guided the car carefully around the wide bend and waited for the awfulness of the house to hit them both. There it was, somehow squat, dug into the sandy ground that hid its infamous cellar. She pulled up so that they could view it as a whole.

He glanced at her and said in a very matter-of-fact voice, "It's a huge asset, Lucy. I am guessing that the long arm of the L-shape overlooks the sea. And the outbuildings look solid enough to be converted into accommodation."

She appeared not to hear him. "It's not empty," she murmured.

"My dear, you are bound to feel that. It's one of the reasons I would advise you to sell it as soon as possible."

She continued to grip the steering wheel. "I don't mean ghosts. The house is being lived in. There's washing on the line."

He frowned. "So there is. Yet no smoke coming from the chimneys."

She put the car into first and edged over some tractor ruts and on to the yard and as they drew up at the back door, so it opened and a girl came out with a basket of more washing. She wore no shoes and her jeans were rolled to the knee. But an enormous oiled sweater must have given warmth. Above it her face was almost obscured by curtains of brown hair.

She put the laundry basket on the ground, surprised to see them but not shocked.

"Hello!" She walked across, ignoring the small stones littering the concrete of the yard. Her feet and lower legs were red like a chicken's. "Are you lost?"

Lucy, used to the Flower People though most of them had disappeared from Truro in the autumn, smiled. "Not at all. We came to see the farm."

"Oh. Well, come in. There's two of us on duty today and Paul has gone for wood for the fire. I'm doing the washing in cold water but we need firing to cook."

Lucy got out of the car and stood holding the door and looking at the girl; she was much too thin. "Have you moved in?"

"No. It's not ours but we keep it going for Harry. He lived here and there was a terrible accident and he's in hospital. We're going to look after him when he gets back." She smiled that special beatific smile they all had. "Go on in and look around while I hang up this stuff. It's a lovely house. We're making it beautiful for Harry."

Mesmerized, they both went in through the back door. Lucy girded herself against the long drab passageway and grubby windows; the dark terror of it all. They were opposite the dairy, but not the dairy she remembered from that visit when she had been looking for Harry. The Flower People had covered the brick walls in paper . . . an enormous collage. All she could see was colour. It looked like a multicoloured patchwork quilt. Hardly hearing William's remarks about squatting rights, she put a hand behind her and he took it. She whispered, "It's different, William. It's completely different . . ."

He said, "Those people must have done it. It — it's amazing. My God, it's right down this passage — look."

She looked. They walked slowly down the passage, looking into the rooms. Great swags of coloured nylon material framed the windows. In the kitchen, the whole ceiling was covered with open, up-ended umbrellas.

The girl came up behind them. "This is particularly good, we thought. Kitchen ceilings get so mucky. You just take down the umbrellas and wash them under the tap and hang them back up." She smiled. "We started finding all these brollies when the summer visitors went back. They were washed up or left in the dunes. And the drapes were old tents and . . . well, anything we found really. Then we stuck layers of newspapers on the walls to warm the place up. And on top we've all had a go. We got most of the stuff from wallpaper shops. Magazines. Catalogues . . . you know." She pushed her hair behind her ears and looked about fifteen. "It's beautiful, isn't it?"

"Harry will love it." Lucy smiled at the girl; she had Ellie's enthusiasm and desire to please. "He will be so happy here. It's just the right thing to do."

The girl's eyes opened wide. She said, "Oh my God. You are Harry's angel, aren't you? And it must be your house!"

"I hope my friend here can fix it —" there she was, using Margaret's word "— for Harry to have it. 'Harry's House' . . . sounds just right, don't you think?"

"It sounds . . . wonderful." The girl had that look of adoration that Lucy had seen in Harry's eyes and which so exasperated her.

She said, "Listen. Can you give my friend and me just a few minutes to go on looking around? Then we'll go and you can light the fire in the range and cook your food."

"Of course, of course. I want to go and tell the others anyway." She gave that dreamy smile. "My name is Beatrice but they call me Bee. I'm always busy. And now I am bringing good news!"

She was gone. Lucy found she was still clutching William's hand and she released it quickly. "Well," she said, shaking her head slowly.

He grinned. "I think the phrase is — a turn-up for the books! But be careful, Lucy. Do you really want your mother's old home turned into a commune?"

She grinned back. "You know I'm not an angel, William. Far from it. I wanted to give the place to

Harry anyway. I thought he'd be able to work it enough to keep body and soul together. That's what he came back to Cornwall to do, live off the land. He's a romantic. And I am not." She made a face. "You should have heard some of the gossip going around the village when I bought Pardoe Cottage with one hand and sold it with the other!"

"I've picked up bits from Carthew. You weathered it all, Lucy. That's what you must remember."

"Let them have a go at this latest transaction then. I'm proposing to give the house to Harry Membury and I'm going to advise him to let part of it in the summer months. Either to the Flower People or to birdwatchers or fishermen. It's a full-time job with maintenance and suchlike but it will be just the kind of thing he's looking for. And give him a chance to live his life exactly how he wants to live it. Then if it doesn't prove to be the dream he's chasing, he can sell it and start again somewhere else."

William went to the window and peered out. "On a crisp winter day like this it's probably as attractive as in the summer. But it does depend on the weather, Lucy. You are 'advising' Harry to live here on his own from — what — October to May?"

"Or not. The choice is his. He can sell it and take the money back to Avis. She'd have him back then. But if he can make a go of it here, his two girls will want to spend time with him. And soon they will be old enough to make their own choices."

She was moving around, trying out the electrical appliances. They were all dead. She looked up at the

354

inverted umbrellas and smiled. She knew he would choose to live here. At last, at last she had done something . . . good.

She came and stood by William and stared out at the dunes rolling down to the sea. She felt suddenly as if a great weight had fallen from her. She whispered, "It must have been near here somewhere that I went into the sea that night."

He turned his head and looked at her. Her whisper became a thread. "Ellie stopped me. I've never done it again." He put his arm around her shoulders and held her to his side. She breathed audibly, once, twice and then said in a normal voice, "Margaret wants us all to swim together in the sea. She thinks it will take away some of the nightmare. We were going to do it last summer but . . . other things happened."

He said, "Connie has not swum since that afternoon."

She lifted her face and looked at him and saw that all was not well. Without thinking, she put her free hand up to his head and drew it down. She felt the shock go from his body into hers. She held the kiss for too long and he broke from her and started babbling apologies. She wondered what had possessed her and said harshly, "It was me. Stop saying sorry — you know it was me." She moved from the window and went straight to the cellar door. "Let's see what they've done in the dungeon —" she forced a laugh "— then we must go."

She opened the door. The ladder had gone. She had intended going down and her foot was extended into mid-air before she realized the steps were no more. She could easily have pulled back her foot; she was hanging on to the lintel anyway. There was no danger. But William pulled her back as if she might be going to throw herself forward into oblivion. And then he held her to him and as she put her head against his shirtfront she realized she was weeping.

"I am sorry, Lucy. So sorry." His voice was broken, jagged. "If I hadn't brought Connie down to Cornwall . . . Chasing a client, that's what I was doing . . . All our motives were wrong. And your son drowned. And my poor Connie, my poor Connie, will never forgive herself."

She held on to him as if she were indeed about to crash into the darkness of the cellar. He stroked her hair; she thought he might be kissing the top of her head. His comfort flowed around her. She relaxed against him. But still she said, "That girl will be back. Bee. She will be back."

"Yes." He did not stop stroking her hair. She did not want him to stop.

She said, "Let's go. Let's slip away before they all come in and want to talk to us."

She turned within his arm and he shepherded her back down the passage as if she were an invalid. She felt in her pocket and gave him the car key. "You drive," she said, not looking at him.

She thought that if he pulled in nearer the towans and took her in his arms again, she would let it happen. But he did not stop until they were in the drive of the rectory. And then he made brief farewells to Matthew and Harry and got into his own car to leave. She stood

356

there, waving to him, until Harry called, "I've made some soup, Lucy. Can you spare the time to have some with us?"

She could spare the time. She smiled congratulations at him. "You're cooking again, are you? I just hope this isn't mushroom soup."

He promised her it was not. Matthew was already eating his appreciatively and she frowned at him. The very people you expected to have manners certainly did not. If Barbara or Denny started before grace was said they would have got a good rap on the knuckles.

Harry said, "You look rather pleased with yourself, Lucy. You weren't put off by the house any more?"

"No." She sat down and picked up her spoon. "And neither will you be, Harry." She told them both about the psychedelic wallpaper and the umbrellas and laughed at their expressions. "You'll really like it, Harry. The Flower People did it for you." He said something about squatting and she said, "They're borrowing it, that's all. Once you're in they'll probably leave till next summer."

He stared at her. "I thought the grand plan was that I was going back to Avis?"

"I don't want the house, Harry. Seriously. It's yours. William is going to draw up the necessary papers. Apparently it will make quite a big difference to my income tax!" She laughed. "That's why I'm looking pleased with myself. So please don't spoil it."

She ate her soup. They both babbled on. It was delicious; Harry was a good cook even if he was a vegetarian. She voiced this and he told her in no uncertain terms that Avis could keep the vegetarian cookbooks.

They all smiled at each other and before Harry could start up again she said, "There's something else too. I feel pleased because I don't hate Connie Vickers — Connie Mather — any more."

She got up to clear the plates and thought with surprise that she meant that. She couldn't still be hating Connie if she had actually avoided kissing William again. And probably again and again.

CHAPTER
SIXTEEN

Later, Lucy thought that she should have known the Trips were returning to America for good. But they left a stock of Tad's food as usual and some special plant food for the berberis and Gus made plans for the spring term; they could not have known themselves. But she had had a gut feeling for some time now; Margaret's enthusiasm was still there but her restless mind was looking for something else. Even so, she appeared to have to tear herself away for her "duty Christmas", as she called it. Everything was as usual on the surface. Margaret was pleased that William Mather had taken the trouble to come down and be an advocate for Lucy over the farm business. More so that he had gone with her to the house and discovered the Flower People still there. For some reason Lucy did not tell her that she was gifting the place to Harry Membury; Margaret had never really taken to him. And she could never tell anyone that she had kissed William.

The Trips had opened so many doors for them; the television, the telephone, the car, had all been instigated by them. The swimming had died a death since the weather became colder; even the warm water of the pool could not tempt them. But Lucy and the girls had kept up the allotment and were back to using only home-grown vegetables. That was their own thing; the skill they had brought with them from the towans. Lucy did not mention it but some time during the late autumn Margaret had given up helping with the allotment. She pleaded a bad back.

They left for America before the end of the school term. Ellie and Gus actually appeared to enjoy a tearful farewell. Gus cuddled Denny and Barbara and stroked the cats. Ellie asked her at least three times to write every day. Margaret put a Christmas sack of presents under the tree and Lucy gave her the lightweight package specially requested. "Something that will poke down the side of one of the cases without breaking," Margaret had stipulated. The outer brown paper was so pliable it obviously contained either scarves, ties or handkerchiefs or all three.

Margaret said, "Well done, Luce. You did listen to me for once!" She laughed and pecked at Lucy's cheek. Lucy smiled back and just for a moment saw something in Margaret's face that almost frightened her. Without stopping to think, she flung her arms around the thin frame and held her tightly, and after a startled moment Margaret put her own long arms right around her friend and lifted her off her feet.

Marvin stepped in. "Come on, you two girls! No tears now. Just because Gus and Ellie want to make a drama of it, there's no need for you to follow suit!" He drew Lucy away and kissed her cheek. And then they were gone.

Lucy had assumed that Margaret was deliberately cooling their friendship because of Marvin. He was not possessive but there were certain social occasions Margaret was expected to attend and she had twice begged off working on the allotment because she had to keep her nails decent. "Marvin knew I was a farm girl when he asked me to marry him so I don't know what all the fuss is about!" she had said. Yet Marvin had been so generous and easy-going it was hard to imagine him making a fuss about a broken nail. And then came that moment when Margaret's face had opened to her and shown her such misery that she had responded with a hug like a python's.

She worked hard to dispel that look from her memory. She baked and roasted and checked on her chutneys and jams; cleaned the house from top to bottom; took Harry to Roach's farm and on the journeys there and back told herself sternly that of course Margaret was not dying of some terrible cancer and keeping it a dreadful secret.

Ellie's new job helped. As soon as the Laurels closed for the holiday she wrote an introductory letter to the librarian at Truro Central, suggesting a storytelling session once a week. She listed the books she had used with her little groups in Hayle library and left her telephone number too. The librarian responded immediately and asked whether Monday afternoons would suit Ellie. "The main library is closed on that day while we catalogue and do repairs in the back room. You could have all that space for action drama if you felt like it. Some mothers will come in case you need help and we're just a knock on the door away." Ellie was slightly overwhelmed and the librarian picked up on that and immediately said, "Look. Just try it. One session — I will advertise one session only. If it works . . . well, who knows?"

It worked very well. Barbara and Denny were inclined to be over-helpful but by the end of the session they were very willing to "sit quietly" and "just listen". The pile of books they had accumulated for Ellie to read were all put back neatly, the biscuit crumbs swept up and thanks from the mothers accepted.

"We done it back in Hayle," Denny said, nodding graciously.

"How would you feel about having sessions twice a week?" asked the librarian, watching one of the mothers hoist a child on to her left hip then another on to the right. "I think there's quite a need for this during the Christmas period."

Barbara and Denny were all for it, Ellie doubtful. "Leaving Mum twice a week for a whole afternoon . . ." Ellie was very protective of her mother; she imagined her own dear father rescuing Lucy and a five-year-old Egg from that house and that cellar and she wanted to do the same.

Barbara interrupted. "Make her come, Ellie! She's really good at cuddling."

Lucy had half planned to take the girls to the rectory for Christmas Day. She could cook a chicken and do vegetables. They might get there in time for the family service over in the church, and then after their meal they could walk across the towans and the girls could see Roach's farm. She had told them about the collage work and knew they would be entranced with the umbrellas and the swags of nylon . . . It would give her a base for talking to them about the really old days when her mother had shown her what a wonderful thing the world was. She knew that Ellie had told them concisely about their grandfather. She needed to give them alternatives — to share some treasured memories to offset the nightmares.

It was a surprise when the girls did not show much enthusiasm for her plans. Barbara said very practically, "It's awful cold in the rectory, Mum. And I don't want to see the farm."

"Not even when Harry is living there?" Lucy asked.

"P'raps. Don't know."

"Can we come home for the carols in the k'feedral?" Denny said from where she was squatting by Matthew's saucer of milk, "helping" him to drink.

"She means the cathedral carols in the afternoon, Ma." Ellie lifted Mark to the other side of the saucer, leaving no room for Denny's pudgy fingers. She led Denny to the sink for a wash. "You remember, we went last year just before teatime. It was lovely."

Lucy had thought last year was only slightly better than the two terrible years before; their first Christmas without Egg and then their first in Truro. Last year they still didn't know many people in the city and the Trips of course had gone to America. But she had forced herself to wrap the girls up and take them to the cathedral service in a desperate attempt to find some kind of meaning before the day ended. She had thought it was a failure, yet here was Ellie telling her it had been lovely.

She said, "Well, of course we will stay here if that is what you want. I thought you would so enjoy an afternoon walk on the towans."

Barbara said, "It will be windy. It's always windy. And Daddy's cottage has gone. Ellie told us."

"I want to stay with Matthew and Mark," Denny said firmly.

Lucy laughed incredulously. "Home is best!" She should be relieved — she was relieved — but wondered when Steep Street had become "home" and the towans without Pardoe Cottage had become simply "windy".

Ellie put Denny on a chair and moved it close to the table. "We have to hurry. Ma, please come to the library with us. It's really nice. Bigger than at Hayle, of course, but the children are just the same."

Lucy looked doubtful. "It's not for adults, surely?"

"Well, some mums go. And you could help . . . you know, the toilet and things."

Lucy grinned, accepting a role. She was proud of Ellie for seeing the librarian and offering to read stories through the Christmas holidays. She said, "OK, I'll do that. And in return can we have the two rectory boys for Christmas dinner? Here?"

The girls looked puzzled then Ellie laughed aloud. "I'll tell them that. The rectory boys! They will love it!"

On Christmas Eve the last bundle of cards arrived. There was a big white envelope from the States with a

364

star sticker and the words "silent night" written in silver across it. Lucy put it on the mantelpiece to be opened later; but she was certain that there would be no letter enclosed. She had written two weeks ago, the day after they had flown. It had been unwise, to say the least; she could not remember her exact words but she did remember feeling frantic.

There was a reproduction of an old Giles cartoon in aid of the lifeboats, which she knew would be from Josh. No message, just the signature. There was a Victorian scene from Harry and a photograph of the church from Matthew, both saying they were looking forward to seeing all of them on Christmas Day. And Dr Carthew had sent a printed card. The last one was from Chippy Penberthy with a scrawled message to say he was very well but his poor wife was failing and soon he would be "free". Lucy stared at it in disbelief and then threw it on the back of the fire in disgust.

The day itself went very quickly. The rectory boys arrived at one o'clock, the back of Matthew's car full of presents. The meal was completely traditional but the table decorations were different. Ellie had wedged a tall red candle in a large bowl and surrounded it with everything she could think of: silver balls, fir cones, a few fallen twigs from the Christmas tree and her old hair ribbons. Barbara and Denny had cut pictures from magazines and propped them against water glasses and under cutlery. They wore some of their presents, a tiara each and a jangling collection of wire bracelets from the market.

Matthew gave them each a Book of Common Prayer bound in white leather. They handled them with awe. "Everything you need for a church service is in there," he told them, trying to look suitably solemn. "The liturgy, hymns, psalms, funeral services . . . weddings." He remembered jocular uncles from the past. "You will need to know about weddings, that's for sure."

Barbara and Denny giggled and clutched their beautiful books to them. Matthew looked at Ellie and thought what a wonderful wife she would make for a parish priest. He was surprised to see a momentary look of distaste cross her perfect heart-shaped face. But then she said, "We have already needed the funeral service twice — that's for sure." And he thought he understood.

Harry gave them what he called a "family present". On his walks along the towans before and after his "accident", he had gathered the many dead palm leaves littering the dunes and dried them in the cluttered kitchen of the rectory. He had enlisted the help of the therapist who had been making visits that winter and produced a large basket.

"I have varnished it but I doubt it is fully waterproof so it won't last long outdoors."

They were all delighted with it. Lucy tucked it in under the tree almost reverently and turned to Harry. "It is completely beautiful," she said. "A piece of the towans for all of us." The girls agreed vociferously and hugged him and, after a moment's hesitation, so did Lucy. Harry held himself very still and looked as if he might cry and it could have become embarrassing but the cats, prowling curiously through wrapping paper and string, found the basket and settled into it with loud purrs. And everyone laughed.

The cathedral service was well attended, mostly by families with small children who brought their gifts to "show Jesus". The lights were extinguished and candles lit and handed out for the pilgrimage around the crib. In the melee afterwards the girls saw schoolfriends and grinned widely. Ellie introduced her history teacher and Harry shook her hand and listened to her eulogy on Ellie's "sense of time". Matthew talked to one of the clergy. A young man put a hand on Lucy's shoulder and said, "You don't recognize me. I gave you lilacs last spring."

Lucy looked at a very ordinary young man, conventional enough in an enormous oiled wool sweater and jeans. She glanced at his feet and saw comfortable-looking desert boots. "So you did. They were lovely but . . ."

He took her up. "They didn't last. That was part of the message. Happiness, like beauty, is ephemeral."

"Oh dear." She looked towards the crib where children were gathered more informally now, listening to the story the bishop was telling them. "So . . . we have to make up our minds to put up with human misery?" She smiled. She knew suddenly that in spite of everything she had a sort of content.

"No. That is ephemeral too. But there is something else." He grinned even as he began to move away. "We're looking for it."

Denny said, "Who was that, Mummy?"

"That was the lilac man, my maid."

"What is he looking for?"

"He doesn't know yet."

They were swept towards the west doors, where various clerics were shaking hands and wishing happiness right, left and centre. Outside, across the big apron towards the little shops, the lanterns and fairy lights flickered through the trees in the gusts of wind. Denny clasped her hands. "It's magic!" she said.

"I think it must be," Lucy agreed.

They waited for the others and struggled back up Steep Street for tea and ginger beer and then sang carols and told stories until supper. And all the time the cats slumbered and woke in Harry's basket and accepted titbits from eager hands like Roman emperors.

When it was time for bed, Matthew kissed Barbara and Denny and took Ellie's extended hand in one of his and Lucy's in the other. He said, "It's been a very special time. Thank you." Harry smiled and nodded and waited until the younger girls jumped up at him for a kiss. Then he opened the door and went outside to Matthew's car without a word.

Lucy closed the door, turned, and held out her arms. The three girls stood within them. No one spoke for a few seconds, then Denny, unable to stay still any longer, jumped up and down and said, "Can we do this every year till we die, Mum?"

Lucy saved her letter from Margaret until Boxing Day. Since her marriage to Daniel the day after Christmas

368

had been probably her favourite day of the year. Meals were all ready, every leftover vegetable was fried in her biggest iron pan, cut into crisp slices and topped with cold poultry and stuffing. This year she had agreed to have a picnic in front of the television to watch the *Snow White* cartoon. She spread a sheet on the floor instead of a tablecloth and pulled the sofa round to enclose both fire and television set. After she had cleared the plates she put out dishes of mince pies and jelly and settled herself in a corner of the sofa with the precious card. The girls sat on the floor and leaned against her legs. She smiled; for two pins she could have put her head down and had an afternoon sleep. She slid out the card and tucked inside was a letter. The letter. The dwarves were singing as they marched to work in the mine . . . Doc's glasses were slipping down his button nose, Sneezy was sneezing prolifically . . . and she read,

My most precious friend, there is only one way to end this and that is quickly. A knife cut. A knife that hurts terribly and then heals fast. I think you knew — just at the last you knew. I could not believe — before then — that you did not understand my love for you. I thought you were acting up, like Denny, like you did with the lilac man — that you were trying to make me jealous. A couple of times you hugged me like you really cared and then you would get on with seeing to Harry as if you really were in love with *him*! And the bloody car. I was the one who talked you into learning to drive a car — dammit, Luce, I taught you how to do it! And then off you go. You called it your key to freedom — what did that mean? Freedom from me? And then, when we said goodbye, I saw that you had not understood anything. You've gone through what you've gone through, Luce, and you didn't see — understand — my love for you. You read it in my face then, didn't you, my dearest? And you tried to hold me, tried to keep me from leaving. And then, like me, you knew you couldn't. We're ashamed, Luce. Ashamed of our love. It's unnatural, against nature, against the law. It's illegal for men so it must be for women. But for us it's worse than that, isn't it? Because of Marvin, because of Gus, I can never live with you. And because of Harry and your three lovely girls you could never live with me . . .

Lucy had read so far in leaps, certain she was still misunderstanding, certain this was one of Margaret's crazy jokes. But at that point she knew this was no joke. She put her hand palm down over the page and took a deep breath that was almost a gasp.

Ellie looked up, "You OK, Mum?"

Lucy cleared her throat. "Bit of mince pie went the wrong way."

Denny started to sing with the dwarves as they marched off to work. Ellie laughed, still looking at her mother. Lucy joggled her knees in time to the song and

Denny pretended to collapse. They all went back to the film.

Lucy stayed very still, laughing when they laughed, ruffling Barbara's hair, rubbing her own throat as if it were sore. After a long time she looked again at the letter. This was from Margaret. Her friend, Margaret. In a strangely numb way she began to read again.

Here comes the knife, Luce. You are so sensible that you will know instantly it is the only way. Marvin has taken a job with General Motors. Detroit, in other words. He has been so kind. He could have been disgusted and chucked me out, I guess. But he just held me when I cried, which was a lot and often. He talked about love being love and that nothing could alter that. But he thinks we can go back to being how we were before you and I met. Maybe we can. One thing is certain, we have to try.

That's it, my dearest. That's the knife done with. Forgive me, Luce.

One last thing. I wanted to do something splendid for you. Something that would make you love me as I loved you. Marvin found your Bertie McKinley's parents. They live in Florida. I phoned them and they told me to give you their address and then leave it to you. I didn't do that, Luce. I pretended, even to myself, that I had not traced them. I did not want you to go to America and find someone else and leave me behind . . . I will print the address on a separate page and you will do what you have to do. I'm sorry, Luce. I'm really sorry. What we had was so sweet and I wanted more. I still want more. Or nothing.

She put her hand over the page again and squashed it into her palm. Ellie looked up and said again, "OK, Mum?"

"Yes. A lovely card from Margaret and Gus and Marvin. Look." She slid the card away from her hand and Ellie took it. On the screen Snow White sang that one day her prince would come. Lucy put the two sheets of crumpled paper into her sleeve with one of her new handkerchiefs. Barbara was weeping sentimental tears and she picked her up and held her beneath her own chin and stared at the cartoon and said steadily, "Daddy told me that the artists had to draw hundreds of pictures just to make Snow White lift her arm like that."

Ellie looked up and smiled. "There's a book about it at the library — they call it a flicker book. I'll show you when we go next." She stood up. "I'll put Margaret's card on the tree, shall I?"

The snow came with the new year. The news programmes had been showing "snow chaos" for three days up-country and the locals had looked smug and said such weather never reached Cornwall. But 1963 was to prove them wrong. During the first week Matthew telephoned to say that "that idiot" had moved into the farm and was now cut off and had got no phone and probably no food.

372

"The people at Home Farm will take him some groceries," Lucy tried to reassure him.

"They don't know he's there. And he's not strong — still has to use his stick some days."

Lucy knew he had not used his stick at Christmas and though he was as skinny as a bean pole, she thought he was probably fitter than the reverend.

She cut to the chase. "How are you managing without him?"

"Mrs Penberthy has been bringing me the occasional meal. She's no cook but it keeps body and soul together."

Lucy grinned; so Mrs Penberthy was not failing after all. "I bet she charges highly for doing that."

"She certainly does. She has blackmailed me into including the three grandkids in the Confirmation classes. They're much too young of course but I moved the goalposts slightly — the bishop was surprisingly co-operative."

Lucy stifled her laughter. She said, "Don't worry about Harry, he's not alone out there."

There was a pause while Matthew worked that out, then he said, "You are surprisingly open-minded about Harry and those damned Flower People."

"I want him to be happy. I know it's ephem . . . ephem . . . I know it won't last but he needs something, someone. Avis is . . . like a viper. It must have been awful. And the sooner he is settled the sooner he can send for the girls."

Matthew said, "You really did go through that notebook, Lucy."

373

"I suppose I did." If only Margaret had kept a similar notebook. Lucy handed the telephone to Ellie, who wanted the name of an author he had been recommending. They were all going to the library for one of Ellie's readings and Barbara and Denny looked marvellous in fur-trimmed caps and mittens. They crowded to the door and waited impatiently while Ellie wrote down something laboriously letter by letter, then they squashed through the door as quickly as possible so that Lucy could close it against the cold.

The snow was piled from pavements to road but across the wide expanse of the quay it was smooth and almost unsullied. Even Lucy enjoyed the complicated footprint game which involved them walking in line and backtracking now and then so that looking back they could convince themselves a wild animal was on the prowl in Truro. "The yeti," Ellie shouted and clasped her chest in pretended terror. "Half a dozen whatever-you-said," her mother commented drily. They were convulsed the next day when a picture of the snow prints was on the front page of the local paper and the headline asked, "*A visitor from the Himalayas?*"

But that night Ellie said, "Will the weather mean that Gus can't get back for the new term, Ma?"

Lucy took a deep breath and told them that Marvin had been offered a wonderful new job and the Trips had decided to stay in America. "It's their home . . . their real home. And this sort of opportunity . . . well, they had no choice really." The girls stared, stunned. The Trips were part of their lives. Lucy said, "There was a note in the Christmas card. I didn't know how to tell you."

Ellie said, "I knew there was something. Oh Ma, you will miss Margaret so much. And Gus . . . Gus is my best friend."

"Yes. But you will be all right, Ellie, won't you?"

"Oh, at school. Yes. But Gus was here. All the time."

Barbara said, "What about Tad? And the house?"

"I don't know." Lucy felt helpless again as the pain of Margaret's love washed over her. "We'll go on feeding Tad and wait to see what happens."

Barbara said, "They were funny. And happy." And Denny, looking from one to the other, started to cry.

Strangely, the weather helped them through most of that spring term. It was a constant challenge every time they left the house. They would crowd to the kitchen window as it got light and watch Matthew and Mark leap like tiny gazelles through the fresh powder and run up on to the wall, scattering snow, slipping and clawing frantically at the ivy and then pausing for a quick wash before making their perilous way to the ridge and the warmth of the chimney pot and their own special view of the sea.

After the first week Lucy brought Tad back with her and he needed no persuasion to settle by the fire in Harry's palm-leaf basket. He loved them all but he was always Lucy's cat. Because he purred so loudly when he was on her lap, she sat down more often. The afternoons were short and she took to eating lunch by the fire and dozing for an hour before collecting the girls. She could have dreamed of Margaret or simply thought about her but in the no-man's-land between sleeping and waking, with one hand on Tad's soft fur, it was as if they walked together. The shock of Margaret's disclosure then the suspicion that their friendship had not been true friendship at all walked between them. She hardly knew when the suspicion melted and became Margaret's pain; one afternoon her eyes opened quite suddenly and she understood that pain. She understood why Margaret had been unable to talk to her, had been forced to plan her own escape so secretly. And she was able to separate her own feelings; betrayal and anger, grief and loss . . . They were nothing compared with Margaret's pain.

Lucy looked down at Tad, who lifted his head and smiled sleepily. She whispered, "I can cope with this. And so can the girls." She put him down very gently and went for the flimsy air letter she had bought. She sat at the kitchen table and began to write.

It is already getting dark though the snow will stay light because there's a full moon hanging over the quay. I have been dreaming that we are walking up towards the allotment, no snow, the smell of growing things pushing up through the earth. There is no stopping life, Margaret. We might as well just let it happen. Perhaps enjoy it. I do hope so. I am going to meet the girls now. It takes ages to wrap up against the weather, this is how it must be for you every winter. It is a shock to us. Tad is fine. Ellie has probably already written to Gus so I

will get news of you now and then and you of me.
God bless and keep you always. Luce.

She folded the thin paper along all the dotted lines,
stuck it down and printed Margaret's name and
address on one side and her own on the other. Then she
donned an extra cardigan, her coat, scarf, woollen hat,
gloves and boots and left the house, clutching the letter.
She dropped it into the postbox with a murmured "love
to you".

It was almost Easter before she got out her "key to
freedom" and drove along the old A30 to Portreath and
the coast road. It had been a waiting time, a time of
hibernation, a time of survival too.

Now she must go and see Harry Membury.

CHAPTER
SEVENTEEN

Connie so wanted a son for William; *another* son for William. And the fact that William was cautious seemed to make it more urgent. They had both agreed to wait until May "settled down". After May's birth it seemed there was no time to discuss anything, but, as Greta kept saying, "Give her a year to get used to things and she'll be fine."

It seemed that Greta was right.

May had not liked the long night watches and wailed for her mother — for anyone — every two hours. They had been advised by health visitors, their doctor, the other young mothers Connie met at Frankie's playgroup — everyone except Rosemary and Greta — that May should sleep in her own room. May told them in the only way she knew that this was not the case. Every two hours she told them. Connie padded back and forth across the landing, gave her boiled water and a cuddle and stayed until she was asleep again.

Rosemary said, "Darling, you look a bit on the gaunt side. Why don't you have the cot right next to your bed and just reach over to her now and then?"

Greta was worse. "Listen, Connie. Have her in with you. Let her feel you and smell you."

Connie was amazed at both of them. "Mummy, William wouldn't get any sleep at all then! And I can catch up in the day — she's an angel all day long. Well, almost."

She shook her head at Greta. "It's absolutely *out* these days to take your baby into bed with you. You could roll over and smother it."

At eight months May learned to crawl. Two weeks later she could climb. The day after her first birthday, probably accidentally, she found she could let down the side of her cot and drop down on to the floor without too much trouble. Connie found her at the top of the stairs.

They put her in with Frankie next door to their room. He was as sunny as ever and welcomed her with his usual clapping and cries of "Maybe Maybe", which Rosemary reckoned was an amalgamation of May and baby. Arnie said it simply meant perhaps, and perhaps Perhaps was a good name for May. Rosemary took a long time to work that one out and then did not even smile.

Connie was doubtful for Frankie's sake but he had slept through it all so far and she crossed her fingers and agreed to try it. They could hardly tie her into her cot; they decided that before they brought her in with them they would try the night nursery.

At last May had got it across that she needed company. When she woke up that first night, the dimmed light showed her brother contentedly asleep in the little bed next to her cot, arms upflung. When she woke again, it was morning.

Connie was overjoyed in every way.

"A lovely month to conceive a new baby," she said. "August, high summer. And the baby would be born in May, like the others . . . Oh darling, I'm so happy. Shall we try? What do you say?"

"I say we've got a boy and we've got a girl. Just a year between them. Don't you feel we're rather well set up as things are?"

"Of course. But I also feel that we haven't finished yet. You did actually mention a cricket side to Arnold a few years ago."

"In an attempt to be jocular."

"Yes. Eleven children would take too long. I did think two pairs. For tennis."

He was almost asleep. Arnold had come into the office today and disrupted everything. He murmured, "Who's for tennis?"

"Me," she breathed into his ear.

And because he found her irresistible he made languorous love to her and then could not sleep for ages because he was certain that she imagined having babies would assuage her guilt for being alive when Egg Pardoe was not. She slept like a top, woke at six o'clock and started kissing him all over again. He protested but, as she pointed out, she wanted to start the day really well before May came crashing in. At thirteen months May Mather could climb over the side of her cot with ease, open the door of the nursery and scramble into her parents' bed without any trouble. She had tried to get in with Frank but the bed was too narrow and she kept slipping out. She was sure of a welcome next door; she had tested her parents for a year and they had passed the test with flying colours. When her grandmother told her she was spoiled she clapped her hands delightedly. Rosemary shook her head in mock despair; she too had passed that particular test many months ago.

After the instant conceptions of Frankie and May, pregnancy had eluded Connie and she had begun to panic. The meaning of her existence seemed to hang on giving birth. And then one very hot day, she was horribly sick. She checked the calendar and realized it was almost the anniversary of Frankie's conception. She refused to remember the tidal wave, refused to remember Philip Pardoe. It had been the time she had let her dear William stay in her room all night long. It simply had to be a good omen.

She waited the prescribed three months before consulting their doctor; it was a formality and the pregnancy was confirmed in November 1963. The next day, as the news cameras flashed the terrifying pictures of John Kennedy's death across the world, she knew that the pregnancy was over. She did everything she could, took to her bed, feet higher than body, kept calm as the doctor said she should. It made no difference. She wept. "I know now how Lucy Pardoe felt," she said to William that night as he administered the medicine that would hopefully help her to sleep.

He looked at her in the glow of the bedside lamps. It was a year since he had gone to see Lucy to sort out her father's estate, a year since she had kissed him and he had had a glimpse of her life and her losses. He whispered, "Oh my darling, I hope you never will."

And she, who knew as much as William knew about Lucy Pardoe except for that kiss, and was linked to her by ties that had no name, whispered, "So do I, William. Oh, so do I."

He watched her until her eyelids began to droop and then undressed and put on his pyjamas and dressing gown, and went into the nursery to check on the children. He thought of his brothers and parents, then of Arnhem, then of Lucy Pardoe. He held the edge of the cot and could not stop the flow — the torrent — of thoughts. The young president shot in front of his people at a moment of triumph. Maurice Heatherington soldiering on without Greta, a hero instead of a rotter. Rosemary Vickers bringing up her daughter on her own. And the baby, Connie's and his new baby, dead before life even began.

May sighed prodigiously and flung up a pudgy hand. He smiled, tucked it under the honeycomb blanket and remembered how she had cried every night when the snows had come last winter and they had been terrified something was really wrong.

And then he let himself think of Arnold and Rosemary, and then, blessedly, of Connie and himself. In spite of their loss, they had so much.

He went to Frank's small bed and looked down at the golden boy. He seemed, quite suddenly, to hold the promise of . . . everything.

William went to his own bed and held his wife gently to his shoulder. He was in exactly the same position when he woke the next morning to feel May climbing in beside him. He smiled at her and helped her up and thought he had probably been smiling all night too.

Rosemary woke to a grey November dawn and the memory of Connie's desperate phone call yesterday. "Mummy, I've lost him! He's dying . . . he's leaving me . . . Oh Mummy, I can't spare him!"

For an appalled moment Rosemary had thought she was talking about William and sat down with a bump on the hall chair. Arnold emerged from the kitchen, eating a piece of toast. "What's up?"

She said, "I'll be with you in half an hour."

"No. William is with me. The doctor is on the way. All I can do is to lie down and . . . hope." There came a little sob that tore at Rosemary's heart. Then Connie said, "I don't know how I will bear this."

Rosemary held out a hand to Arnie and he took it and held it.

"Listen, Connie. You will bear whatever comes. Perhaps this baby is not meant to be . . ." She sounded heartless and trite and bit her lip fiercely. "If you have to lose him then it is better now than — than . . ." She stopped speaking, hearing her own words. She sobbed, "Darling, let me come and be with you."

"No, Mummy. You are right. And it is something William and I have to do by ourselves. Honestly. Let me speak to Arnie."

Arnie put the last of his toast into his mouth and took the receiver with his spare hand. Connie's voice was urgent in his ear.

"Don't let Mummy leave the house today, Arnie. I need her to be there."

He was about to reassure her but she replaced her receiver.

"She's gone," he said. "She wants you to stay here." He leaned over Rosemary and replaced their receiver. "Darling, I have picked up that she's having a miscarriage. But nothing terrible can happen, can it? Surely she's only been pregnant five minutes?"

Rosemary looked at him. Then she drew his face down and kissed him. "Dear Arnie. When we got married you didn't realize that you were taking on so much, did you? You weren't too keen about May at first, if you remember. Especially when poor William arrived at the office unshaven. Twice. This is worse. Much worse, my love."

She went to kiss him again and he drew back. "Sweetheart, your lip is bleeding and the taste of blood does not go well with buttered toast."

She had known he was trying to cheer her up but somehow it hadn't helped and she had spent the rest of the day doing housework as if her life depended on it. No one had phoned until late that night, then it had been William.

"Greta came and took the children out in the twin pram thing. They're in bed now and the doctor has given me some medicine for Connie. It's all right, Rosie. She's inconsolable at the moment. But I'll phone tomorrow. Try not to worry."

And here was tomorrow, already eight thirty and he hadn't phoned. She looked at Arnie, on his side, fast asleep. She eased herself out of bed and went downstairs, put breakfast on a tray and took it up. He did not open his eyes but smiled widely and said, "I love you. And yes, of course we will drive over to Edgbaston and take the kids out for a few hours."

She put down the tray and poured tea. "No. They will ask for help if they need it. And I rather think that Connie needs Frank and May as much as they need her. I will do a Lancashire hotpot and we can take it in on our way to see Maurice and Greta."

He opened his eyes and hauled himself up against the pillows, watching her as she put a splash of milk in the mug of tea and placed it on the bedside table. She sipped her own tea and answered one of his unspoken questions.

"We arranged to see Maurice and Greta today. About the Brighton sale. You remember."

"Yes. I thought you would not want to go. In the circumstances."

"I particularly want to go. It was good of Greta to take the babies out yesterday. I used to think she'd got a thing for William like she had for you, but she is very close to Connie."

"Couldn't get much closer than sharing her labour pains." He reached for some toast. "That was strange."

"It was. And before that, if you remember, Connie dreamed of seeing Maurice in Brighton. She visited there just once and remembered the Pavilion. And that was where she saw him."

He rolled his eyes. "Women!" he said.

"I'm a woman."

"Yes, but you stick to your own labour pains and you don't dream."

"As a matter of fact I had the strangest dream the night after Maria's wedding. I dreamed we were making mad passionate love — I didn't know where and it was pitch black. And then suddenly a spotlight came on and we were on the set of *Sink and Swim* and the auditorium was absolutely packed with people and they all started to applaud."

He was stunned. Then he said, "You're making it up."

She nodded smugly. "It wasn't even at night actually. I dreamed it up when we were in the cathedral and Maria was coming down the aisle. It would have nobbled all her thunder and served her right after she and Vallender spied on us all through that summer and autumn."

"Challenger, darling. And don't you think we might have been slightly embarrassed?"

"Not a bit. I forgot to tell you we were fully clothed and you had your Sherlock Holmes overcoat on."

He managed to swallow his toast without choking and then he grabbed her and pulled her on top of him and told her she was a wicked wanton woman but that she tasted better today; lemon marmalade was nicer than human blood. And she replied with a scream of horror.

Greta was delighted to see them. "I did wonder whether you would come. Connie is so sad, I thought she might need you."

386

"She's got William. She's up today. We left them all by the fire playing with Frank's engine. We have to play it down, Greta. She was only three months."

"Yes." She sighed deeply. "I thought I might have shared this one too. Perhaps I should be feeling her grief for her."

Rosemary shrugged out of her coat and looked at Arnold. He said bracingly, "Come on now. They will have another baby. Not too quickly, I hope."

Maurice took their coats and produced two pairs of slippers, gloriously warm from the fireside. "I listened to what you said about this slipper thing." He grinned at Arnie. "You were quite right. Any more tips?"

"I reckon you're doing well on your own." Arnold eased his feet into knitted slippers topped with pom-poms. "I take it Greta made these?"

"Pinched them from the theatre," Maurice said. "I'd quite forgotten that she's low on morals."

"I've got my own morals, thank you, Moll." Greta kissed him forgivingly then turned to Rosemary. "They're pulling down the old theatre — the Cochrane. Did you know? Most of the costumes went with the cast on tour so I took what I could. Waste not, want not."

"How goes the tour?"

"Pretty good. The author has done something else for them. Roger asked me if I would like to go back when they have a read-through." She smiled. "It was nice to be asked but I said thanks but no thanks."

She sat them around her oval gate-leg table. Arnold almost closed it with his right knee. He held the leaf up while Rosemary pulled out the leg again. There was laughter and references to "hanky-panky". They ate sausages and mash and then cabinet pudding. Greta told them that she and Connie had first met over cabinet pudding. "Only three years ago," she sighed. "What a lot has happened since then. Two babies and three weddings . . . well, two really because we were already married." She told Moll about it and how Connie had looked at the crumpled wedding snap and never forgotten it. "She dreamed about you, you know. That's how we tracked you down."

He could have told her that he had heard about Connie's dream several times before, but he did not.

Greta cleared the table, folded it down and drew the armchairs around the fire. Rosemary was surprised by this new aspect of someone she had tried hard to dismiss at first and then cautiously to appreciate as a "good friend to Connie". Now suddenly she had become as good a home-maker as Rosemary herself. They all watched the news on a tiny television and talked about President Kennedy and what he might have done had he lived and how his wife and children would now manage. Greta brought out an album of pictures from *Sink and Swim*. In spite of her proxy labour pains that first night, she had managed to snap a page labelled "Frank Fotos". There was Arnold, glass held high, gloriously drunk. Rosemary holding his other arm in case he fell off his chair. There was Maria, her eyes wide as she announced that Marcus's car was being towed away. The stage manager and her partner looking into each other's eyes with total love. Connie and William laughing and leaning in towards each other so that their heads touched . . . Other pages showed swatches of materials, the cast modelling-dressing gowns, Greta herself at a sewing machine, glasses on the end of her nose . . . "Don't bother with that, Rosie. I look about a hundred!" But Rosemary had discovered yet another Greta and said, "You look like an artist — nineteen twenties. You look beautiful." And Maurice — Moll, as Arnold was already calling him — crowed, "What did I tell you?"

At last they got down to the business of selling Maurice's newsagent's. It was straightforward enough. His father had let him take it on when Maurice married Jessie back in 1920 but there had been no legal contract, and when his father died twenty years later the Battle of Britain was at its height and paperwork had not been a priority. "Don't even know where Dad kept the deeds of the property," Maurice admitted ruefully. "And I'm pretty sure he never left a will. But I am the only child."

"That's good," Arnold said. "New deeds can be drawn up if necessary. After the war a lot of vital paperwork had to be reinvented. I've got your bank details and I'll see if they know anything. Let me have your father's death certificate and your birth certificate and we'll go ahead."

Maurice grinned, relieved. "I haven't got a head for all this stuff. Jessie did the accounts and dealt with the suppliers when she was able. Don't suppose anything is up to date. She was pretty bad towards the end."

Greta reached for his hand.

"Don't worry." Arnold became 100 per cent reassuring and Rosemary felt beneath the table and put her hand on his knee.

Later, as they were leaving, Greta said, "I should take you and Moll to Cornwall some time. It's a beautiful place and where we stayed had something special about it in spite of what happened to Connie and Philip." She smiled at her husband's expression. "It's what she called the boy who drowned. He was fixated on the American detective yarns he was reading. And she called him Philip. After Philip Marlowe, the private eye." She tucked Arnold's scarf into his coat and Rosemary felt her usual twinge of annoyance.

Greta went on sentimentally, "Actually I think that dreadful drowning brought Connie and William closer than ever. They should go back too. See the good things that happened."

"I don't think Connie could bear that," Rosemary said. "Not with May yelling the place down every night and this latest disaster."

Arnold said, "Darling, May is fine now. And perhaps the miscarriage is not a disaster. Mother nature and all that." He looked at her. "We could go with them. Next summer perhaps."

Greta said eagerly, "We could all go! Wouldn't it be fun? All of us on holiday together!"

Arnold hurried Rosemary down the steps and into the car. He waved at the two Heatheringtons standing under their porch light, arms around each other. He was suddenly overwhelmed by the fact that Greta was happy. Properly happy. He turned a beaming face to Rosemary and said, "Isn't it wonderful?"

She hugged her coat around her and said, "What? Exactly what is wonderful?"

"Love," he said simply. "Love is wonderful."

And quite suddenly she surrendered her small moment of irritability to the foggy November night and transferred her hug to his upper arm.

"Oh darling Arnie. It is indeed. Perhaps it really does conquer all."

"I'm sure of it."

"Even for poor Jackie Kennedy?"

"Yes. Even for her."

And they drove into the night.

All through that summer Lucy Pardoe visited Harry Membury occasionally at her old home on the dunes. After the snow and ice it was wonderful for her to get into her green Hillman Minx and feel again that heady freedom of the road. And she missed Harry. He still irritated her at times but after reading his notebook she had begun to see him differently. His bid for a new life had seemed foolish and irresponsible to her at first. Gradually it attained something like an aura of heroism. He too was testing out a sense of freedom. And that first visit had been almost involuntary; as if they were joined by a long length of elastic.

He never knew when she was coming; she did not know herself. He had no phone so there was no way of inviting herself to the farm. Now and then she had an irresistible urge to see him and if he was planting or digging or just weeding she would join him immediately and work as hard as he did.

He said, "You know this soil, don't you? How can you bear to do this work of your own free will?"

She smiled at him. "That's why. Because I choose to do it." She turned the hoe and lifted a dandelion, root and all. "Anyway, this was my escape in a strange sort of way. My father hounded me out of the house to work the land but once I started he never touched me. I was too useful."

As the summer "took hold", as he put it, the Flower People began to come back. They used his kitchen and bathroom and on rainy days they would gather in the living room and strum their guitars. Some of them helped Harry with his project to make the barn habitable. The girls fed the hens, which seemed to be everywhere. It became apparent that they were not all penniless beggars and they paid Harry for board and lodging. Some of them found work in the fields. And Lucy grew used to them. She taught two of the girls to bake and when the autumn gales began and they drifted away, she and Harry went on beachcombing, delighted when they found an umbrella or a battered nylon tent.

Once she said, "Do you mind me coming here, Harry? It is your place now, legally yours. You don't have to put up with me if it's difficult in any way."

He answered her question with another. "Why do you come, Lucy?"

She hesitated, then said uncertainly, "I think I'm trying to get rid of nightmares." She grinned suddenly.

"That sounds the sort of thing Margaret would say. I'm getting used to the place again — that's what it boils down to."

He went to fetch another bucket for the weeds. "That's why I like to see you. You help me to get used to this place. I still see it as yours. When we're sharing it . . . well, it helps." He laughed, embarrassed, then changed the subject. "You must miss Margaret."

"I do, of course. But there was no choice for her. Not really."

When she came oftener than once a week he knew that her underlying loneliness was overwhelming. She had three daughters and a large house to look after; through schools, through Margaret, she had acquaintances who were almost friends. But on one level she was still terribly lonely. He had seen that loneliness the day that her son had drowned and he had recognized it because it was his; he had thought nobody else could feel it.

In early October there was an outbreak of chicken pox in Truro and all three Pardoe girls caught it within a week of each other. Three weeks later, Lucy got it and because she was nearly forty it was much worse than theirs and she was laid low until Christmas.

Matthew drove in to see them and was shocked to find Ellie coping with all three invalids, opening tins of soup and boiling kettles for hot-water bottles and lugging coal buckets in from the outside coal house. He drove home via the farm to unload his worries on to Harry.

"She's not fifteen yet and she's being used as a drudge! I'm surprised at Lucy letting things get to this pass. She can afford to pay for someone to come in and clean the house and do some cooking, surely to goodness?"

"Did you sort them out?" Harry looked satisfyingly worried. "I mean — the coal, for instance. You could stack buckets along the hall to last for a few days. And do some shopping perhaps? What about the cats?"

Matthew exploded. "Bugger the cats — three of them, for goodness' sake! They don't need looking after anyway — put them out and let them catch the mice. I'm certain they've got mice in the downstairs cloakroom."

"I doubt it. Listen, can I borrow the car tomorrow? I'll go over and help out for a bit."

Matthew nodded thankfully. "You should get a car. And have a telephone installed. Stuck out here by yourself. Not safe."

"I'll think about it. Really. And meanwhile I'll be over when it's light tomorrow morning."

Harry drove with exaggerated care along the A30 and turned off for Truro at nine o'clock. He went straight into the shopping area and loaded up with groceries, arriving outside Steep Street just before ten. Even the outside of the house looked drab and when Ellie opened the front door, the inside did as well. He should have guessed it was bad because Matthew had actually noticed it. All the Pardoes had loved and cared for this tall narrow house and now they were too poorly to care about anything.

Harry held Ellie to him and she wept thankfully and let him lead her into the kitchen and sit her down in front of the gas cooker. He lit the gas and opened the oven door and she crouched towards the heat while he fetched her coat and wrapped it around her.

He made tea and gave her a mugful, very hot and sweet, and she inhaled the steam and held the mug gratefully. Her rash was fading fast; she would be all right. He went into the living room and lit the fire with some difficulty. The kindling was not dry and even the newspapers were damp. Eventually, after smouldering its way through to the coal, it burst into life and he heard the radiators cracking as they heated through. He piled cushions and some rugs from the chairs and made a bed for Ellie on the sofa. She sank into it gratefully.

"Ma's really ill," she said. "I came downstairs for some more aspirin. The girls are still asleep. Anyway, they're not too bad, just grizzly."

He went upstairs with tea and aspirin. Lucy's room overlooked the street and was full of the quiet November morning light. He had never been in there before and peered tentatively around the door for permission to enter. She seemed to be asleep and had slipped down in her bed so that only the top of her head was visible. He hurried over, put down the tea and moved the sheet to uncover her face. It was scarred with the distinctive rash, her eyes sunk deeply into the larger pustules and her lips, slightly parted, were dry and cracked. She gave a small moan as the light hit her.

Then she saw him and tried to say his name. Then she tried to ask him what he was doing there. And then she hung on to him while he hoisted her on to her crumpled pillows.

He made her as comfortable as he could and held the tea for her to sip and answered her questions.

"Yes, it is Harry. And I am doing here what you did at the rectory for me last year. I have lit the fire and settled Ellie on the sofa. I haven't seen the girls yet because Ellie said they were still asleep. And I haven't seen the cats, so probably Ellie let them out. Yes, here are the aspirin. Two every four hours . . . well done." He replaced the bottle top. "What has the doctor left for you, Lucy?"

She tried to tell him that she still had not registered with a new doctor. He seemed to understand but said he would telephone for a prescription. She shook her head and gave up, pulling the sheet over her face again.

"Listen, Lucy. Finish this tea. Then I'll look in on the girls. Then I'm going to get you and Ellie some food. Is that all right, my dear?"

She nodded and tried to smile. "Glad," she whispered hoarsely. "To see you."

"Likewise." He grinned at her and then as a tear gathered in a corner of one eye, he smoothed her hair and kissed it gently. "Everything's going to be all right, my darling. Don't think. Try to relax."

He went across the landing to the back bedroom. Barbara and Denny were both awake, staring at the big square sash window framing a view of grey sky. Denny was whimpering with each breath, Barbara scratching

396

her arm. They turned, saw Harry and started to cry in unison. He gathered Denny into one arm and Barbara scrambled into the other.

"We told Matthew to tell you we were ill," Barbara hiccoughed. "We knew you would come."

Denny wailed loudly, "Don't leave us, Harry — please don't leave us!"

He calmed them down. "Listen. These are the plans. I've got more aspirins and more tissues and more fruity drinks in the car. So . . . what would you like to eat? Sausages? Eggs? Soup?"

"Not soup," Barbara said, suddenly interested. "We had soup yesterday and the day before. Ice cream. And celery. Sausages would be nice. And bread and butter and banana and sugar sandwiches."

Denny managed a smile. "And some jelly babies too."

He persuaded them to stay in their beds until the fire in the living room had warmed everything up. Then they could come down for a feast.

He ran down, reassured Ellie, fetched the shopping from the car and set to. Lunch was fruit juice and banana sandwiches and aspirin for the girls. He spooned scrambled egg into Lucy's dry mouth and held the glass while she sipped her fruit juice. "The fire is red hot. Perhaps later you could come downstairs but I need to ask Doc Carthew about that. I'm going to phone him now while you have a sleep."

Mrs Kervis answered the phone. "It's his day off, Mr Membury. You know that."

"I'd forgotten. Mrs Pardoe and her three girls have this chicken pox and I want some advice. Could he come to the phone?"

She said grudgingly, "I'll ask him."

He came to the phone but sounded immediately annoyed. "Honestly, Harry. You know I can't poach another preserve. You must ring her doctor in Truro."

"She hasn't registered with anyone yet." Harry hardened his tone. "She is still your patient. I need to know whether she can be moved. I am with them at the moment — I have Matthew's car, which, as you know, is a decent size. I want to take them back with me. To the farm. I've got chickens to feed tonight."

"Dammit, man, you can ask the Godolphins to do that for you. They've been helpful enough since you moved in — and before that."

"I can do. I will probably do that for tonight. But then I would prefer to look after them down on the dunes. It's what they're used to, John. The air, the sea . . ."

Dr Carthew said thoughtfully, "They were never ill when they lived there, I have to admit. And if Lucy hasn't bothered to find herself another doctor it would be easier all round if she was a bit nearer. What's the matter with the woman, is she trying to keep a foot in both camps?"

Harry was about to reply angrily and then paused. "Perhaps that is exactly what she is doing," he said slowly.

"Well, in that case, let's see what we can do." There were sounds of rustling. "I'll have to examine them all, make sure they're fit to be driven to your place. If so, I can take Lucy. You can take the girls and the bloody cats. You'll have to take blankets and clothes and food . . . This is ridiculous, Harry."

"No. It's not. I collect milk from Home Farm each day. They will supply other provisions." He paused, then rushed on, "Matthew will be our link. He wants to help — he looked after me."

"Lucy looked after you," Carthew said heavily. "But yes, he will see this as an opportunity to serve. I've got no calls tomorrow afternoon. I will be with you at two. If I don't think Lucy should be moved then I will see to re-registering the whole family. They will be entitled to a home help and will be far more comfortable in their own home. We'll discuss it when I arrive."

He replaced his receiver with a definite click and left Harry holding his, full of doubts. He had been so certain that the Pardoe women would be better back on the dunes . . . but Carthew was right. They had everything they needed right here and if a home help could be provided just like that . . . He looked into the living room; the three girls were cocooned in blankets, the fire was settling comfortably into a hot glow and the television was on. He bit his lip. He had no television.

He cleared up in the kitchen, made tea and took it upstairs to Lucy. She was in the bathroom but came out immediately and managed a smile. She looked very pink. Her hair was combed flatly to her head.

"Calamine." She pointed to her face and arms. "Takes away the itch." She moved haltingly back to bed. "Feel much better, Harry. Thank you. How are the girls?"

He described the scene in the living room and she forced another smile. "I really don't know how we would manage without the dratted television now," she said. "Marvin brought us into the modern world well and truly!" She stopped smiling as she pulled the bedclothes around her. Harry plumped the pillows and tucked her in, then sat down and told her of his conversation with Dr Carthew.

"I thought it would be so good for you all out on the dunes again. But you've got everything here. I'm pretty certain that the doctor is even now on the phone arranging for a home help . . . I'm so sorry, Lucy. I feel I am failing you badly. You looked after me and . . ."

She held up her hand to silence him. "Listen. There are four of us, Harry. Can you stay tonight?" When he nodded emphatically she closed her eyes with sheer relief. "I am so glad." She gathered strength visibly, then said, "Tomorrow, go home in Matthew's car. See to things. Come back the next day on the bus. Take my car. Come to see us . . . often. Will you?"

"My dear girl . . ."

"Thank you, Harry." She put her head back on the pillows, eyes still closed. He held the tea to her lips but she was already asleep. He gathered a glass and an empty aspirin bottle and crept downstairs.

It worked out exactly like that. Harry knew a deep contentment that transcended all the sheer hard work of the next three weeks. He knew all the Pardoe females were going to be well, given time and loving care, and simply to drive the green car from one coast to the other every day made him supremely happy. He left when it was dark and came home when it was dark but he still found time to do his normal chores and to get the house ready for . . . anything. Avis's solicitors sent him half the sale price of the house and he immediately bought a large freezer and gradually filled it. The cowman on Home Farm let him have three single beds and he began to furnish the bedrooms. Matthew offered him a television one of the parishioners had thrown out; at first it did not work but Harry spent time perched precariously on the roof turning the aerial this way and that until magically there was Andy Pandy getting into his box. He watched it avidly.

At the end of November the girls went back to school for the final weeks of term. They were still listless and on their first Monday Denny wept because she had missed the school party and Ellie was very quiet because she was missing Gus all over again. Barbara told them they were wet wallies and they hadn't missed the carol singing on the quay, nor the shopping, nor Christmas. Ellie managed a smile and Lucy said weakly, "Well done, Barbara!" And Harry, wheeling in a trolley loaded with tea and sandwiches, said, "Listen, all of you. How would you like to come and stay on the farm for Christmas? I've got the rooms all ready and I've put up new umbrellas everywhere and all down the hallway I've stuck pictures of Santa Claus in his sleigh. And . . . guess what . . . I've got a television set! I'm longing for you to see everything. It's different in one way but in another it's probably back to how it must have been when your grandmother was a little girl."

Denny cheered up instantly and Barbara clapped her hands; Ellie and Lucy exchanged glances. Ellie said, "We'd love it, of course. But Mum . . . she is still very weak, Harry. And everything is laid on here. Wouldn't it be better if you came to us?"

"Of course, if that's what you would prefer." Harry forced a grin. "Christmas is Christmas wherever we are."

The little ones were disappointed for only a moment. Harry was always right and Christmas certainly was Christmas.

When he arrived the next day, the girls had already left for school and Lucy was lighting the fire in the living room. He was horrified and reminded her that she was not well yet by a long chalk. She was on her hands and knees and she looked up at him and smiled. "Help me on to the sofa, Harry. And then sit and let's see if that fire will behave itself."

He shrugged out of his coat and lifted her easily; she had lost a great deal of weight. When they sat down he put his arm round her and she did not move it. The fire worked its way through the paper knots and the kindling and licked around the coals and her head was still on his shoulder. He held her carefully, leaning back so that they were both resting against the cushions. The centre of a flame burned bright blue and he said quietly, "Frost tonight."

He felt her face stretch into a smile. "Where did you hear that old wives' tale?"

"From you. After my accident you lit a fire in my room at the rectory and you told me. Blue flame today, frost on the way." He held her closer and she rubbed her forehead very gently against his chest.

"Ah. Harry. That must have been when the seed began to germinate."

He waited, then prompted her. "Go on."

She said, "Your love ... gentle, undemanding. I thought it was irritating me and then when you went missing, I knew that it wasn't. I still couldn't admit that I loved you. I was frantic but did not connect it with anything but guilt. He was my father, that was all I saw or understood, and I had to make amends somehow." She sighed. "Often I felt cross with you, Harry. As if you ought to take a part of that guilt." The fire was established now and she held out her free hand to it. "If I told you about the frost-flame, which was something my mother told me, then ... then I must have started to let you into my life properly. That must have been the beginning. Do you see?" She tilted her head so that she could see his face; he nodded slightly.

She snuggled down again, dropped her hand back into her lap and was silent for a long time. The flames seemed to be dancing; there were three of them; they leaped and then intertwined. She took another breath.

"Did you understand about Margaret? I did not. Perhaps I still do not. She had to leave England because she was in love with me. In love with me. I loved her but she was in love with me."

His hold tightened. She whispered, "It's all right now. I was terrified at first . . . but then I felt . . ." She buried her head in his shoulder and tried to laugh.

"Go on," he said, holding his breath, his eyes on that centre parting in her hair.

She whispered, "Desirable. I felt desirable." She looked up, put her hand behind his head and reached with her own to kiss him.

They held each other until the room was warm. And then they both began to talk at once. Then they laughed and inevitably, with infinite care and tenderness, they made love.

Christmas 1963 was very different from the previous one. Eventually they decided to spend their joint Christmas at the farm and they drove over on Christmas Eve, tired after the end-of-term festivities. The girls loved their room and the umbrellas spilling over with ivy and trailing berberis. Lucy had told them that one day she and Harry would be married but they would keep the Truro house and live there until things "were settled". Barbara and Denny had been overjoyed; Ellie a little less so. Her face flamed when it became obvious that Harry was sharing her mother's bedroom. At the farm it was different; Harry had put single beds in all the rooms to accommodate his "over-nighters," as he called the Flower People. She preferred that somehow.

For her, the dunes and the enormous seas brought something unique to the usual quiet joy of the nativity.

And then something happened that changed her view of . . . everything.

Christmas morning was a jumble of paper and string and dolls' clothes and jigsaw puzzles. Matthew came over after the morning service and said how good it was to see them minus spots. They opened presents, ate one of Harry's hens and listened to Ellie reading from her Charles Dickens complete works. Then they went out and walked the length of the beach and watched the spray being whipped from the top of the enormous rollers crashing along the rocks. Ellie had let her hair grow for almost a year now and she climbed on a rock and let it stream out behind her and the girls ran around screaming for no reason at all except the joy of being alive.

"Someone else up there!" Ellie shouted against the noise of the sea. "It looks like . . . no, it's all right. Just another walker."

Lucy too had seen him and her thoughts had run with Ellie's. As the boy drew into view, she too saw it was not Egg. Nothing like Egg. Summer-bleached hair dulled to brown, nose and fingers red with cold. It was the lilac man.

Ellie remembered him from last year's cathedral service. She was as excited as if they'd met in the desert. "D'you remember, Mum? You told me he was the lilac man!"

She jumped off the rock and ran to him and he let himself be included in the gathering.

"I remember you," he said to Lucy. "You and your friend. And the cats. You were growing all your own vegetables and I thought you must be one of us — our first converts!"

He laughed, suddenly coming alive. The girls jumped up and down around him and Harry insisted he must come back for tea. He shook his head; he had to get to Truro before complete darkness.

Matthew said, "I'll run you to Truro. I'm a visitor too."

"I came to your service this morning, vicar." The young man pumped Matthew's hand. "I'd heard about your sermons and I wanted to hear one. You really are inspirational."

Matthew looked shocked. He had been in Cornwall for nearly four years and had felt often that he was completely out of touch with his parishioners.

But Lucy nodded as if he really was inspirational and said, "We could not manage without him."

And they all trooped back to the farm.

He stayed. Ellie fell in love with him. She was still weak from the chicken pox and his wiry strength seemed to strengthen her. His name was Peter but she called him Lilac and teased him constantly and he smiled and smiled at her till she thought she might faint at his feet. Lucy was anxious and Harry told her not to worry. "She's just a child still," he insisted. She said, "How would you feel if it was Rosalie?" And he had no answer to that.

Every day Lilac walked over the dunes and around the holiday camp grounds to the rectory. Ellie went with him whether he liked it or not. And she talked to

406

him properly, no longer a provocative schoolgirl but a serious young woman, concerned for the people around her. She was surprised when it seemed he knew all about Egg.

"Harry used to speak of it all the time. He wanted to become your mother, live it for her. He was obsessed. Are you obsessed too, Ellie?"

"No. We were all right. We were fine. Gus was my best friend and her mother was like a sister to my mother. But then . . . he came back. Harry. And the kids love him and I do too. Sort of. But he's there. All the time. They're going to get married when he gets divorced from Avis. And I suppose his two girls will live with us sometimes. I don't know what I think about it. I need Egg again. I need Egg badly to tell me how to feel."

"Shall I try to tell you?"

"Yes. Oh yes. Please, Peter — please."

He smiled at her use of his name. Then he said very deliberately, "Live each day as if it were your last, Ellie. From what I hear, that was what Egg did. He lived every moment, didn't he? I've talked about him to people in the village and that's how I see him."

"You're right. That's how he was. Every grain of sand was precious to Egg."

His face lit up. "I would have liked him for that alone." He stopped walking and looked around him. They were on top of the dune that led down to the towans. Across the bay they could see the cove and in the watery sunshine two boats with a spinner trailing behind for mackerel. Ellie looked where he looked, saw what he saw; and something more. She drew a sharp breath and then let it go. It was a random wave, small, curling, lit for an instant by the gold of the sun. She whispered, "I thought . . ." And he said, "You probably saw what you thought you saw." And she looked into his blue eyes and nodded. "Yes. Yes, I think I did."

He went on walking and she ran after him and said breathlessly, "Do you want to be a vicar, Peter?"

He laughed. "Why on earth would you think that, little girl?"

"Because you come to see Matthew every day. And I am fifteen now."

"And I am twenty. Would you like to join our group in the summer? Live on the beach and worship the sun? Swim naked and eat magic mushrooms and reach beyond meditation to the everlasting?"

She hesitated. Her face was pale. "Yes."

"Why?"

Every bit of colour left her skin. She took a breath and blurted, "Because I would be with you all the time."

"And if I tell you that you are not going to do that . . . that you are going to finish school and go to university and make a career and marry me and be a vicar's wife, what would you say to that?"

Quite suddenly the blood rushed back via her neck until she was so hot she could hardly bear it. She looked at him and said, "How dare you treat me like this — as if I were Barbara — even Denny! Do you think I don't know about you? That you don't believe in marriage or commitment of any kind? That when people eat those mushrooms they think they can fly and every now and then they try it and they're killed? Haven't you got a conscience? Is that what you're looking for at Matthew's? Well . . . get on with it then!"

She turned and hurled herself to the top of the dune again, then fell and rolled down the other side to the beach where her mother had gone into the sea to look for Egg. She lay there, stunned, feeling unutterably stupid. She looked back and saw he was not following her. She began to cry and could not stop.

CHAPTER
EIGHTEEN

It took another three years before Rosemary and Greta between them could arrange the holiday in Cornwall. By then the 1960s had reached Birmingham with a vengeance, Flower People were out and hippies were in and the news — instantly accessible on the television — was rarely good. Arnold mourned the loss of Bechuanaland. "Yes, I know it hasn't 'disappeared'," he said irritably. "But Botswana will be totally different. Like Zambia and Malawi!" He rolled his eyes. His mother's family had all been in the diplomatic corps. Although decolonization was morally right and proper, he mourned the loss of those red blobs on the atlas.

He and William worried together and quite differently about Vietnam. Maurice, strangely, about the imprisonment of Nelson Mandela.

Sometimes it seemed that nobody noticed Connie.

In the summer of 1965 she had another miscarriage. She "took it well", according to William and Rosemary. But that winter and into the following year she had a persistent cold and began to lose her schoolgirl face. Something less tangible went out of her too. It was as if she was being drained of vitality; the sturdiness in her small, capable body was going. Yet she made fancy dresses for the children's playgroup and put on another wonderful Christmas for them all.

Rosemary tried to rally Greta, who was starting to worry about Connie doing too much. "She is always smiling — haven't you noticed? She is a fully fledged member of the society of grown-up women now, Greta. She's got past the froth of life and this is the real stuff . . . contentment."

Greta was unconvinced. She and Connie had taken the children to the pantomime the week before, and May, as usual, had been pro-active while Frankie watched with all his being. Greta egged May on to louder screams of delight and turned to Connie to share one of these moments. "Look, Connie — they're playing just to her — they haven't had an audience like this all week!" Connie was smiling as usual; she turned and let her gaze sweep over Greta and May, then put her chin on Frankie's head. That was all. Greta told herself she must not dramatize such a moment. She tried to explain how it had been to Maurice. How she had felt the sheer nothingness flow from that gaze.

He said, "She didn't enjoy it then?"

"I don't think enjoyment comes into much at the moment. But she didn't dislike it either. She was . . . sort of . . . disconnected. In some way."

Greta could not do better than that. Rosemary might have understood in spite of her determination to see Connie as merely stoical. But Greta could not talk to Rosemary about her own daughter. Sometimes Rosemary still made her feel like an outsider. So she mooted the holiday plan again and wrote off to Mrs

Pentwyn, who said she could not take them all but her neighbour would manage any overflow. They booked two weeks in September when the visitors would be thinning out. But in August Connie had a third miscarriage.

She smiled at William as if it was an achievement. "It's the actual anniversary of our first time together."

He looked at her and hated what was happening. On the pretext of inspecting their holiday digs he had gone down to the cove only the previous week and had visited Harry Membury and all the Pardoes at the farm. He learned of their peculiar domestic arrangement, which, apart from short breaks for Ellie's activities, meant that they spent all school holidays on the farm, and during term time Harry was with them in Truro as often as he could manage it.

William had kept in touch with events through John Carthew; he remembered that all those years ago Harry Membury had accompanied Josh to Pardoe Cottage to tell the women that they had lost their dearly beloved Egg; he himself had been inclined to put Lucy Pardoe on a pedestal and the way she instinctively recognized the difference between goodness and expediency yet juggled the two so expertly made him smile appreciatively. Somehow her triumphant survival seemed to vindicate some of his personal horrors. Human beings, on the whole, were worth fighting and even dying for.

Now, down at the house in the dunes, he saw those two mismatched people caring for each other. It had taken time and a near-tragedy before it had happened, but they were there, together, evidence of true compassion.

He told them about the holiday. "Late. We're not keen on crowds."

Harry said, "Marvellous. Wish I'd known earlier. I'll be most nights over with the family —" William loved the way he said that "— but if someone could have seen to the hens, you could have had this place all to yourselves."

William was regretful. The farmhouse had no stinging memories for any of them, in fact it had a fairytale charm that would entrance Frankie and May. "We'll see something of you, won't we?" He looked at Lucy as he spoke, deliberately not mentioning Connie.

Even now, after six years, she hesitated. "Come to tea with us in Truro," she said suddenly. "We've got plenty of space. And you might meet Lilac as well."

"Lilac?" William thought this was one of Ellie's school-friends.

"Ellie's in love with him. He's training to be a priest." No other explanations, typical of Lucy.

William smiled. "How . . . wonderful," was all he said.

And now he looked at Connie and said brusquely, "Did you stop taking precautions?"

She kept smiling. "Of course. How else would it have happened?"

He felt a kind of creeping despair. "You know that we are supposed to wait."

"Darling, it's a whole year . . . a whole year."

He realized that for her it was approaching eternity. She tried hard to explain. "All I do is wait."

"Sweetie, if you look at life like that all any of us do is wait." He took her hands. They were cold and damp and it was the hottest day of the year. "Listen, you are bringing up two children, two very happy children. You shop, cook, do the laundry, keep the house going . . ."

"You do the hoovering — anything that you consider to be too heavy for me — you just . . . do it." For an instant that dreadful smile disappeared and then came back. "Anyone could do what I do. What they cannot do is have your babies."

He held her to him and his chest heaved with a gigantic sob. She was appalled.

"Darling . . . William . . . we can still go to Cornwall. September is a whole two weeks away and this time I've only missed two periods so it's not a proper miscarriage at all!"

He could not speak. He wanted to comfort her, he wanted to shake her hard. He could do nothing. He put her from him at last and stood up.

He said finally, managing to sound almost jovial, "Mrs Pentwyn? The cove in the rain? You did mention yesterday that the long-term forecast was rain for September?"

She nodded and made a face. "She thought I was a hussy and brought shame to her house. What on earth will she think now? Two children and three near misses — oh dear Lord!" The smile was back and what she was saying was not in the least amusing.

414

He said, "The others will enjoy it, darling. And we can have our holiday here. I'll stay at home and we can have a drive most days."

The others cancelled the whole holiday. Rosemary borrowed the two children, Connie rested and William gardened in between enormous thunderstorms.

Greta panicked. She said to Maurice, "She's going to die. Right in front of us, with us doing sweet fanny nothing. We've got to get her back down there. She's got to see it again and to understand . . . something."

Maurice, who after all had lived with someone very near death for twenty years, shook his head. "It's a helluva risk, Greta. What if she has got to the pitch where she too walks into the water and forgets to come out again?"

"Oh . . . Christ! Maurice, don't talk like that. Connie's not like that — she's got Frankie and May to consider and she adores William."

"OK. I'm just pointing out that there's no answer to this. She's got to get out of her hole all by herself."

"And she only knows one way to do it," Greta said sadly. "Produce children."

She asked William very tentatively if they could try again the next year. Frankie would be six, May five. They would just adore the place.

He told her about Harry and Lucy. "They offered the whole house. It's big, it's almost self-sufficient . . . it would be great fun. And it's not Mrs Pentwyn and it's not quite the cove." Suddenly he took her hand. "Greta, I have to say this while I can. Without you,

Connie and I . . . would not be Connie and I. It's not only that you bullied me into Worcester Cathedral that day but that you have been so — so — *staunch*." He lifted her hand and kissed it and felt the arthritic lumps along the knuckles and kissed each one. She said nothing and he looked up expecting tears. She was starting past him, seeing nothing. On her face was Connie's small determined smile.

"William. There won't be any more babies after the next time." She spoke slowly, very clearly. And then the smile expanded properly. She patted William's arm with her free hand and said, "Listen. You do the booking, darling. Will you? You know Harry Membury — I thought he was an absolute wimp actually! You sort it out with him and Mrs Pardoe. Let's try again!" It sounded like a rallying call, typical of Greta. William wondered if he had imagined that moment when she had *not* wept sentimental tears. Later he wondered whether he had made his small speech to provoke those tears, so that he could comfort and be comforted. As it was, he had been given a job to do. Next year.

Arnold was sixty that November. He did not relish it at all and refused all celebrations. "What is there to celebrate? Anyone can manage it so long as they keep breathing."

Rosemary had already invited Greta and Maurice to lunch and was about to ring Maria and Marcus. It would be an interesting mix; a stimulating one too. Maurice was an easy companion and Marcus was even more pompous than before his marriage. The sort of company that would spur Arnold on to his provocative best. Greta giggled over the phone, "I hope you can keep Arnold in check, Rosie. Maurice is easily shocked, you know." They both laughed inordinately. In the background Arnold muttered something about wicked and conniving women.

She replaced the receiver and left her hand on it. "What's so awful about being sixty? The alternative of not breathing is better, is it?"

"I haven't tried it yet," he responded gloomily.

She picked up a cushion by its tassel and dangled it in front of him. "We can always arrange something."

"OK." He lay back in his chair, spreadeagled, offering himself for sacrifice.

She dropped the cushion in disgust. "I'm not trying to play games, Arnie! I'm trying to arrange a quiet lunch here that could be entertaining if you would only co-operate. I know you'll go along with William's plans for the actual day — but this was going to be something for you. Just you." She left the phone and stood looking at him until he felt ridiculous and struggled up in the chair. Then she went and knelt by him.

She said, "Arnie. I am so thankful you are sixty. Please go on and on. Be seventy and then eighty and then ninety."

He made room for her in the chair and she tucked herself neatly into his shoulder. They sat there for some time, looking out at the November day. They did this quite often. Arnold called it "savouring the moment".

He was the first to speak. "I don't want to leave you. Ever."

"No. I feel the same. You know that."

"I do."

"What about Greta? And . . . the others."

She felt a chuckle beginning in his abdomen but all he said was "I don't want to leave them either. But you know very well that in one sense I left them immediately I . . . left them." She did know that and was ashamed at her own insecurity.

He said gently, "What about your first husband?"

She was surprised. It never occurred to her that Arnie might feel any insecurity where her past was concerned.

She thought about it carefully and was shamed again. "I can hardly remember how it was. I was devastated when he was reported missing so I must have loved him. Everything was different then, Arnie. I was a different person."

"I know." He used her own words. "I feel the same." He kissed the top of her head. "Your very small difficulty with Greta, my lamb, is nothing to do with me. It's to do with her feelings for Connie. Try not to begrudge her loving Connie. She would have made a smashing mother."

"It's easy for you, Arnie. I sometimes think you love the whole world."

He laughed at that. "Like heck."

"There were just the two of us. Connie and me. For . . . quite a while. I constructed a life for us — in my head — and tried to live it."

He kissed her hair and left his face there. His voice was muffled. "Then you *constructed* another life — for you on your own. And I came along and messed it up."

She chuckled and lifted her face and they clung together for a while. When they surfaced she said, "I put the remains of the curry in our lunchtime soup. D'you think it'll be all right?"

"Was it Lord Woolton who said waste not, want not?"

"Who is Lord Woolton?"

"He was the Minister of Food. In the war. Rosie, I am surprised you can't remember that. You live by his book."

"Oh." She clung again, then said, "Arnie, I do so love you."

And he said, "She's going to be all right, my love. Connie is stronger than you think."

They stood up reluctantly; it was after all past lunchtime and the soup was waiting. Rosemary said, "D'you know, William and Greta have already booked that farmhouse for next September."

He took her hand and they went towards the kitchen. He said, "After lunch I'll ring Maria. You never know, I might get Marcus and I can ginger him up a bit, ready for the fray."

She laughed.

Greta asked Connie if she had "felt anything". "Just before Arnie's birthday party, darling. I had one of my funny feelings when I sort of connect with you. You know. Like when our tummies touched that time and I felt May kicking in me. And then, of course . . . the labour pains." May would be five that late spring and nothing had "connected" them since then. They never spoke of it. Greta had a horrible moment of disbelief. Had she imagined the whole thing?

But Connie had never forgotten. She stopped smiling and looked up sharply from the sink, where she was washing up their few things from lunch.

"I don't think so. But it didn't work like that before. Your feeling did not transfer itself to me. I simply . . . believed you."

"Oh Connie . . ."

"What was it, Greta? Another baby? Tell me — don't try to wrap it up — please — just tell me." She took dripping hands from the sink and held them out and Greta took them.

"I was talking to William about the holiday. And it happened. And I said to him — interrupted him, I think — that after the next baby there would be no more."

She paused and added, "It didn't mean you could not have any more. It meant that you would be happy then." Another pause, then, "I think." She squeezed Connie's slippery fingers and let them go. "It was before Christmas, darling. I can't really remember. What I do hang on to is . . . there will be another pregnancy and it will go full term." She swallowed, wondering whether that was what had really happened. "That was the sort of . . . message."

It was enough for Connie. She stood there, taking it in. Gradually — Greta saw it happening and said to

420

Maurice that it was like an electric fire growing warm
— Connie became radiant.

She breathed, "Oh . . . Greta."

Greta said hurriedly, "Listen, just because of what
happened when May . . ."

Connie said, "You were right then, darling. You were
right!"

"I wasn't right or wrong, Connie. It just happened."

"There's something between us, Greta. Remember I
dreamed about Maurice in Brighton."

"Darling, please don't set too much store by this
time. I wish I hadn't told you now."

"You wish you hadn't made me happy?"

"Connie . . ." Greta watched helplessly as Connie
dried her hands and took off her apron. Connie saw her
anxiety and laughed; actually laughed properly. She
said, "Come on, it's time to meet the kids from school.
The daffodils are all out in the park, it's Frankie's
birthday next month and May's straight after." She
shrugged into her coat and said thoughtfully, "Nineteen
sixty-seven. I like the sound of that. I think seven is my
favourite number. It rhymes with heaven."

They went outside. Connie tucked her arm into
Greta's. Greta felt frightened yet so special.

Connie talked to William after they had put May and
Frankie to bed that night. He was wary; she realized
that he was frightened, just as Greta was frightened.
She hated the fact that she was a source of such anxiety
to them and wondered if her mother felt the same. Her
mother would be better at hiding her feelings of course.

William nodded and moved the fireguard so that they got the full heat of the crumbling fire. "I was there when it happened. It was very strange. She did not really understand it herself. But if it has helped you, Connie . . ."

"Stop it!" She was angry. "Stop pretending everything will be all right if I rest and recuperate. I am not *ill*, William! I simply need us — you and me — to be complete! Can't you see that?"

"No. You and me . . . that could have been completion. You, me and Frankie, that too. You, me, Frankie and May . . ."

She held up her hand. "You're right. Of course you are. But darling, just tell me this. Do you still love me?"

He looked at her. She cupped his face with her hands and made a sound. Then she whispered, "Then . . . why can't you trust me in this?"

Still he was unable to speak. She brushed beneath his eyes with her thumbs.

"All right, I know that too. I thought that Greta's . . . what? Experience? I thought it would help you to believe that in this I might know best." She sighed. "Greta knows that there is another child for us. Waiting. I know it too."

He continued to stare into her velvet brown eyes though he could scarcely see them. He thought of his parents and his brothers. Killed so randomly. He thought of Arnhem. And he thought of Connie and their two children. He dealt in reason and logic and it had deserted him. He held on to her fragile body as if they might both be drowning. Just as he had held on to her as he dragged her from the sheer weight of water in the cove seven years ago.

So, in September they arrived at the farmhouse set in the sandy soil of the dunes and decorated with upturned umbrellas and strips and swathes of nylon tenting like insubstantial arras. Hens clucked and scooted around their feet as they unloaded their luggage and Harry came from the slopes of the garden holding an enormous chip basket of kidney beans and a smaller one of late raspberries. He put them down, shook hands all round and pretended not to notice Connie's enormous abdomen, then took them in to show them how to work the hot-water system.

"Lucy has left a hotpot. And there are new potatoes and these beans."

William remembered the house from before. "You've extended the kitchen somehow," he said, admiring the long table and the sideways view of the lighthouse in the distance.

"Yes. We started to use the old range and we needed to take full advantage of the heat from it. So we knocked the living room into the kitchen. It works well. Lucy likes it."

"You can turn your hand to most things?"

"I learned when I was at the rectory. Matthew borrows Doc Carthew's housekeeper now and then. She tells me she is doing a correspondence course in plumbing!" Harry grinned. He was looking well. For a time after he and Lucy had set up together the locals had taken against them. Chippy Penberthy had broken all the windows on Lucy's car during one of her weekend visits to the farm. One of the fishermen had left buckets of rotting fish around the house. Josh had dealt with that, probably using his fists; Matthew had dealt with Chippy by the simple threat of eternal damnation. Chippy's grandchildren had converted their grandmother — and therefore Chippy — and though he did not believe in hell he felt it was too big a risk to take for someone so downright immoral as Lucy Pardoe. "It's them two what'll burn. Not me!" he was heard to say on several occasions.

It was a good reason for keeping their main base in Truro. Since the arrival of the Flower People everybody seemed to live with everybody else. After all, Harry and Lucy were not summer visitors.

Soon the house sang with voices. Frankie and May called it the Magic House and May had discovered the tea tray at the top of the stairs on which she could hurtle down to the passage. Frankie, more cautious, fetched pillows and threw them down to provide a soft landing for himself. There was a cat, grey with rings around his tail and paws and a white bib.

"He's Tad," Harry told them. "He lived with Matthew and Mark in Truro but they are getting very elderly and he got on their nerves. So he lives out here now and makes sure we don't get mice in the house."

"Oh thank God," said Rosemary, clutching her blouse theatrically. "May! You are NOT to come down the stairs head first. Ever again!"

May looked at her well-trained grandmother with surprise then began to crumple her face up. Harry said,

"Would you care to help me collect the eggs from the hen coops?"

"Ooh! Yes, please!" She put her hand confidingly into Harry's. "We got a book at home called *Polly and Peter* and they live on a farm and c'llect eggs every day."

"You could do that for me. If you wouldn't mind. Look, here is the trug and the tray fits inside it and you put one egg into each of those holes so that they don't break or crack. Can you do that?"

"I can do anyfing really," May said airily. "Anyfing Frankie can do I can do. An' he's a year older'n me."

"That's good because he can look after you, can't he?"

She hesitated then said, "Yes. I s'pose so. Come on, Frankie. You can be Peter an' I'll be Polly . . ." Her voice grew less strident as they made their way to the hen coops.

Rosemary sighed. "It was a long journey, Arnie. Don't let's take May back in our car. Let's have Frankie instead."

Arnie looked at her and grinned. "OK," he said.

Harry left and they settled in. The sunset was amazing and they all walked on the beach and watched the enormous red ball drown in the sea. The children went to bed and William and Connie read to them until they were asleep. They left the others to themselves and went to bed. William massaged Connie's back and she pretended to purr with delight. He was still so frightened; she had told him after three months that everything was all right this time but he could not overcome the terrifying sensation of not being in control. The sense of being lost at sea came upon him at times and he had to gasp for air. Once, only once, he had called out in his sleep, "What have I done?" Connie had wrapped herself around him and whispered, "We're all right, darling. We're really all right." Their roles had changed that night; he had given himself up to fate and she had surrendered stoicism for gratitude.

Greta said, "I wish I could give you things . . . like you give to me. The sheer sweetness of love, for instance."

Connie had crowed with delight. "That is what it is, Greta! So sweet, so very sweet!" She revelled in it and tried hard to pass it on to William. The massage sessions were part of it and that first night at the farm when she rolled over and let him feel movement in her womb, he smiled.

"Ah. Connie. Dear Connie. So practical."

"Women often are, darling. Think of the women you know really well. Mummy and Greta and Lucy Pardoe . . . all very practical."

"Yes."

"All will be well, my dearest. The forecast is splendid for tomorrow. I thought I might float my tummy in the sea. What do you think?" He started to voice his doubts and she kissed him, curled into his shoulder and said, "We'll see."

He knew that she would consult Greta before she went into the water. How was it that Greta could be practical yet so other-worldly? It all seemed part of the near-chaos that made up the universe. The only comfort was that he was sure Greta would shake her head at the idea of swimming. He held his wife carefully within his arm and closed his eyes. He slept right through the night.

Greta did not shake her head. The weather was glorious and they spent a short morning setting up a miniature market stall with pieces of driftwood and plenty of sand. The children sold tiny portions of raspberries and cream from eggcups, paid for with shells and unusual pebbles. Then they sold the pebbles for more shells. Connie went with them into the shallows to wash the eggcups and spoons and then the shells.

In the afternoon William and Maurice drove into Truro to get more provisions and the children rested indoors. Arnie and Rosemary went to sleep in their chairs. It was then that Greta and Connie had their dip. Greta had not swum since before the war; she was nervous about it. But she could not shake her head to Connie and if Connie went in she most certainly was going in with her. They entered cautiously, gasping as the salt water stung their red skin. Then Connie realized that the heavy load she carried these days was being borne by the sea and she turned on to her back and floated luxuriously. "Greta — look!" She pointed to her pregnancy, which emerged from the water like an island. "Oh, this is lovely. Oh . . ." She lifted her head and spoke to the lump. "Are you all right down there? Isn't it great!"

Greta started to laugh and took on a mouthful of water and choked. Rosemary, slipping and sliding down the dune to join them, stopped and watched them, smiling, wondering why she had ever felt odd about their friendship. Greta was older than Arnie and looked every inch her years in a costume that was wired like a corset. Rosemary was wearing shorts and a vest and without any hesitation she joined the two of them. They floated around, laughing inanely for ten minutes or so, then Greta took one of Connie's hands and Rosemary took the other and they towed her slowly to the shore, helped her to her feet and hugged her. It was such a natural thing to do, yet they imagined it was the first time it had ever happened. Connie hugged them gratefully. "I'm so glad you're so glad," she said.

Rosemary smiled. She had not been a bit happy about this pregnancy until she had heard about Greta's strange pronouncement. And then, quite suddenly, it had been all right.

The holiday moved slowly around Connie. Sometimes Maurice and Greta would take Arnie's car and explore Penwith, its coves and inlets and standing stones and ancient churches. Sometimes Arnie and Rosemary would go with them, other times they would take the children to Newquay or Falmouth. They drove to Plymouth and went aboard a naval destroyer and the children came back with miniature caps, May with a lanyard and bosun's whistle. She piped them in and out of the house until they begged for mercy.

Always Connie was the anchor at the farm. When the weather was grey for a few days, she and Tad the cat might be found in the garden picking beans. There was an orchard further up protected by an ancient Cornish

428

"hedge" of granite slabs overgrown with wild flowers. She picked plums and made jam and pies. Then the sun came back and she relaxed on the beach, hat tilted over her face while the children buried her feet in sand. They went with her into the sea; she taught Frankie to swim. May shouted that she could swim already and she crawled along the seabed flailing her arms energetically and spitting water like a whale. Tad sat well back on shore watching them disapprovingly, following them back to the house with tail erect. Connie felt at home here; something frozen inside her had started to melt some time ago now and living like this down here she found she could monitor it consciously. She loved it when they gathered around the table in the evenings and talked about what they had done and seen during the day. She felt at ease; mistress of herself at last.

William spent time with Matthew and heard a great deal about Peter Stephenson, renamed Lilac by Ellie Pardoe. He was amused and interested by Matthew's progress in his rambling parish. His success with Ellie and then, later, with Lilac Stephenson had given him a confidence he had almost lost. The sense of being useless amid all the drama of Harry's so-called accident, of being practically pushed aside by Lucy every morning, the business of the magic mushrooms, Chippy Penberthy bullying him into confirming his illegitimate grandchildren, his dwindling congregation . . . Discouragement had descended on him like a cloud. And then Lilac came to the towans church especially to hear him preach on that Christmas morning. He had thought all along that Ellie would make a wonderful clerical wife. And it looked as if things were moving that way.

William did not like that bit of the story. "Not yet surely? She's only eighteen and he's not ordained."

"No, not yet. She's got a place at a teacher training college in Exeter. She's always wanted to work with children." Matthew grinned. "Funny how things work out. Lucy met him when she and her friend were working on an allotment in Truro. He gave them armfuls of lilac. He was at the cathedral on Christmas afternoon and she remembered him. I think he reminded her of her son."

Matthew fell silent and William said, "That was a terrible thing to happen. It affected all of us."

"She's getting over it slowly. Harry's doing, of course."

"Yes. I think Connie will. Eventually." William looked at the younger man. "Lucy is so often in my thoughts."

"Mine too. John Carthew says the same. He has known her since the war years. He delivered Egg Pardoe. Looked after him when he had his seizures."

"I want to see Carthew before we leave. Does he still take a Monday off?"

"I believe so. You can ask Mrs Kervis. She's somewhere around."

So he dropped in on the good doctor and was surprised that on his departure Carthew said, "No help from me either? The vicar telephoned and said you needed reassurance. I take it nothing from him?"

William was somehow mortified. He said, "I hadn't realized I was so . . . obvious."

430

"The only person who can help any of us is Lucy. By continuing to be happy with Harry Membury she will do that. If you want anything quickly you should ask her straight out."

"How?"

Dr Carthew cleared his throat and adopted an actorish voice. "Lucy, have you come to terms with your son drowning alongside my wife?"

William was appalled. If the doctor was serious it was awful and if he was joking it was . . . macabre.

Carthew shook his head. "That's not right, is it? She is good at the direct approach but that might be —"

"Brutal," William supplied flatly, wondering what Cornwall did to people who ought to be sensitive to others.

Carthew put up a hand. "Listen. All you can do is to see her and then play it by ear. She often picks up feelings — a lot of Cornish women can do that — and she might bring it up herself. But whatever, go and see her. She speaks of you often, and kindly."

William looked at him sharply, wondering how much he really knew and understood about Lucy Pardoe.

The holiday was drawing to a close when he eventually announced that he was going into Truro to see Lucy. May looked up sharply from her cornflakes.

"Not us, Daddy."

"Well, she would probably like to see you."

May was silent, weighing up the possibilities of seeing Ellie, Barbara and Denny. Frankie said, "Please not, Dad. Moll is helping us to make a raft with those tyres what were caught in the rocks."

William might have resisted May but not Frankie. He grinned. "Perhaps next year then. We are all coming again next year, aren't we?"

There was a spluttering cheer from both children.

William could not get anyone on the telephone but he decided to go to Truro anyway. Even if they were both out Lucy would come home at four when the girls were home from school.

He left the car on Steep Street and knocked on the door. Two pint bottles of milk waited on the top step. One of the cats looked out of the living room window.

William scribbled a note, pushed it through the letter box and walked down the hill to the allotments. On the way, he bought two hot pasties and a bottle of lemonade.

Lucy was pleased to see him. He knew that for certain because she immediately told him he shouldn't have bothered and what on earth was he thinking, bringing food and drink with him when she'd got a thermos of tea and some bread and cheese in the shed. He said nothing, stood there in his shorts and polo shirt, smiling at her, delighted that she was looking tanned and younger than her forty-three years.

She said uncomfortably, "What is it, Mr Mather?"

"William."

"What is it, William?"

"I didn't think I'd have you to myself. And for a picnic. And in your allotment. You can show me round."

She led him between rows of lettuce and radish — "They grow at any time. This will be the third harvest this year." Then through the beansticks. She talked about soil and compost and a new cabbage called Little Princess. She realized she was talking too much and brought two folding chairs from the shed. They settled down with the pasties and it was as if they had synchronized that first bite. They both laughed at the same time.

He swallowed with some difficulty and waited until she had too, then he said, "We are so close, Lucy. I can't imagine why that is."

"You were there. That day."

"But I let him — I let Egg go, Lucy. You blamed Connie. Not me."

"It was not your fault."

"That day when you showed me the farm . . . why did you kiss me?"

She gasped and was silent, embarrassed for a moment. Then she looked up and said honestly, "I wanted to. If you had asked for more I would have given you what I could. I sensed that something was not fully right. With your life. If I could have comforted you it would have been a small thing to do."

He looked at her and nodded slowly, then started again on his pasty. She hesitated. "We are bound together somehow, you and me, William. I think we are the same age. We are easy together. It helps us if we know that the other is content."

He lifted his brows, finished his pasty and poured some lemonade into her beaker. He drank a long draught from the bottle, choked a little and said, blinking, "It would make me very content indeed if you came to see Connie and my children before we go home."

She sipped more decorously but shook her head. "You know I cannot, William. I am really pleased she is making you happy but if I see her and talk to her, that will go." She looked across the patchwork of gardens. "When I kissed you I stopped hating her, stopped blaming her. But . . ." she hesitated then added quietly, "bitterness is bad for the soul."

He flinched slightly as he put the top on the bottle.

"Please, Lucy. I do not believe you will feel bitter. But . . . please do it."

They packed up and she locked the shed; he carried a bag of lettuce and tiny tomatoes and she a trug of Victoria plums as big as apples. Still, like May, he pestered and still she shook her head. When his car was in sight he was within an inch of accepting defeat and she turned on him like Matthew turned on Mark, claws out.

"You have no idea what you are asking of me, William Mather! I did not think you could be so selfish. I have worked hard to forget that day — the girls have been there always and Harry would not go away until there came a time when I did not want him to, when I could not do without him. And somewhere

434

in the awfulness of it all you were there too. You understood completely — you knew I was not strong — I knew you were not either. We suffered together. And no one knew. It was our secret. And now . . . you want to smash all that to pieces for some sentimental claptrap about forgiveness!" She took a deep breath. "If it means that little to you, then so be it. I will bring the girls over tomorrow morning and they can swim with your children. And I will say hello to your wife, who . . . face up to it, William . . . was the cause of my son's death!"

She walked on very fast and William stood on the pavement watching her and wondering whether she was right. Then he went on to the car, put the bag of vegetables next to the milk bottles on the step, turned the car and drove away from Lucy Pardoe.

They were travelling home on the Sunday so the next day was their last and they decided to spend all of it on the beach. William said nothing about Lucy; in truth he did not expect her.

No one heard the arrival of the Hillman Minx in the yard at the back of the house. Frankie and May were in the sea, carrying buckets of water to their latest pond. William and Rosemary were still digging it out, hoping to reach the water table sooner rather than later. Maurice and Arnie were walking the width of the beach, discussing the small black patches floating on the water which might or might not be from the wrecked *Torrey Canyon* in Prussia Cove. When they reached the pond-diggers they were immediately roped

435

in. Greta and Connie were lying in deckchairs discussing what to put in the sandwiches for lunch. There came a shout from behind them and they both looked round to see Denny Pardoe hurtling from the side of the house, already in her swimming costume and making a beeline for Frankie and May. She was closely followed by Barbara Pardoe, now in her third year at the Laurels and therefore dressed in a Laura Ashley print frock with a sunhat worthy of Ascot. She stood at the top of the beach looking down on everyone in more ways than one. Her mother joined her, then Harry brought up the rear with his two girls.

Greta said, "Oh my God. They're little shockers. And of course Ellie's started at college so we'll probably have to deal with them."

Connie hardly saw the children. Her eyes were fixed on Lucy Pardoe. It was the first time she had seen her since that day in 1960 and she had changed. But Connie knew her instantly. Greta glanced at her and said in a low voice, "Go and say hello, Connie. Go on. You can then go on into the house and make drinks. I'll come as soon as I can." She scrambled up and made for Harry.

"My goodness," she said in a loud voice. "You haven't changed in the slightest, Mr Membury. And these are your two girls — they certainly have changed! Rosalie and Lily, isn't it? My dears, you were this high when we last met!" She held a hand about a foot from the ground and the girls laughed. Harry shook her hand. Lucy and Barbara were isolated for a moment. Connie went forward. She felt huge and

436

unwieldy in her smock sundress, her heart beating hard and slow.

She said, "How nice to see you." It sounded pathetic. "It's good of you to come." She wanted to hurl herself on to Lucy and sob and tell her how sorry she was. She said, "I was just going into the house to make some thermoses of coffee."

Barbara looked at her curiously and said, "Mum, did you bring my costume? Rosalie wants to get in the sea and I really think Denny needs me."

Lucy stopped looking at Connie as if she was some kind of freak and said, "Yes. Everything is in the car."

Greta said gaily, "Come on, everyone, let's go and get your stuff and go down to the sea." She struck an attitude. " 'Let's go down to the sea again!' "

The girls looked at each other and followed her unwillingly with Harry urging them on. "I've brought my shorts too. We'll all help with . . . whatever's going on." He turned to Greta. "Marvellous to see you again, Mrs Heatherington. We heard about your husband being found. So romantic."

"It really was," Greta said enthusiastically as they disappeared into the farmyard.

Connie made no move to the house. She stood there, quite unable to put one sandy foot in front of the other. Lucy had moved away from her almost involuntarily, as if pulled down the beach towards the sea. She came to the two empty deck-chairs and sat in one. Connie managed to turn and watch her. Lucy was looking — concentrating with her whole body — at the children with their buckets. Connie followed her stare. It was a typical family holiday scene: the men regressing to roughly ten years old and ordering the digging in loud voices; the children quietly — not so quietly in May's case — subverting them and each other, pouring water willy-nilly then running back through the complicated canal system, breaking down the sand walls unconcernedly.

At first they were simply a group of people playing on the shore. All seemed to be brown-haired and brown-skinned. And then as they grouped and regrouped and ran and poured water and shouted at each other, one stood out from the others. Frankie's golden hair, below his ears as was the fashion at his school, had not darkened with the water; his skin was not the colour of walnuts, it had tanned to gold, and his movements were not random, he went purposefully from sea to pond, running along the smooth beach rather than the canals that William had planned so carefully.

Connie closed her eyes for a moment, wishing she could faint, knowing it would not happen. The time had come. She had always known it would but she had pushed the thought away and "got on". William and Frankie were so close that it was easy to believe they were father and son. Looking down on them now it was so obvious they were not.

She stiffened her spine, forced herself to walk to the two chairs and to sit down. Lucy seemed not to notice her. She continued to stare at that one small figure who was now talking to William, pointing to the sea then the pond.

Then, quite suddenly, she spoke. "He's telling William that there's no need to go on filling up the pond and watching the water soak away!" She chuckled. "The tide's going to do it for them — good and proper — in the next half-hour!"

Connie looked down again. William bent and picked Frankie up and held him high, laughing. Then he kissed him and put him down and they both went into the sea and filled their buckets. Connie could almost hear William saying, "Let's go on pretending — just for May." William never missed an opportunity to put Frankie in charge of his raucous little sister.

Then over the brow of the dune, like the arrival of the cavalry in a film, came Barbara, Rosalie, Lily and Harry. They tore down to the shore to which Denny had just returned from a swim and was now being offered a towel. There were more shouts. William stood still and looked up at the house; he put a hand across his head to shield his eyes from the sun then turned back to the children and Connie realized he was assuming that she and Greta were still sitting there peacefully. Harry started to introduce all the children; Lucy watched that too. They made fresh groups; May, Frankie and Denny; Barbara and Rosalie and Lily. Frankie held May's hand.

Lucy said, "They're close, those two."

Connie forced herself to speak. "Yes."

There was another silence. Lucy was unable to look away from the children, hardly conscious of Connie Mather sitting by her side. Frankie was leading May to the damp pond. They jumped into it. He began to dig at the sides and after a while May joined him. They scooped sand up and out until they had small bucket seats just the right shape for them to sit in comfortably. Frankie leaned towards May and said something and she threw back her head and gave the sort of belly laugh that was worthy of Arnie and Maurice combined.

Lucy said softly, "He'll never be lonely with that one."

Connie knew she was weeping; she could do nothing about it. She whispered somehow, "He is close to William too." She sounded desperate; it was a plea.

Lucy nodded. "William would make sure of that."

At last Lucy looked away. She studied her hands in her lap, wondering what to say. There was so much; too much. She said at last, "Thank you."

From the corner of her eye she saw something drop on to Connie's clenched hands. She swallowed. What else did she want?

She said, "You gave my son something he might never have had otherwise." She flicked her gaze to the children again. "He must have been happy. Everyone said he was and I didn't believe anyone. Now . . . I see his son. And I know."

Connie choked, "William doesn't know. Please . . . Lucy . . . please . . ."

Lucy looked round in surprise. There were the childish brown curls, brown eyes, round face. William was darker again. Did she really think anyone could doubt that Francis Mather was Egg's son?

Lucy blurted before she could think, "William knows. Of course he knows."

440

Connie said, "We were together. It was not a success but . . ."

Lucy waited, staring. Then she said slowly, "Now that I know William . . ." She paused and took a deep breath. "He would never have risked you becoming pregnant. You must know it yourself."

The words came out flat and entirely convincing. Connie thought back. The bathroom; William's embarrassment covered by a thick white bathrobe. She stared at Lucy Pardoe, her eyes wide.

"But — but — he has never ever said . . ."

"Surely you know too that he wouldn't?" Lucy was as surprised as Connie. She knew that the girl was silly and thoughtless but not that she was totally stupid. "He loves you, Connie. Do you know that much?"

She saw the girl withdraw slightly and knew she had trodden private ground. She smiled. "I see you are pregnant again."

Connie took a breath. She said, "Yes." She wanted to give Lucy something, she wanted to share something. "It's twins actually."

Lucy smiled properly. "Frankie and May will have one each."

Connie actually laughed. "I hadn't thought of that."

They talked of families. Lucy had, of course, had four children. She said she recommended it. For a moment Connie was silent then she said, "You could come and stay with us sometimes. You and Harry and the girls."

"They would like that. A big city." She looked at Connie. "Perhaps later. I'm not sure."

"All right." Connie nodded. "Let's wait and see."

She smiled at Lucy; tentatively, still nervous; she gave her the same smile she had given Arnold Jessup when he had interviewed her for the job of filing clerk ten years ago. In that moment Lucy saw her as Egg must have seen her. She stared at her, startled. This girl had understood Egg. In the few hours they had spent together she had known Egg as well as Lucy had known him herself. She had recognized his connection with everything around him. He had transcended the ordinary and mundane without the help of any magic mushroom and with his feet on the ground. And when he had asked this girl for comfort she had given him something wonderful.

Lucy swallowed. Then, suddenly, she reached into the big patch pocket of her skirt and withdrew Margaret's letter. She took off the back page and gave it to Connie.

"It's an address. In America. I think it's the address of his grandparents. Take it. For later. Perhaps."

Connie took it, startled herself, but knowing it was important.

Greta arrived with mugs and two enormous thermos jugs. "I've made sandwiches," she said proudly. "Peanut butter. Banana and sugar. Some of that ham from Home Farm. Hard-boiled eggs . . ."

Lucy laughed, feeling suddenly helpless and not caring.

"Harry and I have brought pasties! They must still be in the car."

Connie watched the two women organizing everything. She walked slowly into the house holding her sundress beneath the bump to support the twins. She found her handbag and slid the sheet of paper inside it, then turned and looked at the long table with its array of sandwiches. This was where it had happened for Lucy Pardoe, Lucy Roach as she had been then. Connie pieced together the things William had told her, the beatings after her mother died, the cellar and the escape. This was where she had found Harry and saved his life. How on earth could she bear to come here so often, work the garden, cook in this kitchen, make happiness where tragedy had been?

She heard them coming back with the pasties, Greta talking nineteen to the dozen, instantly friendly. Connie trusted Greta's instincts. She turned, smiling widely as they came in.

"Look at this! Greta, you must have worked like a trouper to get this lot on the table in half an hour!"

Greta fetched a tray. "I *am* a trouper!" she reminded Connie.

Lucy arranged the pasties on the tray. She was unexpectedly captivated by Greta. She said, "Greta was telling me how you found her husband for her after twenty years!"

"Well . . ." Connie began.

"And how on earth she knew about Barbara and Denny liking banana and sugar sandwiches — and she's not even Cornish!"

Connie laughed. There seemed nothing else to do. She found a chair and sat down and Greta was there, rubbing her back.

Lucy washed her hands at the sink and looked over her shoulder. "I've got some of it. I know that you will go full term and have one of each, a boy and a girl." She laughed as Connie's face opened wide. "Lots of women can make those sort of predictions. But banana sandwiches . . . that's another thing!"

Connie laughed too, suddenly full of excitement. A boy and a girl.

She said, "Why don't you go and watch the pond fill with the tide? That's what Frankie was telling William — no need for the buckets." She swallowed. "Frankie has a natural feel for the sea."

Lucy finished drying her hands on the roller towel. She straightened it carefully. "Yes. He has, hasn't he?" She came over and said again, "Thank you. Thank you, Connie." She knew what she had to do. She leaned over the chair and pecked Connie's cheek one side . . . and thought of William and that kiss. Here in this house. She kissed Connie's other cheek. Then she turned and went.

Connie closed her eyes for a moment, then said, "She can't be that much younger than Mummy. Look at the way she runs!"

"Your mother could run faster than that if she wanted to," Greta said. She hugged Connie's shoulders. "Was it all right, darling? You did so well. I was proud of you."

Connie kissed the gnarled knuckles and said wonderingly, "She thanked me, Greta. Again and again."

"Well, of course she did, darling. Now before we start on all that coffee, I'm going to make you a nice cup of tea. Just sit still. It's all been a bit much."

Rosemary appeared in the doorway. She had obviously run very fast indeed and she hung on to the doorway, panting loudly, taking in the normality of the scene before her.

Even so, she gasped, "Are you all right, Connie? What did she say? I didn't realize you were here. With her. On your own."

"Oh Mummy. Sit down. The dunes . . . so steep . . . sit down."

Rosemary sat and held her side. "When I saw her tearing along like a maniac and sitting in the pond — yes, in the water — by Frankie and May — and William said, 'This is Lucy' — and she said you and I were like peas from the same pod — I did not know what to think." She stopped speaking, then suddenly started to cry.

Greta and Connie gathered her from either side and told her everything was all right and of course Lucy was not going to take Frankie away and Connie told her that Lucy had actually thanked her.

At some point during all the emotion, William joined them and Greta made the tea. William told them how Frankie had made May sit down and wait for the water to arrive because she was getting "all het up". He took his sunglasses off and looked at his mother-in-law. "Rather like you, Rosemary."

Rosemary acknowledged this. "I was never het up until I met Arnie!"

Connie, still held down in her chair by Greta, smiled at William and said, "That's perfectly true, actually." And it was the way she made that matter-of-fact defence of her mother that convinced William that somehow, in some way or other, acceptance and forgiveness had actually happened in this place. He went to her and helped her up and put a hand on the front of her sundress.

"How are the Bisto twins?" he asked. "Would they like a swim?"

She nodded. He said, "Let's do it now. By ourselves."

They waited until everyone was settled with sandwiches and drinks and the noise level was ascending by the second, then they slipped into their room, changed sedately and went down to the dunes almost unnoticed.

Connie floated on the same sea that had taken the lives of Lucy Pardoe's loved ones and felt the water hold her babies for her. William told her the story about Josh watching the Flower People do the same thing. "A pre-natal baptism — that's what the vicar called it." He put a hand in the small of her back and moved her to the shore. "Are we going to be all right, Connie?"

He pulled her gently to her feet and she shaded her eyes and looked back towards the house. Frankie and May were sharing a pasty, starting at either end. Sitting next to them in the sand, Lucy seemed to be telling them a story. She described a big circle in the air and then jiggled her fingers around it.

William said, "That's the Merry Maidens dancing in a ring."

Connie said, "I think it's Lucy Locket who lost her pocket on a summer's day."

He leaned back to look down on her, astonished.

"That's something you danced to in the playground at school," he told her. "We're joined in so many ways . . . of course we're going to be all right."

They clambered back up through the loose sand of the dunes and ate their pasties and sandwiches and drank the rest of the coffee in the thermoses. Harry took over the storytelling and even Barbara sat and listened to the familiar tale of the Mousehole cat. She explained it to Rosalie, who was actually the same age as her but seemed to fit the latest put-down at the Laurels, which was "pretty juvenile".

Arnie slept with his head in Rosemary's lap and when he woke he smiled up at her and said, "I don't mind getting old, Rosie. Actually it just seems to get sweeter and sweeter."

"What does?" She looked down at him and smiled back.

"Love, of course." He reared up and nearly broke her nose as he kissed her.

Then she had to convince him she was laughing, not crying. She held his head and said, "D'you know how that song ends? It's something to do with 'love's old sweet story' — can't quite remember but the word 'old' is definitely there!"

And Lucy, listening to Harry, overhearing Rosemary's words, thought suddenly and inexplicably of Margaret Trip. She had loved Margaret. And Margaret had loved her. Lucy put a hand on Harry's shoulder and squeezed it gently.

Greta and Maurice were washing up. Greta said, "I'm not sure about next year, Moll. How do you feel about it? The twins are going to need so much attention. I rather think William and Connie could do with being en famille — after all, there will be six of them."

Maurice nodded vigorously. "I'm already drawing my pension, love."

Greta rinsed away a bowl of water and drew another one. "Pass those mugs, Moll." She began again. "What about Monte Carlo? Have you ever been to a casino?"

"Never had the time, love." He laughed. "D'you fancy trying a holiday in Monte Carlo? Sounds a bit racy."

"We might break the bank!"

They both giggled and he slapped her with his damp tea towel. "D'you think Arnie and Rosie might come? He speaks French."

"He'd come like a shot. I'm not sure about Rosie."

"She will if he wants to."

She rinsed and dried her hands, thinking sentimentally of Arnie. Then she said, "If it's only his French you want, then don't worry. I speak it like a native. I lived with a Free French captain for three months in the war. He couldn't speak a word of English so I had to learn French!"

He chased her round the kitchen and she let herself be caught.